# Love on the Edge of Time

Julie A. Richman

**Love on the Edge of Time**

Cover Model: Bryce Draper

Front Cover Photograph: Shaun S. Michelsen/Michelsen Studio

Back Cover Photograph: Marina Svetlova (model not cited)

Cover Design: Jena Brignola/Bibliophile Productions

Formatting: Shanoff Designs

Proofing: Elaine York/Allusion Graphics LLC.

# Table of Contents

# Other Books by Julie

Searching for Moore

Moore to Lose

Moore than Forever

Needing Moore: The Complete Series

Bad Son Rising

Henry's End

Slave to Love

The Do-Over

For Mindy,

Because the journey becomes epic when

you've got the perfect person riding shotgun…

Tramps like us…

*"What we learn through love is never forgotten."*
*~ Chani Nicholas*

# Chapter 1

"What the hell is wrong with you?" Bongo Cole was seething mad as he slammed his boss, who also happened to be his oldest friend and leader of their band, into the concrete block wall of the backstage tunnel. "I have a family and every time you fall off the wagon, Jesse, you hurt my family. Does that mean *anything* to you?"

Hitting the wall like a ragdoll, Jesse Winslow, lead singer of the chart-topping band, Winslow, unsuccessfully attempted to pull away from his drummer's grasp. Jesse's limbs were having no part of interacting with the limited messages he could access from his substance-polluted brain.

"C'mon, Casey," he addressed Bongo by his given name. "They were crucifying us, man. What was I supposed to do? Just let them crucify us?" The handsome rocker slurred, defiantly defending his crowd-enraging behavior.

"Fuck you, Jesse. Maybe if you weren't too trashed to remember the freaking words and riffs, they wouldn't crucify us. I am so through with you, dude." Bongo turned from his friend, a look of utter disgust marring his long, thin face. Walking away at a brisk pace, he called over his shoulder, without stopping, "This time, I am done with you."

And that was how Winslow ended the highly anticipated Australian leg of their world tour.

· · · · · ·

It was all over social media in a nanosecond. The press loved it. Bad boys of the stage were irresistible. Like Jim Morrison or Billie Jo Armstrong before him, the public could never get enough of the charismatic Jesse Winslow, who couldn't keep his shit together. When he lost it, as he invariably often did, the Internet, TV paparazzi shows, radio, and news broadcasts were sparked to life by his over-the-top antics. This publicist's nightmare was truly a gossip hound's wet dream.

But, more than anything else, like the other bad boys of rock, Jesse was the stuff fangirls and music sales were made of. And luckily for him, bad behavior and swoon-worthy were two of his strongest attributes. Hot. Sexy. Talented. And fucked up. Jesse Winslow was pure eye candy with intrigue and charm.

What more could you ask for in a rock star?

Embodying bad boy and then taking it to the next level, his backstage after-parties were legendary, although he probably possessed very few actual memories of them. Tennessee whiskey and blow, all while he was getting blown, was his nightly version of a relaxation technique. Rock star meditation, he'd been quoted as calling it.

When performing, the man prowled the stage like a caged animal, releasing pheromones in palpable waves that made females in the audience drip with desire and male fans feel like they were big-cocked stars, fist-punching the air along with him. When he looked out into the audience, every woman, right up to the last row of the nosebleed seats, swore he was singing to her with his low, raspy growl. He was begging her, and only her, when he sang the words,

*Please come back.*

*Baby, please come back,*

*Please come back to me*

There wasn't a woman in the arena who didn't want to fix him, heal the hurt residing behind those words and his sexy, clear grey-blue eyes.

When Jesse held it together, there was no doubt why this charismatic, talented man had throngs of loyal fans–men and woman alike. Men wanted to be him, they aspired to duplicate his effortless cool, his every-man working-class hero style and women wanted to be his lover and confidante, exploring the darkness in his soul and being the one to finally fix him.

When Jesse lost it, allowing his first teen lover bourbon access through the door he'd slammed on her a million times before, there hardly seemed to be a soul who didn't want every detail of his latest fall from grace. The public could not get enough of him. The worse the behavior, the more they loved him. And the media outlets loved him for it.

He truly was a tabloid's wet dream.

. . . . . .

Looking over her notes from the late-night emergency phone call, Claire Stoddard thought, *Jesse, Jesse, Jesse, how do I get through to you?*

Out of rehab for the third time in less than four years, she wondered if her exceedingly sexy, rock star patient would make it to his thirtieth birthday. Hell bent on letting his demons have their way with him, Jesse Winslow was a tortured soul. Of that there was no doubt.

*But why?*

And that was the question that plagued psychiatrist, Dr. Claire Stoddard, as she sat with her psychiatric supervisor, Dr. Marshall Reid, early on a Monday morning.

"How long have you been treating him now?" Marshall pushed up his glasses from the bridge of his nose.

"Just over a year," Claire's eyebrows were drawn together forming a pair of twin arches, that screamed frustration from their rounded tops.

"Have you done regression hypnosis with him? Explored childhood trauma he might be repressing?" Marshall continued to make notes without looking up at Claire.

"We've talked about it, but he didn't want to begin the process prior to his last tour. He's just about to return from a tour in Asia and Australia with his band. I think he'll be home, or at least in the states, for the better part of a year, so I'm hoping it's a topic we can broach again."

"Potentially that gives you time to work with him in a concentrated and in-depth capacity. Hopefully, that will provide the opportunity to see if you can get to the root of some of his self-destructive issues."

Continuing to look through her notes, "I'm almost fearful of the demons I'm going to find," she sighed, shaking her head. "He's definitely a tortured soul. Are you familiar with his music? His lyrics are a dark poetry and the melodies are positively haunting."

"My son's a fan," Marshall confessed. Giving Claire a pointed look, "Let's talk about you, Claire. Your interest in this patient has been almost obsessive. You've had other high-profile patients before, and I have never noted anything but a detached professionalism from you. So, that makes me question if there is some countertransference going on between you and Jesse Winslow."

"That's absurd," she shot back, her spine straightening as her shoulders squared for battle. *Countertransference. Seriously, did he think she was falling in love with her own patient?*

"Is it?" Marshall's tone remained even, his face betraying nothing, as he pinned her with his unwavering stare.

And for the first time, Dr. Claire Stoddard came face to face with the shocking realization that like most women on the planet, she was not immune to the mystery and charms of bad-boy rocker, Jesse Winslow. And she *was* in a position to actually fix him, something most women only dreamed of.

Except for her, as his therapist, these feelings were forbidden. And she knew better.

Claire Stoddard was the only woman not allowed to have a crush on the blue-eyed soul master and yet, she had to admit that Marshall was right. She was more than a little obsessed with her patient. There was just something about him.

*Could she be falling in love with Jesse Winslow?*

# Chapter 2

Kylie Martin shifted from side to side in the big overstuffed chair, a chair that felt oddly out of place in a shrink's waiting room. Sucking mindlessly on the straw of her Starbucks Salted Caramel Mocha Frappuccino, she shifted left, then right, then left again. To the casual observer, it would appear she just couldn't get comfortable as she flicked through the pages of the waiting room's copy of *People* magazine.

But there was nothing casual in Kylie's movement. It was deliberate. Very deliberate. Peering over her magazine, she checked out the very proper receptionist, a total mini-me clone of her employer, and was thrilled to see that the girl was thoroughly wrapped up in her work and paying no attention to Kylie.

"Fucking Brazilian," Kylie muttered under her breath as she continued to squirm. And then, there it was, the right spot. She'd found it and began to rub against it in an almost imperceptible movement. Scratch that itch.

*Ahhh, relief.*

There was nothing worse than the itching and pain from a Brazilian wax that was just beginning to grow in. Another torturous thing women had to endure.

*Yes. Yes. Yes.*

Snickering, Kylie knew if she kept up the motion the Brazilian wouldn't be the *only* itch she'd be scratching. *How funny is that!* she thought and for a second wondered if she could pull off a silent orgasm just feet away from Miss Prim and Proper right there in her shrink's waiting room. Just the act of doing the nasty in a place she wasn't supposed to be doing it, sent a shiver-inducing jolt to the apex of her thighs.

*Serves Claire right for making me wait. If I come now, I'm just going to want to sleep during our session. If we do a regression today, good luck in keeping me awake.*

Closing her eyes, Kylie placed the magazine on the table next to her and sucked on the Frappuccino, continuing the almost undetectable motion with a smug smirk on her pretty face. Feeling the pressure build, she wanted to unbutton her already too tight jeans, unzip the fly and stick her right hand down her pants. She always did herself with her right hand, she mused, with a barely audible chuckle. Mmm, felt so good and she couldn't believe how quickly she was getting closer, even without using her hands. She had no idea that the excitement of doing a selfie-nasty with someone just feet away, who didn't have a clue or did she? *Maybe I'm a closet exhibitionist? Or some other kind of weirdo perv. Note to self: Discuss with Claire. Not!*

*So close.* She pressed against the seam in her jeans. *So fucking close.*

The surprising click of the entrance door opening behind her instantaneously plucked Kylie from the amorphous electric edge of orgasm and deposited her with a thud under the harsh lights of the waiting room. Left to quickly scramble to regain a straight-backed, seated position, she attempted to act like nothing was going on.

It was the door from the outer hallway. No one ever came when another patient was there. Ever. Claire spaced out her patients to ensure privacy. *What the fuck? The UPS man?*

Opening her eyes, he was as shocked to see her as she was to see him.

Flustered, he turned to the receptionist. "M-my appointment," he stammered in a gravelly voice that Kylie would've recognized even if she'd been blindfolded.

Miss Prim and Proper was as flummoxed as he was, "Your appointment is on Wednesday."

"Well, isn't today…" his voice trailed off, the confusion evident in the tilt of his head and the furrow that appeared between his brows as he quickly raised his mirrored aviator shades. He looked rough, as if he hadn't slept in days, dark circles betraying his truth, yet at the same time, this was the most clean-cut Kylie had ever seen him look. Under his low-slung baseball cap, his hair was cut neatly at the sideburns, around his ears and neckline, transforming the appearance he was known for with his trademark rocker locks, to more of a model with his sculpted features finally being given their due. Almost immediately, he dropped the glasses back into place.

"Today's Tuesday," she corrected his non-verbalized thought.

"Oh," he appeared genuinely confused. Turning toward Kylie, "Sorry, I recently got back from Australia and have kinda lost track of days since then. I-I'll come back tomorrow."

Responding to her smile with one of his own, she felt as if they were the only two people on the planet sharing a great secret.

And in a way, they were.

Kylie now knew that Jesse Winslow, one of the sexiest bad-boy rockers on the planet, was a patient of the preeminent psychiatrist, Dr. Claire Stoddard. And Jesse Winslow knew that a very pretty, full-figured girl with the most gorgeous natural auburn hair he'd ever seen, who liked to drink frozen drinks in the dead of winter, saw Claire, too.

With a smirk and a slight smile, "Sorry." He shrugged his shoulders. The distressed leather of his jacket making a slight creaking sound.

Kylie smiled wider. The tip of the straw still in her teeth. With a slight nod of her head she acknowledged his apology for the intrusion.

And then he was gone.

Kylie could feel the energy charge in the air dissipate. Had it been because Jesse had been in the room, or her unfulfilled orgasm, or was it her reaction to Jesse. She wasn't quite sure, but Kylie had felt it leave in a whoosh.

It wasn't two minutes later that Dr. Claire Stoddard opened the door to her office. *The Inner Sanctum*, Kylie had dubbed it.

"Kylie, I'll see you now." Her demeanor was detached and formal, her clothes polished and professional, if not a little bland. The Ivy League-trained doctor had perfected perfection. Never seen with a hair out of place or a wrinkle in the impeccable fabric of one of her earth-tone suits, Claire Stoddard personified *aloof,* or at least that was what Kylie thought.

Brushing past her, Kylie stopped. "So, Jesse Winslow is a patient of yours, huh? I'd love to get inside both his head and those painted on ripped jeans. That man has a seriously beautiful ass." With that, Kylie plopped herself down on the big leather couch, smiling like a Cheshire cat.

*Turd aimed at the punchbowl.*

*She shoots.*

*She scores!*

Knowing exactly how much she'd just freaked out her psychiatrist, Kylie let the bombshell sink in for a moment. When Claire had nervously readjusted her glasses twice, Kylie finally offered up an explanation, "I guess he thought it was Wednesday, because he showed up here." Again, she let it sink in, "You're lucky I'm not a stalker, Claire, because I could totally be waiting for him on Wednesdays." She stopped and thought for a moment, "How rude of me, I just should have invited him to stay for a group session." Kylie took great pleasure in antagonizing her shrink. She didn't quite know why, but she got such satisfaction from fucking with her. Which generally was not her style of dealing with people, but with Claire, she had these unresolved antagonistic feelings. Which, even she had to admit, was odd.

Dr. Stoddard was not amused by her patient. "I'm sorry you were disturbed and your anonymity was compromised. Would you like to be rescheduled for an alternate time?"

"No, not necessary. He doesn't know who the heck I am." *Just another random chick,* Kylie thought. *He's certainly not going to be stalking fat chicks who see shrinks. And there's no way he has any recollection of the one-time our paths actually did cross.*

Getting right to business, Claire reviewed her notes.

"You had committed in the last session to engage the service of a trainer." She looked up from her notepad, waiting for Kylie's response.

"Didn't happen." Kylie clicked the straw in her teeth and secretly took delight from Claire's slight flinches.

"And why is that?"

Kylie shrugged, "I just didn't get around to it."

"What do you think is holding you back?"

Another shrug, "I dunno."

Claire remained silent.

"Maybe I don't want to be thin again."

Claire waited.

"Maybe I'm happy being fat."

"Are you?" The psychiatrist tipped her head.

"Yes. In some ways, yes, I am." Kylie sat forward on the couch. "Do you know how hard it is to compete solely on your looks? To constantly be judged on your looks."

"Everyone is judged on their looks, Kylie. We make snap judgments all the time on everyone we encounter based on visual impressions."

"But there is not pressure for them in that. Not like what I went through."

"There are many strategies you can employ to work on the pressure and get your life back."

"Why do you assume I want it back, Claire? Maybe I don't equate thin and perfect looking to happiness. I was thin and perfect and I wasn't remotely happy. Why the hell would I want to go back to that?" Kylie visibly shuddered, memories of starving herself, hours in make-up before pageants and the stress and competitiveness rolling off her mother and the other parents. It was Hell. And it certainly wasn't her dream.

Claire remained silent for a few moments. "I had you scheduled for a regression today. Is that something you would still like to pursue?"

Kylie shrugged her shoulders and took another sip of her Frappuccino. "Sure. Why not?" She seemed resigned. She wanted the process to work, but up until now, all she'd seen were some hazy images, like viewing an old slide show, and who knew if that was even real. Although she desperately wanted it to be, mainly because lack of a truly successful regression in her first twelve attempts was making her feel like a failure. Yup, add that to the pile.

With the press of a remote, the window shades darkened, giving the Inner Sanctum an insulated, cocoon-like feel.

Immediately relaxing in the darkness, Kylie reached over to the side-table next to the couch, feeling around with her hands as her eyes adjusted to the darkness, she picked up a pair of what appeared to be oversized sunglasses. Situating them on her face, she played with a small scroll button that adjusted speed and intensity of colored light flashes. Placing headphones on as she laid back on the couch, soft drumbeats played and the lights before her eyes danced to the music.

And then they started. Just like they had done a dozen times before.

"Are you in a comfortable position?"

"Yes." She could hear Claire's soothing voice through her headphones. *Her voice is so soothing, so why does she grate on my nerves so much?* Kylie wondered, before shooing the thought from her consciousness and finding a comfortable spot lying down on the couch.

"Good. Now, let's begin. Start with a few deep, cleansing breaths. Each breath is like a gust of wind, blowing all concerns and stresses from your mind. Concentrate on your breathing and where the breath is going. It's traveling down into your lungs and oxygenating and relaxing your chest and your shoulders. Feel it flow into your arms, relaxing them as it enters your fingers and along the trunk of your body as your lower back melts effortlessly into the couch. Your thighs relax as the oxygen moves down your legs, relaxing your quadriceps and your knees. Let your calves sink into the couch as the arches of your feet become oxygenated and finally allow your toes to relax. That's right, sink into the couch, concentrate on your breathing. Feel the white light that surrounds your body. Envision it entering through the crown of your head. Feel the warm, calming glow as the light slowly spreads down the pathways opened up by the oxygen. On one of your hands I want you to touch your thumb to your forefinger. This is your anchor. At any time, should you need to stop, or if this gets overwhelming, touch your thumb to your forefinger and it will activate your anchor and take you out of your hypnotic state. Do you understand, Kylie?"

"Yes," her answer was slow.

Concentrating, Kylie could feel all the tension leave her body, as she listened to the dulcet tones of Claire's voice.

"I want you to go back and find a happy memory from when you were around five years old. Visualize it. Who was there with you? What can you smell? What are you wearing? I want you to concentrate on what you were feeling."

Claire remained quiet for a few moments, allowing Kylie to visualize the memory.

*Sitting in Grandpa's lap and playing with my new doll. She's so pretty. I want to look like her. Her hair is black and shiny and her eyes are so blue. Daddy just mowed the lawn this morning and it's making my nose itch. It feels like there's a line of ants walking in there. I'm so tired. I want to nap, but if I do, I might miss the barber Q.*

"Now, I want you to go back to just after your birth. Take note of your surroundings. Your feelings. Your needs."

Again, Claire went silent.

*So cold. I'm shivering. I think it's hunger I feel. I'm so cold. The light hurts. And I'm so cold.*

"Focus on a time before your birth. You'll be able to communicate with me, describing things with your knowledge from today, from current times. Do you understand?"

"Yes."

"Where are you, Kylie?"

Shaking her head, "I don't know."

"Look down at your feet. What are you wearing?"

"Oh, they're cute," there was surprise and emotion in her voice. "Lace-up boots. Practical. Not fancy. Pointy toe, low, curvy heel."

"Do you know what year it is?

"1870."

"Where are you?"

"Strasbourg."

"Is that France?" Claire asked, trying to visualize the region on a map.

"It was. We are now under German rule. The city fell a few months ago."

"What is your name?"

"Noëlle."

"And you are French, Noëlle?"

"Yes. I am."

"What is your last name?"

"Regensburg."

"Hmm, that sounds German," the doctor mused.

"I am Alsatian." Noëlle was quick to insert.

"What are you seeing, Noëlle?"

"There are so many wounded. Not enough of us to take care of them. And they are so young. We need more supplies. We're losing boys we should be able to save. We don't have enough medicine for the pain or the infections."

"Are you a nurse?"

"Yes."

"How old are you?"

"I am twenty-two."

"Tell me what you are seeing."

"It is after hours. My shift is long over. But I am still at the hospital. I am with a patient. He is the enemy, but someone special because we are treating him at this hospital and not a field hospital. He was in custody and shot trying to escape. But the commanders want him kept alive. He is very important to them."

Claire watched as her patient's demeanor became almost giddy, her shoulders alternately lifting in a flirtatious manner. She made note of the physical manifestation on her iPad.

"What is his name?" the psychiatrist probed.

"Gunther."

"Do you remember his last name?"

"Wolff."

"And he is a patient of yours?"

"He was, but now I come to read to him and spend my free time with him. He makes me laugh and tells me that I am the most beautiful girl he's ever seen and that someday he will marry me. He said that Berlin will become the capital of the German Empire and he will take me there to meet his family and to live and I will have servants and maids." She stopped speaking, although the twitches in her cheek and jaw muscles indicate that the story was continuing. "He's so handsome and every day I grow more attached to him. But his fever is still high and we can't find the source of the infection."

"What do you see?"

"His eyes. So clear. They are the color of the sky after a rain storm has blown through. I have never seen so much love in eyes. They tell me a story, and if I look deeply enough into them, I can see our future and the smiles of our children. But I am so afraid of what will happen when he recuperates and I know he is scared for me being in a war-torn region if he isn't with me. He wants to take care of me, protect me.

"He told me that if he leaves, that I should wait for him. He will come back for me or send for me. I don't know what they are planning to do to him once he is well enough to leave the hospital. I'm scared."

Kylie falls silent again, her face contorted as tears stream down the sides of her cheeks and drip to their final resting place, buried within her thick, auburn hair.

Claire waits, remaining still.

"What has happened?" she finally asks.

"We could hear the sounds in the dormitory. Gunshots. And when I went in the morning to see him, he was gone. But my heart already knew. I knew the minute I heard the shots."

"Gone? What happened?"

"He was executed trying to escape. They killed him. He was just trying to get home and they killed him."

Writing continuous notes as her client spoke, "What happened to you after that?" Claire asked without looking up.

"It took a long time, but I finally married. He was much older. Very stern. But he kept me fed."

"What was your husband's name?"

"Christophe."

"Did Christophe know about Gunther?"

"He did. But I wasn't permitted to speak of him. Only in my heart. If I spoke of him, even aloud in my sleep, Christophe would get very angry. Feel that I was betraying him and he would make me apologize," she visibly shivered. "He would hurt me, physically. Sexually, he was rough. He'd lock me in the basement for days."

Kylie's chin sank to her chest, her eyes remained closed.

"Are you still here?"

"No. I am gone."

"What did you learn in that lifetime?" the psychiatrist ended with a question she always asked.

"That love has no borders."

**Patient: Kylie Martin**

**Session #59**

**Regression #13**

**November 4, 2014**

**Regression Length: 10:25 A.M.–10:48 A.M.**

**Entity: Noëlle**

**Location: Strasbourg, Alsace-Lorraine**

**Year: 1870**

· · · · · ·

Bundled up in her faux fur jacket and scarf, Kylie rode the elevator down from Claire's office remaining firmly entrenched inside her own head as she fought to retain her grasp on the fading visuals of a world so foreign, yet so familiar. And the feeling. She couldn't shake the feeling. Gunther's eyes. The emotion in them. He didn't need to speak to her. She knew the depth of his love and devotion, even though their time together had been short, and now she felt empty, positively hollow without him, without someone loving her so deeply, so purely.

As the elevator doors opened in the lobby, Kylie wandered to a trash can, mindlessly tossing in her now empty Starbucks cup. Stepping out onto the sidewalk, the blast of frozen air on her face caused her head to snap back, as if she'd just been slapped by an overbearing stage mother. Although the sky was gray and threatening snow, she scrounged around the bottom of her purse feeling desperately for her sunglasses. Finding herself surprisingly overwhelmed, she needed a barrier, not yet ready for this world.

A man. A man she loved deeply. The thought running through her head was *it was us against the world.* We didn't care if they called us French, Germans, Prussians. It didn't matter as long as we were together, because our love was right.

*How do I know this?*

None of the other regressions had left her with such a strong, lingering emotional imprint. Claire had warned her that as they continued their work, what were initially snippets of visuals or feelings would become more complex and richer in nature. But this was a feeling she couldn't shake. It was so real. So emotionally real that it had her yearning.

*But for what?*

Crossing 63$^{rd}$ Street, Gunther's eyes, as she saw them in that last vision, were the only thing she could see now. The traffic and noise and smells of New York City evaporated to the far side of a translucent veil, parallel to the space she was currently inhabiting. The overwhelming pull on her heart as she and Gunther were separated forever, felt like a fresh wound.

The rhythmic sound of tapping swiftly catapulted her back to the streets of New York and out of the netherworld she had been caught in while walking the previous block. He was gently rapping on the glass with his knuckles and when she turned toward the sound, there sat Jesse Fucking Winslow, in his full camouflage, on a stool at the counter along the window. With a sexy as-fuck lopsided grin on his face, he held up a frozen drink, and motioned for her to come inside Starbucks.

Entering the warm coffee shop, the heady aroma of the dark roast and rough-hewn brick walls brought immediate comfort and much-needed grounding, although walking toward freaking Jesse Winslow was anything but grounding, she mused. Weaving her way through the tables and overstuffed chairs toward where he sat, Kylie wondered how many people in the coffee shop realized the camouflaged man sitting on a stool by the window was the one and only leader of the iconic rock band, Winslow. The man who'd been the focus of more press, in the past month or so, than any world leader.

Somewhere in a former life, not the kind of former lives Claire brought her to, but one of just eighteen months before, the former Miss New Jersey would have had the balls to stroll up to a man as gorgeous and famous as Jesse Winslow, and know with the utmost confidence, that just the sight of her was causing his testosterone to run amok and fever-ishly race toward both his heads, obliterating all sound logic and reason in his northern one.

But today, size eighteen Kylie Martin, would have willingly vowed to never, ever again eat another spoonful of Ben & Jerry's Cherry Garcia ice cream just to possess the super-power to make herself invisible, or at least a size four, as she walked toward one of the most famous, sexiest men ever to have sauntered a rock 'n' roll stage.

"I think I got it right." He held up the drink and handed it to her as she slid onto the high stool next to him. With his lopsided grin, he added, "I asked the guy what the cold drink was that the gorgeous redhead had gotten about an hour ago."

Slipping the straw between her teeth for instant pacification, Kylie took a sip. The Salted Caramel Mocha Frappuccino was perfect. She smiled, straw still in her mouth. "You done good." *Gorgeous redhead? Seriously? This man needs to go back into rehab because he's on the good stuff.*

Jesse laughed and nodded his head, spiky bangs flowing out the edge of his baseball cap and over the shiny rims of his sunglasses. "I'm Jesse."

Kylie just smiled, but didn't say anything.

"Okay, so you knew that." He was off balance. This girl wasn't gushing. "So, Dr. S would shit right now if she walked by here and saw us together."

Kylie's smile broadened as she clicked the straw between her teeth. "I told her I saw you."

"Did she freak?" Jesse looked amused, his tone suddenly conspirato-rial.

"It was awesome," Kyle confided. "I'm surprised she didn't excuse herself to change her panty liner."

Choking on the hot coffee he'd just swallowed, Kylie reached out and patted Jesse on the back. "Take another sip, it will help."

"You are funny." He sized her up.

"Yeah, hilarious," her voice dripped sarcasm in a way only confident girls from the northeast could pull off. Had she taken off her sunglasses, he would've seen her rolling her eyes.

But neither Kylie nor Jesse would remove their sunglasses that day and give the other a glimpse into psyches that neither one was prepared to expose. Just knowing the other was one of Claire's patients was enough exposure for one day.

"So, I have something really personal to ask you." Jesse's demeanor had turned serious.

"Okay, shoot."

"Well, first, what's your name?" He leaned in close to her.

Kylie could feel the intensity of his gaze from behind the mirrored glasses.

"Kylie."

"Kylie," he smiled. "That's a pretty name." He reached out and let a long lock of her hair absentmindedly slip through his fingers.

Looking down at his hand, Kylie watched the movement, stunned. He had just invaded her personal space, with a very intimate gesture. She could immediately feel the contraction in her muscles pulling away from his touch.

Realizing his overture was not being well received, "I'm sorry. I don't know why I did that. When I saw you in Dr. S's office today, I couldn't help but notice how beautiful your hair was and I don't know why I just reached out and did that. I'm sorry," He was actually stammering, seemingly almost confused as he apologized to a woman for touching her, something clearly not a staple in his repertoire.

Kylie remained silent. Jesse was in a very public, media-fixated relationship with a supermodel named, Claudine. *Claudine.* Just Claudine. Nothing else.

The only other time Kylie had ever been near Jesse Winslow was during Fashion Week, nearly three years before, when she modeled at a runway show for a designer friend of hers. Her buddy, Travis, was the "Opening Act" to the mega-popular lingerie company where Claudine held the exalted role of top model. She remembered catching his lop-sided smile that day, and returning it with one of her own, as she confidently strolled the catwalk. But she knew she was one of many models catching Jesse's eye at the show as he waited for the main event to appear. *Claudine.*

Usually quick with a retort, Kylie was left speechless. Embarrassed that she had backed away from Jesse's touch, and yet, aching desperately, wanting him to touch her again. Needing another chance, this time not shying away.

Beyond her oversized, dark glasses, she was trying to remember where she had experienced this feeling gripping her, and wondered if maybe it had been in a movie. A woman backed up against a wall. The man, dangerous. A knife to her throat as he slipped his fingers inside her underwear, discovering her wet with desire beyond her control. Turned on. Scared. Helpless. Captive. Captivated. Wanting his fingers to continue their slow, deliberate strokes. Needing him to go even farther. Breathless with fear and desire.

"I'm sorry," he repeated.

Kylie shook her head. "No, I'm sorry. I just had an intense morning and I'm a little spaced out."

"That's what I want to talk to you about. I know this is really personal."

Feeling an immediate pang of fear, Kylie's radar immediately propelled off the charts. *How does he know about the knife to the throat, the man's fingers stroking me?*

Jesse continued, bringing Kylie back to the here and now, "As you know from my little appointment faux pas this morning, I recently got back from Australia. And I'm home now. I'm not going to be out on tour for a while."

Elation flooded Kylie and she internally smacked herself to *stop that,* but she couldn't stop herself and immediately went to the possibility that if he were home, maybe this would not be the only time they'd ever meet. Maybe they would meet again someday.

"I had made a promise to Dr. S that when I got back from this tour that I would commit myself to getting healthy. Body, mind, and spirit." He played with his coffee cup, lips moving slightly, but no sound emerged as he formulated his thought, "And between you and me, if I'm still going to have a band, I really need to get my shit together." Looking down, he shook his head, "I can't believe I just told you that."

"It's okay." Not seeing herself as particularly nurturing, Kylie was surprised to find she was reassuring him. Wanting to reach out and touch him, she didn't, fearing he'd see her like every other fan tugging at pieces of him until he was fragmented.

"Anyway, now that I'm back, I want to make a commitment to get serious and..." he paused.

"Begin regression analysis via hypnosis," Kylie finished his sentence.

Jesse looked up from his feet. Stunned. Then slowly nodded his head. "Are you doing it?"

With an almost imperceptible nod, she confirmed.

Kylie could feel pulses of tension radiating off Jesse as his right leg bounced to a beat only he could hear. "Are you concerned about doing it?" she probed his anxiety.

"I am. Lord knows what demons I'll unleash. Aren't you afraid of that?"

"No." She shook her head. "I keep searching for my demons, hoping that maybe they have the answers."

"Are you finding them?" With his elbows on the wooden bar, he leaned close. "There's so much I want to know." He paused. "Are you okay with talking to me about this?"

Clicking the straw between her front teeth, "Yeah, I guess so. I dunno. I'm not really good at sharing stuff with people, sharing feelings. So, I don't know how helpful I'll be." Absentmindedly gnawing at the straw as she thought through it, "I have no one to talk to about this, so that would be good." *And you're Jesse Fucking Winslow and you want to have deep conversations with me regarding stuff that if I talked to most people about, they would think I'm bat shit crazy.*

"Did it happen right away?"

"No. Not really." Kylie slurped at the bottom of her drink. "I mean initially there was nothing. Then it was like a still picture or a word or a pervasive thought that would just permeate my brain."

"Let me get you another one of those." He pointed to her now-empty drink.

"No, I think you should stay right here. I'll get it. Miraculously, people have not figured out you're in here. If you get up, someone is bound to notice."

Jesse nodded. "Well, at least let me pay for you."

Kylie waved him off, but he insisted until she finally took the twenty dollars he offered. "What can I get you?"

"Venti drip, black, with three sugars."

Laughing, "That should keep you revved up," she called over her shoulder, smiling broadly at his lopsided grin. *Oh, God, I should have let you get the coffee. Now you're seeing my ass as I walk away.* Kylie went into pageant girl mode, it was as easy as flipping a switch as she tossed her hair and gracefully maneuvered through tables that didn't seem to be placed so close together when she was thinner.

Pretending she looked like she did the day he saw her on the catwalk–wanting to look like that for the first time in forever–Kylie shook her head. *Fool, he lives with one of the most beautiful women on the planet. Do you really think he's going to give a flying fuck if your ass looks like it's in a relationship with Colonel Sanders or is starved to near perfection? Umm, no. Just get the coffees. One of the hottest musicians of our time is just here to pick your brain, not pluck your body like a six-string.*

"Thanks." He took the coffee from her and brought it to his lips.

Kylie watched him sip it, his full, sensual mouth on the lid. It was impossible not to imagine what the bow of his beautiful top lip would feel like pressed just under her jawline.

"What?" he asked, smiling.

"This is just really bizarre. Who you are and what we are talking about. It's totally surreal and," lowering her voice, "oddly intimate." As the tail end of the sentence filled the space between them, she could feel the heat emanating from her face.

"I really had no right asking you." The apology tumbled from his lips.

"No, it's okay." Kylie felt the supple smoothness of the leather under her fingers as she reached out and laid a hand on his arm, this time being the trespasser. Looking down, she was appalled that she had entered his space, like a groupie making her play for the night, her soft caress suggesting an intimacy far outside the boundaries of her comfort zone, boundaries she had established when he ran his fingers through her hair. With a jerking motion that made both of them jump, Kylie pulled her hand back, viewing her renegade fingertips with disdain. She felt like she'd cheapened the moment and didn't know how to get back what she felt was a special and unique connection.

Jesse changed that for her. "I'm really glad I found you," he started.

Then stopped. A scowl forming a twin set of parallel lines between his eyes. "I mean," he stumbled, "I mean, maybe I won't have to go through this alone. And you won't either, if you don't want to."

Kylie couldn't look at him. For some reason she didn't want him to look at her as a groupie. But, what was shocking was that she wanted him to view her as a partner in this process.

*Jesse Winslow's partner. How could that even be?*

"I saw something today," she confessed. "It was a really long time ago. Like 1870. I don't know." She shook her head. "And I can't shake it. I can't shake the feeling. I was a nurse and it was during a war and I was in love with one of the patients. He was a wounded enemy soldier and everyone told me I couldn't love him. But I did. He was my sunshine in a dark and rotting world. And I cared for him for months and we dreamed of our future."

"Do you know if you ever had that future?" The intensity of needing to know was evident in the way he leaned in when he spoke.

Kylie reached under her sunglasses, not removing them, to swipe away sudden tears. "No. I wasn't able to save him in the end. He was executed trying to escape. It was so emotional. My pain at losing him. Having to live on without him. The love. How much I loved him. It was overwhelming." Thoughts shot out in staccato bursts, ripping through her heart.

Jesse raised a hand, covering his own heart, as if trying to quell his own pain. "Wow. That's intense. And you knew he was an enemy soldier?"

"Yes. I just knew so much. It was like it all downloaded in a nanosecond. His name was Gunther. And, Jesse, I'd give anything to see him for one more second. To feel that overwhelming love. It was intense." Kylie lifted her frozen drink, pacifying herself with the straw. "Claire said it would get more intense the more we did it and this was how it started."

Leaning in, his tone low, "How many times have you done it before?"

"Today was the thirteenth. I mean it didn't last long or anything, but this was the first time I didn't walk out wondering did something really happen or not? Was I just making it all up?"

His lopsided grin almost made her gasp. "Okay, I'm going to do this." He nodded. "I'm so fucked up and out of control." And then, "I guess I'm not so out of control or I wouldn't know how fucked up I was or give a shit about losing it all. And I do. I give a shit. I just can't stop myself from fucking up."

With a smile that she had no inkling was causing emotions he couldn't grasp and forming stanzas he would one day write, she said, "I hear ya."

"I'm going to do this," he muttered again.

"Well, good luck with it. And don't beat yourself up if nothing comes to you for a while. Like I said, today was my first big breakthrough and it was my thirteenth regression." Kylie zipped up her faux fur.

"Did it give you any answers to your problems?"

Shrugging, "I don't know. None of it makes sense yet."

Taking in her words, he observed, "You don't seem to be in a bad place."

Kylie laughed as she turned to walk away. "My name is Kylie Martin. Google me."

And with that, the former Miss New Jersey left rock 'n' roll bad boy, Jesse Winslow, seated on a high stool in a Starbucks wondering what overwhelming issues could be so prevalent in her life that she was resorting to regression therapy with a very pricey uptown psychiatrist.

# Chapter 3

*"I didn't know you smoked," Kylie's nose scrunched up and he thought how cute she was, in a kid sister kind of way.*

*"Only when I'm stressed."*

*"What are you stressed out about?"*

*"Everything. I haven't written a single song since I've been back, the guys in my band aren't talking to me, my girlfriend puts a load of pressure on me, I'm detoxing myself from alcohol and all the other shit I put into my system."*

*"Shouldn't you be doing that with a doctor or a sponsor?"*

*"I've done it so many times with doctors, I could open my own clinic."*

*"Why do you want to die?"*

*"I dunno. Sometimes the pain is overwhelming."*

*"What pain is that, Jesse?"*

*"I dunno. I just know it's there. Don't you feel it, too?"*

*"Yes. I do. I can't find what I'm looking for."*

*"Yes. Yes. That is exactly it." He was astounded that she understood.*

*"You smell like a goat."*

*"I smell like a goat?"*

*"Yeah, those cigarettes smell like goat shit and you smell like a goat."* Kylie smiled at him.

*"A goat,"* he mused, laughing. *"You just told me I smell like a goat."*

The hand on his shoulder was rocking him hard. "I have to go. C'mon, Jesse, wake up, I have to go."

Rolling over, his hand raised to shield his half-stuck lids, "You're a goat?" he asked, quickly trying to bridge the gap from his dream to the screwed-up face of Claudine's early morning wrath.

"I'm not a goat. I said I have to go." She was annoyed. "You knew I was leaving for Paris this morning. It's 7:15 and I have to go."

"You're taking a day flight?"

"Ugh, Jesse." She tossed her long blonde hair over her shoulder with the mere flick of her head. "You are still planning on meeting me there in two weeks, aren't you?"

"Yeah, sure." He sat up in bed and ruffled his hair. "Martin," he said aloud, not meaning to.

"Martin?" she repeated, regarding him suspiciously.

"Yeah, it was just a name I couldn't remember." She had told him to Google her. It seemed like a lifetime ago, on the other side of his detox. The initial physical trauma was already behind him when they had met, and that day had been a good day, a rare early good day, that was finally becoming more the norm.

Three weeks had passed. Each Tuesday he had planned on going to Starbucks and wait there, hoping to catch her as she passed by after her appointment with Dr. S. But he couldn't do it. The anxiety, nervousness, and mood swings during that phase of his detox were not pretty. Getting his ass to Dr. S's and to the holistic center that was guiding him was work enough. Calcium, magnesium, and herbs were helping him sleep a lot, easing the conscious hours, and he knew that was what would get him through.

His mind had felt dulled, and for the life of him, he could not remember her last name. As hard as he tried, it was out there but he couldn't quite grasp it. He thought about calling her in a few weak moments when things got overwhelming, but what would he say? When she had gotten up to get them coffee, he had programmed his number into her phone, taking a selfie of himself in camouflage. He could see her face so clearly these last few weeks, but his mind felt too vacuous, incapable of making the necessary connections to remember her name.

*Kylie Martin.*

Later in the day, he dragged his laptop onto the bed and Googled the name.

*Miss New Jersey Tossed Out of the Miss America Pageant.* There was the headline, almost two years old, and the image was of a beautiful redheaded girl with green eyes and an enticing, full, pouty mouth.

The mocking wit in her eyes and lustrous wave of her dark titian hair were the giveaway. *Wow. What made you do this to yourself?* And Jesse instantly knew she was hiding. He could almost feel her trauma. The Kylie Martin pageant queen he was stalking on Google images, had to have been at least sixty to seventy pounds, or more, lighter than Dr. S's patient, the girl he'd met up with at Starbucks.

Examining screen after screen of the poised beauty in pageants and fashion shows, he kept expecting to find a light in the girl, something to show him that she was happier when she was thin and successfully building a modeling career. But there was no such light. Her eyes flashed *vacancy*, her vacuous, camera-perfect smile confirmed the void.

*What are you hiding from, Kylie? Women would give their left arm to look like you. Rare beauty*, were the two words resounding in his brain.

Setting the laptop on the bed, he reached over and plucked his old Gibson acoustic from its home, leaning against his nightstand.

Em, G, Gm

Jesse closed his eyes as his fingers took flight over the strings, a warm bass tone emanating from deep in the body of the forty-year-old six-string.

*Where ya gonna run when there's no place left to go*

*Where ya gonna run when there's no place left to hide*

*Those are skyscrapers I can't scale*

*Chasms I can't cross*

*Shells that can't be broken*

*Oh, baby, I'm at a loss*

*I want to tell you all my secrets*

*I want to bare to you the depths of my soul*

*I want to take you on a journey*

*If only you would go*

Who would have ever thought that the former Miss New Jersey would be his muse? With his favorite acoustic spooned under his arm, paper, journal, pen, pencil, and laptop strewn about around him, Jesse Winslow sat in the middle of his bed, in an empty apartment, and wrote the first four songs for his next album.

In interviews, he would later describe the experience as if he were being guided and comment that this newfound sobriety was the greatest and most creative high he'd ever experienced.

Filling the apartment with soaring guitar riffs, haunting piano solos, honest words from deep, dark places and empty take-out food containers, the bones of Jesse Winslow's next album, *Fade to White*, were born of a wanting, a need to know, and a deep-stirring gnawing at his soul begging to be recognized, as the lead singer reveled in two weeks of solitude.

. . . . . .

**I felt something today.** He texted after a session with Dr. S.

**Jesse?**

**Yes. I put my number in your phone when you went to get us coffee.**

**You sneak!** ☺

**I'm hoping by that smile it means you're not mad at me.**

**Not mad. What did you feel?**

**It was only a passing glimpse. The buildings were old and stone. Maybe Ireland.**

**So, you saw something?**

**Yes, but it was really fleeting and the feeling was stronger than the visual. You know how when you think of a certain time in your life, there's a whole "feeling" that goes with it. It's like multiple senses all come together to form that imprint that will always signify that time.**

**Yes, I think I know what you are talking about. Sometimes a smell can bring it back for me.** She wrote back to him.

**Well, that is what it was. For a split second, it all came together. And then it was gone. And I wracked my brain, was it something I know? And it's not anything I know. But it was real and it was part of my *memories*. Does that make sense?**

**Totally. I totally get it. I'm so excited for you. You're chipping through.**

**LOL. Break on through to the other side.** He couldn't help himself and wondered if she'd get the reference.

**Now you're stealing the other guy's material.**

Jesse smiled at her response. *Miss New Jersey knew the classics. Impressive, indeed.*

**LOL...he's dead, he won't know. Or maybe he will. It is real, isn't it?**

**I think so.**

**I think you might be right.** He found himself nodding as he typed the words. **Have you seen more?**

**Yes. But nothing major.**

**Gunther?**

**You remember ☺. No, not Gunther. A different time. In France.**

**Really? I'm headed to Paris for a few days. Need me to check out anything, Miss New Jersey?**

**Ah, so you stalked me?**

**Yeah, it was weird. I'm usually the stalked, not the stalker.**

**I'll bet you've had your share of stalkers.**

**The stories I could tell you!**

When there was no response, he pinged her again. **Want to meet at Starbucks after your next session with Dr. S. I'll be back from Paris by then.**

**Okay. Hey, go have an éclair for me at Patisserie Stohrer when**

**you're in Paris. I love that place.**

**I'm more of a Napoleon kind of guy.**

**LOL. Nah, you're way too tall.**

**LOL. That's true. You are funny. Okay, I'll see you next Tuesday.**

Jesse was smiling as he tossed his phone onto the bed and grabbed his laptop.

Patisserie Stohrer. There it was. He clicked on the link. Perusing the pastries, Jesse's mouth watered. A gorgeously photographed fruit tart nearly jumped off his screen. He could taste the fresh raspberries, both tart and sweet on his tongue, feel the little seeds crunch between his teeth.

Putting the address into his phone. 51 Rue Montorgueil. Second Arrondissement. He'd have plenty of free time while Claudine was working. Back on his laptop, he clicked on Google Maps and dragged the little person icon to street level.

As he navigated through the cobblestone streets, past alleyways and sidewalk cafés, attempting not to slam into buildings, while trying hard to negotiate Google Earth on the laptop's touchpad, there was one prevalent thought ricocheting through his brain, loud and clear, so clear that it felt as if it were on a frequency that was being broadcast from deep within his temporal lobe. The message kept repeating as if it were on a loop.

*I've died here before.*

# Chapter 4

Kylie looked at her phone shaking her head and smiling. Not only had Jesse Winslow programmed his number into her phone, he had taken a selfie, lopsided smile and all. She had no idea it was in there.

It had been well over a month since their conversation in Starbucks and Kylie had secretly been hoping that she'd hear the tapping on the window after each of her sessions with Claire. But it didn't happen and after the first few weeks she was convinced it never would again.

That day in Starbucks had been so emotionally charged, she thought, and although they'd only just met, and he was who he was, Jesse Freaking Winslow, she really felt something special had gone down, an affinity only the two of them could ever share.

She replayed that morning in her mind, scarcely believing it was true and allowed her mind to wander. Could she be his friend? His confidante? The person with whom he shared secrets and demons? He would understand what she was going through and she would understand him in a way that no one else would. Well maybe Claire, but she was a doctor, and not the one visiting these other worlds they'd lived.

The initial thought that she might see him the following week after Starbucks motivated a purge in her refrigerator and freezer, a Whole Foods run resulting in a shopping cart filled with brightly colored fresh foods, and a trip to the dreaded health club where she purchased a dozen-session package with a personal trainer. *Ding. Check that one off the list, Claire. I hired a personal trainer.*

But with each week, that glimmer of sharing this other world, this strange and parallel universe with Jesse grew dimmer, receding to a pinpoint on a distant horizon. She'd blown off her training session the week before, her motivation waning. A new wave of self-loathing encroached. *Were you really trying to get healthy for some guy who doesn't even remember you? What you won't do for yourself, you were doing for him? Pathetic, Kylie!*

And now here she was back at the gym, just a week and a text conversation later, with newly found incentive to work out, to want to look good.

Standing there with a smile on his handsome face, arms crossed over his muscular chest, "Okay, Gorgeous," he greeted her. "I'm going to work your ass double-time for missing your last session. I don't like to be stood up."

"I'm betting not a lot of female clients stand you up," she mumbled, as he led her to the mats to stretch out.

Tall, blonde and handsome. Zac had a smile that could melt hearts, yet Kylie found his faraway blue eyes to be his most interesting feature. "You were my first and a man never forgets his first."

"I'll bet not," Kylie laughed. "Was your first good for you?" The sear in her calf made her choke slightly on her words, but it was clear she had changed the meaning to talk about his personal life.

"My first? My first was, umm … inappropriate, to say the least." He continued to position her to get optimum stretch on her muscles. "Have you ever done Pilates?"

"I used to."

"Did you like it?" He pressed down on her shoulder, nearly flattening her to the floor.

"Yes," she squeaked out.

"I think we should add that into what you are doing. I think it'll really center you. Get your head back into taking care of you, for you."

*Shit, what is he? Psychic?*

"Not yoga?" Kylie was surprised he wasn't pushing yoga.

"Let Pilates help get you the flexibility back so that if you want to move into yoga you're positioned for success. Both are great for a holistic approach to health. Okay, now let's go get your heart rate up."

An hour later, Kylie was drenched, her muscles spent and aching.

"I told you I'd make you pay," Zac smiled his sexy smile. "Drink a lot of water today, take a hot bath tonight." With hands on both shoulders, he looked her straight in the eyes, "We're going to get you back to loving you."

"What makes you think I don't love myself?" Kylie searched his distant blue eyes.

"Just a hunch." He gave her shoulders a squeeze and released her. Turning back as he was walking away, Zac pointed a finger at Kylie, "Don't stand me up again."

"I won't." She smiled back at him. He's right, I need to love myself. That removed look in his eyes made her wonder if what he recognized in her was something he knew all too well because he had seen it so often in the mirror. *We all hide demons*, she thought. Some we know and others are hidden deep in the recesses of our brains.

. . . . . .

"Bomp bomp-bomp-bomp-bomp. Bomp." Jesse scatted along, using his index and middle fingers to keep beat on the edge of his tablet's keyboard. Stopping to hit a few notes on the onscreen keyboard, he made the notation in his leather-bound journal, a journal he had found hidden in a secret compartment of his mother's prized, eighteenth-century tiger maple secretary desk. The old leather wrapper was casted with a chariot and cherub design attached to leather string, making Jesse always think its origins had been Italy. The only thing that had been inside was an old, worn deck of playing cards with a red-plaid back and surprisingly colorful and beautifully detailed face cards. He assumed the cards were possibly a few hundred years old and the journal wrapper potentially significantly older than that. Adding bound pages to the journal, and replacing them as necessary, Jesse filled the ancient diary with two things: hit song after hit song and the antique card deck.

"Stop that." Claudine pulled a pillow over her head. "You know I have a night shoot."

Tomorrow Jesse would fly home and he wondered why Claudine had even wanted him to join her in Paris. Shutting down his tablet, "Okay, I'll get out of here for a bit and let you sleep." Pulling the pillow off her head, he smiled down at the exquisite beauty. "Want to go for a light bite before your shoot?"

"Are you high?" she snarled.

The accusation ripped deep. The last month and a half had been hell, but he'd fought like a motherfucker to get through it, to take on the responsibility of toughing it out on his own to get clean and sober, without the coddling support of a spa-like, Malibu-based facility. Jesse also knew he couldn't blame her for throwing out the snarky comment, she had lived through his over-the-top addictive behavior for nearly four years, as he watched her voluntarily starve herself to climb the modeling ranks.

"You know I don't eat before shoots," she continued and then pulled the pillow back down.

He did know that, but he wasn't thinking. He was thinking it would be the last time they'd have to spend together before he headed back to the States and they were separated for another few weeks while she remained, shooting at multiple locales throughout Europe.

Packing his tablet, journal and headphones into a fraying messenger bag, he silently slipped from the room, headed for the Paris streets to find an out-of-the-way café where he could get lost in his latest composition. Camouflaged in his uniform of a leather jacket, baseball cap, mirrored aviators and a loosely wrapped scarf, Jesse headed down to the Seine, walking east on the river bank and enjoying the cold air stinging his cheeks. With a gray sky looming and a stiff wind prevailing, the pedestrian walkway had a fraction of its usual crowd. The openness was a stark contrast to the hotel room's claustrophobic presence.

At Rue du Louvre, he headed north back onto the streets, suddenly knowing exactly where he was going. For as deserted as the Seine was of pedestrians, the Rue Montorgueil's foot traffic was still robust with Parisians braving the cold to people watch at the cafés over steaming, bowl-like cups of cappuccino and latté.

Without knowing for sure, he somehow knew it was up ahead on his left as he strolled the narrow cobblestone street, picking up on the energy of the locals and propelling him onward toward the blue and gold awning. And there it was. Patisserie Stohrer, the oldest bakery in Paris. Maison foundee 1730 was painted on the building's stone façade. *1730,* Jesse marveled.

Approaching the window, it was impossible to contain his smile as his eyes roved the neatly lined rows of beautiful pastries. Fruit tartes, baba au rhum, a colorful display of macarons, napoleons, cream puffs, and éclairs. He could feel his frozen cheeks broaden into an even bigger smile. He had to go in and get one for her.

Once inside the warmth of the small shop, he was overwhelmed by the sweet aroma of choux pastry, dark chocolate and sugar.

"Deux éclair, s'il vous plait."

Exiting the shop with a small, smartly wrapped box and an accomplished feeling, he hoped they would stay fresh long enough for her to enjoy them. *What would her face look like when she saw this little surprise,* he wondered? It really had been quite some time since that day he'd ambushed her in Starbucks. And then to go from such an intensely personal first encounter to dead silence must have been confusing to her. *Bet she thought douche rock star. And although she wasn't wrong, I wasn't not back in touch because I was being a douche. I was de-douching.* In a few days, he'd get to explain it to her. Come clean on the silence and his disappearing act. *De-douching,* he chuckled.

Strolling into Café Marie Stuart he noticed the inside was fairly empty and headed for a small table in the corner where he faced the wall, his back to the street and the crowd eating and drinking on the sidewalk.

"Café crème, s'il vous plait." He didn't remove his scarf and sunglasses until the waitress had delivered the coffee. Earbuds in, he dove back into the creation he had halted when Claudine had gotten annoyed with his scatting.

Claudine was often annoyed with him and Jesse had the feeling they were probably pretty close to running their course. Beneath the surface of being a "super-couple" there wasn't a lot of glue holding the fractured pieces together. They'd probably been together for as long as they had because their careers forced extended absences. On some level, Jesse knew if he was being totally honest that he actually feared what extended time together would bring, besides the end. That was inevitable. It was the ugliness in between that was going to be problematic. But then again, maybe being clean and around, as well as undergoing intensive therapy, he'd be able to be a better partner to her than he'd been in the past.

Drug addicts and alcoholics were selfish and he knew it. He wondered why she had stayed. Love? Prestige? Laziness? Some combination of those things. Convenience? Press?

**Where are you shooting?** he texted.

**Opéra de Paris Garnier,** the answer arrived twenty minutes later.

Looking up from composing, he glanced at his phone, pleased to see that she was within walking distance. He then returned his focus to the melody he needed to get out of his head.

Another two hours had passed before he emerged onto the Rue Montorgueil, the frosty air and rough-hewn cobblestones immediately pulled him back to the now from the far away reaches of his consciousness, where he had sojourned during the creative process. Passing the cafés lining both sides of the street he wondered how close the mental state he would achieve during Dr. S's regressions would be to where he went while composing. He concluded there might be a link to hitting that alternate-reality zone that was his creative treasure trove.

Across the street, a small market had large white buckets of brightly colored tulips lining the sidewalk. There was something so European about the kaleidoscopic blooms in the dead of winter, Jesse thought. *They didn't have far to travel from Holland, did they now?* Wandering across the street, Jesse walked up and down past the flowers until he finally settled on a pale purple, knowing how much Claudine loved anything lavender.

With a large bouquet in hand, as he continued down the cobblestone and marble-tiled street, something different in the stonework caught the corner of his eye, and he noted lettering on a plaque near his foot. Stopping, he read the bronze plate inlaid into the sidewalk.

**Le 4 Janvier 1750**
**Rue Montorgueil**
**Entre La Rue Saint-Sauveur**
**Et L'Ancienne Rue Beaurepaire**
**Furent Arretés**
**BRUNO LENOIR et JEAN DIOT**
**Condamnés Pour Homosexualité**
**Ils Furent Brulés En Place De Grève**
**Le 6 Juillet 1750**
**Ce Fut La Dernière Exécution**
**Pour Homosexualité En France**

Shaking his head in surprise and disgust, the movement ignited a wave of dizziness, as if brought on by a lack of oxygenated air. Accompanying the vertigo-like sensation was a burning in his eyes, causing them to tear up and blurring his vision, momentarily disorienting the rocker. Jesse loosened his already untied scarf even more, and opened his jacket. Taking a few deep breaths, trying to calm down after the physical onslaught that assaulted his body, he didn't need a perfect understanding of the French language to understand the plaque's meaning–Bruno Lenoir and Jean Diot were executed right here in Paris, burned at the stake, just for being gay.

. . . . . .

Reaching the Opéra de Paris Garnier, they had a defined perimeter roped off, not permitting anyone in who wasn't directly involved in the shoot. Approaching the guard, Jesse removed his baseball cap, shaking his spiky hair into messy perfection. The guard didn't need to ask for ID.

"Monsieur Winslow, comment-allez vous?" the elder man greeted.

"Ça va, merci. Et vous?"

"Trés bien, merci. Madamoiselle Claudine est en la caravane." He pointed to a trailer on the right.

Thanking him again, Jesse took off in the direction of Claudine's trailer.

Knocking, an unfamiliar voice told him to enter. Stepping up, he could see she was undergoing a hair and make-up change.

Their eyes met in the mirror.

"Surprise." Jesse smiled at her and held up the tulips.

She spoke without any actual movement in her face, a beautiful ventriloquist, "You're here." There was surprise in her tone. "Get those out of here," her eyes had settled on the purple flowers in the mirror. "I don't need anything to make me sneeze."

Jesse was laying them down on a table at the far end of the trailer, feeling overwhelmingly like the ventriloquist's dummy, when he spied an ornate floral arrangement across the way. Sauntering over, he pulled the card, it had a single word ~*Nick*.

He slowly turned back. She was watching him intently in the mirror, clearly waiting for his reaction. The stylist stood there, hairbrush and spray in hand, frozen mid-air.

Meeting the reflection of her eyes, his lopsided grin appeared slowly and like the masterful showman he was, he let the silence of the moment gain power before he spoke. "I need to find out who Nick uses as a florist. Hypo-allergenic flowers. Now *that* was *really* thoughtful."

Sitting down on the couch, he pulled out his laptop and opened his Sibelius First program to get back to not only his composition, but also to a place he actually wanted to be.

The stylist turned from the mirror to view him on the couch, shocked by Jesse's lack of reaction. But Jesse had escaped the confines of his current physical reality and never saw the hairdresser's surprised expression, or Claudine's.

# Chapter 5

"Where are you, Kylie?"

"Je suis à Paris." Her diction was perfect and authentic, no trace of a New Jersey accent in her now sweet, child-like voice.

"Please speak in English, Kylie."

"I'm in Paris." Her accent was distinctly French.

"Are you in the same place in France as in your previous session?"

"Non," she shook her head. Even her monosyllabic response was heavily accented.

"What year is it?" Claire probed.

"It is the year of our Lord, seventeen hundred and forty-nine."

"And what is your name?"

"Geneviève."

"Geneviève what?" Claire wanted specifics. It would be hard to validate a Parisian citizen from 1749.

"Geneviève Lenoir," she said matter-of-factly, as if the doctor should know.

"How old are you?"

"Je suis douze ans."

"In English, please," Claire reminded her patient.

"I am twelve."

"Who is currently sitting on the throne? Who is your king?"

"King Louis Quinze." There was not a moment's hesitation in her response.

Louis the Fifteenth. Claire immediately began to Google for information without so much as a momentary lapse in her rapid-fire questioning of the girl.

"Do you go to school?"

"Oui, à l'eglise Saint-Eustache," she lapsed back into French.

"In English, please," Claire reminded her. 1749. According to Google, Louis XV would have been on the throne, validating the information. The hairs on the back of Claire's next stood at attention.

"Je me regrette," she began. "I am sorry. I go to the church school at Saint-Eustache."

"What do you learn there?"

"Sewing. Embroidery," she trailed off.

"Have you been taught to read?"

"No. I am a girl and a commoner."

"Do you also work?"

"Yes, I am a chambermaid for Mme. Michaud."

"Does she treat you well?" Claire noticed that Kylie/Geneviève was twirling her hair. It was not a habit she'd ever noted Kylie to do before. She made a note of the physical manifestation on her iPad.

"Oui." Again, she lapsed into French, but immediately caught herself. "I think she is nice to me because she wants to find out more about my older brother. I see the way she looks at him. She makes wolf eyes at him."

"How old is your brother?"

"He is twenty-one."

"Is he married?"

She laughed. More of a giggle than a laugh, covering her mouth with her hand. "Non, mon frère est un bon vivant." She caught herself and self-corrected to English, without prompting. "My brother likes to have a very good time. I tell him to watch out or a husband will come after him with a hatchet."

Claire laughed to herself, "So, he likes married women?"

"They like him. He likes many woman and they all like him, too. He is very handsome." Another giggle.

"And what do your parents have to say about that?"

Looking down at her hands, but seeing nothing, a lone tear ran down her cheek. "My parents perished in a fire."

"I'm sorry to hear that, Geneviève," Claire addressed her by the name of the life she was seeing and noted the physical manifestation of tears.

"I was eight," she volunteered.

"So, who takes care of you?"

"My brother," she offered cheerfully.


*Geneviève ...*

*"Wake up, Ma Petite Chou, or you will be late for school."*

*Wiping the sleep from my eyes, I smile at my brother's handsome face. "I did not hear you come in last night."*

*"I had to work late."* He pokes the wood in the fireplace that is heating the black iron pot.

*"Mme. Michaud again?"*

*"Oui."*

He doesn't turn around to face me.

*"Do you like her?"* I can't imagine him kissing her pinched face.

*"She pays well for the tasks she needs done."*

I know she pays him for odd jobs: chimney sweeping, roof tiling, replacing rotting floor boards, but I suspect most of his money is made in her bed satisfying her womanly cravings.

*"You had better be careful or she will smother you in that giant bosom of hers and you will never escape."*

Putting a bowl of steaming porridge in front of me, he shakes his head, his dark blue eyes laughing at me.

*"I really should sell you to the gypsies,"* he teases and reaches forward to let a long lock of my hair run through his fingers. *"That red hair will get me a good price."* Laughing, *"Finish up, I need to get you to school."*

*"I can walk alone. It is only a few blocks down to the churchyard."*

Shaking his head, his handsome face becomes very serious. *"No, Geneviève. Two more children have gone missing these past few days. We are one of the neighborhoods being targeted. I will not let you walk alone."*

*"But will you not be late for work?"* I do not know how we would survive if he were to lose his job. And I cannot fathom how I would survive without him.

As if reading my mind, something my big brother is always able to do with the precision of a clockmaker, *"Trust me, she is not going to relieve me of my duties. I have got this under control," he laughs. "It is good that I make her wait. Now if only you would stop making me wait, ma moitié."*

*He knows I love when he calls me that. Ma moitié. My half.*

*"I will make you wait for me forever, mon moitié," I tease back.*

*"I believe this to be true." And he swats me on the bottom to keep me moving.*

*We could always count on him to be standing in the doorway of the charcuiterie on Rue Montorgueil, just like he did every morning. Shirt sleeves rolled, exposing well-defined muscular arms covered in dark hair, he always appeared oblivious to the chill of winter's air.*

*"Bonjour, Monsieur Diot," I call to him.*

*I am greeted by his handsome smile.*

*"C'est la belle, Geneviève. Bonjour, Madamoiselle."*

*Giggling at being called beautiful by this big, rough handsome man, I see a look pass between him and my brother.*

*"Monsieur Lenoir."*

*"Monsieur Diot." My brother nods in acknowledgement.*

*We are beyond his shop when I hear him call to my brother, "Are you working tonight?"*

*My brother's smile is bright as he calls back, "Not if I can help it."*

*"A drink?" the charcuitier poses.*

*My brother answers with an even brighter smile, his head turned around still looking at the handsome older man.*

*It occurs to me that they are becoming friends, meeting often for drinks. He is so much older than my brother, that I am a little surprised that they have taken up to be friends. Maybe he is a father figure. I know how much my brother misses our father.*

*Approaching the great stone walls of Saint-Eustache, my brother puts his hands on my shoulders, "Today you walk home with Lilette and you stay with her until her mother can walk you to Mme. Michaud's. I will meet you there later."*

*Looking up at him through my lashes, I hold out my hand.*

*Laughing, "I should really sell you to the gypsies," he teases, as he places a denier in my palm.*

*"They might like me."*

*His eyes take on a serious cast, "That is my fear, my rare beauty." Turning to walk away, he looks back, "I will pick you up from Mme. Michaud's. Be careful, ma moitié."*

· · · · · ·

*Lilette and I skip down the Rue Montorgueil trying not to step on the cracks in the cobblestones, laughing about the l'hermitagoise who will come eat us if we do.*

*Looking through the frosty windows of Patisserie Stohrer, I pull out from my cloth pouch the denier from my brother.*

*"The two most beautiful little girls in all of Paris," Monsieur Stohrer gushes as we enter into the warmth of the store, the yeasty smell of dough mingling with the nose-tingling scent of rum and other liquors that the cakes absorb like fat sponges. "The Bourbons cannot compare," he teases, comparing us to the royal family. "What would you two princesses like today?" He does not really have to ask. We get the same thing every day and he is already plucking them from the counter and wrapping them in paper for us.*

*The first bite of choux pastry squirts crème chocolat onto my tongue. The rare dark chocolate frosting of the éclair is the most delicious thing on Earth, I have decided, as it joins the choux and crème in my mouth. Slowly, I take small bites so that it will last longer and I can keep it in my memory. This is my luxury. My one luxury. A gift my brother works hard to make sure puts a smile on my face every day. For that alone, I love him more than all the stars in the night's sky.*

*We walk six flights up the curving staircase to Lilette's flat. Her mother is breastfeeding the baby. Both have had coughs for months now. She has mending for us to do and we sit in the stream of light coming in through the window trying to capture the afternoon sun's warmth as we work. Lilette's mother will later walk me over to Mme. Michaud's where today I will launder her dresses.*

*My brother is very concerned that I not walk alone for fear that I will be abducted and sold. Lone girls are disappearing with frequency, being sold to agents of Louisiana silk factory owners in the New World.*

*It is two days later that I sit quietly by the fire in Mme. Michaud's salon mending a green silk and brocade dress. Her bosom has grown so large that I am now repairing my repairs. The thought of my brother's face pressed into her jiggly flesh makes me queasy.*

*"Geneviève, Madame would like to see you," her chambermaid Chantal informs me.*

*I follow Chantal through the moderately decorated rooms to where Mme. Michaud sits at the dining table. Next to her, a place is set, and a steaming bowl of soup is placed.*

*I curtsy as I enter the room, "Madame." I greet her, hoping that my voice is louder than the growl in my stomach. The aroma from the soup is making my hunger burn.*

*"Geneviève, come sit by me." There is a false sweetness to her voice. I know it is false because it is a tone I've never heard before.*

*She must be reading the confusion on my face–servants don't sit at the dining table with their employers, because she comments, "It is alright, come sit next to me." And she pats the chair.*

*Taking the seat next to her, I note the fine silk of the fabric. The fragrant steam from the soup rises to my nose. I close my eyes breathing it in and silently telling my verbose stomach tais-toi,* be quiet.

*"You are looking so slim and pale these days, Geneviève. I am so worried about you."*

*I am not sure how to respond. She has never taken much of an interest in me. Now, my brother, on the other hand...*

*"Eat," she commands me, motioning to the bowl of soup. Again, she nods her head to let me know that it is alright for me to begin eating.*

*"This is delicious." I consciously slow myself down when I realize I am shoveling spoonfuls of soup into my mouth at an alarmingly fast pace.*

*Mme. Michaud is looking at me with a mask I can see through. There is disgust behind it. But she continues to smile and then calls the cook in to bring me another bowl and crusty bread.*

*By the time I go back to my mending, I want to curl up like a cat in front of the fire and go to sleep. My stomach almost hurts it feels so good.*

*A few days later she feeds me fatty mutton. The rich, stringy meat takes away my hunger for the whole night. When I curl up on my mattress that night, I don't feel any pains.*

*I know she has a reason for all this and I wonder. Will she marry my brother? But I know that even though she craves him, she could never cross the line to marry him, he is a servant. But if she did, possibly this is practice for taking me on like the daughter she never had.*

*Maybe if she is nice to me, my brother will satisfy her more. I decide that is the answer.*

*"Where is this meat on your bones coming from?" My brother asks weeks later. "I am going to have to stop giving you deniers for éclairs," he teases, "or the gypsies will no longer want you. Your upkeep will be too expensive."*

*I laugh. "Mme. Michaud has taken a liking to me. She has been making sure I have hot food in my belly."*

*His back is to me as I say that and he spins like a coin on the edge of a tavern table to face me. "She has been doing what?"*

*"Feeding me," I stutter, suddenly looking down at the warped floor boards. "And letting me try on her jewels and creams."*

*"Chou, look at me," his fingers are on my chin, tipping my head back. "You need to be careful. Very, very careful."*

*"I am." I stick my chin farther into his hand, part to be defiant, after all, I am a big girl and I can take care of myself, and partly because I like when he takes my chin in his hand and looks at me with serious eyes. My protector.*

*"Has she asked you about me?"*

*My eyes are starting to burn as I try to fight back tears. Maybe I've done something wrong, after all. Maybe I've been a fool.*

*"Tell me, Chou. It is alright," he implores, gently running his thumb up and down on my chin to calm me.*

*"Some days she asks me if you had a good time the night before."*

*"What days are those?" His jaw muscles twitch.*

*"Usually when you've been at the tavern." I'm beginning to shake with panic.*

*"And what have you told her?"*

*"I've told her I think you did because you came home very late."*

*"What else?" He looks angry, his dark hair partially obscuring his deep blue eyes.*

*"She has asked if you've brought anyone home."*

*"And what have you told her?"*

*His fingers on my chin are beginning to hurt and I avert his eyes, focusing on the cast iron pot hanging in the fireplace.*

*"Geneviève, answer me."*

*"I have told her the truth. That you have brought no one."*

*"Good. Good girl." He lets go of my chin, his hand going to cover his own mouth, as he stalks the room.*

*"Have I done something wrong, mon moitié?"*

*He crosses the room quickly and sinks to one knee in front of me. Stroking my hair and letting a lock slip through his fingers, "No, ma moitié. You have done nothing wrong. She is just a jealous, crazy old woman and I don't want her using you to spy on me."*

*I gasp, shaking my head. "I would never do anything to hurt you."*

*"I know that, ma petite chou. But she is crafty. Very crafty and I want you to be careful."*

*I nod, promising I will be.*

*"I will take care of her," he vows. "Now promise me you will pretend that we did not have this conversation so that she does not know that I am on to her treachery."*

*"Treachery?" I am alarmed at that.*

*"I do not want you to worry. I will take care of this. I have got this under control. She will not harm you."*

*"But will she harm you?" I have a sudden foreboding fear of*

*something terrible happening to my brother. He is all I have. I cannot lose him.*

*Bending down, he kisses the top of my head, "No, she cannot harm me. I am invincible." And he shares a smile, the one that makes the ladies swoon.*

. . . . . .

*I have been giving her the same answer for weeks now, telling her the weather is so cold that my brother stays in all night. I know that she has begun to doubt me, because there is no more special food and she has me cleaning chamber pots, a task that has never been given to me before. My stomach had become familiar with the extra food and now craves it more, and I am hungry all the time. But I cannot tell her the truth.*

*I cannot tell her that he is out late at night, every night, returning in the small hours of the morning.*

*"Madame, that salon window is drafty," my brother comments to her when he comes to retrieve me one evening. "I could try to come earlier tomorrow and fix the sash, if that would please Madame."*

*The pinches in her face instantly smooth at his offer and her overly large breasts puff out like a molting bird's plumage. Even the tone of her voice changes, becoming breathier as she speaks.*

*I know he is doing this for me. She will no longer dare to assign the cleaning of the chamber pots to me if he is tending to her. I do not care if she does not feed me, I just want to go back to being left alone with my mending and sewing.*

*Using the pretense of odd jobs, they often disappear behind locked doors in her chamber or the salon. One day the door was slightly ajar and one of her male servants stood outside, peering through the crack as he stroked himself through his clothes. He scurried off like a cock-*

*roach when he saw me.*

*I went and stood in the spot where the man-servant had been. My brother had her facing the wall as he plowed into her.*

*"You are a dirty whore," he snarled into her ear. "Your pussy is here to please me, only me, whore. You need to be fucked by a dirty peasant. I am the only man good enough for you." And he grabbed her by a handful of hair and yanked her head.*

*Hearing her swine-like grunt brought me to the edge of nausea and I quickly hurried back to my sewing.*

*It was not long after my brother's regular visits began again that Mme. Michaud resumed feeding me. As thankful as I was for the warm food in my belly, I was also saddened that there was a cost to my brother. To quell my hunger, he had to satisfy hers.*

*We left there nightly, often in silence.*

*"Maybe you should sell me to the gypsies," I announced one night, "then you could have your freedom and would not have to service that horrid woman to keep me fed and working."*

*Putting an arm around my shoulder, he smiled as he gazed off into the frigid night air. With his free hand, he touched his chest, covering his heart. "Ma moitié, there is nothing I would not do for you. You are my heart. My one true heart. We do what we have to do to keep our true heart safe. Do you understand? One protects their true heart at any cost." He looked down at me.*

*"But what about you?" I searched his face.*

*With a secret smile, he dipped his head down, "It is all taken care of," he confided.*

*And I knew he was referring to his late-night visits. Satisfied, I smiled, as we walked on.*

*"Good evening." We were greeted by one of the members of the*

*night watch as we approached our street. Many neighborhoods throughout Paris had recently increased their night watch as more and more children had gone missing. In addition to seeing our usual night watchmen, we were now crossing paths with several new ones who had appeared in the neighborhood.*

*My brother makes sure I am bolted in when he leaves in the evening. Many workers live in quarters provided by their employers, but we have remained in the rooms that belonged to our parents, barely scraping by to pay rent and taxes. My father's miserly cousin was at the door looking for payment immediately upon my parents' death, and together we have worked to keep our small space.*

. . . . . .

*"Geneviève, I have the theatre tonight." Mme. Michaud fills the doorway, a royal blue velvet cape fastened over her pale blue silk dress, a garment I added fabric to just last week to accommodate her expanding girth. Next to her stands a man who looks familiar, yet, I cannot quite place him. I have the distinct feeling that I know him, but I don't. Something is out of context.*

*"Your brother left this here last night when he left me." Mme. Michaud hands me a small leather pouch. Without opening the sack, I can tell by the weight and sound that the bag is filled with coins.*

*I find it odd that she is being so open about her affairs in front of this other man, potentially sacrificing her reputation.*

*"Thank you, I shall see that he gets it back."*

*My brother has been working a steady job at a cobbler's shop on the Il de la Cité in the days and not doing odd jobs for Mme. Michaud. I was concerned that with him gone, she would start treating me poorly again, but he calmed my fears. "Don't worry, ma chou, she knows I am working for the cobbler on Il de la Cité and the money is good. She will not take that out on you."*

*The night before when he arrived to retrieve me, he waited in the entrance until I was finished, his coat still buttoned, so he could not have left the pouch then. He must have come back here last night, I decide, and he left it when he was with her.*

*As he and I walk home, I remember the pouch. "Madame gave me this to return to you."*

*"Return to me?" he asks questioningly, his face filled with confusion.*

*"Yes, she said you left it last night."*

*My brother stops in his tracks, "Geneviève, what did you say to her?"*

*"I told her I would give it to you."*

*"Merde!" The anger in my brother's face transforms him, his eyes wild, darting left to right and back again.*

*"What is wrong?" I am alarmed by his response.*

*"I was not with her last night. This was a trap to see if you would say that I was home last night."*

*I realize I have failed him and my heart cracks. I try to speak but nothing comes out. My voice is failing me as I have failed him.*

*"This was her way to spy on me. She knows I am working at the cobbler shop during the day and I told her I cannot leave you at night."*

*"I did not know. I wish I had known," I mutter.*

*"I am not blaming you, ma moitié. It is my mistake. Do not worry, I will fix this. I will not permit her to abuse you over it." He kisses my head as we continue down cobblestone streets on our way home.*

*"Bon soir," Monsieur Gauthier calls to us as he makes his night watch rounds.*

*"Bon soir," I call back to him, sadness in my usual bright tone.*

*Something is bothering me, besides Mme. Michaud's trick. But I cannot figure out what it is. It is just out of the reach of my mind.*

· · · · · ·

*Even though my brother has taken on some jobs for Mme. Michaud and spent time satisfying her cravings, I feel a chill from her. Her smile is different with me; there is a different tone to her speech. It feels as if my brother has not been able to make it right with her.*

*"Do you feel a difference?" I ask him as we walk home one night.*

*"A little bit." He thinks for a moment. "She will come around eventually."*

*"She has not had me cleaning chamber pots, so for that, I am thankful." And we both laugh.*

*"Bon soir," we greet the night watch as we pass the man, one of the newer ones.*

*"Monsieur Gauthier must have the night off," my brother comments.*

*"It is so cold, I do not blame him for not wanting to be out." I watch the white smoke from my breath curl into the dark January night.*

*"Lock up after me, ma moitié," my brother says as he prepares to leave after dinner. Every night he says the same thing to me, and kisses me on each cheek, then my forehead before he goes.*

*Once in my sleeping gown, I blow out all the candles and crawl into my box bed, drawing the curtain. As I drift off, it comes to me. I know who he is. I sit up in bed. Alarmed. I know who the man is.*

*The man on the night watch. It is the man who took Mme. Michaud to the theatre.*

. . . . . .

*It is morning and my brother is not there. He never returned the night before. My stomach hurts. Not from hunger. I feel fear. Something is very, very wrong.*

*Dressing quickly, I run down to the street. Someone must know where he is. Small groups of people are huddled on street corners, whispering. I feel their sideways glances. Something is very, very wrong.*

*The charcuterie shop is closed. Merde! I had hoped that my brother's friend, Monsieur Diot, might know where he was. Maybe they had been at the tavern together. But the shop is closed when it should already be open.*

*I lift my skirts so as not to trip as I run down Rue Montorgueil toward Saint-Eustache. As I go to enter the side door into the school rooms I am met by the imposing figure of the priest, tall and smelling of incense, a heavy gold and bead crucifix hangs down the front of his frock.*

*"Arretez-vous." Stop!" he commands. "Sortez-vous." Leave! "Maintenant." Now!*

*"Pourquoi?" Why? I ask, tears beginning to stream down my face. What has happened? Where is mon moitié?*

*"Sodomites and criminals will not bring filth into our hallowed halls," he bellows, his ugly words reverberating off the gray stone walls.*

*What is he talking about? I am so confused by what is going on. Something is very, very wrong and I need my brother. I need my brother now.*

*He shoos me off the property like I'm dirt under a servant's broom and I stand at the start of Rue Montorgueil not knowing where to go. Again, I lift my skirts and begin to run, tripping over cobblestones I can barely see through my tears.*

*Lilette's mother will know what to do, I decide, and run toward their apartment. Climbing the stairs, I stand before their door, tear stained and out of breath. Opening the door with Lilette's baby brother still latched onto her breast, my confused story spills out between sobs.*

*"Calm down, we will find out what is going on."*

*She makes me tea, which I sip while she finishes feeding the baby.*

*"Did you eat?" she asks.*

*I shake my head and she points to some bread on the table. I thank her, but I cannot even look at food without my nausea rising. My stomach and heart are sick with worry.*

*Where is my brother?*

*Out on the street we see a small group of people talking. She tells me to stay where I am and hands me the baby to hold while she goes and talks to the neighbors across the street.*

*Watching her face grow grave with concern, I start to choke on my own tears and hide my face in the baby's neck. She comes back across the street and takes me by the arm.*

*"Where is my brother? Do you know where my brother is?" I am distraught. I cannot lose him. I just cannot.*

*"Oui," she whispers, barely moving her mouth. "He was taken to Bicêtre."*

*"Bicêtre," I gasp. "The hospital?"*

*She stops and turns to face me, taking the baby back. "No, Geneviève. Not the hospital. He was taken to the prison."*

*My knees are gone and I sink to the cobblestones. Lilette's mother reaches under one of my arms and pulls me up. She continues to talk in a whispered tone. "He was caught and arrested by the night watch."*

*"The night watch," I spit out. That man. Madame Michaud's spy. "For what? What did he do?"*

*She looks away and then continues to look at the ground as she tells me, "For performing sodomy. For homosexual activity."*

*"What? My brother? Who would my brother do that with?" I am shocked.*

*"With Monsieur Diot, the charcuitier."*

*I cannot breathe. I have to get to my brother. Bicêtre is far away. How will I get there?*

*"I need to see him. This is all a mistake." Breathing deeply, I try and gather my thoughts. "Mme. Michaud. I need Mme. Michaud to help me. She has a carriage. It can take me to my brother. She can help me."*

*Lilette's mother walks with me to Mme. Michaud's home. A man-servant answers the door, but will not permit me in. I ask to speak to Madame and he tells me that she is indisposed. I beg and plead, but to no avail.*

*"Leave, Madamoiselle."*

*I tell him my brother is in trouble and he shuts the heavy wood door without another word.*

*Staring at the weathered planks, I am shocked. How is this happening? Mme. Michaud was my only hope to travel to Bicêtre and now it is rapidly slipping away. Stepping back from the entrance, I gaze up. There, in the third-floor salon, at the window where my brother recently repaired the sash, stands Mme. Michaud, her dress a claret red silk.*

*Our eyes meet and she smiles, then draws the curtain.*

As she listens to her patient's story, Dr. Claire Stoddard literally finds herself gasping for air. The detail is so exquisite that she can feel it. She can visualize it as if it is swimming before her eyes, a motion picture so vivid. She can see that little redhaired girl, looking up from the rough-hewn grey cobblestone street, as if she herself is the one looking down from that salon window in Paris. She can feel the texture of the woman's silk brocade dress, the color of dark cherries in summer and the slightly scratchy texture of the lace curtains she peers through.

"Were you able to see your brother again?" she asked her patient.

"No. Not until that sham of a trial. I was told that they wanted to make an example of him and Monsieur Diot."

"So, they were found guilty?" the psychiatrist continued to probe.

Kylie is almost violently twirling a lock of hair. "Yes, they were sentenced to death." Her voice is a mix of sorrow and anger.

"Did you speak to him?"

"No. He saw me in the courtroom and pounded his heart. I watched him mouth the words, "Ma moitié.""

*"You should not go, Geneviève. You should not see this." Both Lilette and her mother plead with me, but there is nothing that will keep me away. I cannot stay away and neither can the throngs of Parisians who make their way through the squalid summer heat to the Place de Grève to witness yet another debacle of humanity.*

*I press my way through the crowd, Lilette follows. Her family has been the only ones at my side, while everyone else has abandoned me. The smell of sulphur is thick in the air and the people are cheering. As I make it to the front edge of the crowd, I can see the stake. My brother and Monsieur Diot are bound to it with heavy rope. The flames from the kindling are licking up their legs. I can see from the position of my brother's head, hanging to his chest, that he is already gone. There were rumors that they would be strangled first to make their deaths more humane. There is nothing humane about any of this.*

*"Mon moitié," I cry. "Mon moitié."*

*I continue to push trying to get to him. I must get to him and pull him down, take him far away from this vile, ugly crowd. I cannot lose another family member to fire.*

*"Mon moitié." I am reaching out, arms outstretched, but they are pulling me back. Pulling me away from mon moitié. "No. No. No," I cry. "My brother needs me. Let me go to my brother. Get him down from there. He did not do anything wrong."*

*Two large men have me pinioned. I cannot get to my brother, although I continue to try and fight their binds. The fire climbs their bodies, igniting their shirts which combust into brilliant blue engulfing flames. I realize that their shirts have been stuffed with sulphur as part of their eternal damnation, for we have now smelled Hell.*

*"Bruno," I wail, as I try to break loose. "Bruno...."*

"Who is Bruno?" The psychiatrist is quickly typing into her iPad.

"Mon frère. My brother. My brother is Bruno."

"Bruno is your brother's name?" Quickly, Claire tries to corroborate.

"Yes."

Checking her notes, "So, your brother is named Bruno Lenoir?"

"Oui," the response a reverent whisper.

Pulling up Google, Claire types in Bruno Lenoir. The first entry reads, "France: Plaque Unveiled for Last Men Executed for Being Gay."

With shaking hands, the psychiatrist placed her iPad on her desk, quickly skimming the article. 1750. Rue Montorgueil. Bruno Lenoir. Jean Diot. Burned at the stake. Place de Grève.

Grasping the edge of her desk, nearing the point of hyperventilation, the enormity of what has just occurred washes over Claire Stoddard, engulfing her, momentarily robbing her senses. *Oh, my God. I must tell Marshall. I have to document every detail.*

For those psychiatrists utilizing hypnosis and regression analysis with patients, it has proven nearly impossible in their discipline to corroborate the facts and tie them back to actual individuals in history. But Kylie Martin/Geneviève Lenoir had just provided a credible account of a historical event. It wasn't an event that one could say, "Oh, they just read about that in their history book." At least not as an American student, who would not have been privy to the details of a foreign event that wasn't of world magnitude. Yet, from what Claire could see, Kylie's recounting of the event was remarkably accurate.

Not only did this provide significance in the field of psychiatry and regression therapy, but the ramifications for the belief in reincarnation and of souls living on, surviving death, was earth-shattering. As a scientifically trained professional, Claire's left brain was ready to mount an attack to debunk what had just happened, yet her gut knew that this was, in fact, one of those breakthroughs into dimensions we did not yet fully understand.

Regaining her composure, Claire pressed on, "Please tell me what happened after Bruno's death."

"I was taken."

"What do you mean taken? Please be more specific."

"Two men grabbed me. They kept me in a building with others who were taken. They hurt us. Treated us like wild animals. Abused us. Turned us from children to women. Weeks passed before they loaded us onto a barge and from there a ship."

"Where did the ship take you?"

"They were taking me to Louisiana."

"To work in the silk factories?" Claire surmised.

Kylie nodded.

"What happened in Louisiana?" Claire knew she could check ship manifests to corroborate.

"I never made it."

"What happened? Where did you end up instead?"

"I died. I was sick and malnourished. Too weak to fight for my food. People would steal my rations. I had no clean water. They stole my water from me because they knew I could no longer fight them. The pain of starvation." She rocked, her arms wrapped around her stomach. "I thought I had known hunger. I knew nothing."

"And you died during the voyage?"

"Yes. I starved." Kylie was curled up on the couch, remaining quiet for a few moments. "I ended up in the ocean."

"Are you gone now?" Claire was fascinated, hoping she'd get more.

"I'm gone."

"Tell me what you learned from that lifetime."

"Tolerance and independence. And what it's like to truly have a love bond with another person." Kylie fell silent. "We never said goodbye," her whisper was barely audible, but the glistening tears that streamed along her cheeks with that last statement were highly visible.

"Okay Kylie, I am going to count to three and on the count of three, Geneviève will be back in her time and you will be in present day."

"One," she paused. "Two," another pause. "Three."

Wrapping her arms around herself tightly, Kylie took a series of slow, deep breaths, removing the RGB glasses and headphones, yet her eyes remained closed. Across her face traversed a myriad of emotions, which Claire wished she could have captured digitally. Sadness. Pain. Relief. Confusion.

When her eyes finally opened, she blinked a few times, yet remained unfocused. A moment passed before she looked up at Claire, locking eyes with the therapist.

"And you wonder why I have weight problems. I was starved to death."

**Patient: Kylie Martin**

**Session #65**

**Regression #16**

**December 16, 2014**

**Regression Length: 10:15 A.M.–10:50 A.M.**

**Entity: Geneviève Lenoir**

**Location: Paris, France**

**Year: 1749-1750**

. . . . . .

Shell shocked would be an understatement. *Holy fucking shit. Holy fucking shit.* It was all she could repeat in her head. *Holy fucking shit.* Bruno. He couldn't stay out of trouble. *He was so charismatic*, thought

Kylie. Even looking at him from the viewpoint of a sibling, it was obviously impossible for men and women alike not to be taken in by his charm and dark, handsome looks.

The tightening around her heart, squeezing, cutting, bursting. The pain of losing him. First Gunther and now Bruno. These losses felt so absolute. And the love was overwhelmingly real. She thought Gunther had been painful, but seeing Bruno strapped to a post in the Place de Grève was still unbearable as she crossed 63$^{rd}$ Street in Manhattan.

*Post-regression come-downs*, as she had named them, were getting tougher and tougher as her regressions revealed more and more details and the entities became three-dimensional strangers who she knew intimately and loved deeply.

*I never want to be hungry and thirsty like that again. Those pageant bitches can starve themselves into some neurotic designer's delusion of perfection, but I don't ever want to go hungry again. Fuck that shit.*

*And abused and taken advantage of by men that way. What a horrible, helpless feeling. Ugh. I'd rather they not look at me. Not touch me.*

The rhythmic sound of tapping snapped her back from the netherworlds, bringing an instant smile to her face, and all felt right again within that moment. *He showed!* He was there and oddly she needed him on this day more than she had imagined, and that felt a little shocking, yet good. He was the only one who could be a salve for the hurt in her soul today.

On the other side of the window, the camouflaged rock star's lopsided grin shone like a beacon only she could see. Jesse fuckin' Winslow, you are a sight for sore eyes and not just because you are one sexy man.

Kylie made her way to the upfront corner where he sat at the window bar. Taking the seat next to him, it was impossible not to match his smile with one of her own. It was so good to see him. Amazingly good.

He slid a small box over so that it was in front of her, followed by her favorite frozen drink that he had waiting. Immediately, she recognized the blue inscribed logo on the box. Had she just tasted these minutes before or well over two hundred years ago. It was confusing, hard to separate the merge. And today is the day Jesse showed up with this. Seriously? *Universe, you are so fucking with me.*

"You didn't." Her hand was on the top of the flap.

Laughing, "I did. But I have a confession to make."

Kylie stopped, her hand not moving.

"I ate one," Jesse confessed.

Bursting into laughter at an admission she did not expect, Kylie opened the box to find a lone éclair. Realizing she needed this, the levity and laughter, made her want to throw her arms around the charismatic rocker to thank him just for his mere presence on this emotional day. What was that saying? *There are no coincidences.*

"I'm really sorry," he was so sincere. "It was a moment of weakness. These things should be used as drug replacement therapy."

Trying hard to not laugh, "I understand," she deadpanned at the serious nature of his crime.

Picking up the fine pastry, Kylie broke it in half, holding out one of the pieces to Jesse.

"No, it's for you," he protested.

"You brought it all the way from Paris. That was so thoughtful. Please share it with me." Kylie wanted to laugh, how funny that she was offering him her food after her thoughts walking over from Claire's office about foolish starving pageant girls, and now here she was, giving away her food.

Reaching out, Jesse took the treat, his fingers grazing Kylie's. *Clitoral jolt,* she thought. *Damn, title that one The Awakening. This man is too sexy for his own good.*

She watched his lips and tongue savor the rich chocolate crème tunneled in the flaky layers of choux pastry and as he licked the dark chocolate from his top lip, she could see by his expression that he was lost to the rich texture and flavor explosion in his mouth.

And then he surprised her. Removing his sunglasses, she was overwhelmed by the intensity of emotion in his eyes as they sought and held her gaze. Close up, his eyes were more expressive than she had imagined they would be, yet just as captivating as she had suspected.

"Thank you for sharing and giving me half." He finished his last bite, savoring it.

Half. *Mon moitié.*

Kylie sat there for a moment, half an éclair in hand, before extending her hand to Jesse and offering him the remainder of the pastry. Her half. His eyes never left hers, as he smiled and wrapped both his hands around her outstretched hand and brought the éclair to his mouth. Taking the tip of his tongue, he took a swipe of the crème at the center, and then slowly brought the pastry, still wrapped in both their hands, back to her mouth.

"This is your half. It was my gift to you."

She opened her mouth and he grazed her lips with the treat, rubbing crème on them. The same crème his tongue had just swiped. As he fed her the confection, she let the rich chocolate roll over her tongue. This sublime flavor had the hairs on her forearms standing at attention. Did I just taste this? Or was it the last time I was in Paris? Or 1749? All senses were on overload as she savored the smooth crème. When was it? When was it last? When was the first time? Why today? Twice.

The sticker on the box sitting between them on the counter said, *A Paris depuis 1730.* In Paris since 1730. *I knew that,* Kylie mused, though she suspected they cost more than a denier these days.

He had still not let go of her hand, his gaze intent and serious, as if he needed her to eat her half of the treat, his gift to her that must be consumed. Closing her eyes, Kylie took the last bite of the éclair that remained in their hold.

Her half.

It was a taste she had not forgotten and would never, ever forget.

"Jesse, can I get a selfie with you."

The moment was broken as three girls approached, pulling Kylie to interrupted reality as if she'd been plucked off the cobblestones of Rue Montorgueil. Jesse's eyes flashed sadness and regret, as his mirrored lenses quickly made their way back to obscure their connection as the girls' cell phones clicked away.

Leaning forward, he quickly whispered in Kylie's ear, the anxiety in his voice apparent, "I've gotta bolt."

She nodded, but he was making his way out the door before she could verbally respond.

Sitting quietly for a few minutes, trying to process the overwhelming events of the day and Jesse's hasty departure, Kylie was quickly losing a grasp on containing her emotions, and a public meltdown in Starbucks, after being seen with Jesse Winslow, would not be a good thing.

Pulling out her phone, she opened their text thread as she stepped back onto the sidewalk.

**I didn't get to thank you. And I didn't get to say goodbye.**

And those two things hung over her for the remainder of the day, keeping her shrouded in a sadness that was hard to comprehend. Falling into an uneasy sleep that night, where worlds began to collide and new faces from millennia past walked alongside contemporaries, she found relief from the need to try and make sense of something that would never, ever be possible.

It was shortly after four a.m. when the text tone from her phone woke her.

**You don't ever have to thank me and you don't ever have to say goodbye.**

Smiling at the text, Kylie thought, *I'd love to never say goodbye to you. But this stop/start is so frustrating. There was so much I needed to share with you. And today was just not a good day to not say goodbye. You weren't the first.*

**I'm sorry you got busted and had to bolt.**

**LOL. Yeah, me, too. The minute my sunglasses came off, I was toast. We'll figure out someplace new to meet.**

*Someplace new to meet? Kylie could feel the dark shroud lifting off her.*

**OK**

**Now sleep, Toots.**

**Night**

*Toots?* Only Jesse Winslow could get away with calling a woman Toots and make it sound coveted and sexy. *Toots,* she laughed. Soft and sweet like a Tootsie Roll.

*Please don't make it another month before I hear from you or see you again, Jesse. Please. I have to tell this shit to someone and not have them think I'm totally crazy. You're the only one I can talk to.*

And like an epiphany, *I could have told Bruno* was the last thought that ran through her head, before both physical and emotional exhaustion won the battle, stealing the remaining vestiges of her consciousness.

# Chapter 6

"She's a friend from therapy," he said for the fourth time, his tone terse, as his patience clearly waned.

"Well, you look very friendly eating out of one another's hands." The photos were everywhere and everyone wanted to know who was the mystery woman sharing an intimate moment with the famous rocker.

Thirty-six hundred miles away didn't diminish the weight of her anger pressing down on him like a lead blanket, the kind dentists use as a precaution when snapping X-rays. In his mind's eye, he could see the look on her face, that look, the one he knew so well, and he knew she was pressing next, next, next on her keyboard, scrutinizing the photos of him and Kylie in Starbucks.

After a solid minute of silence, he finally asked, "Are you still getting home next Thursday?"

Another silence followed, "I was thinking maybe I'd take a few extra days and join some of the girls in Formentera. One of their families has a ranch with bungalows on the beach right off of Platja de Migjorn."

"Formentera?" It wasn't really a question, just more of a surprise at her seemingly sudden decision to vacate to the quiet island off Spain's coast. The models typically headed to Ibiza for the pulsating nightlife, not chilled-out Formentera.

The first thought that crossed his mind was, *I'll bet Nick has a place on Formentera,* and that was followed by an immediate instinctual testosterone surge that rapidly cooled and dwindled, replaced by relief. *Nah, I don't want to beat the shit out of the guy. Take her. Just take her.*

"Sounds like the perfect relaxing break." He wasn't quite sure whether he was talking to her or himself.

. . . . . .

Looking at the picture brightening her phone screen as it accompanied the opening strains of Faith Hill's "Mississippi Girl" ringtone, Kylie couldn't help but smile.

"Sip," Kylie greeted the caller.

"Gracie," the heavily southern accented voice returned.

"What's up?" Tossing herself down onto her couch, Kylie was thrilled to hear the voice of her old pageant circuit roommate, Hayley Taylor, the reigning Miss Mississippi, hence the nickname, Sip.

"You tell me. You seem to be having all the fun adventures these days."

Kylie laughed. "I assume you're talking about my little java rendezvous."

"Heck yes. Give it up, Gracie." Hayley's nickname for the former Miss New Jersey referencing another Miss New Jersey, the diamond-in-the-rough movie character, Gracie Hart, from the *Miss Congeniality* movie franchise.

"Nothing to give up, Sip. He and I have an acquaintance in common and were just having coffee." Kylie knew it wasn't her place to reveal that the acquaintance was a psychiatrist and that Jesse was in therapy.

"Sugar, your voice is like an octave higher when you are lying or talking about your commitment to world peace," Hayley chuckled. "When you're ready to divulge this little secret, you know I'm here to listen. And I want every single detail about that hot, hot man."

Kylie was smiling as she listened to her friend speak. DYE-vulj. Her classic southern accent and smoldering emerald eyes could charm the pants off any man or woman and the latter was a huge issue for her on the pageant circuit. Many a night Kylie would cover for her roommate and friend who was successfully seducing yet another sweet young thing.

"I know you are, Sip. And I appreciate it."

"Seriously, Gracie," her voice became soft, almost nurturing. "This is Jesse Winslow we're talking about. Somehow I don't imagine *boyfriend material* is part of his set list."

"It's not like that between us, really. It isn't." She wasn't sure what it was, but it certainly wasn't anything that had her fantasizing about a happily ever after. They were just two souls on a journey of discovery who no longer had to forge an uncharted, scary and potentially painful path alone.

"Are you seriously telling me that you're not attracted to Jesse Winslow?"

Pausing to formulate a response denying any attraction, she wasn't quick enough as Hayley jumped in.

"Hell, woman, I love pussy and even I'm attracted to him. Everything about that man exudes pure carnal energy. So, I don't believe for a single second that you're not attracted to him."

Kylie just sighed. She couldn't even begin to tell her friend the truth. *How insane would all this sound?*

"Gracie, you need to take a look at those pictures. The way the two of you are looking at each other, mmm...mmm...mmm hotter than an egg frying on a Texas pick-up truck in July. It's like there's no one else in the world. You have the look of absolute bliss on your face. What was he feeding you?"

"An éclair."

"An éclair? Seriously, sugar? Our backwoods Starbucks don't carry éclairs."

"Ours don't either. Jesse brought it for me from my favorite bakery in Paris."

There was a snicker on the other end of the phone. "Paris? As in Paris, France? He brought you éclairs from Paris?"

"Yes. From my favorite bakery. It wasn't éclairs. It was just one single, lone éclair. He ate the other one," Kylie giggled.

"Did he know it was your favorite bakery?" Hayley was digging.

"I may have mentioned it."

"May have mentioned it," she laughed. "Claudine, your days are numbered, you stuck-up bitch."

"Seriously, Sip, it's not like that."

"Gracie, turn on your PC and take a look at those pictures and the way you two are looking at each other. Every woman dreams of a man looking at her like that. And for you, it's a man half the women on the planet have fantasized about."

Hanging up the phone, Kylie grabbed her iPad and googled Jesse Winslow. Her screen immediately populated with hits.

"Jesse Takes a Bite"

"Rockers Prefer Redheads"

"Claudine Who?"

"Rocker and Mystery Woman Share a Moment"

"Jesse's New Love"

The same four pictures appeared in all the articles. As Kylie studied them closely several things crossed her mind. *I need to see Zac more often and work out harder because I look like a beast in profile* and *Hayley is right! Look at the way we are looking at each other.*

There was no denying it. She and Jesse Winslow were sharing a connection. A very special connection. But it wasn't the connection the rest of the world, including his very famous girlfriend, thought it was. But even Kylie couldn't tell them exactly what their bond actually was.

. . . . . .

"We were scheduled for a regression today," Claire commented, perusing her notes.

"We'll see," the tone in Jesse's response revealed a dark mood.

"Let's talk about what has you out of sorts today."

Unlacing his boots, the rocker kicked them off, lying down on the couch and pulling a throw pillow behind his neck.

"Lots of shit. Detoxing is hard. Staying sober is hard. I'm trying to substitute positive things for the destructive, but I'm on edge, my fuse feels short. People say shit to me and I just want to punch their faces in."

With a pencil in her mouth, Claire absentmindedly ran it back and forth through her lips. "So, what are you doing to counteract all the aggression and negativity?"

Running his fingers slowly through the long dark spikes of hair, Jesse remained silent as he focused on a spot on the ceiling. Finally, "I've been working out like a motherfucker and I do it at the gym so that I'm getting my ass out of the apartment."

"You don't have a problem being stalked in the gym?" Claire was envisioning the gym packed with women in brightly colored, tight sports bras and yoga pants on the days Jesse worked out.

He laughed. "The owner has a gym within the gym set-up for people who need privacy. It's card access only with the owner's permission."

"Well, that is certainly convenient," her remark ended with a smirk.

"Yeah. It is. So, when I was in Paris with Claudine there was no connection there between us and I'm pretty sure there's some guy in her life. I know making more changes in my life while in recovery is probably not the smartest thing I can do for myself," his thought trailed off.

"Changes are triggers. We know that. But staying in a situation that is either negative or destructive is not healthy either. Is staying going to make it easier? How do your interactions with her leave you feeling?"

Snickering, Jesse shook his head, "Like shit. We're both miserable."

"Are you happier when she is not around?"

"Infinitely," he didn't miss a beat in responding. Chuckling, "Well, there's my answer. You know what, Doc?" Turning his head, he looked at her. "I really think I'm okay this time. I'm not in some bullshit place in Malibu. I'm taking responsibility for myself, by myself. I'm writing. I'm working out. I haven't missed a session with you."

Just verbalizing his accomplishments lifted the funk that had walked through the door with him. "Ya know what, let's try this thing." And he reached over to the end table for the headphones and glasses.

Closing the shades and dimming the lights, Claire began her relaxation monologue, listening intently for the changes in Jesse's breathing patterns. As they became deep and regulated, more so than she had seen in previous sessions, she began to ask him to focus on events in his childhood.

"Jesse, can you take me back to when you were three years old." She paused and watched the expression on his face change. His brows drew together in a questioning line. "Where are you?"

"In the basement." His voice was tentative.

"At your house?" Claire probed.

"Yes."

"Are you alone?"

"No. Daddy is here with his band. They are practicing. The music is loud."

"Do they know you are there, Jesse?"

Shaking his head, "Nope, I'm sitting on the stairs. They can't see me from there. Daddy is really mad at Marco."

"Who is Marco?"

"He plays bass. They are taking a break now. Daddy is still mad. I can smell smoke. They are all smoking."

"Cigarettes?" Claire clarified.

"Yeah and a pipe, too. Marco is putting a lighter under a spoon. And Scotty, the drummer sounds mad, too."

Holding her breath, Claire could feel the hairs on the back of her neck grow stiff. This three-year-old was about to watch a man shoot up.

"Icky. He's getting a shot and he's not even at the doctor's office."

"Tell me what you see, Jesse." Maybe this would shed light on some of his demons.

"Marco has his head back on the couch. I think he's going to take a nap. Scotty is slapping him. Telling him to wake up. Daddy's trying to help but Marco is just shivering and shaking, except it's not cold. His eyes are white and he's turning red and now purple. Everyone is screaming. Mommy is running down the stairs. She sees me and is screaming my name. Now Daddy sees me. Daddy is yelling at her to get me out of there. He looks like he's mad at me." His face crumbles.

"What happened next, Jesse?" Claire makes note of his shallow, rapid breathing.

"Mommy is trying to pick me up but I'm holding onto the handrail. I'm scared. I don't know what I did wrong to make Daddy so mad at me. I just wanted to hear the music. I love the music." Pulling at his spiky bangs, his anxiety is manifesting physically.

"Go on, Jesse."

"They are trying to carry Marco up the stairs, but I'm in the way. Daddy is yelling at me to move and I'm crying." His face screws up in pain, "Oww," as he grabs his right shoulder.

"Jesse, tell me what's going on." Claire's voice remains calm, detached.

"He just picked me up and threw me to get me out of the way. I hit the wall."

"Okay, I'm going to count to three now, Jesse. I want you to take a deep, cleansing breath with each count and at three you will be back here and present."

Claire counted. At three, Jesse's exhale emptied his lungs as he stared into her eyes.

"I had no conscious memory of that." His voice was shaky. Putting his face in his hands, he shook his head. "At three years old, I watched a man overdose and die. Ironic, huh?"

"He died?"

Nodding, "Yeah and I'd always known that my Dad's bass player overdosed. I just didn't know that I was there watching it. I didn't think that I remembered anything from that far back."

"It was there. Just not a conscious memory."

"Wow." Jesse continued to shake his head as he absentmindedly kneaded his shoulder. Finally, he looked up at Claire and smiled. "Big breakthrough today."

"Very big. You'll find the process will accelerate quickly now."

**Patient: Jesse Winslow**

**Session: #36**

**Date: January 7, 2015**

**Regression: #7**

**Length: 10:15 A.M.–10:35 A.M.**

**Entity: Jesse Winslow (age 3)**

**Location: Basement of his childhood home**

**Year: 1991**

· · · · · ·

**Just leaving Dr. S's. I had a memory,** he texted as soon as he got down to the street. **Meet me**

**Where?** The response was almost immediate.

**Are you familiar with L9?**

**I'm a member.**

**Excellent.** Jesse typed with both thumbs. **Meet me in an hour.**

**See you then.**

· · · · · ·

"Hey Red, you're not on my schedule today." Zac was walking past as Kylie entered the vast rotunda of L9/NYC. It was almost impossible not to gasp every time you entered the iconic space with its mythological figures painted on the domed ceiling above the SkyTrack.

"Surprised to see me, huh, when I don't have you cracking the whip." Smiling at her trainer, the shock on his handsome face was almost comical.

"Understatement doesn't begin to sum it up."

"I'm meeting a friend," Kylie explained, her eyes scanning the premises.

Zac followed her gaze, which had landed on two men, his father, the owner of the facility, and a very famous bad boy of rock 'n' roll.

With eyebrows raised, he smiled at his client. "You *are* full of surprises today." And then, "Have a great workout." He patted her on the shoulder, leaving her to meet a client as she headed toward the two men.

Seeing her approach, Jesse acknowledged with a smile, causing the taller man to turn in her direction. Kylie was struck at the man's resemblance to Zac, older and just as handsome, she immediately decided it must be his father.

"Kylie, you made it." Jesse looked pleased.

The older man greeted her with a warm smile. "Hello. How are you today?"

"Hi. I'm great." Kylie returned the greeting.

The man turned back to Jesse, handing him a keycard. "Same door as you used last time." He motioned with his head to the far right.

"Thank you so much for this. It's truly brilliant." Jesse looked at the keycard.

"Let me know if you need anything else. You should find everything you require in there, but if you need any assistance at all, just pick up the house phone and we'll take care of whatever it is."

"Where are we going?" Kylie asked when the man left.

Leaning in to whisper in her ear, "To a secret gym within L9."

"Seriously?" Kylie broke into a huge grin.

Nodding, "Seriously. Is that not the coolest thing?" Jesse steered her to the door and swiped the keycard.

Entering the private space, they gave one another conspiratorial looks like two kids who just hopped a fence and were going to explore the haunted house on the edge of town.

Motion sensor lights lit the space. Gasping, Kylie took it all in, "I want to move in here. This is like a gorgeous apartment."

Retaining the tall ceilings and ornate moldings from its turn-of-the-century origins, the private gym had a living room area with couches, reclining chairs and tables, a large-screen TV mounted to the wall, sound system, fully equipped kitchen with breakfast bar and two VitaMix blenders for making smoothies, multi-stall and private bath-rooms, massage room, sauna, steam room, hot tub and state-of-the-art exercise equipment.

"Perfect, isn't it." Jesse looked around, trying to take it all in from Kylie's first-time perspective. "I just need to call ahead or book it for times I know we'll want to use it."

*We'll want to use it.* Kylie's heart skipped a beat.

"I'm sorry I bolted on you at Starbucks," he began.

"I'm sorry that they got those photos of us."

Smiling, "Well, redheaded mystery woman, you've definitely caused me some grief."

Kylie's eyes misted slightly at his words, not wanting to cause him pain. Ever.

"No. No, no. Don't feel bad." He reached for her hand and squeezed it, before leading her over to the couch.

"With your girlfriend?"

Nodding, "Yes, my girlfriend who is shacking up with some guy named Nick on an island off the coast of Spain."

"I'm sorry, you must be upset." Kylie was surprised the rocker was confiding in her.

"From an ego standpoint, I'm kinda pissed. But honestly, it's a relief not to have her around. There's a whole stress factor to everything about our relationship, from expectations we have of each other to the public's expectations of us. And right now, I just need to worry about me getting clean and staying clean."

Kylie nodded and Jesse went on. "Also, I'm a shitty boyfriend. Addicts and drunks are notoriously self-centered and self-absorbed."

"Did you cheat a lot?" she asked, wanting to know everything and fearful of the blatant truth.

"Did I cheat a lot?" he repeated the question and looked Kylie straight in the eyes. "You are really direct and I like that."

She held her breath waiting for him to answer what was now his question.

"I had a lot of sex with other people. I really didn't consider it cheating, though."

"Seriously?" she laughed, wondering what set of personalized rules he had created for his life.

"Seriously," he was now chuckling. "Had I fallen in love with someone or even grown an attachment, then that would have felt like cheating, because my heart would have been involved."

"So, sex to you is what?" She was trying hard to understand.

"Release," he answered without giving it any thought.

Kylie nodded. *Note to self: This is not a guy to get involved with in any serious way. Raise walls. Engage force field.*

As if reading her mind, he began to explain. "Kylie," he reached forward and took a long lock of her hair and let it run slowly through his fingers. This time, although she didn't back away physically, she was emotionally preparing barriers. "Kylie, after a show I'm spent. I've expended all my energy, given everything I have to give. It's a control thing for me when I'm up there. I not only have complete control over my own life, but also the surroundings and the energy and the people engaged in this magic with me. And that makes it very safe for me." He laughed, "It *is* my circus. And they *are* my monkeys. It's the only time in my life that I get to be the puppet master of all the variables. And I'm focused because it is my responsibility to deliver something that transcends just the here and now. And to create a moment that is alive with so much energy that it lives for a million years. Like light from the stars making its way to Earth. And that is my responsibility and usually I do a good job with it, because I really take it very seriously. But every so often, like in Australia, I fuck up. The pain becomes too great. And I'm lost and even the footlights can't illuminate my way." Stopping for a moment, he ran his hand through his spiky bangs. "When I walk off stage, I am done. And then the adrenaline leaves my bloodstream and I am totally depleted. Gone. So, when I sit down and someone hands me a cold beer and throws some lines on a mirror, I am kicking back and stepping out of myself. I'm kinda gone already. Next thing I know I'm inside someone's mouth and looking at the top of their head. I close my eyes and I haven't got a clue who I've been with. Half the time I don't see a face."

The rush of emotions momentarily overwhelmed Kylie, rendering her speechless. He wanted to make everyone happy, relieve them of their pain and transport them elsewhere. "But you're clean now."

"Yeah, and not on tour," he paused, then laughed. "And celibate."

The conflict in her mind, heart and soul began waging a fierce battle. Was he like no man she'd ever met before? Or were all men like this and he was just the first honest one? It was hard to tell, but this conversation had pulled her too far out of her comfort zone, making the real Kylie want to shrink deep within her outer shell. As he shared deep truths with her, retreat was her response instead of meeting him with some of her own. She needed to steer the course back to her comfort zone and away from any nook the raw truth might reside.

"Tell me what happened in your session." Changing the subject quickly put her back on ground that was easier to navigate.

Jesse's face lit up. His eyes wide. Putting his hand on his forehead, he began to shake his head. "I can't believe it happened. It was a memory from when I was three. I'd totally repressed it because it was really freaking traumatic."

"What happened?" Kylie leaned in. They were back on safe ground.

"I was three and I snuck down into the basement to watch my dad's band practice. They didn't know I was there and I watched his bass player shoot up and OD."

"Holy crap. That's horrible." Kylie pictured this little boy trying to make sense of it all. "What happened to him?"

"He was convulsing and they took him out of there. And he died. The guy died."

"That's not something a three-year-old, or anyone for that matter, should see." Horrified, Kylie wasn't sure what to say, as her feelings were now turning protective. And her next thought was, *it's going to be impossible to protect myself from him.*

"I was on the stairs and I wouldn't leave. My dad literally picked me up and threw me against a wall. I thought he was mad at me. That somehow everything was my fault." Jesse was visualizing the memory as his fingers absentmindedly slid up and down a lock of Kylie's hair.

"I think it takes time to process it and figure it out and to understand how to apply it to how it's impacted other things in your life."

He nodded. "Yeah, I have no clue yet. Pretty ironic that I've had a substance abuse issue most of my life. I can only think that I was trying to hide from this, keep it repressed and music and writing have been my release and my savior."

"I think the more you get to see, the picture builds and pieces fit and make sense."

"Is yours making sense yet? Have you put any puzzle pieces together?" he probed as if Kylie held the key to unleash all his secrets.

She nodded, "Yeah, it's definitely starting to. I had a really significant regression." Pausing, she took a deep breath before being able to verbalize her fate. "I was going to tell you about it when we got made in Starbucks. I had just come from Claire's and I was still reeling at that point." She paused, and looking him straight in the eye, confessed her painful truth. "I starved to death in a past life."

Jesse's eyes widened as his head snapped sharply. "Really?"

Nodding, "Mmm-hmm. How's that for telling."

"That is crazy. How did it happen?"

"I was traveling across the Atlantic by ship, being sent to Louisiana to work in a silk factory. I became ill on the journey and other passengers were stealing my food rations and water."

As Kylie shared her tale she could see the emotion in Jesse's eyes, gathering like storm clouds on the horizon. "Where was your family? They couldn't protect you from the thieves?"

Shaking her head, she looked down at her lap, "I was an orphan by then, so I was an easy target. I had been abducted. That's how I ended up on the ship in the first place."

"Abducted?" he repeated in a ghost of a whisper.

"I'd lost my last living relative. My brother." Mon moitié. Kylie could feel the pressure at the back of her eyes as tears threatened and she thought they felt like the storm clouds bursting in Jesse's eyes.

"Wow. The amount of detail you know." He was entranced by her tale.

Nodding, Kylie searched for the words to share with him. "It's not just what I can remember, it's how heightened all my senses are of the memories." Her nose twitched, as if just mentioning her senses overwhelmed the limbic portion of her brain with the horrible stench of sulphur and now it would forever be equated with death. Quickly pushing that away, she refocused. "And the feelings. Love, hatred, fear. I can feel them. They are so strong. How can I feel such deep love for someone I don't know?"

"Was it a boyfriend or your husband?" Jesse's hand stopped midway down the lock of Kylie's hair that he absentmindedly continued to stroke as if running a strand of beads through his fingers.

"No. It was my brother. He took care of me. We'd lost the rest of our family, so it was just us." Looking at the famous rocker, she continued. "My heart aches at the loss of him. This person I don't know, who died like two hundred and sixty-five years ago. How could that be?"

"This is intense, Kylie. The fact that you now possess memories." His hand dropped from her hair and he grasped her hand. "It's like you never thought you'd see someone again and you just saw him." Squeezing her hand, he was clearly trying to process it.

"But only a memory and I'm feeling pain from someone else's memory. Not mine. It's really overwhelming. I'm not sure how to deal with it."

In a move that surprised them both, Jesse pulled Kylie into his chest, wrapping both arms around her. "Know you can call me, day or night, Toots. If you need to talk through it or the emotions are closing in on you. Text me. Call me. I know what I went through with unlocking my memory was overpowering, I can't imagine yet what it is like to unlock someone else's memory that is yours."

Pulling her face off his chest to look at him, "If anyone heard this conversation, Jesse, they'd think we were nuts."

Laughing, "Well, then we'd better pray Schooner doesn't have hidden cameras with recorders in here."

"Who?"

"Schooner Moore, the owner of L9 who you met earlier," he explained, standing and reaching for her hand. "Treadmills?"

Kylie just nodded as she followed Jesse to the side-by-side treadmills. Outwardly, a silence accompanied them as they walked and jogged mile after mile. Inwardly, loud dialogues raged as they each sought answers to questions they were yet to formulate.

. . . . . .

"There's always the possibility that she was walking down that street in Paris and saw the plaque and it somehow stayed in her subconscious memory."

Looking at Marshall, Claire shook her head in disagreement. She knew in her gut after watching and listening to Kylie recount her tale, and the detail in which she told it, that her patient was truly experiencing a past life memory.

"Marshall, unless she researched it–and then had no recollection of doing so–she was relating a memory. Let's consider some of the historically accurate details. To know that Bicêtre was a prison as well as a hospital in 1749 or that the accuseds' shirts were stuffed with sulphur or that they were executed at the Place de Grève versus the Place de la Concorde, which is much more famous because of Marie Antoinette's execution, is pretty remarkable," Claire plead her case.

"It is compelling. I'll give you that." The older psychiatrist acquiesced. "What bothers me here is that they weren't just obscure people. There is a researchable history to the story. Have you been able to locate a Geneviève?"

Shaking her head. "Not yet, but I am working on it. I'm waiting to hear back from an archivist at Saint-Eustache."

"It will be interesting to see what they come back with." Moving on, Marshall flipped the page on his legal pad, a vestige of the past of which he couldn't let go. "Any success with your star patient?"

With a telltale squirm in her seat, Claire tapped her iPad screen. "As a matter of fact, we're actually making headway. We achieved a first full memory under hypnosis."

"Oh?"

"I was able to successfully regress him back to a traumatic memory from when he was about three. And it was haunting and harrowing."

"What happened?" Marshall encouraged her to continue.

"He saw a member of his father's band shoot up and overdose in their basement."

Looking up from his legal pad, Marshall's trademark implacability disintegrated. "Did the man die?"

Nodding. Claire offered one word. "Yes."

"Did his parents seek help for him?" Marshall was no longer looking at his pad.

"Sadly, no. And what makes it even worse, they never sat him down to explain it to him, so this three-year-old somehow thought his presence had been the culprit. That he was responsible for the man's death. He had repressed the memory."

"That is an unfortunate burden for a small child. Especially a sensitive one. So, he is actually punishing himself for this event through his own addiction."

Claire nodded. "It would appear so."

"Interesting." Marshall flipped over the pages on his pad now that their session was nearing completion.

"Very," Claire agreed. "My self-proclaimed narcissist is, in fact, an empath."

"Not a surprise when you look at the lyrics he pens. Clearly the work of a highly sensitive person."

*How did I miss it?* Claire wondered. *Was I just buying the rock-star hype?*

With a rare smile, Marshall's gaze took on an almost amused look. "Now that he is successfully regressing, I look forward to seeing if he is able to access any pre-birth memory. Will there be any correlation to the magnitude of his personality and fame in this lifetime with past experiences? Or was he just a common man? I can't wait to see what you uncover."

Leaving Marshall's office and stepping out onto upper Fifth Avenue, Claire stood for a moment looking out over the winter's bare tree branches of Central Park. Something was bothering her about her supervisor's last statement, "I can't wait to see what you uncover." But she couldn't quite put her finger on the source of her discomfort.

# Chapter 7

He saw the movement out of the corner of his eye and, in one sweeping arc motion, ripped the headphones from his head. The shock on their faces mirrored his as they entered the apartment.

"Jesse," Alexa Seurley, one of the most well-known faces in fashion modeling, stumbled on her words as she stopped abruptly in the doorway. "I didn't think you were going to..." her words trailed before she completed her sentence.

"Be here." Jesse picked up without skipping a beat.

The statuesque brunette, accompanied by a younger model and two burly tatted guys closely stacked behind her looked confused as to their next move.

Standing up from the rough-hewn wood table, Jesse approached the supermodel, hand outstretched. "My keys, please."

Not sure what to do, Alexa, moved her hand down to her side, "These are Claudine's."

"I own this apartment," Jesse's voice was soft, his tone even. "So, we can play this one of two ways. You hand me my keys or I call the cops and have you arrested."

Alexa looked back to the guys behind her for guidance.

The guy pulling up the rear spoke, "Give the man his keys, Alexa. I'm not getting arrested for one of your flaky friends." Recognizing the rocker, "Hey Jesse, I had no idea this was what she was getting me into when she asked for help."

"Why are you here, Alexa?" Crossing his arms over his chest, Jesse approached her, standing nose to nose with the model.

"Claudine asked me to clear her stuff out." As she spoke, her eyes cast downward, no longer able to make eye contact with the famous rocker.

It was a blindside blow. And yet, it wasn't. The real sucker-punch was the sharp and unexpected pain in his gut and solar plexus. That was the surprise. Reminding himself to breathe, and outwardly showing no emotion, Jesse, the showman had arrived on the scene to save Jesse, the songwriter and the boyfriend.

"Shipping it to Nick's?" He cast the red herring.

"Yeah." Alexa nodded, confirming Jesse's suspicions.

Looking at his watch, "You have five minutes. I'm calling my security now and in five minutes I call NYPD and report a break-in. Your five minutes starts now." And he pointed down the hall where they could find Claudine's clothes and personal items.

"Hey, take this," the guy in the way back handed Alexa and her friend several empty duffel bags. "Man Code invoked here, I can't help you." Turning to Jesse, "Dude, I'm sorry. I had no idea this was the shit they were getting me into. This is some crazy bullshit."

The other guy, who had yet to speak, finally broke his silence. "Jesse, so sorry, man," he apologized to the rock icon. "So, so sorry." And with that, the two guys were out the door, leaving the two super-models to forage through Claudine's closet and dressers.

"You have three minutes," Jesse appeared in the doorway to the room. "Three minutes and I call the cops."

"What about the rest of her stuff?" Alexa's wide-eyed accomplice asked.

"She can buy it back from Goodwill." Jesse was dead serious.

At four minutes, Jesse snapped pictures with his phone of the two women franticly going through drawers. At four-and-a-half minutes, he announced, "You have thirty seconds to zip those bags and get your skinny asses down the hall and out of my home."

Blocking the entrance to the room, he once again found himself toe to toe with Alexa. "Forget something?" the venom in his tone was chilling.

Reaching into the pocket of her skintight jeans, she pulled out the keys, and with a sigh and an eye roll, slapped them in his hand.

Leaning forward, he growled in her ear, "Now get the fuck out of my house."

Sitting back down in front of his laptop, he imagined a cold beer and his taste buds craved the acrid flavor almost as much as his blood stream yearned for the calming rush.

"Fuck that and fuck her." He got up and stormed into the kitchen. Prowling through cabinets and the refrigerator with purpose, he pulled an odd variety of ingredients: an avocado, which squeezing it he found was bordering on overripe, a carton of blueberries, plain Greek yogurt, and a jar containing Maca Root powder. Dumping everything into a smoothie maker with ice, Jesse proceeded to make himself a smoothie from these high Vitamin B ingredients that he knew would have a calming effect on his body. He then poured almonds into a bowl and carried the drink and snack back to the table where he had been working.

Proud that instead of pursuing the initial craving for a beer, he proactively made himself a calming holistic alternative. Jesse sat back and drank his shake, wondering what the hell Claudine was thinking sending people over to gather her belongings versus having a conversation with him to end their relationship. Their multi-year relationship. Was it because she'd have to confess to her relationship with Nick?

The one Alexa confirmed tonight when he threw out the red herring.

Dialing her cell, he wondered was she back in New York? Or was she on Formentera? If she'd ever actually even gone there. After three rings, the call went to voice mail and he hung up.

**Classy move, Claud.**

He texted.

**I didn't think you'd be there.**

**Seriously, you didn't think this deserved a conversation? We deserved a conversation?**

**We've been over for a long time, Jesse.**

He couldn't disagree with that.

**Had it been me, I would've shown you more respect.** He was pissed at her cowardice. Doing the right thing was not easy, as he was well finding out.

**I've had enough of your respect over the years, Jesse. Your idea of respect was calling me from somewhere in the world to say goodnight with a groupie attached to your dick. So please don't talk to me about respect.**

She wasn't wrong. The waters under their bridge had become a toxic pollutant long before tonight and most likely long before the mysterious Nick had emerged onto the scene.

**I'm sorry that we ended this way, Claud.**

But he also knew, that he wasn't sorry they ended.

First inclination, a habit born of repetition, was to scour the liquor cabinet and see if a bottle of Jack Daniel's No. 27 Gold was hiding back there. The seductive mellow of the first sip coursing through his bloodstream made his body quiver. Tennessee whiskey had always been his unrivaled lover. The Juliet to his Romeo. *Heh,* he thought.

*Well, that didn't end up too good.*

Picking up his phone again. He shot off another text.

**I'm sober. And I'd like to stay this way. Can you meet me?**

. . . . . .

Faith Hill's "Mississippi Girl" blared from Kylie's phone at a volume way too loud for eight a.m. on a Friday morning.

"Looks like your boyfriend is making headlines again," Hayley informed her.

"Huh? What are you talking about?" Kylie's voice was rough from sleep.

"Did I wake you?"

"Yeah, I worked last night. I actually had a modeling gig and we shot until about two a.m. on the steps of the New York Public Library.

"Well, turn on the NBC morning show, Gracie. They are just about to talk about your boyfriend."

Reaching over for the remote, Kylie got herself into a comfortable position to watch the TV.

"Here it comes," Hayley sounded excited.

Kylie watched as the camera focused in on the attractive blonde. Behind her was a still photo of Jesse on stage.

"It's been several months since the onstage meltdown in Sydney, Australia of rock 'n' roll bad boy, Jesse Winslow. The uncontainable half of super-couple, Claudesse, with fashion model, Claudine, Jesse Winslow has been keeping a low profile. That was until fans photographed him three weeks ago, feeding a pastry to a mystery woman in a Starbucks on Manhattan's Upper East Side. That woman has now been identified as former Miss New Jersey, Kylie Martin."

Groaning, Kylie smushed her face into her pillow. She'd just been outed.

"Today new video of Jesse has surfaced checking into the exclusive Crossroads Centre, located on the island of Antigua. Crossroads is a residential substance abuse treatment center founded by legendary guitarist Eric Clapton. He's seen here entering the facility accompanied by an unidentified companion. Spokespeople from neither his nor Claudine's camp could be reached for comment.

"We wish you the best for a speedy recovery, Jesse."

The warm, salty tears were threatening to roll off her jaw as Kylie watched a hoodie and sunglasses-shrouded Jesse being escorted into the facility by none other than Dr. Claire Stoddard. A pang of hatred for the psychiatrist soared through her heart, followed immediately by guilt. There was no reason to hate the woman. She was trying to help a patient. But Kylie's instinctual reaction was not born of logic or anything that made sense.

Hitting the back button on her remote, she watched the clip again.

"Gracie, who is that with Jesse?"

She had forgotten that Hayley was still on the phone.

"I dunno," she lied, knowing it would not be cool to divulge the doctor's identity and expose Jesse that way.

Pausing the TV, she tried to see Jesse's face, but his head was down and the hood of his sweatshirt obscured any chance of capturing his facial expression.

*What happened, Jess?* she wondered. *You were doing so great. You were writing, exercising, eating healthy. You were the one getting* **me** *healthy. What the heck happened?*

*And why didn't you tell me?*

Her heart ached at the realization that she was an outsider in her new friend's life. Intellectually she knew it was ridiculous to think he would turn to her, I mean, what could she really do anyway? Yet, there was an annoying stabbing in her craw that he turned to Claire. Again, intellectually she knew he did the right thing to insure his health by seeking medical help. It just bothered her deeply, and in a way she couldn't quite grasp.

"Do not get involved with that man, Gracie. He is nothing but heartache and trouble and hot ass. You are never going to fix him," Hayley warned, still on the phone.

Holding on tightly to the phone she had forgotten was still in her hand, "Don't worry, Sip. We're just friends."

And Kylie wondered if they were even that as she hit the back button on her remote and attempted another glimpse of Jesse's face through her tears.

· · · · · ·

"How's Jesse doing?" It was the first question out of her mouth upon entering Claire's Inner Sanctum.

With a lack of any kind of expression on her face or in her voice, "You know I cannot answer that, Kylie."

*Bitch.* But Kylie hadn't expected any other answer.

"Can you give him a message from me?" Kylie sat on the couch.

"Kylie," Claire began, her tone already betraying annoyance.

Cutting her off, "Geez, Claire, it's not like I'm asking you to pass the guy meth. Ask him if he's okay with getting a message from me and if he says yes, tell him I'm thinking about him and sending good, healing thoughts." And just to piss off Claire and because it was true, "And tell him, I miss…," her voice trailed off. "No, forget that. Just tell him I'm sending good, healing thoughts. And if he tells you he doesn't want a message from me, that's fine, too. Can you do that?"

"What you are asking is highly unorthodox."

"Yeah, well, what we do in here is highly unorthodox. It doesn't make it wrong," Kylie pushed back. "If he says no, he says no. If he says yes, it's not going to disrupt his treatment to know someone is pulling for him."

Three days later the text came.

**I'm okay, Toots.**

**Jesse! OMG. I've been so worried about you. Seriously, are you okay???**

**Yeah. I'm good. It's gorgeous down here.**

**What happened? If you don't mind my asking?**

**Claudine sent some friends over to move her shit out. I was just sitting in the living room writing a friggin' song and four people walked into my apartment (said 'ex-'girlfriend was not one of them)**

**Oh, shit. I'm so sorry. How are you doing with that? That's a huge change. Are you devastated?**

**Nah, I'm fine. It's the removal of a toxic relationship from my life. So, that's a healthy thing. It's a big change, though, and I knew something like that could potentially be a trigger and I didn't want to relapse. I worked very hard getting clean, Toots. And I was feeling really good. Honestly, my relationship with her was one of the last negative things in my life.**

**So, you didn't start using or drinking again?**

**No. I stayed clean.**

**I am so proud of you, Jess.**

**I'm proud of me, too, Toots. How are you? Are you okay?**

Looking at the text for a few minutes, Kylie started multiple responses and stopped, deleting each one. She wanted to tell him, but she didn't want him to feel any pressure.

**Yeah. I'm okay.**

**Really?**

It felt as if he were reading her.

**Yeah, really. I just miss you. I miss our "sessions."** There she said it. It was out there in the universe.

**I miss you, too. I'll be home in a few weeks. We'll get that special key for L9 and hang out there and catch up on everything, okay. I'll even make you a smoothie ☺**

Kylie, couldn't help but smile. For the first time in weeks, she felt whole. He was getting in deeper than she'd allowed herself to admit.

**You're on.**

A picture came across her phone. Jesse must've been standing on a hill at the facility and shooting across the water at another part of the island. Rising from the sea, a volcanic remnant basked in solitude under the equatorial sun.

Gasping, not the reaction she knew Jesse intended to evoke from her upon sending it, Kylie looked at the lone stretch of island, as she felt bile burning dangerously close to the back of her throat. Gazing at the beautiful image, a photo that looked as if it were publication quality for an exclusive and remote resort, she questioned why the icky, overall feeling had seized her. Why not a Zen-like feeling when looking at the beautiful Caribbean island? But there was nothing soothing in the pains that were wracking her stomach, making every muscle in her body ache, sending cold shivers up her spine and an even colder sweat across her forehead. She might as well have just looked at a photo of snakes based on her extreme visceral response.

*Jesse come home,* was the overwhelming thought pattern wrapping itself tightly around her brain. *Jesse, come home.*

# Chapter 8

"You look well rested," Claire commented as Jesse entered the Inner Sanctum.

"I am. I feel good. A month on Antigua will do that to you." Tanned and relaxed, he sprawled on the couch, arm muscles bulging from the tight sleeves of his black, vintage Sex Pistols tee-shirt.

"The reports I got back from your doctors were exceptional. And taking a proactive role in ensuring you stayed healthy during a transition time was a very sound decision. This is the most committed I think you have been after a detox, Jesse."

"I worked too hard to get where I was and there is no shame in asking for a little help if you need it. I was afraid I'd do what I always do. And I didn't want that to be my fate again. This is the first facility that I felt really got me. I really liked the holistic approach, and the fact that I wasn't going through treatment and detoxing at the same time, gave me the opportunity to get a lot out of it with a clarity I'd never experienced before in rehab. It was also amazing for my creativity. The ocean is a seductive muse."

"And now that you're back? How are you feeling about your life and living in your space without Claudine?"

"I feel good. One of the things that I've been thinking about a lot is that maybe I don't feel like other people do, I mean, when I'm in a relationship. Except for my ego, it wasn't painful to let her go, because I just don't feel deeply for others. Or maybe I just didn't feel deeply for her. I actually really wonder if I have the capacity to feel great, deep love for another person. So, to your question about living in my space without Claudine, it's nice not to have the burden of disappointing another person. Bad enough that I disappoint myself."

"Are you disappointed in yourself?" Claire looked up from her iPad.

"Not at all. I feel very strong and in control. I'm eating healthy foods, sleeping normal hours, and working out regularly at L9. And now I'm ready to move forward with regressions and get back to work here. I thought about them a lot while I was gone. Remembering that scene in my parents' basement and then my subsequent abuse problems was a topic I explored a lot this past month."

"In therapy?" She reached over to her desk and grabbed a folder, perusing several sheets stapled to the inner cover.

"And in meditation." Giving her a smile that never failed to drive fans wild, "I had a lot of time out there on the island. Now that I'm back, I'm ready to get to this."

Looking shocked, Claire offered an out, "We don't have to begin exploring via regression again until you are ready. We can just talk this session."

"Dr. S., I'm ready. The time I spent meditating really made me feel like we are on the right path with regression. I want to explore areas of my consciousness that may hold keys to help me work through my shit. I really want to know why I do the self-destructive things that I do and why I seemingly don't have that capacity to really love another human being." Picking up the headphones and RGB glasses, the seductive smile was going to ensure he got his way. "Let's do this."

Jesse Winslow appeared to be on a mission.

Seeing the difference as she walked Jesse through the guided relaxation meditation, his body muscles and facial expression almost immediately became slack, showing no external sign of stress or discomfort. His receptibility to hypnosis was significantly more positive than before he went away. Claire noted this on her iPad, but wasn't surprised as she'd often found that clients who practiced meditation were more susceptible to hypnotic suggestion.

"Jesse, please touch your thumb and forefinger together on your right hand."

Following her direction, she commented, "Very good. This is your anchor. It will always return you to safety. If you are feeling uncomfortable or overwhelmed at any time, create your anchor and it will immediately bring you out of your hypnotic state. Everything you are seeing, you will be able to describe to me in terms you understand from today," she paused. "Are you ready to start."

"Yes," he responded.

"Okay Jesse, look down at your feet and describe to me what you are wearing."

"Calceus," was his one-word response.

"Calceus?" she repeated, typing the word into her iPad. The adrenaline burst made both her head and chest feel as if they were going to explode when the image of a shoe-boot with a studded nail sole appeared on her screen. Calceus was, in fact, a shoe. Claire was fairly certain that the Jesse Winslow she knew in the here and now had never heard the word or used the word calceus before. Heck, she'd never heard of it. She couldn't wait to throw that one out to Marshall and see if it was in his formidable vocabulary.

"Please, describe them to me, Jesse." She tried to stop her hand from shaking so that she could take notes.

"Brown sheep's hide with a hob nail sole."

*Sheep's hide. Interesting,* she thought. "Now, tell me what else you are wearing."

"A toga."

"A toga?" she spontaneously repeated, hearing the surprise in her own voice. "When and where are you?"

"I am a citizen of Rome."

"What year is it, Jesse?"

He squirmed on the couch, but did not answer.

"Are you in the common era? Is this A.D.?" she queried again.

Shaking his head, he still didn't answer.

"Who is ruling Rome?" Claire took a different tact.

"Octavian," he was quick to answer.

"Augustus Caesar?" Claire was actually amused by the shock in her own voice.

"Yes. That name has been bestowed upon him. But I know who he really is." Jesse's lip curled up in a sneer.

This man was definitely not a supporter of the Emperor Augustus. "Who are you? Can you tell me your name?" she probes.

"Gaius Alexander Antonius."

"Gaius." Again, there was surprise in Claire's tone. "Gaius," she repeated. "Are you related to the Caesar family?"

Jesse laughed a deep, throaty laugh, very different from his own. "Madame, I can assure you that all of civilized Rome is related."

"Civilized Rome?" she questioned.

"Members of society," he clarified. He was now sitting up on the couch, his spine straight, his bearing almost regal.

"What can you tell me about yourself, Gaius?"

"I am a soldier," his response was clipped.

"Whose army are you with?"

"Octavian's."

"Based on your name, I would have assumed Mark Antony's." Claire culled her brain quickly for history lessons long ago learned, hoping she was in the right timeframe.

Jesse's face screwed up, as if he were in pain. "He is gone." It was a mere whisper.

"And where are you."

"Returning from war with the Gauls."

"I see," Claire commented. "Are you returning to Rome?"

"I am journeying to Vico Equense."

"Where is that?" She began to Google quickly.

"Bay of Naples," he answered quicker than she could type.

"Why are you going there, Gaius?"

"To be with Julia. That is where Julia is."

*Julia. Julia. Her name is the sweet scent of the first spring flowers on the breeze. Honeysuckle and bees. The fragrance. Their buzz. Julia. And following the early days, the equinox nipping at its heels was always summer and Julia.*

*The ride from Gaul had been arduous. The mountain passes icy and treacherous at the higher elevations and then muddy, and no less precarious, descending the lower peaks.*

*But finally, I am home in Italy, and once again, close to Julia. News of her husband's death reached camp before the first snows, a time that I know Julia was heavy with child from him. Later, I would learn of her son was born posthumously.*

*I am greeted at the villa by the old servant, Seneca, who has known me since boyhood. There is comfort in the new wrinkles of his skin.*

*"How is she?" I ask.*

*"Sad. Tired. Overwhelmed with both grief at her loss and joy of the baby's health. Your presence will be a great salve."*

*"Where is she?" I cannot wait another minute to see her. This time it truly has been years. Nine years. Not attending her last wedding, her second, my mix of emotions exacted a toll. Knowing her father would marry her off again, after the death of her first husband, was no surprise. The second time, marrying her to a man double her age, and my former commander, was a little more of a shock. But, as always, the move satisfied his political agenda and thwarted a toppling of his power. Julia was always his pawn. His beautiful, engaging pawn, collateral to retain all he held dear. Rome was his one true lover, and my goal was to finally set this situation right, now that her second husband had passed.*

*Seneca points through the loggia and I head toward columns that stand like sentinels, silently telling the tale of Julia's lineage and tumultuous life. Leaning against the cold marble, it is nearly impossible to control the beating of my heart as I capture a first glance down the rocky slope to the Bay of Naples. The late day sun shrouds her and I squint, then rub my eyes, it must be an illusion, because I see a golden glow surrounding her.*

*My memory wanders back to what feels like only yesterday, being entranced by her as a child. Summers where we would chase one another through olive groves and I would follow the fiery mane flying like a fine woven carpet behind her. It's golden saffron hue standing out in relief from the gnarled bark and spindly leaves of the ancient olive trees. The gold in her locks is directly inherited from her father. The flame color, I'm not sure. Maybe from within, because that is distinctly Julia, fiery witted and tempered, four seasons flashing by in a mere moment, making those around her always wonder who will show, the heat of deep summer or the icy touch of winter.*

*Navigating down the rocks to the beach, I stand there as she wanders in the other direction, her back still to me. Smiling, I know she will turn at any moment, she'll feel my presence even though I am quite a length away. Julia always knew when I was there. And I her. Time apart had never dulled this, and still would not, of that I am certain.*

*It takes only a heartbeat. As I knew it would. We feel one another's presence. It has always been that way. For as long as I can remember. She spins, the fine pale silk of her stola swirls about her, and it is as if she's rising from the ocean mist, a siren no truer than she.*

*Even at a distance, I can see her smile. And we both begin running. Pumping the muscles in my legs to move faster atop the sinking sand, time has become an evil imp, slowing to a crawl, extending the seconds into millennia until she has returned to me. Back in my arms again.*

*"Gaius." She barely has any breath left.*

*I feel her tears and tighten my hold. "I am so sorry it has taken me this long to get to you. I heard the news."*

*Lifting her face to look at me, "He was a good man. He truly cared for me and took good care of me."*

*"For that, I have always been thankful."*

*"You came for me." Her eyes mist over.*

*"Immediately, and without hesitation." I repeat the words I had spoken to her nearly a decade before.*

*It has been understood through both her marriages that I have only wanted the best for her. As her father has married her off, we have both faced the harsh truth that despite previous familial arrangements, the historical warring of our houses would always preclude our betrothal. Throughout the years, her father has grown to take me on as an ally and trusted officer in his army, but to marry his daughter, well, the familial scars burned a crevice too deep to allow what he once sanctioned among our families. My goal is to mend that and reverse his decision, allow her to finally be mine.*

*Julia and I always understood the difference between obligation and heart. Although our hearts have remained cloaked, because the discovery of the truth would be punishable only by death, no one has, or ever will, replace the other, to dwell deep in our hearts.*

. . . . . .

*I was eleven when we met. She was a mere seven and rather precocious.*

*"I am betrothed to your older brother," she advised me. "So, do not look at me that way."*

*Our fathers, who were still allies at the time, had struck the deal to bring our houses together when Julia was only two.*

*"How am I looking at you?" I challenged her.*

*"Like I belong to you."*

*This girl was wise beyond her years. Even back then.*

*"Well, maybe you do." I advised her, leaning in to place a chaste kiss on her cheek and forever marking my territory.*

*With my brother's execution as a result of my father's treason, Julia was freed of a betrothal until she was twelve. My heart was all over the place, shattered by the loss of my brother, guilty and elated that she would not be giving herself to him. But with blood now spilled between families, her father never would have allowed her to be wed to me.*

*The summer prior to her being wed for the first time, was the first summer spent apart. I rode my first campaign to the eastern states returning just weeks before the nuptials. Her fourteenth birthday had just passed and her betrothed was sixteen, two years younger than I.*

*Finding Julia on the western edge of the olive groves that day, wandering, I watched from afar as she floated amongst the rutted trunks, seemingly in her own world. Stopping abruptly, she turned in my direction. My heart slammed still in that moment, as I felt our energies connect. Lifting the draped fabric of her stola, she began to run in my direction, flinging her body through the air and into my arms, somehow knowing I would catch her.*

*"Gaius, it is you. And you are well." She had covered my cheeks with small kisses.*

*"Of course, I am well. I am invincible," I whisper, drawing her head to my chest and burying my nose in her golden flame curls. She smelled of the sea and the salty sting I felt in my eyes was accompanied by visions of our previous childhood summers together. "Did you not expect my return?"*

*"I do not expect anything anymore." Julia looked forlorn.*

*"So jaded at such a young age," I laughed. "What brings on this melancholia, my dear friend."*

*"I am to be married, Gaius."*

*"Yes. I am aware." I worked hard at making it sound as if it were unimportant to me. No good could come of the truth.*

*But Julia, being Julia, was not going to let this sleeping dog lie.*

*"I have always dreamed," she began, turning her face from me as a lone tear trailed her cheek.*

*"Dreams are frivolous, Julia." I put her down so that her feet were once again on the ground and our eyes no longer mere inches apart.*

*"I just always thought it would be you."*

*"You know that will never be possible with the state of our families. Now that your father has defeated mine, there is no political advantage to our union." Taking Julia's hand, we began to walk past the grove onto the sloping hillside leading to the bay.*

*"Is that the only worth of a daughter? Marriage to solidify a position? Gain political clout?"*

*"You are like a coveted jewel, my friend."*

*Stopping abruptly, Julia placed her hand over my heart, "This jewel cares only to be worn by one man, as a permanent part of his armor, soldier." Tracing a circle on my chest, "Carefully set deep into his breastplate, protecting his heart."*

*Taking her hand from my chest and grabbing her free hand, I bring her soft palms to my lips, bestowing a kiss on each one. "Julia," I whispered. I wanted to tell her again that we can never be.*

*"Gaius, listen to me, please," she begged, cutting me off. Not looking away, I feel the force of her convictions and the strength of all she is. "I have yet to lie with a man and soon that will be expected of me, with this stranger my father brings forth. He is a child, not a man. I do not want to give myself to him. Why should I give myself to him?"*

*"Because he will be your husband and that is your duty."*

*Shaking her head, she informed me, "It is what my father wants for selfish reasons. It is not what I want."*

*"Julia, his reasons are not selfish. He gives you to another because he seeks to maintain peace for Rome."*

*"And I seek to bear your children and have them run through these sun-dappled groves laughing as we chase them on warm summer afternoons. I seek to make you a fine military and political wife and aid you in climbing the ranks of Rome's leadership. I seek to grow old with you and someday lie together as bones within the marble confines of the family crypt. This is what I seek, Gaius."*

*Shaking my head, "Julia, no. You are to be married. It has been so decreed."*

*"He will not take me," she declared with the obstinate defiance of*

*one on the verge of adulthood.*

*"Then who shall?" My laughter at the absurdity ignites her anger's flair.*

*"Beyond you, do you think anyone else will say no?"*

*Closing my eyes, I know she is right. "Why won't you just wait for your marriage?"*

*"Because I want my vow to be to you, right here, right now, Gaius. No matter what Roman law proclaims, my heart, allegiance and love will always be pledged to you. Your seed will be the first to enter my body and claim it. That is forever."*

*Pulling her to me, the raw silk of her stola puddled at her feet as I pushed it roughly from her shoulders, exposing the thin linen tunic that caressed her smooth, unblemished skin.*

*"I've wanted to do what is right," my voice was gruff, choked with emotion and lust.*

*"This, my only love. This is right." Julia's breath had become ragged with desire.*

*I know what she speaks is truth. I've lived to protect her from the time we were young, and not just because it was my sworn duty as a citizen of Rome, and later, as a member of her father's army, but because she was always mine to protect–a self-decreed army of one, protecting a secret, priceless treasure, one that I always knew would be robbed from me. So, I did what was best–I buried the treasure, far, far away from my heart, convincing myself it never actually existed.*

*"Julia." Her small face was in my palms as I searched her eyes. With my fingers entwined in her hair, my control was gone. Years of pent-up lust, knowing she would never, ever be mine and here she stood before me, begging me to claim her, take her womanhood as a prize that only I will possess, forever.*

*My lips were not soft against hers as I forced her mouth open with my tongue and began an exploration that left us both breathless. She wanted to be taken by a man, not a boy, and I would give her that truth. Lifting her tunic over her head, I had her stand before me, naked in the afternoon's sun.*

*"Down," I commanded and she knelt before me.*

*Parting my toga, my hardness stood out before her and I reveled in her slight gasp.*

*"I will teach you to please me."*

*With wide eyes, she silently nodded.*

*"Give me your hands."*

*Raising her hands to me, I took them in mine, placing one at the base of my scrotum and the other around my shaft. "Squeeze with that hand and stroke me with this one," I instructed her and this time it was my turn to gasp as she instinctively knew how to pleasure me.*

*Putting one hand at the back of her head and the other over hers, I guided myself into her mouth, her exquisite, precocious mouth. Her eyes looked up, initially flashing anger, but the sounds emanating from deep in her throat sang a different song, one of love and lust. Soon it was not I moving her head as she took control of the rhythm and depth of her sucking.*

*"Oh, my sweet Julia." Her sucking was pulling me to the edge and I feared I would confess my full feelings to her. To claim what we both wanted would be tantamount to treason, to act upon it, punishable by death. Yet, here we were, throwing caution to the wind and doing just that.*

*Pulling her gently from me, I laid her down on the grass, joining her.*

*"This may be our only time," I advised her, reaching out for a saffron curl and allowing it to slide through my fingers.*

*Nodding, her eyes fill with tears. "Then, dear Gaius, it will be my only true time in life."*

*"That is not what I want for you." I am pained hearing her words. "I want your happiness."*

*"Nothing will reach the depths of joy my heart is experiencing right here. Right now." Her tone was adamant.*

*Dropping her curl, I cupped her cheek, my thumb softly caressing what feels like infant's skin. "Julia, you have a lifetime before you to learn the true depths of love. For your husband. For your children. For their children. I am merely part of your past."*

*Stopping my hand mid-caress, her blue eyes were the color at the base of a flame, glowing hot anger. "If you ever expect to survive my father's army and someday return to me, you must learn to be a much better liar, Gaius. You are my past. My present. My future. And my forever. You know that. And I know that. And we have both known it our entire lives."*

*Her words sucked away the air surrounding me, leaving me breathless and speechless. For one so young, Julia was a force to contend with and I knew for certain that if I was to ever be a warrior strong enough to own such a brave and noble heart, then I must be man enough to speak the truth.*

*"Wherever this life takes me, whomever I lie with and bear children, it is because that is the fate we have been handed and not what I hold deepest in my heart either, Julia. There is only room for one person at that depth, and that is you. Never, ever doubt that you are my one true heart and that will be you for all eternity. If today is the only day we come together, then it will always be what I hold as the best day of my life. Do you understand that?"*

*Nodding, "Gaius, I want to know all of you." And slowly she began to disrobe me of my toga.*

*When I finally laid naked before her, she affectionately ran her hand slowly over my muscles, her touch light and tender in spots, while rough and kneading in others. Watching her small hand take such masterful control caught me by surprise, heightening my arousal and desire for her more than I had ever let myself dare to imagine.*

*With my lips to hers and her small body molded beneath me on the ground of our ancestors, I whispered the only truth I had ever known, "Julia, never will I allow another your place in my heart. Only you shall dwell there as the mistress and sole proprietor. At the moment of my death, I will only have one wish and that is of finding you again, somewhere, someplace, sometime, somehow."*

*Pulling my mouth to hers, I felt her lips and thighs part simultaneously, her invitation clear that I was to enter her home. That I am to make it my home. Julia is my one true home.*

*Three weeks later, she was married. I was heading on campaign to Aquitaine when the news reached us. It was nearly a year later when we learned of the death of her infant son, living for just a few days after his early arrival. To not be able to go to Julia, to be there for her and hold her through her grief was the hardest battle that I'd ever faced, and ultimately lost. My heart knew that this was ours to share together, and yet, by this time, I was stationed faraway, in the region of Achaea, making a hasty return not possible, and inappropriate, as she was now wed to another. Alone, we grieved together.*

**No armor can protect the holes in my chest**

**I hold your precious jewel tight to my breastplate**

**Praying for the healing properties of its energy**

**To make me whole again**

**To make you whole again**

*Scribing these words in my leather-bound journal, I mourned deeply for all that I could not control, all that I could not make right. I mourned the death of moments that would never exist.*

*Another year had not passed when word arrived again, this time bearing news of Julia's husband, who was taken by a fever. Requesting leave from my unit, I began a six-week journey back to Rome, filled with plots and fantasies of how we two could finally be together.*

*I had risen through the ranks of her father's army. My hope was that as a decorated officer, and a member of Roman society, that the blight between our families would finally be obliterated and I could be free to fulfill the berth once promised to my older brother, as that of Julia's husband.*

*But my arrival in Rome was to hold many surprises.*

*Riding into town, although my heart ached to find Julia, I knew that as an honorable man and soldier, I needed to first gain an audience with her father. So, I headed straightaway to Palatine Hill, taking a moment to sit back in my saddle and gather my thoughts before entering the great colonnaded entrance to his home.*

*As grand as it was, he lived more modestly than men who were of a lesser stature, shunning the times' ostentation. As I walked the fresco-lined portico toward his residence, I could not help but note the simple beauty in rich crimson and gold paintings that lined the verandah and how starkly they contrasted to the barrenness of the field tents I called home.*

*His house servants had known me from early childhood and allowed me entrance and permission to proceed unattended through to his residence. As I approached my destination, I continued my inner dialogue of the case I planned on presenting to him for Julia's hand. So deep in my own thoughts was I involved, that initially I did not hear the laughter and familiar voices emanating from his chamber ahead. Reaching the entranceway, I was shocked into stillness, surprised to find Agrippa, my commanding officer, sharing good cheer with her father. They were both startled by my appearance.*

*"Antonius." Agrippa was clearly surprised.*

*"Gaius, you are in Rome," her father announced, clapping me on the back.*

*"This young man has quickly risen through the ranks in my regime," Agrippa boasted. "There is a familial talent for warring that he possesses."*

*"Perhaps I should watch him more closely." Her father squinted at me and both men laughed.*

*"Gaius, now that you are back in Rome, you must join us for the festivities."*

*Looking to Agrippa, I am not sure to what he referred. There was no holiday taking place.*

*"I don't think the young man has heard the news yet."*

*"You have arrived just in time, young Gaius, to attend my nuptials to the beautiful Julia. We are to be married in two days' time."*

*Certain was I that the front of my toga was stained the same crimson as her father's walls because I felt my heart burst. I heard the popping sound ricochet through my eardrums and reverberate throughout my brain like a hollow scream.*

*This time her father was giving her to a man so powerful that it was his only way to ensure he maintained power as it could be passed to Julia's male heirs. Agrippa, although of no noble blood, truly made sense. My commanding officer was a man whom I admired greatly, and had played a key role in my military success and advancement. Agrippa, a man twenty-five years my senior would soon lie with Julia, filling her with his seed.*

*"Congratulations, sir. That is wonderful news," I lied.*

*"You will join us," her father informed me. "I will have a place set for you at my table. You have been like family to Julia her whole life."*

*Nodding my assent, "I'd be honored." I died a little with my lie.*

*Like family? I am her heart. I am her only true family.*

*"Are you here for long?" her father asked.*

*"Just a brief visit."*

*I already felt as if I'd overstayed my time in Rome, a time that now included the death of my dream before even sharing it with Julia. Something I could now never do. Agrippa was a good man and I tried to find solace in knowing he would treat her well and protect her.*

*Leaving the men behind, I made haste to her villa, hoping for what may be our last conversation. Met at the entrance by her servant, Seneca, the older man's greeting took me by surprise. "Let me take you to her. Your presence will set her heart free."*

*Entering her receiving room, although Julia's back was to me, I could tell by the straightening of her spine that she felt my energy. Without even turning around to see who had arrived, she dismissed her chambermaid immediately, demanding the door be closed. The younger woman, a stranger to me, began to protest, and Seneca dispatched her immediately.*

*We stood on opposite corners of the lavish room, silently observing one another as if we were taking in a vision to hold in our mind's eye forever. Opening my arms, she crossed to me, my tiny titian-haired beauty, who was no longer the girl I left, but very much a woman. I momentarily grieved for that innocent child, until she reached my arms, and the woman I held immediately pulled from my heart the pain I did not even know had latched onto it so deeply. For a moment, the burden was removed as I existed only in the here and now, entranced by the lavender scent of her hair and the way her body molded perfectly with mine, as I felt the race of her heart through the thin silk of her stola. Only one word came to mind. Complete.*

*Pulling her face away from my chest, she peered up and again I was lost as I searched her eyes.*

*"I came to you as fast as I could." My words and actions felt*

*inadequate. "But I fear it was not fast enough," I paused. "I have just come from your father's."*

*"You went to him first?"*

*"My intent was to convince him to let us marry. But when I arrived, he was not alone. The general was present and I was informed that you were to be married."*

*With a forlorn smile, she whispered, "But you came for me."*

*"Yes, I did. Immediately, and without hesitation."*

*Nodding, "He will take good care of me, Gaius. Please, rest your mind at ease."*

*"My mind will be at ease, Julia. He is a strong, fair, and just man. But my heart will never bear that same solace. He will grow older with you, fill you with children, protect you. He will take my place in what I know, with all my being, is rightfully mine. My head and my heart are at odds, but I need to accept this marriage and all the safety it brings to you. For that, I am grateful."*

*Nodding again, but remaining silent, Julia appeared to be deep in thought. "He was beautiful," she began and looked up into my eyes. "He had the dimple you have in your chin and his little eyebrows were a pale copper."*

*My son. Our child. She confirmed what I had known instinctively. The creation from our one and only union. Taking her face in my hands, I rested my forehead to hers as hot tears streamed from her eyes.*

*"He was beautiful, Gaius," she repeated and my hold on her body tightened. How can I lose her again? I feel the pain of losing a son whose face I would never know and the burden of letting her go again is much too much to bear as I sank to my knees taking her with me in my arms.*

*I don't know how long we stayed that way, quiet and tangled, but the sun's stream on the floor had moved partially across the room. When Julia finally looked up at me, she was smiling and there was happiness in her eyes. "You came for me."*

*"Always, my love," I assured.*

*"That's all that matters. You came for me."*

*We fell back into an easy silence, wrapped up in one another's arms, still in the middle of the floor. Absentmindedly allowing a lock of Julia's hair to run through my fingers as dusk began to claim the sky with a soft palette of colors, I broke the silence.*

*"Your father asked me to join him at his table for your wedding."*

*"Will you be his guest?"*

*Shaking my head, "No. It's best if I ride out of town. There is solace in knowing you are safe and will be well looked after, but it is too much to ask me to watch you given away to another man."*

*"I understand, Gaius. And I need you to know that I want you to be happy and I will accept your decisions in finding that happiness."*

*She was letting me go.*

*Fate has not been kind to us.*

*Riding out of Rome that night, alone, it was almost impossible to fathom that I had lost so much in less than a day's time. Which part of the loss cut the deepest, was difficult to discern, but I had the distinct feeling that it was the death of a dream that would have the most lasting and devastating impact.*

· · · · · ·

*The wind off the bay whips the sand around us as I hold her close. Her body is still full and soft from the birth of her last child, this son born after his father's death. A child Agrippa will never know, just as I never knew the son Julia bore me so many years before.*

*Holding her in my arms plays tricks with time. It feels like yesterday.*

*"Have you seen my father," she asks.*

*Shaking my head, "No, this time I came straight to you." The memory of last time still bitter.*

*"He has plans," she advises.*

*And I see fear in her eyes.*

*"His wife is plotting for power and he is listening to her, Gaius."*

*I know her father's wife well, and she has always been threatened by Julia's relationship with her father. "What is she plotting?"*

*"Arranging for me to marry her son, so that my father's power will transfer to him."*

*"He's married." I refer to Julia's stepbrother.*

*"Yes, they are pushing him to divorce, so that he may marry me. I don't trust him, Gaius. I don't trust that he will not kill me. Kill my sons." With her latest birth, Julia has three sons, providing a powerful line for succession of family power.*

*Julia's fear is not unfounded. Her stepbrother is an ill-tempered and abusive lout who has always treated her poorly. With her marriage to Agrippa, I knew she was with a good man who would treat her kindly. But her stepbrother would cause reason to fear for Julia's life. My arrival was not a moment too soon.*

*Convincing her father a marriage to me would be advantageous was going to be difficult, if not impossible, but I could not let this man marry into a position where he would have control over Julia's life. The ending chapters of that story were clearly written and the final outcome would not be happy. One did not need to be a seer to foretell that future.*

*"Together we will convince your father to let us marry. I would*

*gladly abdicate rule to your sons, to protect power within the lineage."*

*"But his wife, she is pushing her own bloodlines and my father is listening."*

*"We will have to convince him." I walk with Julia along the beach back toward a stone-stepped path up the cliffs.*

*The villa is quiet when we enter and I have the distinct feeling Seneca has cleared everyone out so that Julia and I may reacquaint properly.*

*"I feel self-conscious around you," she admits. "I'm not that young girl of the last time we came together and I've just had another child."*

*Sitting her on the edge of her bed, I stand before her. "You are more beautiful than I'd remembered. The wild child I once knew has blossomed into a magnificent woman. One who I cannot wait another moment to plunder."*

*"With my father's plans to marry me to my stepbrother he will view this as adultery," she warned.*

*"Then I am an adulterer."*

*Pushing her back down onto the bed, I do not even bother to remove her stola. Pushing the fabric up, the first time I take her, I am rough, taking both what I need and want. I have waited for her to be mine again and I spend the night marking her as if she were my property. By the morning's first light, we are spent, yet still not sated.*

*"No man has ever claimed me so completely." Her head rests on my chest, her hand still wrapped around me, stroking me to hardness again. "I will now always crave what you have done to me." And then in a whisper, "Like an animal." Together, we laugh.*

*Our passion is carnal, we are one another's true match, challenging, taunting, tormenting, and pushing one another to heights so precarious that as we topple together, the pulsating crash is staggering. I have made sure no one will ever be able to satisfy her again. Driving her up and down on me, time after time, I have reached depths in all places she has to offer, and taken what is mine, and always has been. This woman is more entrenched in my soul than my most steadfast of allegiances, bound by blood spilled between our families and a firstborn who should have been the heir to Rome's greatness and a testament to devotion that goes above and beyond love.*

. . . . . .

*Waiting in his chambers for her father's arrival, I am not altogether surprised by a visit from his wife.*

*Shooing her handmaiden from the room, she sits down next to me, smiling. I had never noticed the sharpness of her canine teeth, giving her an almost feral appearance and robbing her of being a great beauty.*

*"Your return is a surprise."*

*"Is it?"*

*"Very much so." She regards me. "You've inherited your father's looks. I always respected him." She laughed, "Not that I could make that known." Her hand now rests in my lap, her fingertips gently stroking my thigh through the material of my toga. Wasting no time, she continues, "With your military accomplishments and your fine stature, you are certain to quickly climb the ranks right here in Rome, Gaius. Is that your plan? Remain in Rome as you rise to prominence?"*

*"You seem to have spent some time pondering the course of my life." I do not trust this woman. Without her father protecting her, this harpy will have Julia either exiled or executed.*

*"You're not really here for Julia, are you?" Digging her nails into my thigh, she bares her pointy incisors. "You're here for my husband. You're here to rule Rome."*

*Laughing, I remove her hand from my leg, "You need to spend more time out in the provinces," I advise. "There's too much intrigue in this city. It makes everyone paranoid. Go, get some fresh air."*

*"You will never get what you want," she threatens.*

*"What I want is to take Julia from here. Leave you Rome."*

*"You are an Anthony by birth. Your ambitions run too deep. That girl is merely a pawn used to sway the prevailing winds of power."*

*I'm sick listening to her. Her influence over Julia's father will destroy us all.*

*"My son will rule Rome," she hisses in a harsh whisper only I can hear. "Even if he has to marry that wretched girl."*

*Staring into the vacuous hollows of her Mediterranean-colored eyes, it is abundantly clear that our only move in this horrid game of chess is to take out the king, for we await certain death if we do not. If we make this bold attempt and do not succeed, a worse fate will be certain to fall upon us.*

· · · · · ·

*The nursemaid takes the baby from Julia's arms as I stalk around her chamber. Our fate appears bleak, with few good options to remain together. I would leave Julia's side and promise to not return, never hold her again, if I knew she would not fall to the hands of abuse. But we both know, if her stepmother gets her way, she will be married to her stepbrother, and her descent into Hell will be rapid.*

*Dismissing the woman from the room, Julia sits on the edge of the bed. "Gaius, come to me."*

*Sitting next to her, I reach for a lock of her titian hair, letting the silken strands slide slowly through my fingers.*

*"We have no choice," she whispers. "We must kill my father."*

*I can clearly see her pain as she voices our only alternative. I remain silent.*

*"Rule will pass to my sons and with my father gone, I will no longer be under patriarchal control. We'll be free to marry. With your connections, you can raise an army against my stepbrother. You will handily defeat him."*

*Reaching forward, I run my fingertips down her cheek. I know she's right, but say, "Maybe your father will protect you."*

*Sadly, she shakes her head, "If he wanted to protect me, he wouldn't be handing me over to that psychotic beast because his power-hungry wife wants to rule Rome. He has chosen that woman over his blood, and my fate, if I am to marry my stepbrother," she paused and looked up at the ceiling, as tears sealing our fate coursed down her cheeks. "If married to him, death will be something I wish for every minute of every day because he will make my life a living hell, and sadistically enjoy every second of his torture."*

*Having known her stepbrother my entire life and well aware of his feelings for Julia, I knew she wasn't exaggerating. "How shall we do this?" I can't believe I'm voicing the words.*

*"Poison."*

*"Who will administer?"*

*"I will," Julia understands her obligation and that it has come to the point of her survival or his.*

*Taking her in my arms, "We could take the children and leave."*

*"Is that what you want?" She knows that is not what I want. I am a soldier. I fight and I win. "I will do this with a heavy heart."*

*That night we lie together, our lovemaking slow and sweet, unlike our usual carnal fervor, as if making a memory that would need to carry us for millennia. Sadness permeated every movement that night in our bed. Each touch was marred by the pain of loss, the realization that we were never fated to love freely and without pain. Our lives would always be secondary, overshadowed by the needs of Rome, where we remained but bit players as the tragedy unfolded.*

"No," Jesse screamed. "No, take me. Leave her. Take me. I am the guilty one."

"Gaius, tell me what you are seeing," Claire implored, as she watched the shallow breathing of her client.

"They know of our plot. They've come to arrest us. They're dragging Julia out. We're being separated. No!" There is a staccato cadence to his statements. "No. No. No. This is my fault. Let her go. She was not complicit. She knew nothing. I did this for power. I'm trying so hard to protect her." Pulling at his hair, his eyes are moist with tears.

"What is happening to you. Describe to me what is going on."

"The Senate has convicted me of treason. The punishment is death. Either execution or suicide. Her father has chosen suicide for me. He wants her to watch. He wants her to be there to see me die at my own hand."

"No. No. No. No." He screamed, his wail sounding more like that of a wounded animal left at the roadside to die than that of a human. "No. Please, don't make her watch me. I know this is going to destroy her. To punish her this way, the vision of my death scorched in her mind and heart for the rest of her days, while she is sentenced to a slow death, knowing her protector is gone, that I will no longer come for her. With my own hand, I create the dual sins of taking my own life and condemning her to the damnation of the rest of her days. Please, don't make her watch as I rob her heart of hope. I will soon be with our son, yet my damnation will be eternal for I failed to protect my only love. I failed her and left her behind to be tortured at the grip of evil."

Claire cringed. "And Julia, what has happened to Julia?"

"She was married off to him and he's called for her exile to Pandanteria after my death. She will die out there. He knows that. It is just a volcanic rock in the ocean. She will starve and die out there. No one returns. No one ever returns. I could not protect her. I should have done more to protect her." With splayed fingers, he runs his hands through his hair, pulling at the spiky strands with frustration.

"Jesse," she called him by his current name. "Jesse, I'm going to count to three. When I reach three, you will come out of your hypnotic state. You will be able to remember everything, but you will be here, safe in my office. Are you ready? One. Two. Three."

The rise of his shoulders immediately deflated as his head lolled to his chest, his breathing shallow and fast as if he'd just stopped running.

"Jesse," Claire's tone was sharp. "Jesse, take some deep, cleansing breaths."

Following her directive, he breathed in deeply and removed the RGB glasses on his exhale, flinging them onto the couch next to him.

"That was insane. That was freaking insane." Putting his face in his hands, he shook his head. "I don't even know where to begin with that. I was there. I was in Rome in the first century B.C. I was in fucking Rome, Dr. S." Putting his hand over his heart, still panting as the adrenaline coursed through his veins, the pain in his eyes was deafening. "Julia. Oh, God, Julia. I tried to save her. To take the blame so that she would be spared. We got caught. It was that fucking nursemaid. She was spying on us. Her father's wife had placed the woman there." Catching his breath momentarily as visions continued to flood in, "And then they made her watch me fall on my sword. God, how brutally cruel. That horrible little shit made her watch me die because he knew how much it would hurt her. We should have killed the whole lot of them."

Remaining silent, Claire waited for Jesse to calm down.

But he didn't calm. "We should have killed them," he yelled. "We should have killed them all." His rage was real. Pulling at his spiky hair, "Oh, God, Dr. S. what am I saying? It's so hard to separate. That was like two thousand years ago. Two thousand." He shook his head, a look of disbelief on his face. "My heart is ripping apart. I want to go to her. I want to save her. But it's not now. And she's not here. I didn't protect her. How did I not see what we really needed to do? How did I miss the whole picture?"

"What did you need to do, Jesse?" Claire's voice was soothing.

Looking up, he stared her in the eye. A sneer overtaking his lips. That beautiful rock-star sneer, the one that she could feel like a live wire placed high between her thighs, jolting her. Until he spoke, and then her blood ran cold. "I should have killed her father, her stepbrother, and her stepmother. That was my mistake, that I did not murder them all."

They sat in silence, the air in her office heavy, not moving, until Jesse began to speak again. This time calmer. He smiled and Claire could tell he was seeing something in his mind's eye. "That's how deeply I loved her. She was part of my soul, from the time we were kids. So, I guess I can love. Or I could love." Again he lapsed into silence, his head nodding with internal thoughts. "I failed at protecting her. Her faith was all in me. I'm sick at how deeply I loved her and how epically I failed her. There's a steep price to loving that deeply."

"You were playing chess in a game that was less than honorable." Claire brought reason back to the conversation.

"And we were checkmated."

"Yes, you were." Putting her iPad down on her desk, "This is a lot to process. I think we should spend our next few sessions looking at parallels and aspects that we think might have lingered to influence current patterns in your life."

"Not to be rude, Doc, but I've gotta get out of here. I need air. I've gotta head down to L9 and work out or something." And grabbing his jacket, Jesse Winslow was out the door.

**Patient: Jesse Winslow**

**Session # 38**

**Date: 2/18/15**

**Regression # 8**

**Regression Length: 10:11 A.M.–10:53 A.M.**

**Entity: Gaius Antonius**

**Location: Rome**

**Year: 1<sup>st</sup> Century BC**

# Chapter 9

He was reaching the point of muscle fatigue on the SkyTrack at L9. As he passed other runners, he could see their heads whip toward him. He knew they were wondering, *is that really Jesse Winslow who just ran by?* His hope was that the thought that immediately followed that was, *damn, he's in good shape.* The month in the Caribbean had really made its mark on his physique.

Hoping physical exhaustion would slow down his mind, Jesse could not only rid himself of the crystal-clear images of a world of two-thousand years ago, but also of the overwhelming feelings of love and loss. He physically felt the depth of both and the hurt was staggering.

After seven miles, he moved off the track to a water station and grabbed a bottle, rolling the cold, sweating plastic across his forehead before finally opening it and taking a swig. Leaning on the SkyTrack's railing, he watched the members below in the club's main rotunda and wondered what the building, with its great circular center, originally had been. A place of worship? Entertainment? There was something about the structure, with its frescoed ceiling of mythical creatures that always reminded him of the circuses of ancient Rome and now, for the first, time he understood why he had always felt so at home in this club.

He had seen the great structures of Rome before they were ruins, felt the energy of the Circus Maximus as chariots kicked up great clouds of yellow dirt. He had learned the glory and the price of loving amongst the hills and olive groves of Rome. *Holy Shit,* Jesse shook his head and wondered if a few more miles on the SkyTrack might do him good.

Looking down from the ceiling-high vantage point of the track, it was the lights glinting off the natural incandescence of her hair that caught his eye, bringing an immediate smile to his face and the first feeling of solace since the regression. Watching her below work with her trainer as he put her through a brutal set of Face Melters, Jesse couldn't help but notice the change in her body from the last time he'd seen her, over a month before. A feeling of pride swelled as he watched her keep up the grueling pace. When it was over, she stood, a look of victory on her sweaty, flushed face.

Her trainer, who Jesse recognized as the L9 owner's son, en-veloped her in a bear hug, clearly pleased with her performance. When they separated, they high-fived. Standing at the railing, watching them below, Jesse felt very voyeuristic, but couldn't get enough of watching her. It occurred to him, now that he'd *met* Julia, how deeply attracted to redheads he was. Kylie's hair, while a deeper, more auburn shade than Julia's, made him feel a connection to both his past and to her. And now, standing in the shadows, nearly two stories above, the rocker was finally beginning to develop an understanding of his feelings, courtesy of another redhead.

Giving her a final squeeze on the shoulder, her trainer turned away, and headed toward an area that housed the free weights and was filled with serious lifters.

Walking over to the smoothie bar, Kylie took a seat on a high metal stool and ordered something. Sitting back with a tall glass, she observed the room, her eyes scanning as if she were looking for someone. As she looked up, scanning the SkyTrack, *she feels me,* was the thought that fleeted through Jesse's mind, but he realized that from the angle she was looking, she would not be able to see him.

A built, dark-haired guy came and leaned on the bar next to her, he appeared to order and then turned to Kylie and began to chat. It looked as if she was giving him a *polite* look and Jesse laughed to himself that he could already decipher her faces. The girl was smart as a whip and Jesse wondered if she was inwardly rolling her eyes at this steroidhead. The guy leaned in toward her, his stance becoming more aggressive and Jesse could see the distinct change in Kylie's body language in response. Leaning back, there was nowhere for her to retreat, as a wall was to her back.

Quickly jogging over to the elevator located across the SkyTrack, he stabbed the call button with a few hard staccato finger punches. Jesse shifted from leg to leg as he waited for the lift to arrive. He wanted that goon away from her *now*. Reaching the main floor of the rotunda, Jesse could see the back of her head, her lustrous hair shimmering in the club's intricate lighting. Walking toward her, he could feel his heart beating wildly. It had been too long since he had seen his friend. It felt like it was in another lifetime.

As if hearing the distant call of drumming against his breastbone, she suddenly turned around, possibly sensing his presence approach. With an immediate smile that created a dimple in her right cheek that he hadn't noticed until that very moment, he willed her, *come to me.* And she did, nearly knocking over her barstool.

His arms opened for her as she neared, approaching him quickly. "Toots," he whispered into her hair, burying his face as the thought, *back in my arms again,* permeated his brain. Yet, he couldn't remember holding her before that moment and thought, maybe not in my arms, but certainly in my thoughts.

"You look amazing." She continued to hold him. "I've missed hanging out with you."

"Me, too." He caressed the luxurious strands of her at the back of her head. "You are looking amazing, too." He did nothing to hide his eyes appreciatively taking her all in.

Separating from their embrace, he kept an arm casually slung over her shoulder, as they walked toward the smoothie bar. He was fully aware that he was sending the meathead on the next stool a loud and clear message. As Kylie slipped back onto the chair, the guy behind the counter handed Jesse a laminated menu of smoothies.

Laughing, "I'll try the *Zac Attack*." Turning back to Kylie, "I have so much to tell you, Toots."

"Me, too," she was nodding. Things that she had wanted to share with him for weeks, all the way back to the day of her Geneviève regression, when they got swarmed by fans before she could share it with him. "I'm so glad you're home." Kylie could feel her face redden with the admission she had not planned on making.

Reaching for a lock of her hair, he let it slide through his fingers, appearing deep in thought for a moment. "Do you have dinner plans?"

Dipping her head and looking up at him through her lashes, more than a glimpse of bodacious pageant girl was staring Jesse Winslow in the face. "Are you asking me out on a proper date, Mr. Winslow?"

Laughing mid-way through a sip of his very green smoothie, he began to choke. "Yeah, I guess I am." His voice was a rasp as she patted him on the back.

"So, should we send selfies to Claire?" There was a mischievous glint in Kylie's eyes. "I might even flash her my boobs."

"Why do I get the feeling you're a lot to handle?" He was getting lost in her eyes and the depth and brightness of the green.

"Moi?"

Laughing, "I think I've finally met my match."

"Mon moitié," she whispered, without thinking.

Tipping his head, as he looked at her, questioningly. He knew he wanted to say something to that, to whatever it was she just said, but he didn't know what. It was out there, just past the tip of his tongue, but he couldn't quite grasp it.

"Where should we meet?" Kylie filled in the dead air, taking control, as she was not yet ready for him to invade her home turf.

Jesse thought for a moment, his lopsided grin taking on a most amused glint. "Freud. Let's meet at Freud on LaGuardia Place in The Village."

With a sip of her smoothie nearly coming out of her nose, Kylie choked a little before she was able to get out the words. "That is inspired. Truly inspired."

Together they laughed at their little inside joke.

. . . . . .

**I'm at a table in the back-right corner,** he texted.

**In a cab a few blocks away. See you in 5.**

Kylie was running a few minutes late, not rudely late, just fashionably late. She had pulled nearly everything she owned out of her closet, trying to find something that was flattering, yet rock-star cool and 'Yeah, I know his ex- is a top model'. 'So What' chic was the look she was trying to pull off. It wasn't easy. With the recent weight loss, she was between sizes. Her big girl clothes, as she was now referring to them, looked like misshapen potato sacks on her and her pageant days' wardrobe were nowhere near an option yet, and might not ever be.

She made the decision. It's New York, seriously, just pick something black. And so black it was. Black legging jeans, black high boots, a thin, black, cashmere V-neck sweater, all topped with a black leather jacket. Twisting her hair, she clipped it up, then pulled a few strands out to frame her face and a few at the base of her neckline. It was messy and sexy.

Standing in front of the mirror, she wondered for whom she was dressing. Jesse? Well, yeah, you don't want to be seen with a rock star looking like a beast on parade. The paparazzi? Same logic applied as for Jesse. The skinny model ex-girlfriend? Well, not really for her, but for everyone who would make a comparison. For herself? *C'mon, he's Jesse Fucking Winslow. Get real.*

As she made her way to the back of the darkened restaurant, Kylie could feel her spine straighten, shoulders fall back, chin up. The only thing missing was the sash as she gracefully floated past tables, the male occupants covertly attempting to sneak an appreciative look without alerting their female companions.

*I've still got it.*

And her confidence soared as she sat down in the chair next to one of the sexiest, most recognizable men on the planet, and he had watched every man in the restaurant check her out.

"You look gorgeous, Toots."

"Thank you." It was still surreal that she was sitting here with her new buddy.

"I'm going to have to fight half the guys in the restaurant off you."

Laughing, "I doubt that." Kylie rolled her eyes.

Smiling at her, he reached out, allowing the lone curl cascading down her right cheek to slip through his thumb and forefinger. "It's true." Tilting his head, "You're not comfortable with it, are you?"

She shook her head. "I know that's odd, considering I spent years on a stage or a runway, but people treat you different when you're heavier. You kinda become invisible. They're like 'pretty face,' but they're not all over you. Fewer people want something from you. And there's a part of me that kinda likes being invisible."

"I can understand that. It's a bit different, but I can understand it. So, let me ask you something really personal. Is weight a layer of protection?" Instinctually, he felt like he knew so much about this girl.

That he understood her on a level that most people never get to with another human being. And yet they were only first becoming friends, with a special bond through their healing work.

Looking down at his hand on her hair, while he absentmindedly ran his finger up and down the lock, Kylie realized that she now found the gesture oddly comforting, that she yearned for it in his presence, as if it was their connector.

Nodding, "I think it is, and since I started having success with my regressions, I'm beginning to think it's based on past experience."

"Unleashing our demons?" he recalled their first conversation.

Kylie nodded.

"So, I had a really successful regression," Jesse began without preamble, unable to hold it in any longer. "And there was this redhead."

"Oh no, you can't get away from us, can you?" Laughing, Kylie was most amused.

Smiling, "Who would ever want to?" He paused, "Her hair was a lighter copper than yours."

"Where and when was this?" She was excited to hear the details, in that moment feeling so connected to this man, who was experiencing his own parallel journey into the inexplicable.

"Rome. 1$^{st}$ century B.C."

"Wow. That is so cool. Did you remember a lot?"

"Oh, yeah. A crazy amount of detail, Toots. So much so, that I'm feeling trapped between realities and I don't know how to sort that out yet. That's why I went running after Dr. S's today. I was hoping it would somehow help me straighten out my head." His eyes were wide with confusion.

Nodding, "I know. I totally get that. I feel the exact same way. I don't know what to do with myself after these regressions. I don't know where I belong. Which world? I don't even know which world I want to be in."

"Right." He looked astounded. "I'm so glad you get this because I feel like I'm a multiple personality or something." Picking up his large glass of iced green tea, a holdover from his time in the Caribbean rehab, he took a sip and was silent for a moment before he went on. "I was a soldier, born into a well-to-do family. This woman, Julia, was her name; we kind of had this Romeo and Juliet thing happening. Bad blood between the families. Her father marrying her off to others as a pawn for political favor."

"What happened to her?" Kylie leaned closer, elbows on the table.

"In the end, I couldn't protect her. I tried. I spent my life trying. Her stepmother had a maid spying on us and she'd overheard plans we had and they ended up trying us for treason. I was forced to commit suicide, *in front of her.*"

The moment the words were out of his mouth, Kylie was fighting back the tears, crossing her arms over her chest to protect her heart and stop the cold chill wracking her body. *Oh, God. No!*

With eyes tightly shut, his handsome face contorted in pain, he continued after missing just a beat, "And she was forced to marry her sadistic, son-of-a-bitch stepbrother who was sending her off into exile where I'm sure she starved to death. People rarely made it back." He was shaking his head. Disturbed.

Had he not been deep inside the detailed vision in his own head, Jesse would have noticed Kylie's body stiffening at his final words, as the tiny hairs along her hairline quivered. She hadn't yet had the opportunity to tell him all the details of Geneviève and her fate, and now he was telling her about a woman he knew, and loved, who had also starved. And she knew. She knew exactly what that felt like.

"Poor Julia," she whispered, her face a portrait in pain. "So, she lost you and then was condemned?"

"Yes. Basically, to a volcanic rock sticking out of the ocean.

Another shiver wracked her body, her shoulders visibly twitching as the cellphone photo of the island Jesse had sent from Antigua flashed across her eyes. Lone and desolate. A volcanic rock sticking out of the ocean. Kylie could just imagine her, this woman dealing, with her grief and isolation. And starving. The pain and weakness as it all begins to slip away.

Noting her physical reaction. "You're cold," he took her hands in his and began rubbing them to warm her up.

Leaving her cradled in his warmth, where they made her heart feel good, she said, "I never got to tell you all the details about my Paris regression."

"Right, that was that the day we were *discovered* and then at L9 you just told me about how you died and that you'd lived with your brother. "

Nodding, Kylie enjoyed that she and Jesse had clearly begun to make their own set of memories. Then, she began. "I was a little girl, a twelve-year-old, named Geneviève, and I can feel for Julia having starved to death, too. Knowing that pain."

The empathy in Jesse's eyes affirmed his own heartbreak, as he squeezed her hands tighter.

"It's so horrible and I lived it. Or, at least I feel like I lived it." She continued, "So, my heart hurt for Julia when you were telling me that, and all that she went through. And, on top of that, after having to endure watching your death, someone she loved so deeply. I totally get that. I had to live through my whole family's deaths, but my brother's death in that life was like ripping my heart in two," her voice trailed off.

"Getting out of my relationship with Claudine, where I was at the point where I felt nothing, I was really questioning my capacity to feel.

And now, post this regression, I know this is going to sound strange, but the depth of my love and devotion to this woman, I feel like I know I can love. It was that real, Toots."

"I know. Jessie, I have missed him, my brother, so intensely since that regression. A person from over two hundred and fifty years ago, who I don't even know. And I haven't felt whole since that day."

"Yes, yes, that's it, Toots." He threaded his fingers through hers. "That is exactly it. And what I want, I want what I felt. I want that and now that I've experienced it, I know that I can't settle for anything less."

Nodding, "Mon moitié," she mumbled.

Without understanding why, Jesse brought Kylie's hands, still wrapped in his own, to his chest. Placing them over his heart, giving them a final squeeze before letting them go. "I guess we should take a look at this menu." He gave her a lopsided grin.

Nodding, she looked down at the menu's typeface swimming before her eyes, suddenly not hungry.

After dinner they walked, block after block, the conversation still focused on the details they shared from these other worlds they had visited.

As they turned from Park Avenue onto E. 37th Street, nearing Kylie's apartment, Jesse dropped a bombshell. "You know, Toots, I've been thinking about this."

"What?" She looked up at him.

With a grin, he nonchalantly slung an arm around Kylie's shoulder, and just as effortlessly and naturally, her arm encircled his waist.

"Us," his voice was gruff and low.

"Us?" Kylie stopped dead in her tracks, facing him in the quiet of the night-shadowed sidewalk.

"Yeah, how we met. How easy it's been." He reached out for a lock of her hair, letting it slowly slide through his fingers before speaking again. "Do you ever think that my walking into the waiting room that morning was supposed to happen? That we were supposed to meet and to be able to experience all of this together and to share everything we do."

"Share what?" Her spine lengthened an inch as it straightened and stiffened.

"Our stories." Looking down, Jesse began kicking at something on the sidewalk only visible to him. "Maybe more."

"What are you saying, Jesse?"

"I'm saying there's this thing between us, Toots. I know you feel it, too. It's been there since the moment we met. It was undeniable then. And now, it's like almost out of control."

Dropping the strands of her hair, he pulled her into his arms, rocking slowly from side to side, until he felt her relaxing body melt into his. As she filled the empty nuances he'd just recently discovered, he went out on a limb, speaking from his heart and not overthinking the words he spoke. "You're a gift, Kylie. Like an angel who came into my life. I'd be a fool not to see that. And I'm not sure I deserve you, but I'll be damned if I let go."

Burying her face into the now familiar, and comforting, scent of his worn leather jacket, Kylie said nothing. He felt so right. They felt so right. But this was Jesse Fucking Winslow. And the price was steep. Somewhere deep in her psyche, Kylie knew there was no way the final chapter of this one wasn't already written.

Looking up to meet his eyes, Jesse's guard was down; he wasn't hiding behind sunglasses or a drug-induced veil, or a well-crafted rock-star persona. Holding her was a man fighting like a warrior to slay his demons and reach a potential he knew was just out of grasp– he was ready to realize his ability personally and as a musician.

With a heart beating so fast, as her own realizations could no longer be repressed, Kylie leaned in, softly grazing Jesse's full lips with her own, in what he would remember as the sweetest kiss of his lifetime.

And then she was gone, entering her building, with a quick turn-around and a secret smile to the man standing under the streetlamp wearing his very own secret smile.

. . . . . .

Her routine was the same every night. Slip into silky lingerie and take a seat on her antique boudoir vanity chair where she would gaze into the mirror. Pulling her hair from her forehead and cheeks with a wide headband, she would wash the day's grime and her patients' angst from her face, gently patting dry with a soft, microfiber towel. Next, she'd begin applying layer after layer of expensive product, allowing time for her skin to absorb each lotion before applying the next layer.

When she was done, she'd stay seated for a few minutes in the beautiful, wrought-iron chair, just staring at her image, fixated on the gradient of blue in her eyes. This process of getting lost in her own eyes had become a relaxation technique that she had been using for years. By the time she got under the covers for an enjoyable read of either fiction or a magazine on decorating, Claire Stoddard had fully let go of the stresses of the day and rid herself of any lingering energy of her clients, clearing the cache of her consciousness before sleep, which generally came within moments.

*As much as I hate to admit it, she's really quite beautiful. Regal. Sitting and waiting for an audience with her father, servants stopping in to lovingly greet her. She responds in kind with such warmth.*

*Entering the chamber, we exchange greetings as I sit down next to her.*

*"Your father is currently engaged with members of the Senate. Is there something with which I can help you?"*

*She eyes me cautiously, "No. This is a matter between us."*

*"Oh, really." I smooth out the fine silk of my stola.*

*"All matters of the state and family are of interest to me. Everything about your life, Julia, is of interest to me."*

*"Why is that?"*

*"Because you are your father's blood, dear."*

*Julia regards me with open contempt. "Because that is a bloodline you would like to see severed so that you may insert your own." Her eyes have narrowed into slits. "He will never betray me for you, no matter how you poison him."*

*"Poison him? Interesting choice of words. Isn't that exactly your plan? To poison your father before you are betrothed to my son and control comes to me."*

*"You're crazy. I love my father."*

*I am enjoying Julia's agitation as I lean in close and whisper, "Marry my son, without incident, and I will let your handsome lover live, so that he can be mine when you kill your father, Kylie."*

*"Kylie?" Julia's eyes are wide, her pupils dilated. "So, it is Jesse you want. Oh, what a drama this is turning out to be."*

Gasping as she reached for her nightstand light, Claire sat for a moment with her head in her hands taking deep breaths, before opening a drawer and removing her journal and a pen. Wanting to record every detail of her dream, before it was lost, she knew that this very vivid reverie was one that she needed to share with Marshall.

*It's just that Jesse's regression was on my mind,* she told herself.

But the chamber in which she had sat, with its crimson walls and gold leaf paint, the feel of the silk of her stola, Julia's saffron-colored curls, the details were all so crisp, too crisp for it to feel dream-like.

Taking a sip of water, Claire sat back against her cream-colored, padded headboard and wondered how Kylie Martin had worked her way into that dream, a dream stimulated by Jesse's regression. Finally, she surmised it must have been the red hair, although her patient's hair was a deeper, more auburn shade of red than the beautiful girl she had just seen in her dream.

. . . . . .

Claire hadn't yet had the opportunity to relate her dream to Marshall as they'd spent the better part of their hour talking about Jesse's regression to 1$^{st}$ century Rome. Checking her notes again, she wanted to make sure that she hadn't left out any important details.

"You do know who they were planning to kill, don't you?"

"Her father." Claire's response came quick.

Pushing his glasses back up to the bridge of his nose, "They were planning to kill, Augustus, Claire."

"Augustus Caesar?" Claire's voice rose an octave.

"Yes, the Emperor Augustus."

Picking up a glass of water to quench her suddenly dry mouth, "Are you sure, Marshall? I researched Gaius Alexander Antonius and found nothing."

Scrolling through his computer screen, Marshall began to spew facts. "Augustus had only one natural heir to his bloodline, his daughter, Julia the Elder. Married three times, second husband, much older, named Agrippa." Claire could feel the blood drain from her face as she listened to the historical facts Marshall was sharing. "Her third husband was her stepbrother, Tiberius, who treated her poorly. Her father was influenced heavily by his wife, Tiberius's mother, Livia."

"But there was no Gaius Alexander Antonius," she repeated. "He didn't exist. I can't corroborate this, Marshall."

"Wikipedia is the answer to all the lessons we've forgotten," the older psychiatrist laughed. "Well, it appears Julia did have an affair with a member of the Antonius family, Mark Antony's son, Iullus. That would corroborate relationships between the children of the two families."

Claire shook her head, "He clearly identified himself as Gaius Alexander Antonius."

"Iullus was forced to commit suicide because of his affair with Julia and as a member of the Antony family, they would have known each other their entire lives."

Continuing to shake her head as she ran her fingers along the shiny leaf of a potted plant, Claire's head snapped up and she reached for her purse, extracting a small journal. "I had a dream I need to tell you about," and she recounted the very vivid and disturbing dream.

Marshall wrote feverishly, making low "hmm" sounds. "That's very interesting," he said when she ended. "You dreamed of yourself in the Livia role. Willing to sacrifice your husband for power and for Gaius/Jesse."

Marshall sat back in his chair, tapping his lips with his forefinger as he stared at the ceiling. "We've talked about your predilection for this patient. Could it be possible the root of that is because this lifetime is not the first time you've met?"

Claire's heart jumped at Marshall's verbalization.

He went on. "Perhaps it is no coincidence that he ended up as your patient, Claire." He paused and nodded his head. "Or that Kylie did."

The two remained silent, until Claire finally spoke. "It was not

148 | Julie A. Richman

anything I'd ever considered before."

"Hmm." Remaining silent for a few minutes, he looked at Claire pointedly. "Maybe we should think about scheduling a regression for you."

# Chapter 10

**Hey Toots, heading out to LA for a few days to meet with the band and figure out the future. Wanna come?** Was his text message to her early the next week.

**When are you going?**

**Couple of hours.**

**LOL…not much prep time, eh. I've got a photoshoot this week down by the Brooklyn Bridge.**

**Okay, maybe another time. Stay out of trouble.**

**Me? Trouble? No way. You on the other hand…have a safe flight.**

**I'll call you, Toots.**

**Good luck with the band.**

· · · · · ·

"So, is this officially a thing with you and Jesse?" Hayley was in New York for a photoshoot.

"I don't know that you could call it a thing." Kylie picked at her spinach salad. All the bacon pieces were gone and now she dug for the last chunk of hard-boiled egg.

"Are you fucking him?" Miss Mississippi asked in the sweetest tone as if she were asking Kylie if she would like more sweet tea as they sat on her Gran's weathered porch.

"Actually, no. I haven't even kissed him yet. Well, not really kissed." Kylie smiled at the memory of planting a soft one on him on the sidewalk outside her building. "We've mostly been talking by text for the last week. He's been in the studio recording new solo material here in the city and then he just flew out to LA to do a sit-down with members of his band."

"Are they breaking up?" Hayley knew she was on the leading edge to news.

Kylie's voice was barely a whisper. "He doesn't want to. He's out there to talk about what's next."

"They need him." Hayley shrugged it off.

"They do. He's the draw, hands down, as well as being the group's creative center. But from what he's told me, he really wants to make it right with them and show them that they can depend on him, that he can truly lead the band. He has really worked hard on getting his shit together. And you know what, Sip, he needs them. They are his village."

"It sounds like the two of you have had some pretty heavy conversations."

Smiling, Kylie shook her head. "You can't imagine the half of it."

"So, why are you not fucking him?" Hayley turned to eye a passing waitress, giving her an *I'm going to eat you* smile. "Mmm, dessert," she purred.

"Because the time isn't right. We're not there."

"Kylie, I hate to break this to you but Jesse Winslow is *there* in three seconds flat with every woman on the planet. So, don't treat him like you've got a platinum pussy and he needs to earn access."

"So, let him fuck around with every bimbo who throws herself at him."

"You'd be devastated. Don't lie."

Sitting back in her chair, Kylie took a moment, then sighed. *How could she tell Hayley without telling Hayley?* Finally, she shared, if only a little. "What Jesse and I have is different." Realizing the minute it was out of her mouth how pathetic that first line sounded. "We have become one another's confidantes. And if anyone ever heard our conversations, they'd think we were batshit crazy."

"So, he's friend-zoned you?" Hayley was trying hard to understand.

"It's really complicated." *Damn, I'm just spitting out the clichés, aren't I.* She laughed to herself. "I don't think I'm in the friend-zone, but I think we each realize how broken we are, so we're not jumping into anything. And honestly, I haven't really thought about him with another woman. I don't know how I'd feel. I really don't. I guess with someone like Jesse you kinda just expect it. They go backstage from a gig and there's a different chick attached to his dick each night. And the crazy thing is, he doesn't see that as cheating because he's not emotionally involved. We have actually had *that* conversation."

"You'd better protect yourself, Gracie. This is not going to end well. He's not John and you're not Yoko." Hayley pointed a fork at her.

"Yeah, well, that one didn't end so great either."

・・・・・・

An email from Blaise Collins was in Kylie's inbox a moment after she and Hayley stepped out of the restaurant.

"He wants to meet with me tomorrow afternoon," Kylie's tone was filled with surprise.

"A meeting with the owner of the agency. I'll bet there's a major brand that wants you." Over the last several months, Kylie's bookings for modeling plus-sized brands and plus-sized lines had steadily increased. It was shocking how lucrative it was.

But since Jesse and Zac had entered her life, working out had become a serious part of her weekly regimen and the results had been quite extraordinary. She wished there was a category in between, a normal girl category–somewhere between plus and ridiculously starved, for that is where she now best fit.

"Crap, Sip," Kylie looked concerned. "I hope I'm not getting fired from the agency, I'm kind of between modeling sizes. I just don't fit in anywhere. He's going to fire me, I know it." *Fuck, there's no Ben & Jerry's in my freezer,* was her go-to first thought.

"Don't be ridiculous. You are too valuable a face for them to lose. And between your runway and pageant experience, the photographers love working with you. You make it very easy for them." Looking at her watch, Hayley started toward the curb, hand already in the air to hail a cab. "Call me tomorrow and let me know how it goes." And she disappeared into the cab, sliding across the leather seat like butter on a hot griddle.

Standing on the sidewalk for a minute, she thought about Hayley's question, what if there was another woman in Jesse's life? How would she feel? L.A. was packed with gorgeous women. And he was looking even hotter with his new cleaned up look–it really showcased how classically handsome he was. It wasn't just that great hair and that killer ass. He looked like rock star turned movie star.

She certainly wasn't going to admit to Hayley what she was yet to admit to herself. She would be destroyed.

"Fucking photoshoot," she muttered to no one in particular and hailed a cab, heading back to her apartment. *And fucking Sip, for putting that idea in my head. And fucking Jesse, for just living on the same planet as me and for being Jesse Fucking Winslow, who wasn't just some asshole rocker, but this really cool, interesting, incredibly nice, and more than slightly messed-up guy. Ugh!*

Once in her apartment, she knew what she had to do. Tossing her clothes on the bed, Kylie quickly changed into workout gear and packed her gym bag. No Jesse. No training session with Zac. She was just going to go down to L9 on her own and work out, get her head out of this nasty, insecure place where some actress wannabe was hanging off Jesse's dick and she was going to get canned by her agency for not being large enough for plus-sized modeling.

Walking down to L9/NYC, she incessantly checked her phone for texts. *Shit, I'm in deep,* she realized. *This is not good, not good at all. He's Jesse Fucking Winslow.*

Just entering the great rotunda of the iconic health club calmed Kylie immediately, this place was becoming a sanctuary for her, a temple of healing both the mind and body. Even without Jesse waiting for her in their private space, L9 had become her safe place.

Zac's handsome dad saw her from across the main floor, smiled and waved. That small gesture made her heart smile. She was in a place where she belonged, a place that was all about getting healthy and healing. She did the right thing coming here this afternoon after her little emotional meltdown.

Pushing herself hard on the treadmill, Kylie was easily able to slip into the zone. Raising the incline by a few degrees, she pretended she was training in the foothills of the Rockies and that was what was winding her, so she pushed on to an imaginary peak taunting her. *Seriously peak, I've got your ass and the bigger one behind you. Watch me now!*

She was totally in the groove, off on that other plane when her mind began to wander to her appointment the next day. *What should I wear to my meeting with Blaise Collins?* she wondered. *Something that makes me look thinner or something that makes me look heavier, so that I don't lose the plus-sized work?* She wished she knew why he had summoned her.

At five miles, she looked up to see an amused Zac standing before her. Pulling out an earbud, she asked, "How long have you been standing there?"

"Probably for your last mile and a half or so," he smiled at her.

Decreasing both the incline and speed, she began her cool down, glad to see Zac's friendly face.

"What are you doing out here?" It was a surprise to see her on the main floor.

"Working out."

Zac laughed at his sassy client.

"I'm here alone. Jesse is in L.A.," she explained.

"I'm really proud to see you here on a day when we don't have a training session and Jesse isn't here. That is a huge move, Red."

"Well, there was no Ben & Jerry's in the apartment and I couldn't think of anything better to do."

"I'll buy you a smoothie." The handsome blonde offered.

"You get them free."

He laughed, lapsing into an easy smile that Kylie thought should definitely be in front of a camera, and with a nonchalant shrug confessed, "I'm just a lucky motherfucker."

"Two Zac Attacks," he told the guy behind the juice bar.

"So, what's your story?" Kylie wanted to know the secrets she was certain he'd become a master of concealing behind mesmerizing pale blue eyes.

"Well, my dad owns this place."

"Yeah, I know that. Do you work here full-time?"

"I'm in school, too."

"Where and what for?"

"Urban Engineering here at City College."

"Really, City College?" She had expected a pricey private school.

Zac laughed and in a low, conspiratorial tone confessed, "Well, would you believe me if I told you that I'd been kicked out of Bryson?"

Taking a sip of her Zac Attack at the moment of his confession, the green concoction went up her nose, causing her to cough. When she was able to speak again, Kylie had a most amused look on her face. "I wouldn't expect anything less and that's quite a feat because I'm sure your dad was paying full boat for you to go there."

"Go big or go home. I went big and I went home," he admitted.

"I'll bet there's a great story behind it."

From the look on his face, Kylie knew she hit the nail on the head. "Ya know, Zac," she continued, "I think you and I might be kindred spirits."

"I knew that the first time I laid eyes on you, Red."

"Yeah?" With her fingertip, she drew in the condensation on her smoothie cup. "Demons that don't want to take a back seat?"

Again, Zac laughed, "Mine prefer a starring role. I think a few of them might be negotiating for their own cable series. Got a good shrink?" he asked laughing again.

Kylie smiled, clearly to herself, "People say she's good. I don't know if that's the word I'd use to describe her."

"No?" Zac leaned closer. "What word would you use to describe her?"

"I'm not sure. Nothing complimentary though. I feel like we have an almost adversarial relationship. I harbor really bad feelings toward her. As a matter of fact, I cannot stand her and I really don't know why. She just really rubs me the wrong way." Kylie verbalized for the first time, admitting the feelings not only to Zac, but to herself.

"Wow. Then why are you seeing her?" Zac looked confused. "Why not find someone else to treat you? Someone you actually like. There are like a gazillion shrinks in this city."

Kylie was silent, clearly considering the question her new friend had posed. "I don't know. Ya know, I'm not really sure. Just this feeling that she's the one who is supposed to be treating me. And I kind of like getting in her face. I get this total satisfaction from it and I don't know why, but I just do."

Finishing off his smoothie and putting his cup on the counter, he leaned down and whispered in her ear. "My money is on you, Red.

. . . . . .

**Toots, you around?** It was after three a.m. when she got the text.

Reaching over, Kylie grabbed her phone. **Barely.**

**Bare-ly? Mmm-mmm. I like that. Can I call?**

**Sure.** She really needed to hear his voice after her insecurity meltdown earlier in the day.

The phone rang a moment later.

"So, are you really bare, Toots?" His raspy tone sounded even sexier in the dark of night.

"No, I can't sleep naked," Kylie admitted.

"That's because you are not sleeping next to me."

"Well, there are a million and one women who would kill to sleep naked next to you, you really don't need me for that."

"Ah, Toots, it's not about needing you for that, although I do. It's about wanting you for it."

Kylie didn't answer. Being half asleep, she felt like her guard wasn't fully engaged as she listened to his seductive declarations. Running her fingers up and down a lock of her hair, the way Jesse always did, elicited a full body quiver, making Kylie feel like he was there with her in the dark.

"Kylie, I miss you. I like having you around me."

"I miss you, too, Jesse." Kylie could feel the tension returning. She was giving away too much and he was getting too close. It was starting to feel uncomfortable. "So, what's going on with the band." Changing the subject would immediately return the conversation to safer ground.

"I had a really good meeting with them. Talked about songs I'm working on. I've got lunch with Bongo tomorrow. He's my only real roadblock, so we'll see how that goes."

"Do you think you'll get back together?" Kylie hoped he said yes, but feared that would mean more time in L.A.

"I let them down. I let our fans down. I let me down. I lost control and stopped delivering what I promised. What the music promises. I get that now."

As Kylie listened, she wondered if he was generally this honest with women or if it was because he was talking to her and they had shared things they would never share with anyone else. "I'm now in control of things that I've never been in control of my entire life. Being onstage for me was the only place I felt I had complete control before, or what I thought was complete control. Control of the band. Control of the crowd. Control of the music. Onstage was my redemption. Does that make sense?"

"I think so."

"I could avoid danger through control. I guess danger and guilt were the two things right below the surface of my consciousness."

"For your father's bandmate's death?" Kylie tried to follow.

"Yeah. And I didn't even remember that, and obviously never coped with it. So, when I could control everything by performing, I could avoid danger through control," he paused. "You know love is dangerous."

Surprised and thrown by the non-sequitur, Kylie needed to know more. "What makes you say that?"

"Redheaded women who make my heart beat out of control."

"Julia?"

Laughing, "Shit, what that woman did to me. There was nothing more important in life. I had zero control when it came to that one. In the end, I wasn't using my head, I was over-confident and I became careless. It cost us both our lives."

A chill passed through quickly leaving every hair on her arms standing at attention. *I wasn't using my head, I was over-confident and I became careless. It cost us both our lives.* The irony didn't escape her. *That is exactly what you did, Bruno. Those could have been your words.*

*Maybe it's a guy thing,* she wondered.

"But no, silly, not just Julia. There's another redhead who has gotten me all crazy and distracted."

"Oh?" Smiling, she continued stroking the lock of her hair.

"I miss you, Toots. I just want to come home. Now go back to sleep. I just needed to hear your voice before my day ended."

Visions of groupies nestled between his legs quickly dissipated.

. . . . . .

Blaise Collins had style, lots of it.

Definitely not standard good-looking by any means, and probably only five-foot-seven, the man exuded confidence in the way that very few do. Known for his hand-sewn Italian suits, three-hundred-dollar haircuts and very subtle plastic surgery, the guy was actually a head turner. A powerbroker who grew up on the streets of Brooklyn, learning at a young age, what the smart, short wiry kid needed to do, not only to survive, but to thrive. He was wheeling and dealing long before hitting middle school.

"Kylie, so good to see you, love." He took her hand in both of his. "You just keep getting more and more beautiful." He leaned in and kissed her cheek before indicating she should take a seat. "I've been following your bookings, we've been keeping you quite busy."

"Yes, you certainly have," she smiled, "and I truly appreciate it."

"Over the past few years, the plus market has really become lucrative and we follow the trends. Sometimes we help make them," he added with a smug smile. "You've been a great face for us to add."

*Just get to the point,* she wanted to scream at him.

"It's impossible not to notice your weight loss and fit stature."

"Thank you." Kylie smiled sweetly. "I've been working hard on getting healthy."

"What are your plans regarding that?"

"I'm not sure I understand the question." Kylie could feel the tight furrow form in her brow and immediately told herself to stop.

"Are your plans to get back to the size you were in during your previous modeling and pageant days." He paused and added sheepishly, "Especially now, considering your relationship with Jesse Winslow."

*Smile*, she screamed at herself, *smile,* so that you don't go all Gracie Hart on this asshole and deck him. "Well, Blaise," she addressed him by his first name, "that's a pretty complex question, but I'm going to be very honest with you. No, I have no plans at all to get anywhere near my previous weight. I'd like to drop another fifteen or twenty, tops, and continue to get into good shape through exercise. So, I know that is a conundrum for you since I will neither be plus-sized and I'll be far from being model-sized." And with the sweetest smile she could muster, "My plan is to be normal, healthy girl-sized. And I really hope the agency will support me in sending out a message of beauty and positive body-image at all sizes."

"Jesse looks like he's gotten pretty healthy," he changed the subject.

Cocking her head and smiling, Kylie looked the powerful man directly in the eyes, "Yes, he has, he's looking very fine these days."

"I like the cleaned-up look and short hair," the agency head commented.

"Looks like a model himself, doesn't he?" She was surprised at how proud of him she felt, but having accompanied him on his rocky journey, it was impossible not to feel exalted.

"He really does. He's got bone structure most men or women would kill for and the camera just loves him."

"Almost as much as he loves it," Kylie couldn't help but think that was another of Jesse's situations where he felt in control, manipulating a lens to see him exactly the way he wanted to be seen, telling a story he'd crafted like a master.

"Please, give him my best." Blaise stood, indicating the meeting was over.

"I absolutely will."

As Kylie walked out of the meeting, she tried to decipher what had really just happened. Time would tell how hard they would work on her behalf now that she didn't *fit* into a standard group. She had a feeling though that her association with Jesse might remove some of that control from Blaise's hands, and she might be more of an asset and a draw to keep around–no matter what size she was.

Kylie felt conflicted that her fate and her worth lay in the hands of men and not of her own making.

· · · · · ·

Bongo had gone vegan.

*I guess we're all getting healthier,* Jesse thought, as he pulled up to the Crossroads Kitchen Restaurant on Melrose. Upon entering, he immediately saw Bongo at a small table just outside the bar area in the warmly lit dining room.

Noting the recognition in the hostess's eyes, he quickly informed her that he saw the party he was there to meet and immediately headed for the table without waiting for an escort.

"Mr. Cole," Jesse greeted his oldest friend.

"Mr. Winslow." Bongo nodded his head.

In the moment of awkward silence that ensued, Jesse let reality surface. He'd missed his oldest friend and fellow band founder.

"I missed you, Casey." Besides his mother, his wife, and his sisters, Jesse Winslow was the only person to ever call him Casey. It was like calling Ringo, Richard. *Who?*

"You look good, Jess. I've got to admit that. I was watching you yesterday and you really seem to have gotten your shit together."

Picking up the menu, purely to occupy his fidgety hands while they had this conversation, Jesse began, "It's a journey and it's been a lot of work. A lot of internal realizations, admitting that there are issues, big issues in my case, and then figuring out how to deal with them in a productive way, you know." Jesse picked up his sweaty water goblet and took a sip. "I'm sorry, Casey. I'm sorry for what I've put you, your family, and everyone associated with us through."

Casey sat back and looked at his friend, "So what's this? Some make amends with everyone you've wronged step in a Twelve-Step Program?"

Wincing at the affront and attack on his sincerity, Jesse shook his head. "In my case, it's a two-thousand-year program," was his cryptic response. He understood his bandmate's anger, which had probably been festering for months. "Bongo, I know you're angry."

Cutting off his friend, the drummer seethed, leaning across the table. "Angry doesn't begin to describe what I feel."

"I know."

"You are the most self-centered, narcissistic piece of shit I have ever met in my life. You don't give a flying fuck about anyone but yourself. You never stop for one second to consider whose lives you are affecting. You truly don't give a shit about anyone but yourself. You have no idea how to love another human being."

The last point in his rant struck a chord. "You're right, Bong. And you know me better than anyone. I couldn't love. I couldn't. Because loving is dangerous. You lose control when you love and the only way to avoid danger is through control. And I've got a cherry to add on top of that, I didn't think I had the capacity to love. I didn't think I was capable of caring. Not beyond going through the motions. Showing up with flowers or whatever shit you're supposed to do that *shows* you care."

"So, what are you saying? That now you *can* love and care. You've fixed yourself over the course of several months to become a *normal, caring* human being."

While he understood exactly where his friend's anger was coming from and that earning trust back might not be as easy as he thought, he was certainly not going to let his hard work be belittled. "It's a process and I've made huge strides, strides that yes, I am proud of. I'm clean and sober and that was and is no easy task. I did it on my own because it is my responsibility and I am my responsibility. I also knew from being in rehab that it was really all about me and my commitment. And so, I committed. And I haven't looked back. I'm meditating. I'm working out. I'm seeing my therapist regularly and working hard on getting to the root of things. We've uncovered a shitload of stuff that has added to my fucked-up-ness."

"Jesse, you take fucked-up-ness to another level."

"I know, Bong. One of the things I found out in therapy was that I watched my dad's bass player shoot up, OD and die when I was a little kid. I didn't remember any of this shit. I was down in our basement spying on them, I wasn't supposed to be down there. When the whole thing went down and my father found me, he yelled at me and threw me against a wall. I thought the whole thing was my fault somehow and then totally repressed the memory. And I've spent my life subconsciously thinking I was responsible for killing this man. This man who used to always have a Tootsie Roll in his pocket for me. I was three years old. I was Cecelia's age, Casey." Choked up, Jesse grabbed for his water again.

Bongo wasn't able to speak for a moment. "Were you able to corroborate if this really happened?"

"Yeah. I approached my mom about it and my memory of that day was spot on. But back then nobody was thinking stuff like maybe the kid should go see a shrink, this could seriously fuck him up. And since it was a drug death, if they had brought me to someone, Child Protective Services would have been all over it and maybe taken me from my family. So, we never talked about it. Ever."

Being able to visualize his young daughter going through a harrowing experience and not having his and his wife's support, was something

Casey couldn't even imagine. It made it easier to understand why his friend had such a wide self-destructive streak.

"My mom feels really bad." He stopped talking when the waitress appeared tableside to take their order. "I'll have the Impossible Burger."

"Great choice," she smiled at him as if she were the entire dessert menu and dessert was being served in the bathroom.

It didn't go unnoticed. "She your next course?"

Jesse laughed. "Nope. I am not on the market."

"Did you get back with Claud?"

"Bite your tongue. Claudine not being in my life is part of my recovery. Ridding myself of toxic energy. Best thing I've done beyond getting clean."

"So, you're celibate?" Casey's face was a cross between amused and astonished.

Jesse sat back in the comfortable wing-backed chair. "Celibate," he pondered the word. "Well, emotionally no. Physically, we need to change that."

"What do you mean emotionally no?"

"There's someone in my life who is beyond amazing." Jesse smiled. "I'm out here and I miss her. I wish I'd brought her with me. It gets harder and harder for me when we are apart. You know how it is, when you just wanna be with someone."

"Are you talking about that fat girl with the red hair that the paparazzi caught you with?"

The waitress delivered the burgers hoping for a moment of flirtation with the rock star, but he and his lunch partner were locked in a death stare that needed their strongest chef's knife to cut apart. Even she picked up on the vibe and left as soon as she'd laid down the plates.

"That fat girl," Jesse repeated in a scoffing tone, shaking his head. "Her name is Kylie."

"You're serious?"

"Dead serious."

"You could have any woman in the world, Jesse. You were living with a supermodel, for God's sake."

"You ever think," Jesse began, "that the Venus de Milo is much more beautiful than any sculpture of today's skinny women would be? I've been with today's definition of beauty and Kylie is far more gorgeous, feminine, and womanly than Claudine could ever hope to be."

"I never would have taken you for a chubby chaser," Casey taunted.

With a sigh, knowing that Bongo was trying to get him to rise to the anger bait, Jesse's newfound control and resolve kicked in. Old habits were not necessarily good ones. Standing and reaching into his jeans pocket, Jesse threw a crumpled fifty-dollar bill on the table. "If you ever want to play on a stage with me again, you will never disrespect the woman I love."

Turning, he walked from the restaurant knowing two things. Bongo needed him a lot more than he needed Bongo, and that he could love. He could care. He could feel. He would fiercely protect what was his. Because what he'd discovered on this trip to L.A. was that he was in love with Kylie Martin.

Jesse Winslow was in love.

And whether or not he had his old band by his side was yet to be seen. But one thing he did know for sure, moving forward, he wanted to do it with Kylie not just by his side, but also in his arms. And he was going to make that happen. This was one redhead he would not epically fail.

. . . . . .

This time he didn't text. He just called, waking her at two-fifteen a.m.

"Bare-ly dressed again tonight?"

Her laugh, filled with sleep was gruff. "Barely dressed every night."

"What exactly do you have on?"

"A pink tank top and pink silk bikini."

"Take them off," he ordered.

"Excuse me," there was an element of surprise in Kylie's voice.

"You heard me. Take them off. Now." Just hearing rustling on the other end of the line, he could feel his cock stiffen and it felt damn good after all this time. *Baby, I'm back,* he thought.

"We're having phone sex? But, Jesse, we haven't even kissed yet," her protest was weak. And even she knew it.

"Yes, we're having phone sex, and when I get back to New York, we're going to do a lot more than kiss. You've friend-zoned me, Toots, and I'm busting out."

Kylie was smiling on her end of the phone. Friend-zoned Jesse Fucking Winslow? Was he serious? "Nobody puts Jesse in a friend-zone," she couldn't help herself.

"Are they off?" He totally ignored her joke.

"Mmm-hmm."

"What was that?" he asked, his voice gruff and serious.

"Yes, they're off."

"Okay, spread your legs, and with your phone, take a picture of your pussy for me."

"Seriously?" She knew she was blushing in the dark.

"Take the picture, Kylie."

"Okay, but if you sell this to the paparazzi, I *will* kill you." There was a rustling sound, then, "Oh, my God, I can't believe I'm doing this."

He laughed.

"Okay, here it comes. I hope it's photogenic. It would be really embarrassing to have a non-photogenic pussy."

Pulling the phone from his ear to look, Kylie could hear his moan, exciting her even more.

"So photogenic, Toots, just like the rest of you. And I love the red landing strip. It's so hot. Oh, man, I love this. Spread your legs wider and use one hand to spread your lips open for me and send me another."

Following his directions, she did as he requested.

Moaning in her ear, "I need to be inside you. Touch yourself for me."

"I am," she admitted, "and I'm really, really wet. Here, I'm going to put the phone down there so you can hear it." She put the phone between her legs for a few moments, knowing it would kill him. "Could you hear how wet I am?"

"Yeah, and now I want to hear your other sounds. Keep stroking your pussy. Oh God, I can't wait to be buried in you. I want to pull you down on my cock and have you ride me. Ram you down onto me so that I'm deep inside you." As he talked, her sounds escalated. "That's right, baby. Give yourself to me. I want you so badly. I wake up thinking about you. I go to sleep thinking about you, and right now I'm throbbing in my hand fantasizing about that gorgeous pussy I can't wait to claim. It's going to be my pussy, Kylie. And you're going to give me my pussy. Give me my pussy," he growled and could hear her go from panting to whimpering in a split second. "Yeah, that's my girl. That's what I want you to do when I'm buried deep inside you, baby. Come just like that. Just like that. Oh, God." His own moan was out of his mouth, his hand covered in semen he desperately wanted to share with this woman.

"Kylie?" His voice was soft and if she'd been able to see him in that moment, she would have seen a peace in his smile that made him even more handsome.

"Yeah?"

"You okay?"

"I'm great." She stretched in her bed, a satisfied smile on her face as if he were really there.

"That was great."

"Yeah, it was," she admitted. "Hey, Jess, can I ask you a question?"

"Shoot, Toots."

"How long have you wanted to do that?"

"Probably since I saw you trying to do yourself in Dr. S.'s waiting room."

"Oh, my God, you knew? I can't believe you knew," her voice rose an octave. "Oh shit, I am so embarrassed." Kylie pulled her blanket over her head, hiding, even though she was alone in her bedroom.

"Don't be embarrassed, Toots. Walking into a doctor's office and seeing a gorgeous redhead whose face is on the edge of an orgasm is like winning the lottery. And with you, I definitely hit the jackpot."

. . . . . .

Heading straight to her apartment from the airport, without even stopping at home to drop off his bags, Jesse could not wait to feel her body pressed up against his, responding to him. After their late-night phone tryst, his craving to see her, feel her, play with her silky hair, and enjoy the laughter in those gorgeous green eyes became almost painful. He had to get back to New York, needed to get home to her.

After another day of meetings with the band, the decision was not to break up Winslow, but to remain on hiatus. Jesse wanted to continue down the path he'd started on several months before, continue to write, and maybe do some small shows, either solo acoustic or with a few local New York session musicians.

This gave the other band members of Winslow the opportunity to pursue other artistic ventures and the road crew to join onto other tours, without keeping everyone in limbo. For Jesse, he lightened his burden of having to worry about taking care of others when he knew his stress didn't need to extend out that far, at least not yet, not while he was learning to take care of himself.

One thing at a time. And right now, at the top of his priority list was this amazing redhead who, like a ninja warrior in a black cat suit, had infiltrated his heart with such stealth precision, that the hijacking had long been completed by the time he even became aware of it.

"Toots," it was out of his mouth the minute she opened the door. Dropping his luggage, just inches into her apartment, he took her face in both hands, drawing her lips to his for their first real kiss. It was harsh and loving, consuming and cleansing, leaving no need for foreplay, as their mouths took them beyond any exquisite sensations they were yet to explore.

They'd made it as far as a wall before Jesse grabbed Kylie's legs and wrapped them around his waist. "Bedroom," he whispered.

Nodding her head to the hall on the left, she knew this was going to happen quickly. All the slow discovery would happen later. "Do you have condoms?"

"Prepared," he smiled, dropping her on the bed and pulling her into a seated position on the edge. With his hands back on either side of her face, he splayed his fingers through her hair, lowering his head for another savage kiss that left her moaning. Holding her head tightly to his lips, Kylie's body began to thrash. Needing him inside her immediately.

"Jesse, I need you," she managed between gasps for air.

"Then stand up and get undressed for me."

Although she wanted to rip her clothes off, she knew giving him a slow, torturous pageant-girl strip would be much more effective and memorable. And after all, this was Jesse Fucking Winslow she needed to impress.

With subtly exaggerated motions, the former Miss New Jersey began a striptease that was about to destroy rock 'n' roll's famous bad boy. The initial look, as she stood before him, was of shy sweetness and he moaned just gazing into her feline-like green eyes as she unbuttoned her silk blouse, slowly.

By the time the garment hung open, revealing a delicate, pale pink lace bra, her face had taken on a vixen-like confidence and she took a step closer to him, her eyes briefly traveling to her left shoulder and then her right, before landing back on Jesse's face. He read that movement as her invitation for him to slide the fine fabric from her shoulders, and with a mere flick of his thumbs, the blouse skimmed her long legs before coming to its final resting place, puddled seductively around her ankles.

Grabbing her long hair, she ran her fingers through the silky locks, bunching it and pulling it to the side over her right shoulder, as she stood before her soon-to-be-lover in matching silk and lace bra and bikini underwear.

His face could not hide his delight as she stood before him, possibly the most feminine being he'd ever seen. Her curves were soft, her skin creamy. Reaching out, he slowly ran his hand down her side, from her ribcage to her waist, down her hips and around until his hand settled on her rounded ass. It was her body visibly stiffening, more than the slight intake of air, that made Jesse aware of her self-consciousness in that moment and he locked in on her eyes.

"Toots, you are exquisite." And he wasn't kidding, thinking the master painters would have killed their competition to have her stand before their easel. Not letting his eye contact waiver, he put a stop to any self-doubting comment she could make by claiming her mouth with the first soft kiss of the evening. He finished with his lips trailing to her ear, where he whispered, "Exquisite," as he tenderly kneaded her ass. Then, reaching behind his neck, he removed his tee-shirt in one stroke of his arm, leaving them chest-to-chest.

"Has it been awhile?" he asked, wondering if maybe she hadn't been with anyone since her Miss America days.

"Yeah," she nodded.

Confirming his belief, Jesse smiled, "Good. I'm glad."

"How about you?"

He laughed, "Believe it or not, it's been quite a while for me, too." With a hand going back to her cheek, "And I love that this is with you."

"Me too."

"You mean everything to me, Toots." He knew he couldn't yet tell her how he felt, not wanting it to sound like a heat-of-the-moment line versus the revelation he had come to in California. "You really do."

"Jesse."

"Yeah."

"Shut up."

Laughing, because that was exactly why he fell in love with her, he reached around to her back and expertly unclasped her bra, which she eased out of with just a shrug, finally leaving them skin to skin.

"Now I've got something to shut me up." He pulled her back over to the bed, gently pushing her onto her back so that her nipples were ready to occupy his mouth while he slid her panties down, eagerly awaiting to see just how wet he had gotten her. She didn't disappoint.

Running her fingers through his hair, Kylie coaxed his head from her breast. "I think we should save foreplay for dessert."

Quickly unzipping his jeans, his erection gladly sprang free, as he grabbed the condom out of the pocket before tossing his pants to the floor.

As he went to rip open the packet, Kylie stopped him, "Wait, not yet." She smiled at his surprised look. "I have to know what you feel like, taste like, first." And reaching forward, she took him in her hands gently stroking and exploring, lowering her lips she explored the crown with soft swipes of her tongue before taking his shaft as far as she could in her mouth.

"Okay, you can put it on now."

Ruffling her hair, "You feel well acquainted now?" He grabbed the packet again and rolled the condom over his all-too-famous cock. "C'mere, you." Pulling her on top, he held her by the hips, gently lowering her until he was buried deep within her warmth.

"Jesse." Kylie's eyes were shining bright, and instead of riding him, she leaned forward to lay her head on his chest, allowing her legs to stretch out behind her so that the length of them touched while he remained inside her.

Feeling wetness on his chest, he suspected they were tears, causing his eyes to get a little misty. With arms wrapped around her tightly, he drove deeper into her from this most intimate position, with every inch of them connected. And it was right. It felt right. Their entire bodies were touching.

Soon she began to squeeze him when he thrust into her. With one arm tight across her back and the other hand cupping her ass and pressing her into his thrusts, he couldn't get in as deep as he wanted, although he was physically as far as he could be. He needed to claim more of her, this wasn't enough.

Kylie pulled his lips to hers right before she began coming, her sounds pressing into his mouth, eliciting a moan from him right before he unleashed. His final thought was how right this all was.

Later, as they lie together, her head on his chest, their feet tangled, and a lock of her hair between his fingers, she looked up at him and asked, "Still think you scored the jackpot?"

"Toots. I would define this as hitting Powerball."

# Chapter 11

"Working with a new engineer and some really solid studio musicians has me both exploring song construction as well as parts of my voice that I've never really used before. I always shied away from my upper range, stayed out of my falsetto, and that limited my writing in doing that, because there's a vulnerability when you go up into your false, you know. And I'm finally ready to go there. I'm finally ready to explore my vulnerability." Cocking his head, it was as if he finally *got* some inside joke.

"I see," said Claire. "Do you think you are generalizing this into other areas of your life?"

"Well, yeah, it's a mindset to make yourself more vulnerable and to open up."

"And how does that make you feel?" Sliding her glasses down and off her nose, she laid them on the desk, her keen blue eyes focused on her patient.

"Scary. Exciting. Like there are possibilities again." Running his fingers through the spiky front of his hair, he was looking down toward the floor, but the smile on his face was evident. When he looked back up at his psychiatrist, the smile turned to more of a confused look. *What's different?* he wondered. And then realized her hair was no longer pinned up and was flowing freely. It was like he looked up to find himself in the middle of a sexy librarian porn and the sanctity of her office felt somehow compromised.

"Did those possibilities not feel available to you before?" she asked, not skipping a beat.

"Yeah, they were totally closed off. I was totally closed off. My relationship with Claudine was comfortably numb on a good day and that sliding scale could descend all the way to toxic on an average-to-bad day. Maybe we did crappy stuff to each other just to see if the other one could feel. Like any emotion, no matter how hurtful, would have at least been something. It was an easy spiral to get into, Doc."

"And you no longer feel you are on the same trajectory?"

With a smile that broke thousands of hearts on any given night, from the pit to the nosebleed seats, Jesse shook his head, no.

"I feel everything now. And most days it is painfully wonderful. I came out of a dark tunnel, Doc. And greens are really bright. The color of the sky, the blue, it mesmerizes me. I didn't realize how much had been missing."

"You have made a lot of progress since Australia. Be proud," the doctor encouraged.

"I am. The work we've done here, my time in the Caribbean, getting myself clean. I don't take any of it for granted. I really don't. But it was also finding the right person to share it all with…that was key to me working so hard to make it happen."

Picking up her water glass, Claire took a sip before responding. "So, you are involved in another relationship?"

Laughing, "Oh, crap, Doc, I figured you knew. Page 6 and the rest of the paparazzi has been all over us."

"Guess I'm not reading the right publications," her tone was clipped, her smile forced. She picked up her glasses and slid them back up her nose to the bridge, then reached for her water glass again.

"Wow. I thought for sure you knew about me and Kylie." There was pride in his voice.

Her glass came down on the desk a little harder than she had intended. "Kylie Martin?"

"Yeah," Jesse was blinded to the psychiatrist's reaction, so deeply lost in his own feelings. "And I've got you to thank for that. Had I not walked in on the wrong day we probably never would have met."

Claire was still in the process of pulling herself together and attempting to act professional. "Do you think that's a good idea for the two of you to be involved with one another?"

"No. I don't think it's a good idea. I think it's a phenomenal idea. I think she might be the best thing that has happened to me in my entire life." Jesse locked eyes with his doctor.

"And it very well might be," she concurred. "But you are in the midst of recovery and right now you are feeling the full power of the wind under your sails. But winds are unpredictable and fickle and I would hate to have you capsize when you've been doing so well staying on course."

"Yeah, well, Kylie is both my life vest and my anchor. She's my True North. So, I'm not worried about drowning. I've crawled out from the shadows and this is finally my time in the sun."

. . . . . .

"I don't know what is sexier," Jesse smiled at Kylie, "watching you get dressed or watching you get undressed. We should blow this thing off, order Chinese food and eat out of containers, in bed, naked."

Looking over her shoulder, Kylie smiled. "Don't tempt me. Can you zip me up?" She lifted her heavy hair and he came up behind her, simultaneously tugging at the zipper of the marine blue lace dress and kissing the back of her neck.

"Everything will be fine tonight," he reassured her, having seen little stress signs build as the week progressed. Tonight, was the first major event that they were attending as a couple and of course it just couldn't be any event, it was the industry association event for models and modeling agencies. Claudine would be there. Blaise Collins would be there. The paparazzi would be raging in full force. And Jesse Winslow was attending, but this time with a different model.

Tonight, was a night that bitch fights were made of, and not quite fighting weight, Kylie, knew in her gut that everyone was waiting to see what bedlam might transpire between a top model, a former Miss New Jersey and a very famous rock 'n' roll bad boy.

Kylie had chosen a second skin lace dress that proudly showed off every curve. She was owning it tonight, not hiding it. And if the starving girls wanted to call her fat, so be it. Beauty wasn't calculated on the number of bones you had sticking out. And she felt more beautiful tonight in this intimate moment with Jesse zipping her dress than any other night in her life.

Sitting on the edge of the bed, she handed Jesse her high sandals. "Can you do my ankle straps?" She looked up through her long, mascaraed lashes and smiled.

On one knee in front of her, he took the nude-colored strappy sandals from her. "You're killing me, Toots." Lifting her right foot to his mouth, he let his teeth graze her arch, eliciting a moan from Kylie as her thighs clamped together. With thumbs in her arch, he massaged deep into the muscles.

Moaning again, she gazed at him through slitted eyes. "Promise me you'll do this again when we get home tonight and I'm hobbling like an old lady."

Trailing from her arch to her big toe with the tip of his tongue, his grey-blue eyes flashed a contented amusement. "I promise," he whispered, as he gave her toe a nibble.

"Oh, my God," she whimpered. "The Chinese restaurant is on speed-dial. Hand me my phone." She reached a hand out to him.

Laughing, Jesse slipped on the first sandal, fastening the strap around her slim, shapely ankles. "Not a chance, Toots. You look too beautiful in that dress to miss our night on the town."

"You look very handsome, too. You clean up real nice, Winslow." With just a little scruff on his well-defined jaw, black suit jacket, and hair perfectly askew, Kylie knew how crazy both the crowd and the paparazzi were going to go over him. And she prayed Claudine didn't have second thoughts when she laid eyes on her charismatic ex. Or that tomorrow morning's papers weren't too harsh on her for not being a size zero.

"It's now or never, Toots." He pulled her off the bed.

"Let's do this."

The event was in support of literacy and aptly held at the New York Public Library, one of the most elegant classic venues in Manhattan. The Celeste Bartos Forum was pure architectural magic located adjacent the library. It's thirty-foot glass-domed ceiling and twinkling trees and lights scattered throughout the room gave one the feeling of an evening under a star-filled sky in a spun-sugar wonderland.

"This reminds me of a glass version of the L9 rotunda," Kylie noted.

Jesse laughed, "We do spend a lot of our time in circular rooms."

"No beginning and no end." Kylie muttered absentmindedly as she scanned the beautiful crowd for Hayley, excited both for her to meet Jesse and because having a wing-woman in this crowd provided some additional comfort.

"Jesse, can I get a picture?" The photographers were upon them before they were fifteen feet into the room.

"Jesse, over here."

"Jesse, is Winslow breaking up?"

Never dropping her hand, they stopped for a moment and smiled for the cameras flashing around them like fireworks at the Capitol fourth of

July celebration.

"Winslow is not breaking up. But right now, I'm working on some solo material and planning on spending time in the studio."

"Jesse, will you be touring."

"I have no plans for that now, although I would really love to do some small club dates. Maybe something acoustic." A small cheer went up from a group of guests who had gathered around.

"Are you two a couple?" A heavy-set male reporter from one of the network gossip shows yelled out.

Jesse turned to look at Kylie and smiled. "Yes, we are very much a couple. And if you haven't met her yet, this gorgeous lady is my girl-friend, Kylie Martin." Jesse squeezed Kylie's hand as the room felt like it was exploding with the popping of lights around them. Kylie smiled at the camera, a smile she had perfected prior to pre-school.

Jesse waved at the press, "Thanks, everyone," and guided Kylie away from cameras. "Glad we got that done early. We gave them enough for them to be happy and leave us alone."

"They love you," Kylie was in awe of how the press adored him.

"For the most part, I'm really positive and giving with them. When I can be."

"Well, I think our next photo op for them is about to happen." Kylie crooked her head slightly to the right.

Following her eyes, there was a group of three people about twenty feet away. Claudine listened intently to FACES USA CEO, Johnny Spinelli. The third person was a tall, elegant man not bothering to hide his boredom.

"You think that's Nick?"

"Gotta be." Jesse checked him out from head to toe.

"What do you want to do? You, me, Claudine, and Nick are the elephant in the room tonight." Kylie tried to read his expression.

"Let's get it over with so that we can deal with the rest of the evening." Squeezing Kylie's hand, he asked, "You're okay with this?"

Her answer was her smile and the tug of his hand in Claudine's direction.

"Hello, Claud," he leaned in and kissed her cheek as if they were old friends and nothing more. "Johnny." They shook hands. And then he turned to the other man, "You must be Nick." The man extended a hand. "I'd like you all to meet my girlfriend, Kylie Martin."

"Girlfriend?" Claudine raised her eyebrows. "And I thought you were just friends." Her tone had an edge.

Ignoring the barb, Jesse looked at Kylie and smiled. "Yes, that's how we started out. As friends."

"Kylie, who are you with?" Johnny asked.

"Blaise Collins and Siren." She was glad for the distraction.

"Ah, Blaise. Is he treating you good?"

Before Kylie could answer, "Is that my name I heard? Are you trying to poach one of my top girls?"

"Damn right." The two modeling moguls shook hands. "I could double your contracts," he winked at Kylie.

"Promises, promises," sighed Kylie, making the two men laugh and extricating herself from an awkward situation.

Still holding Jesse's hand, she gave it a slight squeeze. Picking up on her hint, "Toots, listen to what the band is playing," and he smiled at her as if no one else was in the big crystal-topped ballroom with them. "May I have this dance?"

Smiling back at him, she couldn't help but think what a formidable pair they were, so effortlessly picking up on one another's cues, as if they'd been negotiating delicate situations together for years.

"Excuse us, everyone, but this fine gentleman owes me a dance."

The tiny lights reflected off the dance floor creating the impression that the guests were dancing amongst the stars. As Jesse led her to the center of the floor, Kylie was aware of all the eyes in the room that were on them as she floated into his arms.

"We did pretty good." She smiled at him as they danced to the slow Big Band anthem.

"Boy, did we ever. I'm glad that's over. Not that I ever think it's going to be comfortable, but the first time is the worst and everyone in the room was watching that."

"Show's over."

"Toots, don't get too comfortable, the show is never over," he warned, then laughed at the scared look on her face. Sliding his right hand up into her long waves, he guided her lips to his for a romantic kiss under the stars.

When their lips broke, she asked, "So, what song is this? Now that it's *our* song," her lips quivered into a smile.

"You really don't know?" Searching her face, smiling, "This one is a classic. It's 'Moonlight Serenade', Glenn Miller's theme song."

She smiled and shook her head. "Well, I'm not as old as you," she teased. "But now I'll never forget it." And with the smile still on her face, she rested her head on his shoulder as they floated between the stars.

Absentmindedly, he stroked her hair as they danced, concentrating on both how good she felt in his arms and how good he felt holding her. Lost in their own world, two songs later, their bubble was burst.

"I'd like to borrow him for a song," Claudine tapped Kylie's shoulder.

"That's really not necessary." Jesse's hold remained firm.

"It's okay. Really." Looking into his eyes, Kylie wanted him to know she believed in them enough not to let this be an issue.

And with a quick kiss on Jesse's full lips, she disengaged from his embrace, smiled at Claudine and left the dance floor.

"So, you really cleaned up this time." It was more of a statement than a question.

"One day at a time." It occurred to him how strange her bone-thin frame felt in his arms and the more she pressed herself against him attempting to elicit a response that she was still the one, the more foreign and uncomfortable the feeling became, making him yearn for the restorative solace of Kylie.

"Well, you look great. I really love the shorter hair and cleaned-up look."

"Thanks." *What did she want?*

"I'm sorry about the moving out thing." Her look was both self-effacing and flirtatious.

*Oh, how well I know her,* he thought, *and I'm not going to get played.*

"It was a really classy move, Claud. But I'm glad you did it. You see, it was the best gift you ever gave me. I wanted to stay straight so badly that when your friends left, I called my shrink and hopped a plane to Antigua where I spent a month getting even healthier and more in touch with what was right and wrong in my life. That month was the turning point for me. I came back home strong, centered and ready to move on."

"Is that when the girlfriend came in?" There was an edge to her voice.

"I never cheated on you, if that is what you are asking."

"You never cheated on me? Seriously, Jesse?"

"What I meant was I never cheated on you with her. What I did in the years before is despicable behavior and I apologize for it. I know those words don't make it better, but I am sorry I was such an asshole for so long."

"So, she gets the best of you now? She gets faithful Jesse?"

"She brings out the best in me, Claud. I want to be a great man for her."

"For *her*?" Without saying it, Claudine was judging Kylie's worth by her size and in Claud's warped mind, the larger the woman, the less she was worth.

"Absolutely, for her." *Make no bones about it.* Pun totally intended.

Claudine's face went from screwed up to shocked when she felt a hand on her shoulder. As Jesse looked into the arresting emerald eyes that were splitting up this dance, he silently thanked the stranger.

"Sugar," *Sugah*, she addressed him with a ravishing smile. "Finally." *Fine-al-LEE.*

And in those two words, he knew the emerald eyes belonged to the infamous Miss Mississippi.

"Excuse me, but could you not see that we are in the middle of a conversation?" Claudine was pulling model rank on this clearly beautiful woman who was unknown to her.

"Where *are* your manners?" She eyed the tall blonde with disdain. "And could *you* not read the man's body language? Your conversation was as over as a raccoon caught in my granddaddy's wood chipper."

Jesse wondered how Hayley was doing this with a straight face.

"Leave us alone." The top model was becoming increasingly annoyed by this unknown.

"Actually, Long, Tall and Toxic, it's time for you to move on." Her meaning was literal and metaphorical, and that escaped no one, as she turned her gaze to Jesse. "Mr. Winslow," and stepped in between Jesse and Claudine, breaking apart the former super couple.

"I've heard a lot about you, Sip," Jesse addressed her by Kylie's nickname, as a stunned Claudine walked away.

Smiling, her voice dripping honey, her words more of a vinegary tang, "And where is our girl?"

"You know, I'm not sure, we were dancing, when Claudine broke in."

"Epic fail," she informed him, causing an immediate stiffness to ensue in his well-built frame.

"She said it was okay."

"Letting your ex literally get in between you two. It's never okay. Ever."

"No. She's fine. She knows how I feel about her," he tried to convince Hayley.

"Oh, really, with Long, Tall and Toxic draped all over you. Don't you hurt my friend, Jesse. Do not make her your rebound person and humiliate her."

"I would never do that, Sip. I adore Kylie. I need to go find her."

"Yes. You do," her friend agreed and the two left the dance floor, headed in different directions, in search of the same redhead.

· · · · · ·

Hayley knew the first place to look for her friend was the ladies' room, even though this evening she was going to find very few actual ladies there, but rather an exorbitant amount of very nasty bitches. Swinging open the door, she gave herself a virtual pat on the back for getting it right. Getting it all right–Kylie and the nasty bitches were all located in one fell swoop.

Kylie was just exiting a stall, much to the surprise of Claudine and two of her lingerie- model friends, one with long, lustrous black hair and the other with a short, trendy platinum pixie. They were clearly talking about Kylie, unaware that she was there.

"I had no idea they made lace, second-skin dresses in that size. You've got to give her balls for wearing it," the raven-haired model quipped.

"Big balls, just like the rest of her," remarked the platinum friend.

Gazing into the mirror as she put on fresh lipstick, Claudine's laughter came to an abrupt halt as Kylie exited a stall with Hayley simultaneously entering the bathroom with the clockwork precision of a synchronized swim team.

"Oh, would you just look," Hayley drawled. "It's a headquarters meeting of the Bitchy Models Society being chaired by none other than their fearless leader, Long, Tall and Toxic."

"Who the hell are you, Miss Nobody?" The dark-haired model was the first to respond.

When the short-haired model's mouth began to move, a stare-down from Hayley's emerald eyes, stopped her from uttering a word.

"That's right, be a good girl and stay quiet. Save your energy. You're going to need it for later tonight when I'm eating your pussy," Hayley paused to let that sink in. She had the trio so off balance. "And then you'll be begging me for my phone number." And somehow, they all knew it wasn't a lie.

Hayley's crazy energy had helped bolster Kylie to a place where she could take on Claudine like a pro.

Approaching the sink next to Claudine and washing her hands, Kylie was in full command as she confronted the famous woman. "If you have something to say about me, I would hope you are enough of a woman to say it to me directly and not as part of a catty bathroom chat." She paused, looking the other woman directly in the eyes in the mirror. "Nick seems fabulous, so why all this venom?"

Taken aback by Kylie's frankness, it took the supermodel a few moments to collect and verbalize her thoughts. "Because you are getting the Jesse I never got."

"Did you ever think you might be a lot happier if you were happy for him? Happy to see him healthy. Happy to see him work through the things that were destroying his life and we all know were going to kill him. You really can't be happy for that?"

Claudine's silence shocked Kylie. How could this woman have loved him and not be elated at his progress? His health? Even Sip was shocked into silence.

Shaking her head, she had no words for the super model as she continued to hold her gaze in the mirror. Grabbing a hand towel, Kylie finally looked away, as she dried her hands. Tossing the towel into a wicker basket, she took one more long look at Claudine, not afraid to face her or to express her disdain.

Heading out of the bathroom with her friend, Kylie felt both beautiful and empowered. There was not a single thing to ever feel insecure about when it came to Jesse and Claudine's ex-relationship. There was nothing there. It was a sham. A shell, just like Claudine. And as far as feeling less than, because of her size, that exchange clearly showed her the beauty in loving and caring for others. The positive and healing energy she was putting out into the universe, that was not only changing her life but was also integral in Jesse's healing, was already coming back to her, threefold. And that energy was the essence of beauty, because it was rooted in love.

Claudine and her friends could make fun of her dress size or correlate her beauty to a number on the scale. But what became crystal clear as she stared down the woman in the bathroom mirror was that she was more beautiful, inside and out, than Claudine or any of her friends, and that was what Jesse and every man who had turned his head to appreciatively stare at her all night had seen. Her true beauty.

Jesse was only a few steps away when she and Hayley exited the bathroom.

"Toots," he was upon her with an urgency, wrapping her in a bear hug. "I'm so sorry," he whispered in her ear.

Looking up at him, she smiled as he put a hand on either side of her head and pulled her in for a kiss.

"I never should have let that happen. I'm so sorry. I guess I thought it would be a closure conversation."

"And?" Kylie searched his grey-blue eyes needing to know the conversation accomplished just that.

Putting his forehead to hers, "And I got the gift of a lifetime when Sip broke in and shooed her off. Please, don't ever worry about Claudine, Kylie. She will never come between us. She and I co-existed, we were a brand, a photo-op. We never shared the depth you and I do. And I realize that I had closure long before she moved her stuff out."

"I know." Kylie surprised him.

"How do you know?" The lopsided smile was back.

"Because, Jesse, you are a beautiful person, inside and out, and she is not."

Cocking his head to the side, Kylie could see the emotion in his eyes as he stood there silent for a moment, before nodding his head.

"Can we miss the dinner?" She had had enough for one evening.

"Take-out?" His smile said everything.

"Sip, do you want to blow this joint and join us for Chinese food?" Jesse asked.

"Maybe another time. There's a platinum bitch I need to get my hands on." Her lascivious smile clearly detailed her intent for the short-haired model she'd met in the bathroom.

"Jesse, can I get a picture of you with these gorgeous women?" A photographer was upon them.

"Sure," the rocker smiled, and with Miss New Jersey on his right and Miss Mississippi on his left, they stopped for a shot.

"Do you think we'll make it out the door?" Kylie asked.

"Not without probably ten more photo stops." This was his life.

"That blonde can wait a few minutes," Hayley decided, as she accompanied her friends toward the entrance and took full advantage of being photographed with the infamous rock 'n' roll (former) bad boy.

As they neared the door, Johnny Spinelli joined them for a photo. "You should come work for me." He whispered into Kylie's ear. "I'll treat you the way you should be treated. Blaise has no idea what to do with you."

Kylie's thoughts exactly after the last meeting with him.

"Jackson Cohen is my agent." She smiled at him sweetly and bid him goodnight.

· · · · · ·

"I'm glad we went tonight," was Kylie's conclusion as she brought chopsticks filled with lo mein to Jessie's lips.

"Me too." He slurped in the tasty noodles. "I'm glad that shit with Claudine is behind me now. And it was really great being able to show you off."

"You showed me off?" she laughed.

"I did. No mistaking it now, the beautiful girl I was seen with in Starbucks is my girlfriend. We will be in every paper tomorrow morning,

I can guarantee you that. And the tabloids are going to go insane with pictures of us and Claudine that we didn't even know were being taken. You're going to read all sorts of shit about us, Toots." He brought a dumpling to her lips. "Ignore it as much as you can, okay."

"I'll try."

"You just need to know one thing."

"And what is that?" *Tell me, Jesse.*

"How I feel about you." Reaching over, he took the white paper container from her hands and placed it on the nightstand.

Kylie remained quiet. Reaching forward, Jesse took a lock of her hair and let it slide through his fingers. "Toots, I've known this for the longest time, but I didn't want to scare you. I think you already know how I feel about you, whether I've said it or not. You see, you make me want to fight every day to be better than I was the day before. You make me scared that I will fail you, that I won't be the man you deserve, because as we know, I have been fucked up in relationships. I've questioned if I even had the capacity to love. And then you showed up in my life and there's no doubt that I have the capacity to love. It turns out that I have the capacity to love deeply. I just didn't have you before. I love you, Kylie. I know, without a doubt, that we will always be together. That someday, some little stinker is going to ask you, "Grandma, did Grandpa *really* play in a band?" He stopped and smiled, "And you are going to be the hottest grandmother on the planet and we're going to still be fucking like wild animals."

Kylie laughed at his last sentence, but there were no words, because the tears were coming too quickly. Smiling as he wiped them from her cheeks, he knew how moved she was by his admission, her reaction was from her heart and it filled his heart with more love than he could have ever imagined.

Finally, the tears subsided. "Jesse Fucking Winslow, am I dreaming? Did you just tell me you love me?"

"Toots, this ain't no dream. Just the here and the now."

"Makes me want to stay in this reality. Forever."

"Yeah, this is the best one yet," he agreed.

Picking up a waxed paper bag, Kylie dug in and pulled out a fortune cookie, gently tossing it to Jesse, before going back in and pulling out one for herself.

Jesse's face broke into a smile, as he read from the slip of paper, "The love of your life will appear in front of you unexpectedly." Leaning forward, he kissed Kylie softly. "Yes, she did." Folding the fortune in thirds lengthwise, he inserted one end into the other, forming a ring and slipped it onto her finger with a lopsided grin and a raise of his eyebrows.

Admiring her new accessory, Kylie looked up at him through her dark lashes before smiling and doing a one-handed crush on her cookie. Pulling out her fortune, she let out a single, loud laugh which she tried to snuff, turning it into a snort. She handed Jesse the fortune, "You read it." She was trying hard not to crack up.

Taking it from her hands, he began to read out loud, "Love is on the horizon. The stars predict he will be tall, dark and a centaur." Laughing, Jesse lustfully gazed at Kylie. "That's right, baby, hung like a horse. Now get in my lap," he pulled her to him, "and come take a ride to Heaven."

# Chapter 12

"I know Jesse told you about our relationship."

"Yes, I'm aware of it."

*Is Claire even colder than usual or am I imagining this?* Kylie wondered.

"Alrightee, then." Kylie smiled at the shrink.

"Are you trying to convey something to me, Kylie."

She shrugged, "I don't think so. I just thought you'd have more to say about it."

Nodding her head, Claire explained, "Since I treat you both as separate patients, I can only address what you each broach with me individually."

"Okay, fair enough."

"It's not about being fair, it's the ethical thing to do and it is the law." The doctor maintained her matter-of-fact demeanor.

"Yeah, whatever." Kylie was trying to not become annoyed with Claire, but it wasn't working. "I think I've struggled in my past relationships a lot. Never really being able to express feelings, never truly being nurturing to my partner, but it's so different with Jesse. I was concerned because of who he is, getting involved with someone of his stature is a huge risk."

"All relationships are risk."

"Yes. Yes, they are." She finally agreed with her shrink on something. "And then add in who he is, his lifestyle, and a recent high-profile break-up and I think the uncertainty of it all increases exponentially. Don't you?"

"Don't I what?"

"Think there is increased risk."

"I think that is your perception, so that becomes the reality that we are dealing with here."

"Well, on paper it seems like a slippery slope, but, in reality, it is the easiest and healthiest relationship I've ever had with a man and it's been like that with him since the day we met. It's just easy and comfortable."

The psychiatrist didn't speak.

Smiling to herself, Kylie finally looked up, visually connecting to her doctor, "The other night he told me he loved me. How crazy is that? I mean, Jesse Winslow telling me he loves me."

"Why is that crazy?"

"Seriously? One of the most well-known men in the world told me he loved me. That's not people's normal reality."

"You sound as if you question it." She crossed her legs the other way.

Kylie shook her head, "No. Not at all. I know what he feels."

"And you returned the sentiment?"

Kylie thought back on the conversation. "No. I didn't. I meant to, but we got swept up in something else." Looking at Claire, she smiled. "I need to change that immediately." And pulling her phone out of her oversized hobo bag, she texted Jesse.

**Did I not say something to you the other night?**

**Well, not in so many words.**

**Gasp, twelve lashings for me**

**If you insist, Toots.**

**Lasher's choice. Talk to you soon. Finishing up with Claire.**

Looking up at the doctor, she smiled again. "Looks like he's going to have a good night."

"And why do you think you didn't return the sentiment when he first expressed it?"

Shrugging, she wasn't going to let Claire turn this into something that she could use against her with Jesse during his session. "I don't think he gave me much of a chance to speak, we were kissing and then I physically told him exactly what I feel. There was no doubt. And when we were done, we just got totally swept up into something else. But tonight, I get the chance to tell him how much I love him. Oh my God, I'm so excited."

*Game. Set. Match. Claire.*

. . . . . .

"What was that about twelve lashings?" Opening the door with his lopsided smile.

"Yeah? What *was* that? Lashings come in all forms and sizes, you know," she informed him, looking up through her lashes, while tossing her purse onto a nearby black leather bucket chair.

"Oh?" His eyes were smoldering as he backed her up against a pale gray wall.

"They can be as simple and delicate as tongue lashings."

She softly swiped the tip of her tongue along his bottom lip, eliciting the lopsided smile.

Inserting his hand between her legs, he cupped her through her jeans, the heat immediately emanating onto his hand being his invitation to give her pussy a rough squeeze. "Delicate wasn't on my agenda," he informed her, rubbing her through the rough fabric and clenching her.

"Mmm," she responded, aching to feel more, with a lot less clothes on. With his other hand, he roughly caressed her breast until her hard nipple grazed his palm.

"So, you've been making me wait." His eyes were laughing, but the rest of his face maintained a fierce intensity. "Maybe I need to make you wait."

"You already told me you loved me," she reminded him.

"Mmm-hmm." His massaging between her legs became rougher, causing Kylie to close her eyes, her concentration being blown to smithereens.

Abruptly, the sublime fondling came to an end and Jesse grabbed Kylie by the hand leading her down the hall toward the bedroom. Walking her over to a chair along the wall, he gave her shoulder a slight nudge indicating for her to sit.

Crossing to the bed, he sat on the edge facing her, a gulf of seven feet between them.

Kylie was charged and coiled and ready to spring, needing Jesse to finish her off.

Smiling at her, he locked eyes. "You're dying, aren't you?" His smile was almost a sneer.

"You know I am," she confessed, wondering why rock stars always had the most beautiful mouths. Without wanting to break his glance, she could see, at the base of her visual field, that he was unbuttoning his jeans, then unzipping them, with its unmistakable sound.

"Look how hot you got me." His right hand was wrapped around his erect cock. "I get so out of control just thinking about you. And now, sitting here, looking at you, look what you've done to me. I can feel your heat across this room."

His thumb started to stroke the shiny purplish crown, rimming the edge and making its way up to the slit at the center. All Kylie could think about was what that felt like between her lips, how the tip of her tongue craved that slit and the slightly salty treat waiting for her there. As his thumb began to move a little quicker, her shallow breaths followed pace.

An expert at holding eye contact for an audience of one or twenty-thousand, Jesse began to slowly stroke himself, his solo attendee mesmerized.

"Feels damn good, but nowhere near as good as it feels inside your tight, warm pussy. I love being buried deep inside you and watching your pupils dilate as you get closer to coming. And the only thing I can think of when I see that is just how much I want to fill you with cum." Using his pre-cum to lubricate his palm, both his breath and his hand accelerated. "Like right now, your eyes are so intense and I know you want my cum as much as I want to come in you. I can see it on your face, in your eyes."

Mesmerized, Kylie sat motionless, barely able to breathe as she watched him get closer to his release.

"I see it in your eyes. You see me," he continued. "And you may be the only person who has ever seen me, who isn't afraid of the ugly, of the cocky asshole who thinks he's got the world under control and blows up everything around him. You're not scared. You'll go toe to toe with me. And that is so sexy. You are so sexy and beautiful," he choked out the last word as a spurt of semen arced, catching the light and glowing iridescent.

Kylie watched, holding her breath as Jesse regained his. Pulling his tee-shirt over his head, he used it to wipe the trail he'd left behind.

Without another word, he stood and made his way to the bathroom. Kylie heard the shower water running and considered, for a brief moment, joining him. But she couldn't move and remained in the chair.

His spiky hair was wet and askew when he returned, a fresh pair of ripped jeans on. Smiling, "Toots, you haven't moved."

Kylie returned his smile but did not speak.

Crossing the room to her, he extended a hand, which she took, standing gingerly, as if she had sea legs or muscle fatigue after sex. Leading her to the edge of the bed, "Sit," his voice was soft, yet firm.

Sitting on the edge of the bed, she looked up at him, trying to figure out what he had in mind.

"Jeans off, missy. Hop to it. We don't have all day. It's time to take those tongue lashings you were promised." Kneeling down next to the bed between her legs he tugged at her now open jeans, whipping them over his shoulder as soon as they'd cleared her. With an unexpected jolt of her calves, he pulled her ass to the edge of the bed, spreading her wide.

"Tongue lashings?" She appeared pleasantly surprised.

"You said lasher's choice," and with those final words, he dove in, finding her secret spots with ease.

Grasping at his wet, spiky hair, she clenched her thighs to his ears, her release coming hard and fast. "I love you, Jesse." The words tumbled out as she crested. "I love you," gasping she said it. She finally said it.

Pulling his face away, he laughed. "Of course, you love me. I just went down on you. Sorry Toots, but that one doesn't count." And with his lopsided grin, he gave a playful slap to the insides of her thighs.

. . . . . .

"What are you doing?" Kylie rubbed the sleep from her eyes as she came up behind Jesse at his desk. With darkness still outside the windows, she surmised it must've been around three in the morning.

"Just clearing my mind." With a click of the playing card, he flipped it from its worn, red-plaid side to its face and placed the seven of diamonds down on a long column of like-suited cards. "I play solitaire when I get stuck writing and it generally frees my mind and helps me through my block."

"That deck has seen better days," Kylie laughed as she watched him continue to count and flip cards. "We need to get you a new deck."

"No. No. No. This is my breakthrough deck," he protested.

"You're a little superstitious," there was surprise in Kylie's voice.

Looking up, he gave her his lopsided grin, "A lot superstitious, Toots. These cards help me break through a barrier. I've had them nearly as far back as I can remember."

Softly Kylie stroked the animal hide journal sitting on the desk. "This is beautiful," she mumbled as she leaned down to kiss the top of Jesse's head. "I'll let you work."

Looking up, he crooked his finger, indicating for her to lean down again, giving her a lush kiss. "That should do it," he smiled, gathered up the playing cards and flipped open the ancient journal to finish the lyrics that were now ready to be written.

# Chapter 13

**Johnny Spinelli called me.**

**And?** He eased into the corner of the worn leather couch in the recording studio as he typed.

**He wants to talk about me doing some work with their clients. Promises to make me the "IT" girl and keep me working more steadily than Blaise.**

**Awesome news, Toots. Will you have any contractual issues?**

**I don't think so. I don't have an exclusive with Siren. Most people are with a few agencies to get good client coverage. But I'll run it past a lawyer.**

**Why don't we have my lawyers take a look at it.**

**Thanks, but I can just send it to my lawyer.** Opening her desk drawer, she unsuccessfully rifled through papers in search of a business card.

**Kylie, I've got a team who have kept me out of a lot of trouble or fixed it when I've gotten into trouble.**

**LOL...then I know they must be good!!** She closed the desk drawer.

**No shit! LOL. That's why I keep a TEAM of them and make them earn their money ☺.**

**Bwahaha...sold! If they've kept your ass out of jail, then I**

**KNOW they can protect me.**

**LOL, ain't that the truth. I'll get you an email address and let them know it's coming. And babe...** He sat up on the couch.

**Yes...**

**Congrats! You totally deserve this. LOL ... I have this feeling I'm going to keep those lawyers busy you know, fighting assholes off you.**

**Oh?**

**Those douches need to understand one thing.**

**And what's that?** Smiling, she could feel his testosterone rising with each text and she was loving it.

**Toots, you're mine.**

The prickle of the hair on her arms made her shiver as she read his text. **Say that again...**

Kylie jumped as the phone in her hand rang. "Yes," she answered with a Cheshire grin.

"Toots, you *are* mine," his gravelly tone couldn't hide his smile.

"But are *you* mine, Jesse?" She challenged.

"Do you really need to ask that?" There was surprise in his tone and a hint of something else.

"I just did." Kylie held her ground.

His sigh was audible, punctuated by loud silence before he spoke again.

*Forever the showman,* she thought, smiling a wide smile he could not see, as she waited for him to speak again.

"Kylie," his voice was gruff, tensed by emotion. "Babe..."

She cut him off. "Jess, I know you love me. I really do. But loving me and being mine are two very different things. You can love a lot of people."

"That's true," he acquiesced. "But not the way I love you. You got under my skin. Slowly. I mean, in the beginning it was just sharing the regression stuff and working out together and getting to know each other and hanging out and talking. You know, becoming friends. And before I knew it, you were a part of me in a way no one else has ever been. It was true and pure. If that makes sense."

Silently, Kylie nodded her head as if he could sense her understanding.

"Toots, you know me. Only a handful of people know me. I have let you in to a place so deep, that it is dangerous. It is dangerous to feel what I feel. And I know you know that. No one else is getting to that place besides you. And there's only room for you for as long as you choose to remain there."

*Would forever work?* she ached to ask, but didn't because she knew the words *I love you* needed to be verbalized first and although she ached to say them, she wasn't going to do it via a phone call.

"I'm not going anywhere," was the depth of the sentiment she was able to share.

"Then, please, don't question if I am yours. Just know, know with everything you are, that you don't have to worry about it. If you're off on shoots or I'm on tour, know with all your heart, that I am yours."

"Does that mean that there won't be groupies attached to your dick after a gig?"

There was a deep chuckle emanating from his throat and she knew he was smiling. "Oh, babe, the only thing attached to my dick will be my hand and hopefully we will be Skyping and you'll be showing me that gorgeous, glistening, pink pussy of yours."

Kylie laughed, "Might need to be the phone if I'm on my back."

"That'll work. Just promise me one thing, Toots."

"What's that?" She wondered what he was going to ask.

"Every day that we are apart because of your work or mine, I want you to send me a picture. It can be intimate, because we do know how much I love your pussy pictures. Or it can be goofy or you in full make-up or just getting out of bed or whatever. I'll do the same. This way we see each other every day when we can't see each other."

"I love that. I promise, I will do that."

"My daily *Mine* fix."

As Kylie searched for the document to send to Jesse's legal team, the realization became clear, she could finally see just how protective of her he had become and how he proved it through the generosity of his spirit. It was the nuances, like making sure she was legally covered, where Jesse not so subtly proved that *mine* was not just an empty word, but rather, a code by which he lived.

*Mine.* For the first time in forever, Kylie Martin truly felt she belonged. They belonged. Together.

. . . . . .

With masterful precision, Bob Kreutzer slid the fader on the sound-board very slowly toward his chest. About halfway down, a thought occurred to him.

"Jesse," he pressed the mic button to talk to his artist. "We got that. That extra riff on the chorus really works. Good add. How about if before we cut for the day, you give me a vocal on that chorus at the very end. I'll play you the mix first so that you can hear it and then let's lay down vocals on the second run through."

Nodding, Jesse perched on the high, three-legged stool and pulled the vocal mic to a comfortable level. With focused intensity, he listened to the segment Bob sent to his headphones. After the first pass-through, he nodded to his engineer to let him know he was ready.

With precision born of many studio hours, Jesse's vocals began at the perfect juncture, laying down the voice track for the very end of his upcoming album's title track, "Fade to White."

On the last of his guitar takes, he began riffing at the end, something Bob had not expected, but captured. He'd gotten caught up in the moment and went where the music took him and now Bob wanted him to let go vocally in the same way.

Closing his eyes, he waited for his moment and the trademark gruff voice filled the recording booth.

*A movie scene fades to darkness*

*But our score never ends*

*After a brilliant crescendo*

*It's always 'til we meet again*

*Fade to White*

As Bob watched through the window above his console, he witnessed the contortion and pain on Jesse's face, knowing the rocker was going someplace deep and dark. When he began to sing again, his voice began as a raspy whisper, surprisingly exposing the top reaches of his falsetto. Bob knew that he was witnessing maybe the most honest and pure moment of Jesse Winslow's recording career as he listened to the haunting melody. Sitting back to cross his arms over his chest, he needed to quell the shiver that had run up his spine and down his arms. The engineer could not remember another moment in his career that had elicited such a strong, visceral reaction. *Pure Gold,* the voice inside his head already knew.

*A movie scene fades to darkness*

*But our score never ends*

*After a brilliant crescendo*

*It's always 'til we meet again*

*Fade to White*

When he finished the stanza, Jesse stood and turned away from Bob. The engineer could tell from the tension in the musician's shoulders that Jesse needed a moment, so he slipped out of the control booth and into the hallway.

When he returned a few minutes later, Jesse was waiting for him in the control booth.

"Do you think we got it?" he asked.

Bob just nodded.

The two sat in silence for a few moments when the engineer turned to him to present a thought that, by the look on his face, had just occurred to him.

"Hey, would you possibly be interested in recording some of the tracks at Abbey Road? I've had time booked for months to work co-engineering with Chris in Studio 3 for Monkey Flesh, but obviously that's not going to happen now."

"Wow. The rest of the band doesn't want it to lay tracks?" Monkey Flesh's lead singer/guitarist was recuperating from a motorcycle accident that left him with more broken bones than ones left intact.

"No. I tried to talk them into that. Psychologically they are all a mess," confided Bob.

"Wow," Jesse's mind was racing a hundred miles per hour. "Studio 3. It's legendary, man. *Dark Side of the Moon.* Amy Winehouse's last tracks. That's some pedigree and a great vibe. And you and Chris. When do you have it?"

"In three weeks, for three weeks."

"Hmm." Jesse tapped his foot. Pulling out his cell phone, he checked his calendar app. "That would get me back in time for my showcase."

"What showcase?" The engineer inquired.

"Just doing a small five-hundred-seat club downtown to test out the tracks solo in front of a live audience."

"You think you'll hook up with the band for any of this?"

Looking down, Jesse shook his head, "No, this stuff is too personal. This is about me in a way I've never been able to share before, and I want that to be a gift for my fans…and do it in a really intimate setting where it's just me, my guitar and them. Totally person-al."

"It's going to go over well in small venues. Fans are going to be clamoring for seats." He paused, "So, London?"

With a lopsided grin, "That's an offer I can't refuse. I've never recorded at Abbey Road and heck, that's every kid with a guitar's fantasy. And Studio 3. Nice. *The lunatic is in the studio,*" he sang taking off on a Pink Floyd riff.

Bob laughed.

"That means I've got a shitload of writing to do between now and then. I'd love to lay down enough tracks for an LP and maybe some extras for an EP, get the whole project, pre-mastering, completed by the time we leave London."

"We can absolutely make that happen. Especially if we're in the groove and I've seen enough of what you've already got written to have a feel for where to take it." Bob's creative wheels were spinning.

. . . . . .

He was on her the minute she opened the door, needing to feel her soft, alluring curves molded against him as his lips crushed down in a bruising kiss. Walking her backwards, he kicked the front door closed behind them. As each day passed, this woman became more and more his partner in all aspects of his life. With her New Jersey street smarts and tell-it-like-it-is persona, she was the rare gem that was always going to give him the truth and not blow smoke up his ass, merely because he was Jesse Winslow.

"Do you want to come with me to London for a few weeks?" The moment their lips parted, he blurted his news out like a kid with a secret he was bursting to contain.

"What? When?" She laughed at his excitement.

"Bob was supposed to work with Monkey Flesh and one of the engineers at Abbey Road in three weeks." Reaching forward, he let a lock of her hair slide through his fingers.

"I could probably come for part of the time."

"Why not all?" He was giving her a look that said I will fuck you to death daily.

"Hopefully, I, too will be working. I'm meeting with Johnny on Tuesday after my appointment with Claire and he said he's got a big surprise for me." She positioned herself across his lap.

"You don't have to," his voice was a whisper and without his eyes leaving hers, his right hand moved slowly up her skirt, tracing small circles on the inside of her thigh with his forefinger. As he reached the lacy edge of her thong, he stopped for a moment before rubbing her heat on the outside of the fabric. Watching her pupils dilate, he laughed and repeated, "You really don't have to work."

Spreading her legs a little for him, hoping to coax his fingers under the fabric for what awaited him, she shook her head no. "I've always supported myself. I can never give up that independence and freedom."

"You are so fucking badass and hot." He smiled down at her. "I still want you with me for as much as possible in London." Laughing, "Damn, I'm being needy."

"I promise, I'll try and spend as much time with you there as I possibly can if you'll put three fingers inside me right now."

"Now who's the needy one? Only three? That all you can handle, Toots?" His cock was aching inside his jeans.

She laughed. "Shut up and get me off." The last word getting garbled in her throat as Jesse plunged three fingers into her and his thumb pressed down on her clit.

. . . . . .

Rolling over in bed, she nestled her head on his warm chest. "I'm blowing off my appointment with Claire today."

"Why?" His voice was thick with sleep.

"I'm certainly not going to do a regression before my meeting with Johnny, and sometimes I walk out of there feeling more fucked up than when I walked in. This way, I can take my time getting ready, look my hottest and be totally clear-headed."

The low growl in his voice was followed by his lopsided smile. "Toots, you look your hottest with my cock rammed all the way into you and your hair spilling all over my chest."

Without wasting a moment, Kylie's hand went in search of the morning hard-on waiting for her. Slowing stroking his rigid length, she clenched her own vaginal muscles, feeling her wetness readying her to take him deep with one plunge. Slinging her legs over his slim hips, she lowered herself all the way down, her gasp drowning out his. Slowly, she lifted all the way up, until he was out of her and she could rub his soft tip along the length of her opening.

"Ready for more?" Her eyes flashed the challenge. Before waiting for a response, she had engulfed him fully yet again.

"Fuck me hard," he demanded and she set a ravenous pace solely focused on getting herself off on his cock. "Sit up a little more, I want to see your tits bounce."

She leaned back on his cock, straightening up.

"Yeah, just like that." Reaching with both hands, he grabbed her nipples, twisting them hard, making her groan from the pleasurable pain. Her reaction made him crave more and he pinched them hard enough to hear her whimper. Pulling her forward by her breasts, he sucked the left nipple into his mouth, flicking it with his tongue to cool down the sharp pain and then sucked the right nipple into his mouth.

Rolling Kylie off him, his cock still buried within her and her nipple firmly entrenched past his teeth, he plowed into her hard as he continued to suck voraciously.

"Suck harder," she could hardly get the words out. "Harder, please," she begged.

Switching back to the left nipple, he complied. As he sucked harder, her muscles tightened around his cock, squeezing him to climax. "Let me know when you're ready." He pulled his lips from her nipple momentarily to say, going back with renewed vigor.

Moving to the rhythm of his thrusts, she tightened her thighs around his hips, simultaneously squeezing his cock hard with her pussy muscles. "Now," the word caught in her throat. "Now. Come in me now."

Plowing into her, he could feel the pressure rising his length, building from his balls, an exquisite fuse erupting into her as he tried to bury himself deeper, sending his seed as far into her as he could get it.

Pulling her to him, he whispered in her ear, "London's going to suck if you're not with me."

. . . . . .

"Have you met Joanna Tivoli, the head of our Women's Division?" Johnny Spinelli ushered Kylie into his all-glass corner office. She couldn't help but notice that not only was the office constructed of glass, the man was a collector of art glass, which was the perfect media for this sunlight-bathed space. The reds, purples and golds glowed and shimmered. Kylie wanted to walk around the office inspecting the beauty of each piece, but with the woman standing right before her, she knew there would be no time for pleasantries.

Her suit was French, her shoes Italian and she was just short of beautiful. The sharp intelligence in her eyes, as they slowly flowed down every inch of Kylie's body, however, made her very attractive. Nothing got past this woman and you definitely wanted to call her friend and not enemy.

Without a word, Joanna looked at Johnny to transmit her approval via an almost imperceptible nod and Kylie instantly felt muscles relax from her abdomen to her cheeks.

"A pleasure," Kylie extended a hand for a firm, yet feminine, shake.

Johnny gestured for them to all take a seat.

"Kylie, you are a natural redhead." Joanna was almost astounded. "What is your ancestry?"

"I'm a UK mutt. English, Scottish, and some Irish in there, too." Kylie smiled.

"What size are you currently wearing?" Joanna cut to the chase.

Without missing a beat or any hint of an apologetic tone, "In general, fourteens are fitting very well now. In some cases, I can go down to twelves on a top and in other cases a sixteen on the bottom, depending on the cut." She wondered what they were thinking as she spit out numbers more than double what they were used to hearing.

The silence was suffocating. Maybe she was just too big for Johnny to make her the 'IT' girl. People wanted to see perfection and society didn't deem double digit sizes as perfect.

"Kylie, I need to tell you something that is not public knowledge at this point and needs to stay that way." He held her stare and she nodded, assenting to keep the information in confidence. "You're familiar with Northern Lights Sportswear?"

Again, she nodded.

"Anika Robinson was chosen as the face of Northern Lights for both spring and fall campaigns. Shoots are set-up in both Alaska and Australia and start in a few weeks."

Kylie wondered what he was getting to, there was some bombshell he was about to drop.

"Anika is very ill," he went on.

"Oh, I'm sorry to hear that." *Here it comes.*

"Truth of the matter is, she has an eating disorder."

*Don't we all,* thought Kylie

"Last week she ended up in Cedars-Sinai after a seizure."

"Oh, my God." Kylie's hand flew to her mouth.

"She needs intensive health care before we'll see her again." He paused, "In addition to Anika, the sixteen-year old daughter of Northern Lights's owner, Ross Eggleston, is also suffering from an eating disorder, so this has hit very close to home for him."

*So, they want the fat girl?* was the first thought that ran through her head. It was almost out of her mouth when Joanna thankfully began to speak.

"Kylie, you are not only stunningly beautiful, but you are actually now smaller than the average size of most U.S. women, which makes you a more realistic body image."

"Maybe too realistic," Kylie couldn't contain her commentary.

The look on Joanna's face indicated that maybe she thought Kylie was too large and would not have been her first choice. That maybe her first choice would have been a single digit- sized model–possibly someone who was a size 6.

"Rubbish," Johnny inserted, sensing the discord between the two women. "You have such a natural look, we think you'll be perfect for their line."

Kylie noted the "we" and felt Johnny was definitely sending Joanna a message.

"I know it's short notice, very short notice, but if you and Jesse are available on Thursday evening, we have a table at the Big Brothers Big Sisters event that Ross Eggleston's wife, Marla, is co-chairing. I'd love for Ross to meet you in person. He's viewed your portfolio and is very interested."

Kylie smiled. *And I bet I become more interesting with Jesse Winslow at my side,* she thought.

"I'd love to meet him." Tipping her head, she smiled at Johnny. "And I'll check with Jesse and see what his schedule looks like. He's in the middle of recording right now."

"So, he's back in the studio?" Joanna was even interested in the scoop on the famous rocker.

Kylie nodded. "Yes. He is."

As if reading her train of thought with the expertise of a clairvoyant, Kylie could see the cogs turning in the modeling executives head. *Maybe size fourteen isn't so hideous after all. They could spin it as beauty comes in all sizes...And still gets the guy. And that is not just any guy. She could so sell this to Ross. And to his wife.*

"An album?" Joanna was her new best friend.

Kylie laughed, "That's what he's working on."

"Tour?" She pressed.

"No. Nothing like that yet. But he is planning a small showcase downtown in one of the clubs." While Kylie loved celebrating Jesse, because she was so proud of the progress he'd made, it was hard admitting that her success was, in part, because her star was hitched to his. Shooing away a wave of self-doubt, she wondered if she'd ever again have an identity that was not associated with the irresistible bad boy of rock. And she knew her name would always evoke his in the same sentence. So, with that fact firmly accepted, there was only one thing to do.

The road to seeing perfection, when you looked in the mirror, was only achievable when you learned to accept and love yourself. Especially the pieces with the jagged edges that didn't quite fit in. Her time in therapy with Claire had shown her that. She loved who she had become through choosing to walk in different shoes than she was raised in. And now, here she was, nowhere near standard model weight, and it *was* her relationship with Jesse that allowed her to share with other women that you don't have to be starved to perfection to have an amazing man by your side. You can be healthy both inside and out by listening to your body and not trying to fit into Madison Avenue's plastic mold.

Maybe out there, some young girl ready to stick her finger down her throat or binge and take laxatives would not destroy their body and their self-esteem, because she, at size fourteen, was truly happy, and deeply loved by a man who was on a poster on their bedroom wall.

And if that is what being hitched to Jesse's star brought into the world, then it was okay to have her success and identity wrapped up in his. *Maybe that is why our paths crossed,* she wondered.

· · · · · ·

"Was that a memory with your grandfather that you'd been conscious of before today?" Claire watched Jesse rustle his spiky hair as he thought about what he'd just experienced.

"No. I had no clue he tried to have me taken away from my parents." He shook his head. "No clue at all."

"And how does that make you feel?" She crossed her legs the other way. The little bit of toe cleavage exposed at the top of her beige pump.

"Loved by my grandparents. At least someone had my best interests at heart. But also pissed as shit at my parents. I was a little kid. I depended on them to take care of me. Make sure I was safe. And they just sucked at it. They really did."

"Are you ready to forgive them?" Claire asked.

"Ya know, Dr. S., I just need to process this all so that I can let go of the bad energy. But I need to understand it. I need to understand who they were back then. I really want to be able to move forward."

"I'm sensing that you're questioning if you'll be able to."

"I'm angry that my parents didn't get me help when I was little, that nobody even talked to me to see if I was okay. I'm angry that my father put his band before me and I'm really pissed that my mom put him before me. My grandparents saw my decline, the change in my personality and they tried to step in. We saw that today with what I remembered. But again, my parents wouldn't do what was in my best interests. They should have let my grandparents take me until they got their shit together." Jesse shook his head, his fingers slowly raking through his hair. "I remember doing drugs at eleven or twelve, hoping my father would accept me, pay attention to me, let me in. That was how I tried to bond with the man."

Claire remained silent as Jesse gathered his thoughts.

"They couldn't help me because they couldn't even help themselves," was his assessment. "A lot to think about." Jesse started gathering up his stuff. "Oh, hey, I'm going to miss a few sessions. I'll be here for the next two and then I'm going to miss three sessions."

"Traveling?" She asked, pushing her glasses up the bridge of her nose.

"To London. To record. This amazing opportunity to record at Abbey Road just fell into my lap and that's just a dream come true for any musician."

"How long will you be gone?"

"I've got the studio space for three weeks and then when I come home, I've got to prepare for a gig, so I think I'll probably miss three sessions."

"Okay, let me mark you out on my calendar. Shall we get in one more regression before you go?"

"Absolutely." He nodded. "And can I put you with a plus one on the guest list for my gig? It's going to be a small acoustic showcase downtown at The Bowery Ballroom. Like five hundred people."

"I'd love to come see you play," Claire smiled at her patient, her shoulder dipping slightly. "That sounds like a very intimate setting." Her tone softened.

"Absolutely. A lot of audience interaction. I'll get really good feedback immediately on the new material. Will this be the first time you've seen me live?"

Claire nodded.

Laughing, "You get Jesse tamed."

Watching her nostrils flare as she sharply exhaled, he wondered if that meant something.

. . . . . .

Big Brothers Big Sisters of NYC's Big Night Out became a paparazzi-worthy event the moment former Miss New Jersey, Kylie Martin, and her plus one showed up. Wandering around the casino-themed night, Kylie spotted Joanna Tivoli, looking ravishing and bored in a red side-drape, plunge gown.

"Come, I'll introduce you to Joanna Tivoli, the head of the Women's Division of FACES USA. I'll bet she's a lot nicer to me with you here." She steered him by the arm through the crowd.

"She didn't like you?"

"She thinks I'm fat."

Stopping abruptly and turning to face her, Jesse let his eyes walk slowly and deliberately over Kylie, lingering on her full breasts. "Is she the one in the red?"

Kylie nodded.

"Lay my cheek on your amazing soft, full tits or ride a bicycle frame? I could ask any man in this room and the result would be the same–her skinny ass would be going home alone. The bitch better not dis you again."

"Come on, Prince Charming," she led him to Joanna.

As cool as people tried to act, both men and women alike, could not help but be starstruck in the presence of Jesse Fucking Winslow. Joanna Tivoli was no different. She stammered, she giggled and she looked positively green with jealousy at the way Jesse touched and looked at Kylie.

It didn't take long for Johnny to find them with Ross Eggleston, his wife, Marla, and their daughter, Sarah, in tow. At their heels, the event photographer was both in shock and awe to come upon Jesse Winslow and took Johnny's direction as he set-up the photo op for the Egglestons, Kylie, Jesse, and himself.

Kylie couldn't take her eyes off Sarah's skeletal limbs. This beautiful little girl was doing this to herself. *Willingly.* It wasn't like Geneviève, who was ill and couldn't fend for herself against people who treated her like worthless garbage. Kylie wanted to help Sarah love herself. But what could she say and this certainly wasn't the time or place. But maybe if Ross Eggleston hired her, she'd have the opportunity to have those conversations with her. To tell her about her journey. Let her know that once she, herself, was pageant girl thin and that she wasn't happy being constrained by others' ideals. And that while weight might always be a struggle for her, there was no comparison to the struggle and pain of starvation.

Ross and Johnny gravitated toward Kylie after the introductions were made. Smoothly, Jesse stepped out, engaging Joanna and the Eggleston women in conversation, who clearly were in seventh heaven, feeling that they had gotten the better part of the deal.

"I told you she was stunning," Johnny oozed confidence when he spoke to Ross.

"You are a very beautiful woman, Kylie," Ross agreed. "Johnny has told you what we are looking to do. Obviously, there's a problem within Northern Lights and the Northern Lights family," he began, glancing at his daughter.

Kylie began to speak, her voice strong, "Mr. Eggleston, the problem has become so universal that it is heartbreaking to see young girls and women robbed of their self-esteem because they don't fit what is, frankly, an unhealthy dynamic. Honestly, the best thing in the world that happened to me was losing my Miss New Jersey title because of the weight I'd gained. Everyone thought I was ruining my life, but it didn't feel that way to me. It felt like one-thousand pounds of pressure to be perfect had been lifted off me. I got into therapy, started looking at what made me happy and what didn't, and I began working out with a trainer who understood I needed to feel beautiful on the inside first." She looked over at Jesse, "And I'm in a really loving relationship with a man who understands that when you get to the darkest depths, you either fight your way back to the surface or you die."

Ross just stood there for a moment. "Help us do something great."

"It would be my pleasure," she smiled.

"We start in two weeks."

"I'll be ready." Smiling, she put a hand on Johnny's arm. "Well, I'll let you gentlemen hammer out what needs to be hammered out, and, in the meantime, I'd love to come down to your offices, meet everyone and get a better feel for things."

Out of the corner of her eye, Kylie could see Johnny Spinelli counting the cash. He'd hit the jackpot without even playing a single casino game.

As they walked toward the buffet and table area, Kylie scanned the room for Jesse who had taken off with Joanna and the Eggleston family, as the two men walked off.

"Well, what a surprise seeing you here," he whispered into her ear.

Turning toward the voice, she plastered a smile on her face as bright as her teeth, "Blaise, how are you?"

"Not so happy at the moment, Ms. Martin."

"Why is that?" Kylie played innocent. *How fucking fast does news travel in this industry?* she wondered.

"I understand you're going to be spending some time in Alaska and Australia."

"So it seems." She looked over his shoulder, still scanning for Jesse.

"No one would look at you twice when you were just that fat girl who left the pageant circuit, disgraced. I saved you," he hissed, a plume of the alcohol on his breath making Kylie's nose twitch.

"Blaise, I thank you for having the confidence in me and for taking a chance. I have done nothing but make you money. The clients have been pleased with the work I've done and I have represented Siren with the utmost professionalism. There are no exclusivity clauses in my contract and nothing that precludes me from accepting assignments through other agencies. And you know, for the most part, models are with multiple agencies, so that they can keep working. I'm not doing anything different than ninety percent of the models you represent."

"Yeah, but I took you when no one else would. Now that you're a novelty because you're Jesse Winslow's chubby girlfriend, yeah, everyone wants to make a quick buck off you before he dumps your fat ass. The minute he has the chance he'll trade you for a couple of grams of coke and you'll deserve it because bitches like you have no loyalty."

As soon as the last syllable of loyalty was out of his mouth, there was a hand on his chest driving him back into the wall.

"What did you just call her?"

The air was knocked out of Blaise, robbing him of the ability to respond. Jesse moved in like a panther, nose to nose with his adversary. "Don't you ever speak to her like that again. Do you understand me? You address her with the respect she deserves."

"Jesse, don't." Kylie was by his side trying to block people from seeing what was happening. She put a hand on his arm and with slight pressure let him know he needed to take his hand off Blaise's chest.

"Blaise, after what you've said to me tonight, you don't deserve the opportunity to represent me. I gave you credit for being a smart businessman, but evidently I was wrong. I'd actually like to thank you for your lack of professionalism this evening. You've made it very clear to me that I do not want my name or my career associated with you." Taking Jesse's arm with her hand, she turned to her boyfriend and said, "Shall we?" Indicating that she was ready to leave.

With sufficient distance between them and the Siren exec, Jesse gave her a smile. "Toots, you were brilliant."

"I really was, wasn't I? I had this flash of Geneviève in my head and how she was controlled by men after she lost Bruno and I just had to do this for her," she paused, "and me." They walked a few more steps, "Thank you for coming to my defense."

"Well, you didn't need it and frankly, you handled it a lot better than I did. I just reacted and went into testosterone-protect mode. No one is going to disrespect you like that in my presence. But, Toots, you showed me tonight, no one is going to abuse you and get away with it, whether I'm there or not."

Kylie laughed, "People should know better. Don't fuck with New Jersey chicks. And you really don't want to fuck with a pageant girl. We will eviscerate you and you'll think we just gave you the solution to world peace."

"Damn, you're hot," he whispered in her ear.

"Let's find Johnny and the Eggleston's and say goodnight. I think I've had enough for one evening."

"I don't know, I think you could still take a few inches."

"Just a few?" She mocked sadness.

Holding up a hand, he wiggled his fingers, "When I pluck you like a six-string." As they made their way across the space, Jesse slung an arm across Kylie's shoulders, pulling her into his side. "I keep getting hard just thinking about how you handled him. You are so badass." He kissed her temple, just as they approached Johnny, Joanna, and the Egglestons.

"There they are," Johnny smiled as they approached. "We were just discussing the trip. We leave for Alaska in two weeks."

"I've never been. I'm excited to go there. I understand it's very beautiful. And that the men are burly and hot." She jabbed Jesse in the ribs with her elbow and laughed.

"I'm gonna get dumped for a salmon fisherman, I know it," he laughed and everyone joined him.

"Come, join us," Ross offered.

"I'd love to. I hear it's gorgeous. But I'm going to be in London for a few weeks recording."

"With the band?" Sarah asked.

"No. This is some solo work I've been doing. It's for my next album. When you guys get back from Australia, I'm doing a small showcase show at The Bowery Ballroom downtown. I'll make sure you're all added to the guest list."

"Can I bring a friend?" Sarah piped in.

Jesse smiled at the teen. "I'll personally make sure you've got a plus one, Sarah."

As Kylie watched her boyfriend make the teen swoon, she hoped that Sarah would be with them in Alaska and Australia, at least part of the time, so that she could have the opportunity to really talk to the teen and maybe help her find the path to healing herself.

· · · · · ·

Rolling over, even in her sleep she knew she needed to savor every moment feeling him next to her. She was going to miss his warmth, the funny little noises he made in his sleep and the talking, the conversations he had aloud with the people in his dreams. So, when her arm found cold, empty space, she woke from her half-sleep state.

Under the door was a slit of light coming from down the hall. *What was he doing up at this hour?* Rubbing her eyes, she grabbed her phone from the night table to see the time. There were still two and a half hours until the alarm before she had to get dressed and begin a long day that would end in Anchorage, Alaska.

Swinging her long legs off the bed, Kylie headed down the hall on her journey to find out what had Jesse up at this hour. His journal was open and there were lines of lyrics, crossed out words and margin notes. He sat playing solitaire with his ancient deck of cards, she had heard them snapping to the table before even entering the room.

"Hey, babe," she said softly to let him know she'd come up behind him.

Turning and smiling, he extended an arm to invite her into his lap. "Hey, Toots."

"What's going on?"

"I had an idea for a song. Got the first two verses out and was just thinking where, if anywhere, I wanted to take it. So, just clearing my mind with a game of solitaire."

"We've got two and a half hours till my alarm, play solitaire after I leave. Come and snuggle." Kissing the tip of his nose, she rose from his lap and headed back to bed, hearing his footsteps almost immediately after hers.

"I'm going to miss you," she whispered once in the comfort of his spoon and strong arms.

"We're not getting out of bed for a month after we both get back."

Kylie laughed. "You really do have this John and Yoko thing."

Hearing the normalized pattern of his breathing, she knew not to wait for a response and snuggled in deeper into his arms for what would be the last time for more than a month.

· · · · · ·

Making sure the doorman had loaded the last of her luggage into the Town Car, he opened the back door for her.

"I'm going to miss you, Toots. I want to get in that car and go with you." He took her face in both hands, kissing each corner of her mouth before going in for a deep kiss. "A picture a day," he reminded her.

Kylie nodded-unable to speak-and ducked into the car. Waving goodbye, she tried to capture a mental image as he stood on the sidewalk watching her leave.

Pulling out her phone, she typed the text message, **Missing you already, your (pageant) Queen of Hearts** and sent off the first photo to him.

She could barely see him, half a block away, when he reached into his pocket for his phone and opened the text.

Smiling as he viewed the first of many daily pictures. This one, handwritten lyrics on a swath of a page in his journal with the Queen of Hearts from his deck sitting diagonally across the page and she'd added a vintage, vignette sepia overlay to frame the image.

He was still smiling as he walked back into the building.

*She certainly is my Queen of Hearts,* he mused.

# Chapter 14

"Yeah. I miss her like crazy, but I'm being really productive and focused. I'm getting ready to leave, and once I'm in London, I'm going to be eating, sleeping, and breathing that recording time. So, I'm really doing okay." Shifting on the couch to pull out his phone, he smiled at yesterday's picture. It was a selfie, her hair sweeping across her face in the wind with majestic snowcapped mountains as her backdrop. Her smile matched his as he wished he were exploring the rugged landscape with her.

Claire crossed her legs from left to right. "Since you're going to be missing three appointments, how do you feel about doing Skype sessions when you're in London?"

"Yeah. Yeah. I think that's a great idea. The time difference might chew us up a little."

"What if we kept it Wednesday mornings, same time for you, and I'll just adjust on my end, so that you have some consistency. Can you comfortably commit to that?"

Nodding, Jesse affirmed. "I like that. I can do that. With being overseas and Kylie almost impossible to communicate with, having this as a constant is a good thing."

Claire smiled. "I'm glad you think so and I have to agree. You've been sober for quite a while now…"

"Two hundred and thirty-nine days," he interrupted.

"Two hundred and thirty-nine days," she repeated. "You are closing in on nine months, Jesse."

"I feel so good, Doc. So good. I've really gotta thank you. I know it's a bit unconventional what we're doing. But it's working and nothing has worked like this before."

Unexpectedly springing from the couch, he closed the space between them in two strides, leaning down to wrap her in a hug. She stood as his arms went around her, falling into his somewhat awkward embrace, her head to his shoulder. Giving her a quick, tight squeeze before placing his hands on her shoulders to disengage, Jesse moved back to his space on the couch, leaving Claire reeling, her emotions swirling too fast to identify.

"So, I was thinking I'd like to get one last regression in before I ship out," he broke the ungainly moment with an amped-up declaration.

"Let's get started." She straightened her skirt, hit the darkener button on the shades and began talking him through the guided meditation. When his head snapped to the left, it appeared as if he were intently listening or staring at something.

"It's more than just wolves, Daniel. Did you hear that cry?" He craned his neck, slowly surveying from left to right.

Claire wished he wasn't wearing the RGB glasses so that she could see his eyes.

"There. There it is again."

"Where are you?" Claire asked.

"We are in the hills above Anathoth."

"Can you tell me where Anathoth is? What country?"

"We are in Roman Judea." The hairs on Claire's neck began to do a line dance. *Israel under Roman rule?* The psychiatrist wondered.

"Who is we?" She asked.

"I am with Daniel."

"Is he your friend, brother?"

"He is my spiritual mentor."

"What year are you in?"

"It is 46."

"AD?" Claire scribbled notes as quickly as she could.

"Yes. It is common era."

"And you are in what is now known as Israel? Is that correct?"

"Yes."

"Is Jesus preaching?" Claire asked, quickly Googling the dates of Jesus's birth and death.

"No. The Great One has been gone for years now."

Corroboration on the existence of Christ. Claire's hands were shaking.

"Did your paths ever cross?"

"No. But he was known by all."

"Who is ruling Israel now?"

"Rome."

"But who specifically has local authority for Rome." She stared at the Wiki chart on her tablet. *There's no way he'll know this.*

"The current procurator is Tiberius Julius Alexander, a traitor to the Jews and to his own heritage."

The chills running up and down her arms stunned the psychiatrist into silence. *There is no way in Hell, Jesse Winslow, bad boy rocker, knows the specifics of Roman history in the middle east. Yes, he could've identified a major, well-known figure like Pontius Pilate, but Tiberius Julius Alexander-not likely.*

Looking to trip him up, she threw out a red herring, "And he reports to Caligula in Rome," her intonation making it a statement of fact.

Jesse shook his head, "No, Caligula was murdered. Claudius now rules Rome."

"I see," was all she said. He was right. After a moment, she asked, "Who are you?" realizing she had never gotten a name.

"I am David."

"What is your full name?"

"David Ben-Abraham."

"And you are a rabbinical student?"

"Always. As God's teachings are eternal, but I already have a ministry of my own."

"And where is that?" she asked, poised to Google.

"It started in Sebastia. Where I'm from. But there are followers throughout the land."

She typed the name into her tablet and looked up at her patient, just as his head whipped around.

"There it is. I heard it again, Daniel. It's coming from that direction." Jesse lifted his arm and pointed at the wall. "Come, we must go. It sounds like a child to me."

*The terrain is rough on our sandaled feet as we utilize the near full moon's light to guide us around rocks and low scrub bushes. The wind howls over the hills and I wonder if that's what I hear and my mind is just playing tricks with me. For a child to be left alone in these hills at night would surely be a death sentence.*

*Quietly, Daniel and I proceed, careful not to alert animals to our presence. Stopping on a ridge, I listen as the wind blows her song through the cedar tree branches, her falsetto as ethereal as the moon's glow.*

*"It must've been the wind," I conclude as we continue to follow the stars and head north toward Sebastia.*

*Falling into easy conversation, we follow the moonlit path, suddenly halted by a blood-curdling scream that is most definitely human...and female.*

*Silently, I point to my left, indicating the cry came from off the path to our north. Changing tracks immediately, we begin to climb the hill, attempting to keep the rustling of our clothes to a minimum. Looking all around us, there is still no one in our line of sight, either close or at a distance, that could have made that sound. That sound. I know if I don't find its source that it will haunt me in dreams forever.*

*Daniel halts me by putting an arm across my chest and gestures with his head to the right. Crouched and growling a dark wolf bares his teeth. Behind him in a bush is a girl. I'm not sure if the animal has her captive or if it is protecting the teen from us.*

*Daniel raises his club, assuming a protective stance as I call out, "Are you hurt?"*

*Shaking her head, "No," she calls out. "I think he's protecting me."*

*"Was that you screaming before?"*

*"Yes, there were snakes. But he killed them."*

*"If my friend lowers his club, will he allow you to walk out to us?" I call to her.*

*"Yes. I think so." She pauses, "Promise you won't hurt me?"*

*"Yes, you have my promise."*

*Nodding to Daniel, he lowers the club and the girl begins to make her way out of the sharp-edged confines of the bushy cedar.*

*"I am David and this is my mentor, Daniel," I indicate pointing to my companion. "What is your name?"*

*"I am Rachel." As she attempts to disengage her snagged garments from the branches, the ripping fabric tears the night's silence, evoking the wolf to bare his teeth. Yet, the imposing animal does not move.*

*It is then that I notice she is here in the wilderness wearing only kethōneth, her undergarments, and there is no sign of her simlāh or any type of outer garment. Quickly stripping off my me'īl, I toss her the cloak as she emerges from the bush, so that she can immediately wrap in it.*

*I remain in a stunned silence, stuck to my place in the dirt as Rachel walks toward me, a vision of the night that makes me wonder if perhaps I am hallucinating. Wrapped in my robe, she seems to float on the darkness, with the wild animal following at her heels. The first thing I notice are her large, wide-set dark eyes as they are almost almond-shaped in appearance and profoundly expressive. They are saying something to me, of that I am sure, telling me a story in a language I have yet to learn. As she nears, I take in the rest of her, admiring her thick ebony hair as it falls past her shoulders, framing her oval face and small, upturned nose, but what I wasn't expecting was her smile, soft, sweet, and shy.*

*What was this beautiful young woman doing out here in the dangerous night? Beyond wild animals, bands of thieves roam these hills regularly.*

*"Rachel, why are you out here alone in the night? This is no place for you to be."*

*"I have been exiled by my family. I've brought disgrace upon them*

*and I am destroying the chances of my sister making a match and being married off. My family can't afford that. My presence puts them all at risk."*

*"Why have they exiled you?" The concern in Daniel's voice is evident.*

*"Because it is too much of a journey, and loss of harvesting time, to take me to the leper colony."*

*Daniel and I look at one another silently. I can tell by his expression that neither of us can breathe in this moment. Having recently visited a leper colony to pray with its occupants for renewed health and healing, there was something we were missing in the beauty standing before us.*

*"Rachel, who told you that you have leprosy?" Daniel's tone remains benevolent and paternal.*

*"Rabbi Ezekial and everyone who knows me." Her head hangs in shame.*

*Rabbis are the healers in most villages and their word is rarely disputed. Yet, this girl standing before us appears to be the picture of health.*

*"Rachel, Daniel and I have helped heal many of our followers, some with leprosy, so maybe we can help you. Is there a diseased area you would be comfortable showing us?"*

*Slightly lifting her kethōneth, she exposes her right leg, a dark red, raised plaque is visible in the moonlight. The patch covers a significant portion of her calf and appears to have an almost silver scale.*

*"Does it itch?"*

*She nods.*

*"And you have it in other places?" Daniel asks.*

*"Mostly my arms and legs, but there are some spots on my back,*

*too." Again, she hangs her head in disgrace.*

*Looking at Daniel, "The Essennoi."*

*He nods.*

*"Rachel, I think we can bring you to some people who can cure you. We will have to go to Jerusalem and borrow some donkeys and a wagon and then it will take a few days. Would you come with us?"*

*"I don't..." she begins.*

*"You will die if we leave you here alone. Please, let us help you. Tonight, we will build a fire to stay warm and we can leave in the morning."*

*"Can you really cure me so that I can live among people again?"*

*Her eyes are wide with hope, and in my heart, I already know I will do whatever I can... call in all the favors owed to me, just to try and give her back all that has been robbed from her.*

*"Yes. We will be taking you to stay with some people in Qumran, on the shores of Lake Asphaltitus. You need to do exactly as they say and you will be cured."*

*"Forever?"*

*I hate to dash her hope. "For a while, at least. And if it returns, you can be healed again."*

*Next to the fire the wolf slumbers. "How long has the animal been with you?" Daniel inquires.*

*"Since the edge of my town. He's been very protective of me."*

*"I've never seen a wild animal be so docile and protect a human in this way."*

*"Perhaps this is not a mere animal," I suggest and the beast lifts his head, looking me directly in the eye, before resuming his slumber.*

*In the morning, the decision is made to split up, with me and Rachel heading to Jerusalem for transportation and Daniel returning to Sebastia in preparation for the upcoming holidays. As we go to leave, the wolf turns and begins to follow Daniel, as if understanding the older man needs him, and in that moment, I know my mentor will return home safely.*

*By the light of day, Rachel is even more beautiful than she had appeared in the moonlight and I find myself trying to banish bad feelings toward her family for exiling her, knowing she would most likely die in the wilderness.*

*"Why are you saving me?" She looks at me out of the corner of her eye, too shy with me yet to be as bold as she might like.*

*"Because I can." I smile down at her.*

*"Are you always that sure of yourself, David?"*

*"Yes, generally I am."*

*She's silent a moment before asking me, "Do you have a lot of followers in your ministry?"*

*"It's growing."*

*"And why should they follow you? What makes the word you preach so different?"*

*"Ah, a skeptic." I tease, "Are you going to make this trip interminably long?"*

*"Well, if you can't answer my questions..." she trails off, looking up at me with a side-glance and her sweet smile.*

*"What I preach is a doctrine of love. There is but one God and He is a God of love here to guide us through this lifetime. I am a student of the Torah and many other scrolls and at the heart of all these writings is goodness, kindness, and love. Love is the music of the universe and the one and only truth."*

*She surprises me with what she does next. While she maintains looking straight ahead, I can see a small smile curl the corners of her mouth as she slips her hand into mine. The second surprise is the immediate warmth that floods my chest and causes a glowing feeling, as if a mint-herb salve has been applied. Silently, I thank God for his intervention in ensuring that my path crossed with Rachel's. My lips join hers in a smile as I realize that our paths will never diverge again. All that is occurring has already been written.*

*Cresting the ridge at Bethphage, Rachel gasps at the expanse of lower hills and valleys before us.*

*"Is that Jerusalem, David?"*

*The excitement in her voice makes me think she is going to charge down the hill to get there as fast as her legs permit. Studying her beautiful face, I can feel her joy as she takes in the sight below for the very first time.*

*"Yes, that is Jerusalem." The pull of the energy, even from this distance, is tangible, the power reserve of thousands of years of prayer and actuated thoughts. Above the city, the air seems to shimmer and I wonder if Rachel, too, is picking up the vibration.*

*Pointing into the valley, her hand sweeps from left to right, "There's an aura. Do you see it, David?"*

*I nod and she looks pleased that she is not alone in what she is witnessing.*

*As we descend toward the Mount of Olives, where the view of Jerusalem is much better and more prominent, Rachel talks non-stop, her excitement eliciting an energy surge.*

*"I've never been to a city. Will we be spending time here for me to see the market? King Herod's temple? Whom will we meet? Do you have family here? Friends? Are we spending the night? Will people stone me for what I look like?" The questions go on and on.*

*"You will be meeting some of my followers. They are friends. They will welcome you and accept you. Tonight, we will stay here and tomorrow we will continue our journey to Qumran. We will leave fed and rested and they will make sure we have food and water for our journey."*

*It is nearly dusk when we enter the lower city, quickly ingested into the crowd that moves rapidly down the maze of stone alleyways. I want to wrap my hand around Rachel's so as not to lose her and make sure she keeps up the pace, but as she is not my wife, I know not to publicly touch her.*

*"Come," I command. "We need to make it to market before they close, so that we can get you some appropriate clothes for the journey, and food." Leading her through the maze of tables and carts, at our first stop we visit the wares of a member of my flock, Joseph, and his wife, Miriam.*

*Bowing their heads to me, "Rabbi," they greet. "We weren't expecting to see you for a few days."*

*From the corner of my eye I can see Rachel's expression as the couple shows deference to me.*

*Pulling Miriam aside, I explain the situation and she takes Rachel, disappearing through an arched, stone doorway. Using the opportunity, I move on to other merchants, following the bold aromas to an area of carts filled with salted fish, olives, fruit, and wine, procuring what we need and return just as Miriam arrives with Rachel, now dressed in new and appropriate clothes, as well as new sandals. I immediately notice the longer length of the sleeves on her simlāh, covering all her skin eruptions. Wrapped in twine are additional clothes for her to take. It is impossible not to notice the buoy of confidence these new garments give her, as she finally has a reprieve from strangers' stares.*

*Bidding them goodbye, once again we find ourselves deep in the maze of alleyways. It is dark now and I detect Rachel's discomfort as her senses are bombarded by this strange and crowded place. Walking very close to me, she keeps reaching for my fingers.*

*"We're almost there," I reassure her by giving her fingers a squeeze before letting go.*

*Tapping on the plain wooden door in a succession of three quick knocks, we hear two knocks from the inside and we complete the sequence with four more raps before the door swings open.*

*Again, the occupants express the same sentiment as Joseph and his wife. Bowing their heads, "Rabbi, we were not expecting you. Please, come in." Ushering us in, they quickly shut and bolt the heavy door behind us, as I hand off to our host the parcels of food we'd purchased to our host. Showing us to pillows on the floor, we take our place among a small group of my followers, Rachel by my side, which already feels familiar and right.*

*"We will be leaving tomorrow for Qumran," I explain, "and Rachel will be staying with the Essennoi for several weeks."*

*She turns to me, surprised at the length of time. "Will you be with me?"*

*I can see the fear of the unknown in her sweet almond eyes and I take her hand, an act that doesn't go unnoticed by the other occupants of the small room, and give it a quick squeeze. "I will be back for you. I promise." Holding her eye contact, I let the sincerity of my words settle in.*

*Two women bring in platters of food and we empty skins of wine into clay tumblers to begin an evening meal lively with discourse, as well as news of the latest squabbles between Jews and the Roman guard.*

*"They've been looking for you, David." Simon, a farmer in his late twenties, informs me.*

*I laugh. "Well, I've been a little scarce. What have you told them?"*

*"That you were not in the city and were in the countryside with your followers."*

*"Go on," I urge.*

*"They were pleased to hear that. I don't think they take numbers of followers as seriously when they are not within the walls of Jerusalem. It's like they are someone else's problem."*

*"They shouldn't be a problem at all. It shouldn't matter to them how many followers you have." Appearing angry, Ephraim pulls at his long, dark beard.*

*"No, it should not. We are peaceful and keep to ourselves. But as long as Tiberius Julius Alexander is the procurator of Judea, we will not rest easy. His inability to accept his own heritage has turned him into the worst kind of self-loather, making him a danger to every Jew in the region."*

*"Just be careful, David," Simon's wife, Leah, warns, her concern for me touching and apparent.*

*"I will," I promise, before adding, "and Rachel and I will be leaving at dawn. They won't even know I was here."*

*Leah sets up a makeshift room in an alcove for Rachel to sleep and Simon and I carry in a divan which Leah dresses with thin quilts.*

*"I'll be in the next room," I reassure her. "I just need to go out for a little bit to check on some of my people."*

*"Can I please come with you?" Her eyes are wide, pleading.*

*Shaking my head, I explain, "No. You need to stay here where it is safe for you."*

*"From tonight's conversation, it doesn't sound as if it is safe for you either. I'm coming with you." She protests, rising from the divan.*

*"No, Rachel. I cannot permit that." My voice comes out sterner than I intended.*

*Her nostrils flare in anger and she rises onto her toes, as if the extra inch will make her more intimidating. "I can take care of myself."*

*"Of that, I am sure." I smile at her. "But when you are with me and I am responsible for your well-being, as I am, then you must obey my rules."*

*Her face is a study in emotion, the prevalent one being anger. "Just go," she hisses, turning her back on me as I leave the house.*

*Looking up to her alcove from the alleyway, I can see her tucked at the window watching me and hope she doesn't follow.*

*With my head down, so as not to bring attention to myself, I negotiate the dusty alleyways of the Lower City until I reach my destination. As the tenth man to join, we now have the quorum necessary to begin our prayers. At the end of the traditional readings, we pray for our people and our city and our land. We pray for our freedom, we pray for the love of God to show us the way to be good and caring and just. And as the service ends, I silently ask God to help me restore Rachel to health so that she can know a life filled with acceptance and joy.*

*It is nearing midnight as I make my way back to Simon's. I can hear his footsteps gaining on me and feel his hatred, without turning around. When he grabs my arm, and spins my back into the stone wall, I am not surprised. Face to face, it takes me only a moment to place him. His name is Cassius Petronius and he ranks high in Tiberius Julius Alexander's order. His fist smashes into my cheekbone before I even have a chance to raise my arms in defense.*

*"Ben Abraham," he addresses me. "I was told you were gone from Jerusalem. Yet, here you stand before me, scurrying like a rat down this alleyway."*

*"I am only here until dawn. Merely passing through."*

*"And why were you out at this hour?" The official demands.*

*"Praying for the well-being of a member of the synagogue."*

*"I should have you arrested for meeting to cause dissent," he*

*threatens me.*

*"No dissent. Just prayers to God." I keep my voice soft in the hopes that I can bring down his negative energy level.*

*"A heathen Jewish God."*

*Slamming me against the wall again to ensure I know who is in charge, he spits, "Get out of here."*

*Continuing on my way, turning down unnecessary alleyways so that my true location stays hidden, I arrive at my destination certain that I have not been followed. Once inside Simon's home, I take a deep breath, leaning against the inside of the door and touch my cheek, feeling the split in my skin. As quietly as I am able, I walk past Rachel's alcove so as not to wake her and sit down on the divan that has been set out for me.*

*I sit for a moment, disheartened. Saddened by the hatred between cultures. Are we really that different that we cannot accept and learn from one another? I remove my sandals. And how can a family turn away their child into the wild to die because they see her as a misfortune and not a blessing? Disrobing from my simlāh, I fold it and place it next to my sandals.*

*Swinging my legs onto the divan, I close my eyes, eyelids heavy with grit and exhaustion. The day had been very long and the next one will be upon us too soon. It feels as if only a few minutes have passed when I hear her scurrying about. Opening my eyes and trying to get them to acclimate in the dark, I feel her before I actually see her. With a rag of cool water, she gently dabs at the cut on my face, cleaning away dirt and dried blood. Her movements are soft and deliberate and whatever anger she had felt toward me earlier in the evening, has now been replaced by concern and care.*

*Dipping the rag again in the cool basin, she wrings it free of excess water and brings it back up, gently cleaning my forehead and brushing my hair away from my face. I lie there silently as she finishes cleansing the wound and dips the rag back into the basin for fresh water. When she resumes, she slowly swipes the side of my neck and I can no longer maintain my silence. A low moan escapes and then a second one when she runs the wet cloth down the other side of my neck. The absence of sleeves on my kethōneth have left my shoulders bare, waiting for her to continue as Rachel begins a stroking motion down my arms.*

*When she finishes washing both my arms, she returns the cloth to the basin and moves it out of the way. Returning to the side of the bed, she stands there a moment looking down at me, her arms hanging at her sides, before she silently crawls in next to me.*

*"Rachel, you can't stay here." The warmth of her body against mine is instantly maddening, igniting a fight within myself not to take her in my arms. "You can't."*

*"I'm not leaving, so you'd better move over and give me a proper amount of space."*

*"Rachel," I try to reason, "we are not married or even betrothed."*

*"David," she lies her head on my chest, as if she's done it a thousand times before. "If you keep talking, we won't get any sleep." And with a small movement of her body, she molds herself to me, the fit so perfect, I can't imagine how I've existed until now without it. Without her. And it is that instant, I know I have neither been complete nor realized how alone I've truly been.*

· · · · · ·

*At first light, we head east toward the city of Tiberius, leaving from Jerusalem with food, water and wine.*

*"Once we get there," I explain, "we're actually going to go a slight bit out of our way and head north."*

*"Why are we doing that?" she asks, looking up at me.*

*"We are going to spend the night in Jericho. There are people there who will give us lodging and food, but tonight we will only go as far as*

*the Ascent of Admummin. Tomorrow we will make our descent from there to Jericho."*

*"What is it like?" she asks, as we walk the road alongside caravans and traders, pilgrims heading in the other direction toward Jerusalem.*

*"It's a lush garden in the middle of the desert. The palm trees produce the sweetest dates you will ever eat," I laugh. "If you can get them off your fingers, they are so fresh and sticky. And the waters from Elisha's Spring are cleansing and pure. I think you will like the city." Smiling, I turn to her, "I will enjoy showing it to you."*

*Slipping her hand in mine, we continue along. "Why are there so many Roman sentry points?"*

*"That is for our protection. Because this road is so heavily used for transporting goods, it is known for bandits and theft."*

*Hearing that, she squeezes my hand tighter and I know she is thinking about the gash under my eye and wondering if the Romans are there to protect us or just the opposite.*

*"Do not worry. God walks with us," I assure her.*

*As we reached our inn that evening, Rachel tugs on my hand, stopping me before we enter. "I want to stay with you."*

*Shaking my head, "It would not be right to ruin your reputation." As much as I want to touch her, I know doing so would rob her of the chances for the future she deserves, once she is cured. I cannot let my selfish needs and desires for her, condemn her.*

*"Did you not like feeling the warmth of my body with yours last night."*

*Although we did nothing but lie together, her presence throughout the night robbed me of sleep as I yearned to feel her hair slip through my fingers and discover the soft curve of her breast. I ached to take a nipple in my mouth and suckle on her until she moaned from the painful pleasure. With my fingers, I wanted to test just how wet my sucking made her as I inserted one, then two, then three fingers into her, preparing her to become mine, so that I might fill her womb with my seed, again and again and again. When she begged me to let her rest, I would take her yet again, because I could, and because she was mine.*

*"I'm staying with you, David," she insists.*

*"God, help me," I mutter, knowing Rachel will find her way into my bed whether or not we rent one room or two. All I can do is pray for the self-control to not do to her, the things I ache to do.*

*Our rooms are next to one another, and as I barely drift off to sleep, exhausted from the exertion of the day's travel, she slips in next to me. Sighing at her relentless nature, I know there is no reason to verbally protest her arrival. It will do no good.*

*Like the night before, she molds her body to mine, finding the place where her head fits into the edge of my chest. Tonight, I let myself touch her hair, allowing long strands to run through my fingers, again and again, the repetitive motion surprisingly calming in the pitch-black room.*

*"David..."*

*"Yes?"*

*She lets out a small sigh before speaking again. "Is the reason you don't touch me because of my diseased skin? I don't think I'm contagious, no one in my family has caught it from me." She rushes on with her words, "I can understand that you don't want to touch me because I'm repulsive."*

*"Rachel, is that what you think?"*

*"I don't know what to think. I feel something between us, but maybe I'm just mistaking your kindness for something more than that. I'm not accustomed to people being kind to me. Usually they just stare and avoid me. People are afraid to touch me or be near me."*

*"People are fools." I hug her to me tighter, my heart hurting for what she has experienced in her short life. "Rachel, soon you will be*

*cured and you will be able to go on and be betrothed to a man your father selects for you. I cannot compromise you."*

*"Is what I feel between us real?" she presses, lifting her head to look at me.*

*With my other hand, I hold her chin. I want to lie and tell her no, that she is mistaking kindness for something more. But as her eyes come into focus in the dark night, I can't lie to her, and I nod.*

*"You are not imagining it."*

*Hearing her sharp intake of breath, I can feel the muscles in her face pull up and I know she is smiling down at me. Pulling on her chin, I guide her lips to mine. "I know I should not do this," I whisper against her warm, parted lips.*

*Knowing she has never been with a man before and that a kiss is all she will be experiencing tonight, I brush her lips softly with mine, not expecting the soft moan it elicits from her, a sound that shoots through me like a lightning bolt, arousing me to hardness.*

*Brushing my lips back with her own, she doesn't wait for me to kiss her again. What began as a soft meetings of our lips, begins to escalate rapidly into something more urgent and primal.*

*"Rachel, we need to stop."*

*She is breathless when she says, "I know, David, but I have never experienced anything that has felt this good or right. I know I must keep my virtue, but I do not want to stop kissing you." And with that, she climbs on top of me.*

*What we are doing has to cease before it takes us to a place of no return. I do not want her to feel my erection. We are both in long linen undergarments that start to bunch up between us, and I'm glad mine are still covering me almost to my knees. When she laid flat on top of me to continue kissing, I knew there was no way she wasn't feeling what my body was boldly saying, covering or no covering.*

*Taking a second to break from kissing, she pulls at her garment to smooth it down, so that it again covers her appropriately. Now with both our garments between us, I breathe slightly easier that we will be able to exhibit some sort of control.*

*With her lips hovering just above mine, I weave my fingers through her long wavy hair and pull her in for a deep kiss. Slightly lifting her body, she repositions herself on me, the tip of my erection poking at her sex.*

*"No, Rachel," I begin to protest, but she silences me with her lips and begins a slow motion of rocking, making my hardness feel like it was in the soft embrace of her sex's outer lips. Back and forth she moves on me, the linen of our undergarments rubbing us both into a frenzy. I ache to press myself into her, but don't, and just let her continue to stroke me with the motion.*

*"David," she calls my name.*

*"Rachel," I whisper back.*

*"Mmm, David."*

*Her guttural sound is almost enough to make me lose control, which I am fighting hard not to do, and failing miserably. Moving both my hands to her bottom, I stop her motion and press her down onto me, knowing my hardness is now pressing exactly where it needs to be to give her release.*

*"I wish you were inside me," her voice is quivering.*

*Totally killing me with her words, for I ache to pull away the linen barrier between us, and drive up into her hard as I fill her. Again and again and again.*

*Holding her to me tightly, I gently moved my hips, showing her what she was doing to me as I rub slowly on the outside of her sex. The sounds she makes in time with my movements are music, creating our unique story and urging me on to the next verse, so that I can be treated to more of our melody.*

*"This feels so good." Her face is buried in the crook of my neck.*

*"Mmm-hmm," is all I can say as I focus on what I am doing to her and to myself.*

*"Will you please let me feel you a little bit?" she asks, breathlessly. And I know just what she is asking of me.*

*Moving my hands from her bottom to the tops of her thighs, I spread her legs and I am rewarded with a gasp that makes me even harder. I then shift her, so the crown of my shaft is positioned on my side of my linen garment to enter her, pushing both garments inward. At first, I just rub gently on the outside, round and round at her opening, until she moans and quivers. Holding her down tightly on me, I raise my hips slightly until I feel her opening's edge surrounding the top of my tip.*

*"David..." She is shaking.*

*With my lips at her forehead, I ask, "Do you want me to stop?"*

*Almost violently, she shakes her head. "No. No. No."*

*Any more pressure and a portion of the crown will be just inside her. I know I should stop. To defile her is not right and not righteous and I cannot come to terms as to why it feels so right. With her.*

*As if reading my thoughts, "David, I know you want to stop because you do not want me to be an outcast. But I am already an outcast. You and Daniel and your friends are the only people I have felt comfortable with in as long as I can remember. What we are doing will not hurt me."*

*Holding her in place, because I am not ready to release the feeling that is binding us, I look up at her. "Rachel, I never want to hurt you. I'd rather hurt myself than hurt you."*

*"Then let me make this decision."*

*And as she presses herself down on me, I can feel her heat surrounding the top half of the crown. I let it remain there a moment, before pulling away and entering again. I don't go deeper, somehow convincing myself that just the tip of the head with two linen garments in the way isn't really violating her.*

*Pulling out again to hear her yearning sound for me, I once again press up, the fabric now wet. As I slip in, Rachel presses down, taking in the entire head and letting out a sensual moan. My entire crown can now feel her glorious heat and I ache for more.*

*"The linen is chafing me, David."*

*"We can't, Rachel."*

*"We already have, David. You have been inside me." She lifts herself, slipping me out of her with the motion and immediately making me ache to be surrounded by her again, craving the warmth. Even if it is only a small portion of me.*

*Moving her undergarment and mine out of the way, she then lowers herself back down to my body, repeating the motion she had begun with, placing me between her sex's outer lips and moving back and forth, stroking both the length of me and herself. Without the garments, the warmth and wetness coats me as she slides effortlessly and the friction between us escalates.*

*Roughly grabbing her hips, I stop her movement. "Rachel, this is as far as we go, for it is already too far." I am finally beginning to gain clarity.*

*"No. No." Shaking her head, her long hair coats my chest in a swirling motion that creates a storm which we are not weathering well.*

*Moving her back toward the base of my shaft and away from the offending head, I again press her down as hard as I can, knowing what the pressure will do to her already swollen sex, and hopefully causing this madness to stop. It takes only a few seconds before she begins to quake on top of me. Sliding my hands up from her hips to her waist and then her back, I don't let up on the pressure until she quiets and then I pull her down to my chest, hug her to me and softly kiss the top of her head.*

*We remain wordless, and in that moment, as the heady rush clears and my blood slows down, I am ashamed.*

*"Did you stop because I look like a monster?" her voice is choked.*

*"No. I stopped because it is my job to protect you. And I failed. And now you need protection from me."*

*"That is not true," she protests. "You did not hurt me."*

*What she doesn't see is that I did. I violated her in multiple ways. My actions were selfish and weak, and in the darkness of this small room, I fill the space with self-loathing. I am appalled.*

*But what I am most ashamed of is that I am fighting every inclination I possess not to flip her onto her back, at this very moment, and plunge into her deeply. For my pleasure, and my pleasure alone. I ache to pump her and fill her and leave her dripping of my seed. Again. And again. And again.*

*Sleep cannot come soon enough and I pray for salvation in the morning's light when we will resume our travels.*

· · · · · ·

*Jericho brings for us a similar experience to Jerusalem.*

*"David, you are so well-known and so loved. Your ministry must be quite a bit larger than you let on. Everyone knows you."*

*"It has grown over the past two years," I admit.*

*"And these women, the way they all look at you, even the married ones."*

*"How do they look at me?" I ask, laughing.*

*"They look at you like I feel."*

*"You feel the way you feel because I have been kind to you and I'm going to help you heal," I explain as we journey from Jericho to Qumran.*

*Smiling, she doesn't say anything, which is unusual for Rachel, I have discovered. Eventually she asks, "Why don't you heal me?"*

*"I am a mere rabbi, not a healer. That is not a gift I possess. Some do, but I am not one of them. But I am bringing you to people who can heal you. That is my role here."*

*Smiling again, she does not speak.*

*"What are you smiling at?" I ask, amused by her happy look.*

*"Don't you see you have healed me. Maybe not my skin, but my spirit. You have brought hope and love and acceptance and that has healed me."*

*I yearn to take this beautiful young woman in my arms and hold her to my chest. She knows what a fraud I am, trying to conceal the depths of my attraction and my feelings for her. I have lain with many women and had many others make their intentions for my affections known, but there never has been another Rachel. With her questioning, her spirit and her bravery, I am as captivated by her internal beauty as by her external. She has stirred in me a need I did not know existed, the need to not only share my life with God, but with a woman I can make my wife and the mother of my offspring. But I have kept her at arm's length the past few days, knowing I must do what is right for her.*

*It is a full day out of Jericho before we reach our destination at Qumran. Entering the central meeting place at the community hall, I can feel Rachel's tension.*

*As we wait for Mendel, an elder healer, to join us, I try and calm her. "The members of this yahad, this community, are very pacifistic. They serve one another and believe in a communal lifestyle. Their life is very simple and guided by both prayer and the work to transcribe scripture. It is just a short walk from the salt sea, Lake Asphaltitus."*

*Dressed in the white robes of this sect, Mendel enters the room and it is impossible not to feel the power of his energy.*

*"David ben Abraham, it is good to see you." He acknowledges Rachel with a nod of his head.*

*"My old friend, it is a blessing that we meet again. I have brought another friend, Rachel, to you, who is in need of your healing. I pray that you can help her and restore her to good health." I indicate for Rachel to come stand by me. "I'm going to show the healer now." And I asked her to remove her outer garment and push up her sleeves. Lifting the hem of her garment, she exposes the lesions on her legs. As I watch her face, it is clear to see her confidence wane. This disease has taken its toll on her spirit and I hurt watching her.*

*Mendel slowly circles Rachel, mindfully taking in the disturbances on her skin. Gesturing for me to follow him out of earshot, his prognosis is positive. He feels that he can help, but Rachel has to commit to stay with them for a month. He explains she will partake in a regimen that includes daily immersion in rain waters that they have stored in tanks. Once cleansed in the rain water, she will next be covered in mud and minerals and lie on white rock in what is known as the solarium, while the mixture completely dries. From there she will walk to the sea to scrub the mud and minerals from her body and float in the sea for an hour and then she will go back to the solarium for the remainder of the afternoon, lying naked on the white rocks until the sun falls behind the boulders' peaks.*

*At night, she will join the community for cooking, serving and eating. As they do not permit animal sacrifices, her meals will consist of fruits, vegetables, nuts, and grains. After that, there is time set aside for meditation. He ends by telling me he feels certain he can cure her. I am elated by his words and excited to share what I have learned with Rachel.*

*Sharing the good news, I walk her through the regimen Mendel has* described. *"You need to remain here for a month."* Was the last of the information I share.

*"You are leaving me?"* For the first time since we've met, her eyes fill with tears.

I nod. *"In the morning. I will help get you settled tonight."*

This doesn't seem to lessen her discomfort.

*"It will go by fast,"* I promise.

*"You will come for me?"* the fear in her voice is palpable.

*"Always, and without hesitation,"* I promise, unconsciously reaching out for a lock of her hair and allowing it to slip through my fingers.

Before being sent to separate sleeping quarters on opposite sides of the compound, I am able to get her alone for a moment, away from other members of the yahad.

*"I will be back for you,"* I promise and lean forward to place a soft kiss on her lips. Her eyes are wide with questions it is not yet time to answer. *"I will be back."*

I understand her fear only too well. With Judea being under the rule of Tiberius Julius Alexander, it is a time marked by tumult, with tomorrows that are never certain. I know this and it hangs over me like a storm cloud ready to strike. Before I left both Jerusalem and Jericho, I gave specific directions to trusted members of my ministry that if something were to happen to me, make sure someone went to Qumran to retrieve Rachel and to bring her straightaway to Daniel, where I know she will be looked after.

I feel a deep responsibility to protect this beautiful young woman and ensure she remains safe, whether I can personally provide that for her or not. Plans were in place if the latter were to become my reality.

. . . . . .

*The month without her by my side proves to be much more challenging than I had anticipated. My thoughts are almost obsessive during our separation as I think not only about that night together, but of the deep conversations we had as we traveled, discussing the nature of man and God, good and evil. I shared with her my beliefs and how they had been shaped, mostly through scripture, and she challenged me with thought-provoking questions that I knew were born of her experiences as an outcast. While I built a life that had been inclusive and created community, Rachel's experiences were those of exclusion, of being judged and sentenced for what was beyond her control.*

*Rachel has proven to be much more than a beautiful young woman in need of healing and it is during this month apart that I realize she has brought me as many, if not more, answers than I have provided for her. I brought her to be healed, but her constant questioning of me made me look at places deep within myself, to study where scripture ends and humanity begins.*

*"Women have always been attracted to you, David. But what I have never seen before is your heart open in more than what is just an empathetic or physical way. This time appears to be different." Daniel knows me better than anyone.*

*"I have never felt like this, Daniel. The time I have spent without her by my side is interminable. So many days I've woken and thought, I'm just going to go there to be with her. But I know that is not what is best. She needs to heal on her own. It will be a reawakening of her spirit and from there she must make her own choices."*

*"Do you really think her choices will not include you?" He absentmindedly strokes the fur on the wolf at his feet. Rachel's wolf. We have concluded that the animal must have been lost from his pack at a very young age and raised by humans. While very protective of his human pack, he is gentle and nurturing and reads the moods of the people*

*who care for him.*

*"I don't know how she'll feel on the other side of this. She may choose to go home to her family and have her father arrange a marriage. I try to remain hopeful that will not be the case."*

*Quietly, Daniel sits there looking at me, appearing so wise in his brocade silk robe. I can tell from his eyes he has something important to say to me. With a direct look, he finally speaks. "Rachel will be by your side the rest of your days, David. You have found one another and I look forward to blessing your union."*

*As the days go on, it feels as if our time in Jerusalem is becoming more precarious as a shifting wind prevails. Members of our congregation and others we know have been harassed with more frequency by Tiberius Julius Alexander's guard. There are never charges that stick, but beatings and jail time are becoming the norm. I stay out of sight as much as I can while I'm here, knowing I need to get to Qumran to retrieve Rachel.*

*"Let me come with you," Daniel offers.*

*"No. I need you here. Our congregation needs you here." Daniel would be leading all prayer in my absence. "I will be back after I take Rachel to Anathoth, to her family."*

*"May God be with you," my old friend blesses me as I begin my journey.*

*Not ten minutes into the journey, I am accosted by Cassius Petronius and his men. My face hits a stone wall before I even know they are upon me. As jagged edges rip the skin beneath my right eye, I have but one thought. None of my people are aware this is happening. There's no one to retrieve Rachel. She'll think I've deserted her.*

*As they drag me off, I know I will be incarcerated, and my best approach is to remain totally pacifistic and not fight them, as that will hopefully result in less jail time.*

*For two days and two nights I sit in a cell that feels like being trapped in a filthy stone box. As the hours slowly pass, I pray for many things and many people. I pray for my flock, that they may all remain safe and free to worship as they choose. I pray for Rachel, that she maintains the faith in her heart to know that I am coming for her. I pray for Tiberius Julius Alexander, born a Jew in Alexandria, the son of wealthy merchants who had contributed the gold and silver for the gates of Herod's second temple here in Jerusalem. I pray that although he turned his back on his ancestral faith, that he will not terrorize and enslave the people who chose to remain Jews. And selfishly, I pray for myself for a speedy release. I need to get to Rachel.*

*On the third day, my prayers are answered.*

*My first inclination is to go back to where Daniel is staying, bathe the filth off me, change clothes, and have my wounds attended. But something tells me better. I need to leave Jerusalem. Immediately. I will find help and all I need along the way, of that I am sure. God will guide me safely.*

*Traveling alone, I cover more ground quickly, attempting to make up lost time. I keep wondering if I will see Rachel on the road coming toward me, if she has left Qumran on her own and I search the faces of all the pilgrims who pass looking for a set of dark almond-shaped eyes. I know if we encountered one another, she will know I was on my way coming to get her.*

*Arriving in Qumran, I silently pray she is still there. And safe. That somehow, she knew, that she could feel me, knowing I'd been detained and that I would still come, as promised.*

*I wait in the great hall for Mendel, watching the white-robed inhabitants as they tend to their business in silence. Everything feels like it has its own flow, in harmony with nature. There is such a peacefulness to the community and I pray that it has provided Rachel with acceptance and solace.*

*Entering from across the long haul, Mendel greets me with a concerned look. My first inclination is to fear for Rachel, but that quickly abates when he speaks.*

*"David, my friend, you have been injured. We need to get that attended."*

*Without even addressing his concern, "Mendel, how is Rachel?"*

*Leading me to a stone bench, we sit. "Rachel has done very well. Her skin responded and cleared."*

*"That is wonderful news." I sigh with relief.*

*"She has been highly agitated the last few days, afraid you would not come for her."*

*"I was afraid of that. As you can see, I encountered some trouble on my way here and lost a few days' travel time." I pause, "Can I see her."*

*"She's down at the solarium. I will have someone show you the way."*

*After a few minutes, a middle-aged woman appears and we walk outside on a path that curves around a rocky area. "How much farther?" I ask.*

*"Not too far."*

*"Does this path lead there directly?"*

*The woman nods.*

*"I can find it from here." I don't want anyone else there, if possible, when I see Rachel for the first time again.*

*As the path veers left, I look down upon what appears to be an open circular area of smooth, white boulders that form an outdoor room. Gleaming off the stones, the sun throws light from every direction. Rachel is at the room's center, lying naked on a bed of white rock. I stand there, for a moment, taking in her deeply tanned, lean body. All the skin lesions have cleared and her small frame appears toned from the natural eating. Not wanting to scare her and just come up upon her, I kick some stones on the path to alert her to someone approaching.*

*Startled, she stands suddenly, at first wobbly on her feet and grabs a garment to hold in front of her. As I round the opening to the solarium, her face is a portrait of the changing seasons of emotion, rapidly fleeting from one to another as her eyes fill with tears.*

*"You look beautiful. And healthy." I walk toward her, knowing my smile is telling her exactly what I'm feeling. Taking the garment from her hands, I let it fall to the floor so that I may enjoy every inch of her exquisite beauty. Her arms, legs, and torso appear clear of the insidious disease.*

*As I stand before her, I drop to my knees, my head bowed as if praying to my goddess. Grabbing the outer portion of her thighs, I pull my head closer, my forehead resting against the soft hairs of her sex, fragrant with eucalyptus and sea air. A moment or two passes before her fingers rake through my hair.*

*"You came for me," her words are choked as she too sinks to her knees where we remain forehead to forehead for a long while. Finally, she asks, "What happened to you, David."*

*"I was leaving Jerusalem to come for you and the Roman guard had different plans for me." I pull my head back to look at her face. "How are you? Physically you look so wonderful. But, how are you?"*

*"I am strong and at peace."*

*"Are you ready to go home?" I brush her hair from her face a second before the confused look appears.*

*"Home? To your home?"*

*"To yours. To your family," I explain.*

*"Family. I have no family. They disowned me and left me for dead. Do not send me back to them. I won't go." She searches my eyes frantically.*

*"You know the law dictates your father makes the decision."*

*"Yes. He already made it. He threw me away and I am not his property anymore."* Her face is becoming red with anger.

*"I want to do this right, Rachel."* My voice is low and calm in an attempt to diminish her anxiety.

*"Do what right, David? Have him reject and humiliate me again? Did I go through all the healing just to cut open the emotional scars?"* The pain in her voice is heartbreaking.

Taking her face in both my hands, *"I have business with your father."*

Her brows crease in confusion. *"Business with my father?"* she repeats.

I nod. *"I need to negotiate a mohar with your father."*

Rachel's mouth drops open at the mention of a mohar, the price the groom's father, in this case the groom, agrees to pay the bride's father to marry his daughter. It is customary for the father to then give the mohar to his daughter, those who keep it for themselves are considered unkind and harsh.

*"Are you saying we will be betrothed, David?"*

*"If your father agrees."*

*"And if he doesn't?"* She looks concerned.

*"Then we leave. He did already disown you. I am doing this out of respect."*

*"But what would happen then?"* I can see the haunting specter of her father's betrayal weighing heavily on her heart.

*"Then, Daniel marries us and we move forward as we would anyway."*

Softly, she caresses my cheek. *"You want to make me your bride?"*

Leaning forward, I whisper in her ear, *"I think I already have."*

*And I am rewarded with her beautiful smile. "Now you've healed my heart, David."*

*Shaking my head, "It is you who has healed mine by giving me back the half I didn't know had gone astray. Because of you, I will be a better man and a better rabbi to the people of Judea. How does one teach others to love when one does not know how himself?"*

Falling quiet for a few minutes with his head down on his chest, Claire waited for him to continue before probing Jesse when he remained silent. "Did you meet with her father?" she asked, looking for more information.

"Yes. He was a lout. Her mother and sister felt bad, I could tell, and I know her mother could rest easy knowing she was with me. I ended up giving the father some silver and gold, which he kept for himself. But that was fine, because we were officially betrothed and she was legally free of him. Rachel was mine and I took her away from there, a place where she was ostracized, to a new community based on love and acceptance."

"What are you seeing now?" Claire asked.

"Nothing. I'm not seeing anything."

"Can you tell me more about David's life?"

"No. I see nothing."

"You don't know what happened with him and Rachel?"

"No."

Putting her tablet down on the desk, she knew the window to question him had closed. "Okay, on the count of three you will be back here in my office and you will leave David behind. One," she paused. "Two," another pause. "Three."

With a flick of his hand, Jesse pulled the RGB glasses from his eyes as he sat up. Putting his face in his hands, with his elbows resting on his thighs, he sat there in silence. Eventually he sat back and exhaled loudly, as if he'd been holding his breath for a lifetime.

"Shit, Dr. S. Just when I think these things can't get any more emotional, boom! Rachel appears. And Daniel."

"What do you think you learned?" she probed, putting her tablet down on the table at her side.

"I'm not sure. I really need to think about this. And I don't know what the outcome was. I was clearly empathetic to the needs of others and a Good Samaritan, but I don't know that I initially had the control to do what was best for Rachel. I learned the power that came with love and I hope I used it wisely. With her and members of the congregation." Stopping, he stared at a point on the floor, eventually shaking his head, "Rachel." His right hand repeatedly raked though the front of his hair. "Oh, God, my heart hurts. My heart physically hurts. What the fuck."

"Let's take a few minutes here." Claire could see her patient struggling, emotionally caught in a world he would never physically exist in again. Overwhelmed by feelings for a woman he'd never see again. "It's like a death coming out of these regressions, isn't it?"

"Yeah. I had a hard time shaking the essence of Julia, she just attached to my soul and now Rachel is there. I want to know what happened." He searched Claire's face for an answer.

"Most likely that will never happen, Jesse. When you get back, we can try, with specifically guided meditation, to see if we can learn more, but I wouldn't get my hopes up. You just have to come to terms with what you do know."

Sitting back on the couch, looking up at the ceiling, "I'm having a rough time with this one. I knew what happened with me and Julia, so there was a kind of closure. I knew how it ended. But with Rachel, I know this is going to sound crazy, but I'm left feeling worried. I don't have the answers. I want the answers."

"I understand, but you need to accept the fact that you may never know. One of the things I find interesting here is that you had a flock, your congregations, which kind of has a synergy with a fan base like you have today. People who follow you. And with Gaius, you had a legion of soldiers you commanded. I can see the parallels. You are very focused on leading and bringing direction to others, and sometimes you get lost in the mix."

When he didn't respond, she went on. "This is a lot to digest, I know. I'm glad we're going to be doing Skype sessions for the next few weeks. I think after today it's really important we don't miss a session. If you need me in between, you've got my emergency contact information."

**Patient: Jesse Winslow**

**Session # 52**

**Date: 6/24/15**

**Regression # 13**

**Regression Length: 10:08A.M. – 10:46 A.M.**

**Entity: David ben Abraham**

**Location: Israel**

**Year: 1$^{st}$ Century AD**

. . . . . .

Checking his phone in the building's lobby, there were no new messages from Kylie. Pulling up the picture from the night before, he smiled at her image as if she could see him. Just seeing her face brought him solace and calm. His snarky Miss Jersey was surprisingly the most grounding person he'd ever met.

**Toots, love the pic with your hair blowing wildly. Hot. Hot. Hot. Missing you something awful. Just had an intense regression with Dr. S. Can't wait to tell you about it. I'm stuck in that nether-**

**world place right now. I know you get that. So, I'm feeling all kinda outta sorts and I just want to stick my face in your soft, gorgeous boobs (I know you get that, too). I miss you. Here's my pic today.** ☺

Holding out the camera, he took a selfie, bottom lip stuck out in a pout. Looking at it, he laughed and then sent it.

# Chapter 15

Today's picture, as you can see, is of my feet. They are KILLING me. I was in boots with six-inch spike heels–on ice! My feet started to go numb after the first hour and then the pain started. It was pure torture and those pics better have come out good because I am not putting my feet in those fuckers again! I will go total NJ bitch diva on these people if I am asked to put anything but flat shearling boots on my feet the rest of the time we are here shooting. By the time we got back to the hotel tonight, it was nearly eleven p.m. and as much as I want to hear your voice, I can't do that to you at three a.m. But if you were here, those two feet you see in that picture would be in your lap and I'd probably be doing something disgusting, like talking baby talk to you, to get you to give me a foot massage. This bitch is not too proud to beg. I'd tell you to do it hard in the arches with your thumbs. Mmm, even harder. The foot that was still in your lap would be rubbing its arch over something else that's hard. And trying to get it even harder. When you put the first foot down and start working on the second one, the first foot takes over rubbing your cock through your jeans until you finally unzip and take that gorgeous baby out for me to rub. With the arch of one of my feet rubbing your cheek, the arch of the other fits perfectly around your dick and rubs in time with the other foot. When you slide my big toe in your mouth and start sucking, I press you hard with my other foot, feeling you harden even more against me. You know how much I love making you hard. Taking my other foot back from you, I put you between my feet so that you fit snuggly between my arches and then I begin to rub up and down. With my legs spread and my knees pointing outward, you can watch my pussy get wetter and wetter as my feet jerk you off. Dropping a few drops of oil in each arch, you put your hands on the outside of my feet, pressing them tighter around you as you take control of the pressure and the rhythm to get yourself off. I'm enjoying the look on your face and I can't wait to see you come. Reaching down, I spread the lips of my pussy, just so you can get a good look at how wet I am, before slipping a finger deep inside. I love watching your face as I do this and what I love even more is that you do not miss a beat pumping my feet up and down on your slick, hard cock. Pulling my finger out of my pussy, it makes a little popping sound and I bring the wet finger to my lips, coating my bottom lip with my juices. When my finger slides into my mouth, your moan makes me quiver and I watch as you close your eyes and a warm load spurts from you, landing all over my feet.

Good morning, baby! Hope you love the picture and my fantasy and that it helps you start your day off right. I miss you so much, too. I can't wait to hear about your session with Claire. We are shooting out near Denali tomorrow and I don't think we'll have cell signal. If we get back at a decent hour, I will call. I miss you so much, Jesse. xoxo ☺ Btw, there's no pouting in rock 'n' roll! (your picture)

· · · · · ·

"I don't think I've ever seen anything so beautiful," Kylie was glancing out the window of the van, watching the sun rise over Denali, bathing the mountain's summit in a warm orange glow and taking pictures with her cell phone. Jesse was going to get more than one picture today. This was just too magnificent not to share and she knew how much the beauty of nature inspired his writing. Jesse Fucking Winslow. He turned out to be an unexpected joy. A pretty boy with a bad reputation was an amazing façade he had built, for the Jesse she knew was deep and spiritual and protective.

"What are you smiling about?" Sarah Eggleston was turned around in the seat in front of her.

"Well, first that gorgeous sunrise and the way it is lighting up the top of the mountain. I shot some pictures to send to Jesse later when we have cell service again. And that got me thinking about Jesse." Kylie couldn't help but smile as her heart warmed at the thought of him.

Getting up from her seat, Sarah moved back a row to sit next to Kylie. "That is so cool you are dating Jesse Winslow."

Kylie laughed. "Cool or a curse?"

"Yeah. Every woman on the planet wants your boyfriend."

Kylie rolled her eyes. "No shit. It's hard not being able to go anywhere without being recognized."

"That's right, you guys got nailed in Starbucks." She laughed, "Those were super-hot pictures. What were you feeding each other?"

"An éclair he brought me back from Paris."

"He brought that all the way back. That is so sweet."

With a conspiratorial tone, Kylie told the teen, "He's really very sweet, but don't let anyone know, 'cause he loves that bad boy persona." She could feel her heart glow just talking about him. A moment passed and when the teen didn't speak, Kylie seized a moment she knew she might never have again. "So, how long have you been battling the eating thing?"

Picking at her chipped pink gel manicure, Sarah admitted, "Two years."

"Binge and toss or are you doing laxatives, too?"

"A little of everything." The teen was clamming up.

Kylie knew that she had the key, so she quickly inserted it in the door and unlocked as fast as she could. "It's fucked up. And you know it's fucked up, but it just kinda takes control, you know. It was a way of life for almost everybody on the pageant circuit. And we all knew it. And we all had convinced ourselves that we had everything under control. Because it's about control when you really have none. None of us have controlled our own lives since we were like three years old when we started getting paraded out on stages."

"The pageant thing starts that young?"

She nodded. "You never have a childhood, not even a pre-school one. And the parents are generally lunatics. Like totally certifiable. Fucked-up insane mothers who are either ex-Miss something or another or total wannabes."

Kylie could see from the teen's face that she found her way in. Sarah was listening, whether it be because she was formerly on the Miss America tour or because Jesse Winslow was her boyfriend, it really didn't matter. Just as long as Kylie could get her to stay open and listen.

"Before pageants were the worst, we would just abuse the shit out of ourselves so that our stomachs were flat for the freaking bathing suit competition. There's just so much pressure, you know." Turning to the teen, "I can't even imagine the pressure you feel."

"My high school is like Fashion Week in New York, every single week. My father owns a major clothes company and I can't keep up with the fashionistas. It is the most judgmental place on the planet."

"The bottom line, Sarah, is you can't let these bitches define how you feel about yourself. Some nasty little twits don't deserve that power. If something they don't like makes you happy, too bad. Think about this, have you ever met a hater who was doing better than you?"

The teen thought for a moment. "No."

"Exactly," Kylie concurred. "These bitches are miserable and they just want to drag you down with them. Most likely they are jealous of you."

"I never thought about it that way."

"My whole life centered around me being thin and looking perfect and my whole self-worth was wrapped up in it. And one day I woke up and thought 'I want to go down to the corner grocery, buy a container of Ben & Jerry's, eat it in one sitting and not feel guilty about it, and not stick my finger down my throat'. I want to be like, *okay, I binged, so what. Next.* And that turned into a rebellion of sorts for me. It was my way of taking my life back. And when I got dethroned as Miss New Jersey, everyone thought I'd ruined my life. But I felt like a nine-hundred-pound boat anchor had been lifted off me and for the first time I could start discovering what made me happy. Not my parents, not my coaches, not the pageant people. Me. What made me happy? Because I had no friggin idea."

"Wow and you're beautiful just the way you look."

"Thank you. And one of the most amazing men on the planet thinks so too. So, you don't have to starve yourself to fit in or because you think it's what you have to do. I've lost friends to eating disorders, Sarah. Please don't go down that rabbit hole. You are smart and beautiful and the people you want around you are people who appreciate you for you. I know it's not easy and sometimes it's about finding the right person to help you, a person you click with."

"I'm seeing this woman, but she feels judgey to me. I just can't warm up to her and confide."

"I know how that is. There's actually something about my shrink that totally rubs me the wrong way," admitted Kylie, "but she is helping me. My friend Krista worked with someone when her eating situation spun out of control on her. She loved this woman and they worked well together. If you're interested, I can text her and get the doctor's info."

"Okay," Sarah nodded.

"You need to feel good about you. And when you do it's amazing what can happen. I'm the poster girl for that." Kylie looked out the window, again struck by the splendor of Denali and thinking about the opportunities that presented themselves in her life once she made the decision to seek out her own dreams.

. . . . . .

**Hey, babes. Check out this picture of the sun coming up and lighting the top of Denali. One of the photographers today told me it's called Alpenglow. There's an actual name for it. How cool is that. The shoot is going great and I had the opportunity this morning to really talk to Sarah. I think she listened, Jesse. I'm not a parent telling her, but more of a contemporary with my own (opposite) eating disorder and I lived under the pressure of having to be thin (before I said fuck this shit!) and I'm dating Jesse Winslow (instant street cred). Anyway, I hope it helped. I'm going to get her the number of a doctor who really helped a friend of mine. I'll try calling you when I get up, before we leave. Hopefully you'll be able to answer. We're going to be shooting on a whale boat or something. So, no cell service again and I need to hear your voice. I know you're leaving for London in two days, so we need to hook up before you go. xoxo Talk to you in the morning.**

. . . . . .

"Pick up, Jess. C'mon," Kylie groaned as his phone went into voicemail. She began talking after the beep. "Grr, you were supposed to pick up. You are probably in the studio laying down a track. I'm off to shoot on a boat today. I'll try calling as soon as I have cell service later. I need to hear your voice. I miss you. Okay, talk to you later."

. . . . . .

"Hey, Toots," his voice was all sleep and gravel.

"Finally," she sighed. "I'm so sorry to wake you, sweetie. It's just been too long."

"It's okay. It's been way too long. So, did you see any whales today?"

Kylie could hear the rustling of his sheets and knew he was stretching. Just the sound made her ache as she pictured the motion in her mind of his right arm going up, biceps bulging and his stomach muscles rippling as they tightened all the way down to the V.

"Yes. That's tomorrow's pictures. I've got one of a whale breaching. It is so cool. I'm really happy I got to experience it. Did you have a good day in the studio?"

"Yeah, crazy busy. We're just preparing everything for the move. I didn't realize there was so much work."

"Have you packed yet?"

"No. I'm going to do that today when I wake up," he laughed.

"I should let you get back to sleep."

"No. Not yet. I need more Kylie time. When do you get to New York?"

"Wednesday and I'll be home for a week. We leave for Australia the following Wednesday."

"Crap. We miss each other on this end and then that time difference is going to totally fuck us." He stretched again, a low moan escaping.

"I know, and with my shooting hours and I know you're going to be making the most out of that studio time and living in that studio, we're so fucked," she laughed.

Laughing, "I'm going to need more foot pictures if we keep this up."

"You liked that, huh?"

"Toots, you totally got me off this morning. And, I thank you. That was a great surprise."

When his breathing got heavy, she knew he was starting to doze.

"Okay, sweets, I'm going to let you get back to sleep. Tell me you love me." She hadn't realized she needed to hear those words so badly until the request came out of her.

Jesse chuckled. "Are you going to tell me you love me?"

"Not over the phone for the first time."

"No? Where then?"

"In your arms."

"Mmm, that works. I love you, Toots."

Every fiber in her being ached to say the words back to him. And the very next time his arms were around her, she would tell him the words he wanted to hear. The words she yearned to share because the sentiment possessed her, heart and soul.

"Goodnight, you." His breathing told her he had already fallen back to sleep.

. . . . . .

**Bed. Lonely, empty bed. Yes. I came home to this. And now I'm the one pouting. Being in New York without you sucks, Jess. It totally sucks. I can't even look at my bed, knowing I won't feel you spooned behind me, playing with my hair. How long is it until we're together again? Oh, that's right, too long. Too fucking long. I walked into L9 today and Zac's dad said, "Where's Jesse?" and it hit me how much we do together, how people know us as a couple. I told him you were in London recording and he was so sweet and asked me if I wanted the private gym. I didn't take it, I just ended up working out on the main floor with Zac, but that was so nice of him to offer. I feel so at home there. Can't wait to wake up to your picture. Make it a good one.**

. . . . . .

**You knew you were going to get this from me, right? I felt kind of like a dumbass doing it, but how could I not, it's iconic. The first one obviously is just me and the second one is me, Chris, Bob (whom you've met), and Ian (one of the Master Engineers). Okay, I feel complete now (well, or as complete as I can feel without you). ☺ So, another great day of recording. This place has got some really good juju, Toots. I feel like Amy Winehouse is looking over my shoulder, pushing me to dig in my soul and go places where it really hurts. I'm excited about what I'm doing and I can't wait to play it for you. That was really cool of Schooner to offer you the private gym. Nice that he's taking care of my baby when I'm not around. I'll need to thank him. Maybe let him and Zac know about the showcase and we can guest list them and their plus ones. If you can do that, I'll get them on the list. Okay, Toots, they want me back in the booth. Love you.**

Kylie smiled, looking at the pictures, flipping back and forth on her phone. She wondered where Jesse had gotten the white suit and shoes. They weren't from his home wardrobe, that she knew. In the picture with the three other men, Jesse led the line, just as one of his personal idols, John Lennon, had done for the iconic album cover in the very same crosswalk. In the picture where it was just him, he faced the camera, huge smile and his left hand held up, fingers forming a peace sign. Not only was he living out his recording studio fantasy, he was getting to play fanboy and pay homage to one of his all-time favorite bands.

A day later, the photos started showing up on the Internet and although she was glad she had seen them first--that for a moment they had just been hers--she couldn't help but feel violated. There was nothing from stopping a random fan on the street from pulling out their cell phone and taking pictures, but these were basically identical to the ones Jesse had sent her. The specialness of their daily picture gift to one another felt sullied. It wasn't there's anymore and it wasn't special. She was used to sharing Jesse with the world, everywhere they went. But this was their personal thing for when they weren't together to alleviate missing one another, not something to distribute to the masses.

Packing for Australia, Kylie felt out of sorts. Was it the travel? Missing Jesse? Being rundown from crazy hours on photoshoots? She wasn't quite sure, but thought it best not to miss her last session with Claire before leaving the country again. She had already missed a few sessions with the Alaska travel and wondered if maybe that contributed to her general malaise.

"I got to do something I'm really glad I had the opportunity to do," she told the psychiatrist, detailing her conversation with Sarah. "And she's already called my friend's doctor and set up an appointment."

"I know your intentions are good, Kylie, but you are really not qualified to give out advice." Claire's eyebrows were raised.

"Seriously? You are seriously saying that to me, someone with an eating disorder. Yeah, I know you've only seen the fat side of my disorder, but I've had my fingers down my throat," and she stopped herself from saying, more than you've had dicks down yours, and instead said, "more times than I care to admit. I lived among a group of women who made a lifestyle out of anorexia and bulimia. I'm highly qualified to talk about it and my conversation has led her to seek help. I think that's pretty damn good."

"Well, I hope it works out for your friend." She smiled at Kylie, then pivoted, "So, have you been able to tell Jesse you love him yet?"

"No. I haven't said it. He's away. I've been away. And he knows I will not say it over the phone to him. I am going to say it to him when we are together."

"Mmm-hmm." She made a note on her iPad. "Do you think you are using the separation as an excuse?"

"No. Not at all. I want to be able to look into his eyes when I say it. I want to see his smile. Feel the reaction throughout his body. I want to take his face in my hands and kiss him. And I want to feel his cock get hard against me." She threw in the final piece for shock value.

"Kylie, have you really taken the time to think about why you might love Jesse the rock star versus Jesse the man? Are you able to parse those two things out?"

*Is she insinuating that I have a groupie crush on Jesse?* Kylie wondered.

"When you say things like that it truly makes me wonder if you even listen to what I say in here. I don't know Jesse Winslow, the rock star, the heart throb. I know Jesse Winslow, my boyfriend. I know a man I laugh so hard with that my face hurts. I know someone I can talk to about anything from feelings to business and he just gets what I'm saying. He's really special and I am honored to be helping him in his sobriety and in discovering the world from a clear place. So, yeah, Claire, I have been able to parse things out and I fell in love with an awesome man."

"You're very passionate in defending your feelings."

"Nothing to defend. I love him. And he loves me. This is without a doubt the single healthiest relationship I have had in my life. So, thank you for having both of us as patients, because without you, our paths might not have crossed. You are responsible for bringing us together. It's no coincidence we are both patients of yours or that Jesse walked in on the one day you kept me waiting out in the reception area. It was meant to be. Meant to happen. So, thank you, Claire," she emphasized the doctor's name.

"So, you feel this was fated?"

"I'd like to think destiny versus fate. With fate it's all predetermined, destiny can be shaped and changed. I think what Jesse and I are both doing with you is making changes in our lives to become healthier. We're both taking responsibility and control, so I'd like to think we are taking an active role in shaping our own destinies." Kylie challenged.

"Interesting concepts, destiny and fate, wouldn't you say?"

"Yeah, it really gives you a lot to think about."

"It does," Claire agreed, "and I think it' a perfect segue for us to begin a regression."

"I agree. Let's do it." Kylie reached for the glasses on the table next to her.

Settling into the couch, she focused on Claire's voice as the doctor led her through the guided meditation, her transition occurring almost immediately and with ease.

"Stop them. Stop them. We have to stop them," she called out, her tone reaching hysteria.

"Kylie, where are you?" Claire interrupted.

"We have to stop them. Please, help me. Help me." Tears were already streaming down her cheeks.

Claire made note of the physical manifestation.

"Kylie, look at your feet. Tell me what you are wearing." Claire needed to migrate away from the hysterics and get her to communicate.

"Sandals."

"What are they made of?" Claire kept her voice even.

"Leather straps."

"Where are you?" She continued, now that she had gotten her to focus.

"Palestine."

"Can you tell me when it is? What year?"

"Long ago."

"BC?"

"I don't think so," she answered. "But maybe around then."

"Do you know who Jesus Christ is?" Claire sat forward in her seat.

"I know of him. But he lived a while ago."

"Can you describe to me what you are wearing?" Claire hoped from the description that maybe she could narrow down a timeframe.

"Stop them. Stop them. Don't you touch me, you filthy animal," her screams were terrifying.

*Running along the dusty road toward the walls of the city, the Roman guards keep pushing me back, trying to stop me. But I need to stop them. I have to stop this whole thing. Can I cause some kind of distraction that will put a stop to this travesty? I wonder if that will work.*

*I'm out of breath and my feet are in pain, cut open from rocks and pottery shards that have worked their way between my sandal's straps. I don't have to look down to know my feet are bleeding. But right now, nothing hurts more than my heart. I have to stop this and so I keep running because I have to catch up and do something. There's got to be something I can do. I can't let this happen.*

*Up ahead, I see the crowds, as if this were sport. Some sick Roman sport. And I know they are coming. Bunching my kethōneth and simlāh in my hands, so that I can run without tripping, I start weaving through the people. Half are crying and the others are the maggots of Rome, there for the spectacle.*

*"Rachel. Rachel." I hear my name. It's Daniel's voice. Stopping, I scan the crowd. I must find him.*

*Standing with Simon, Leah and Ephraim, I notice Daniel is dressed in a heavy silk me'īl, the color of sand with piping the burgundy of a hearty wine. The formal outfit, generally reserved for government meetings, high holy days or funeral processions, I know, is to pay his respects. This can't be happening.*

*"You shouldn't be here. You should not see this. Leah, take her from*

*here," he insists, trying to protect me.*

*"No," I protest. "I won't go. I have to stop this. I can't let them do this. They can't do this to him, Daniel. Can we cause some kind of distraction and stop it?"*

*Tears are streaming down my friends' faces as they know we are powerless. The followers of a man who preached love and tolerance, acceptance and pacifism. And here we are, prisoners of our own beliefs.*

*The crowd seizes into a frenzy and I break away from Daniel, pushing myself through the throngs of people to get out onto the thoroughfare, determined to stop this. Emerging through the crowd, I see David and the three other rabbis approaching. They have all been stripped bare, their hands bound with leather straps to the heavy, wooden crossbeam they carry across their shoulders, as they are marched to their death.*

*I hear a scream. A wounded animal. And somehow, I know it's me. No. No. No. No. This can't be happening.*

*"David," I scream, certain that nothing has actually escaped my throat. "David," I choke on my sobs, barely able to breathe.*

*He knows I'm there and turns his face to see me on the road's edge. "I'll find you," his lips clearly form the words. And he repeats them, "I'll find you."*

*I need to run to him, but my legs won't move, as if I'm nailed to the ground. As he passes, I see his back. He has been scourged and left are raw ribbons of flesh, his skin disintegrated.*

*"No," I scream and my legs finally break from their spot as I fling my body into the thoroughfare. I need to get to David. Get him out of there. Get him to safety. He's moving away from me, his sweet, beautiful face now gone and all I see is the crowd that has filled in behind him and the other rabbis.*

*The soldier's hands grab me from behind, landing roughly on my breasts, digging into the flesh as he rips away my simlāh. Throwing me to the ground, he stands over me, blocking all sunlight. In the shadow, I see his face. It is Cassius Petronius and as I look up into his cold blue eyes, I am certain of what is to come next. I'm only glad David will not see this.*

*Closing my eyes, I envision David's face and his final vow to me, "I'll find you."*

*"No. No. No."*


"Rachel, tell me what happened with Cassius Petronius." Claire's voice is commanding.

"He enslaved me. And raped me and beat me. I was his last way to humiliate David, even though David was gone."

"Were you his slave for the rest of your life?" Claire probed.

"No. For seven years, until he was killed and then I regained my freedom."

"What happened to you then?"

"I went to live in Sebastia with Daniel."

Claire sat there in silence. Every hair on the back of her neck stood at attention and had been since Kylie started this regression. David and Rachel. And Daniel.

"Is Daniel your brother?" This can't be, she thought as she asked the question. These were common names in Judaism.

"No. Daniel was David's rabbinical mentor and closest friend."

Closing her eyes, Claire realized she was straining to breathe. This couldn't be happening.

"Did your skin problem ever return?" Claire threw this out for corroboration, since Kylie had not mentioned it.

"Yes. The years I was a slave, it was very bad. After that it calmed. Daniel brought me back to the Essenoi and they were able to cure me again."

With her hand over her mouth, Claire sat there. None of this was a coincidence. Not the two of them ending up as her clients, not their meeting in her waiting room. None of it. Jesse and Kylie had been lovers before. And he certainly did find her, as promised.

"Okay, Kylie, I'm going to count to three and at three, you will be back here in my office. One...two...three," she rushed through it, needing Kylie to leave Rachel far in the past, immediately.

Kylie sat there, very still, not removing the RGB glasses.

"I don't know," she began, "if I ever want to do another one of these things again." Reaching over to the side table, she grabbed a tissue and blew her nose loudly. "Oh, my God, they crucified him," she screamed. "They fucking crucified him. That is freaking insane. Oh, my God, that poor sweet man. He only wanted to bring good to the world. Why am I seeing those I loved killed so barbarically? And why are my lives so tragically painful?" Putting her face in her hands for a moment, her shoulders heaved, before she finally sat back, her face wet with tears. "That hurt so much."

Finally, she removed the glasses. With a small gasp, her brows knit together and her back tensed and straightened. Silently, she stared at her doctor. The tension in the room thick. "Claire, you have the same eyes as that Roman guard. You and Cassius Petronius have the same exact eyes." The fear in her voice was audible as she voiced her revelation.

**Patient: Kylie Martin**

**Session # 83**

**Date: 7/7/15**

**Regression # 19**

**Regression Length: 10:15 A.M. – 10:36 A.M.**

**Entity: Rachel**

**Location: Israel**

**Year: 1ˢᵗ Century AD**

**\*\*\*NOTE: PULL JESSE WINSLOW'S REGRESSION NOTES FROM DAVID BEN ABRAHAM REGRESSION**

· · · · · ·

Exiting the doctor's office as quickly as she could, she needed to get away from her and the pain in that space. Kylie stood out in the hallway and leaned up against the wall thinking, *Thank God, I'm going to Australia. I need a break from this shit. This is just too much to handle. Way too much. I can't go through this again.*

· · · · · ·

Her hands were shaking when she hit the call button on her cell phone. "Hello, Marshall, it's Claire Stoddard. I need to come in and see you. I know it's not my regularly scheduled appointment. But this is somewhat of an emergency. Can I come in this afternoon?"

· · · · · ·

"So, what are you going to do?" Marshall asked. "Are you going to share it with them?"

"You know I can't with HIPAA laws." Claire shook her head.

"Come on now, Claire. There are ways to get them the information. Perhaps suggest a joint session together. Ask probing questions to lead them to discover it on their own."

Marshall waited for Claire to answer, but she remained silent, clearly not happy with what her supervisor was recommending.

"She could have already shared it with him and they both know."

"That might be true. I'll know tomorrow when I do my Skype session with him. If he knows, it will be the first thing he says to me. She leaves for Australia tomorrow. I'm sure she is packing today. With their travel and time differences, I think they are mostly communicating via text."

"Putting HIPAA aside, why do I feel you are reticent about sharing this information with them?"

"Well, we haven't really corroborated the facts," she began.

"You don't think her identification of Daniel, a skin disease she didn't mention during her regression but had full knowledge of when questioned, and talk of a trip back to the Essenes to clear her lesions was enough? Oh, and Cassius Petronius, whom they both mentioned by name."

Claire shuddered. "She said I had his eyes."

"Whose eyes?" Marshall appeared confused.

"She said I had Cassius Petronius's eyes."

Removing his glasses and tapping the arm against his lips, he held her eye contact, "And?"

"And I don't know," her voice became shrill. "Are you asking me if I was there? I don't know."

"Have any of either of their regressions resonated with you?"

Closing her eyes, she averted his stare.

"Claire?" he pressed.

"I don't know. There have been a few times where I felt like I could see what they were describing and it was like I was seeing it from my own vantage point. But I've dismissed it as just trying to envision what they are seeing and describing to me in such detail.

"You really need to acknowledge that you might be a part of all this and that they aren't your patients merely by chance. Kylie calling you out the way she did after today's regression, and you have mentioned that the two of you have somewhat of a contentious relationship. Add to that your feelings, although you continue to deny them, for Jesse, and I don't think we're looking at any coincidences here."

"Are you saying we're some sort of cosmic love triangle?"

"I don't know about that, but I would not be surprised if there is some karma the three of you need to work out. I think that is at the root of why your feelings for him have always been so acute."

"I can't believe she is Rachel." Claire looked up at the ceiling, shaking her head.

"Does that bother you?"

"No, it just surprises me," her tone was more than slightly defensive.

"Why? Because he loved her?"

Silently, Claire sat there.

"You need to figure out a way to make this right, Claire. Suggest working together as a team, possibly. But if you decide to continue keeping it from them and let them discover it on their own, the outcome for all three of you will be a lot worse. You also really need to ask yourself what your motivations are, because I can assure you they are not all professional."

Without uttering a word to her supervisor, Claire stood and walked out of Marshall's office.

· · · · · ·

Rising early was not a problem for Claire as she preferred the early part of the day when the city was quiet. Often, she would run just after dawn, finding the cool air invigorating and the empty streets welcoming. This morning she didn't go out for a run, instead she sat in her home office, coffee in an aluminum Yeti tumbler at her fingertips. Already up for three hours by the time she needed to initiate the Skype call to Jesse, she had reviewed every one of his and Kylie's regressions, looking at them with a different eye than when they occurred. Now she questioned, could Gaius's red-haired Julia have been Kylie; was Geneviève's beloved brother, Bruno, in fact, Jesse? It was clear they had shared at least one past lifetime. David vowed to find Rachel again, and it appeared he had done just that. But the question was, *how many times,* Claire wondered.

Opening her Skype app, she clicked on the avatar of Jesse to initiate the call.

"Hey Doc," he appeared, smiling.

"Good morning."

"Afternoon here, already. Well, you look nice today." Jesse commented on Claire's deep V-neck, pale sea green silk blouse. "That is a great color for you."

"Thank you," she smiled, knowing he was commenting on what he could see on his screen. "How is it going there?"

"Amazing. Just the fact that it's Abbey Road Studios is such an energy blast."

"I can imagine." It was impossible not to smile at his enthusiasm. "Have you gotten a lot recorded?"

"Yeah and written, too. Creative muse has been paying me a visit. It feels really good, Dr. S. Being able to enjoy the experience sober, I kinda feel like a kid experiencing things for the first time."

"Are you taking care of yourself? Sleeping and eating properly so that you can maintain this and not come crashing down." She was concerned that maybe this was the manic phase.

"You'd be so proud of me. I'm doing everything in moderation. Mostly, I'm just working hard. I need to make the most of my studio time. If I wasted this, it would be a crime. And I would really kick myself in the butt for doing that."

"Are you proud of you?"

"Yes. I am," he admitted with a smile.

"I like seeing you this focused and celebrating your successes. I want you to be realistic that there will be periods where maybe things aren't flowing as well, it happens to everybody, and to make sure you have strategies in place to help pull you through."

"I know. I do need to be realistic. But right now, it's just all so good. I feel like I'm on the right track from doing solo work to my relationship with Kylie."

"And how is that going with this separation?" Claire held her breath, knowing she would have her answer now, even though, based on his demeanor, she didn't think Kylie had told him anything.

"I'm getting more used to it than I was at the beginning. Plus, now that I'm in London and focused on everything in the studio, I'm so consumed, so I have less time to miss her. There are a million times a day that I wish I could share something with her or show her something, but I'm not sad about it, it feels healthy. With the time differences and working, me in the studio and her out on shoots, it's nearly impossible to connect. So, we send each other long texts and it's something to look forward to everyday. You know, it's kind of like old-fashioned letter writing and it's really cool. You learn so much about the other person and divulge so much about yourself through writing. Plus, we can send pictures from our day and stuff. I send audio of riffs I'm working on. So, even though we don't get to talk live a lot, we're communicating daily. It really helps fill the void."

"That sounds great," Claire had to admit, knowing communication like that could help build a relationship. Breathing a sigh of relief, she knew neither of them would write something as important or lengthy as a regression, so that bullet had been dodged. At least for now. "Has she been able to say, 'I love you' back yet?" She couldn't pass up the opportunity to surface that for him.

"I don't think that will happen until we're at least in the same time zone," he laughed.

"Well, you seem to be doing well. How about we check in the same time next week and I'll let you get back into the studio now." She smiled at her client.

"Sounds great. Talk to you next week."

"Have a good week," she bid him before disconnecting.

Sitting back in her chair, she crossed her long legs, pressing them together tightly, a small smile on her face. They hadn't compared notes and the more time that went by, the chances that they would diminished. It would give her time to figure out exactly how she wanted to handle it.

With a little laugh, she amused herself, as handling things was the most pressing issue she needed to deal with at the moment. Uncrossing her legs, she let her hand wander to the wet heat at their apex. She loved that Jesse liked her blouse and wondered what his reaction would have been to knowing the blouse was the only thing she was wearing on her entire body. Under it, there was no bra and her bottom half was totally bare. He was totally unaware that several times during their talk, she had reached down just to see how wet his face and voice were making her, and couldn't resist the opportunity to give her clit a little swipe, sending shock waves through her body and getting an extra thrill by maintaining her composure on the screen.

*Was Marshall right about it all,* she wondered? Was it possible that she, Jesse, and Kylie had been playing out some karmic love triangle for thousands of years. Could she have been Bruno's lover, Mme. Michaud? Angered that he was giving himself to another man.

Or Julia's stepmother, who Marshall thought was Livia, grabbing for power and her stepdaughter's handsome lover, Gaius? Certainly, she wouldn't have been so hell bent on keeping David and Rachel apart that she had the man crucified. Or would she?

Finding Kylie Martin to be an obnoxious, entitled, and yes, beautiful bitch, she had to admit there had been a rub between them right from the start. Claire was actually surprised that she had stayed on as a patient and not found someone else to treat her, but the truth was there were not that many Ivy League-trained MDs who were practicing hypnosis and regression analysis, so Kylie's alternatives were limited. Claire recognized that they both had an amazing talent to get under one another's skin, very quickly, as if they knew the key to the other's pain points.

Quickly pushing Kylie from her thoughts, she sat back in her chair and let her hand wander back between her legs. Smiling, she pictured the beautiful, clear grey-blue color of Jesse's eyes on her Skype screen just minutes before, thinking how amazing it would be to stare into them while he was buried deep inside her.

# Chapter 16

"Toots, it is so good to hear your voice." Jesse opened the refrigerator in his kitchen, taking stock of the contents and realizing three weeks away left nothing that was edible.

"I've got some bad news." The cell connection was poor and she sounded a million miles away. Which she was.

"Tell me, what's going on?"

"We just had two horrible days of torrential rain and we're way behind on our shooting schedule."

"Oh, crap. When do you think you'll be home?"

"Come Hell or high water, I will be back for your showcase. But I might be missing the first thirty minutes, maybe a little more. Unless we have a major delay or I get caught in customs, I should be able to catch most of the show. I'm so sorry, Jess. So, save the best part until last, okay. I want to hear what you've been writing in London."

"Want me to have a car waiting for you to bring you there. I can have them drop you off at the club, take your luggage over to my place and leave it with my doorman?" He offered.

"Yes. That would be awesome not to have to worry about my bags and just come straight to you."

"Consider it done." He picked up a jar of peanut butter in the pantry and looked for an expiration date.

She said something in return, but it was impossible to understand through the static.

"Hey, Kylie, this connection sucks. Call me when you're back to civilization. See you in a few days, babe."

. . . . . .

Three acoustic guitars, a baby grand piano, a stool, a single mic, and multiple glasses of water were all that adorned the stage. Jesse Winslow's return to music after the ill-fated final night of the Australian leg of the Winslow tour was a significantly scaled down version of any show the rocker had played in years. With a house capacity of only five hundred, tonight's showcase was going to be intimate and personal. Fans felt that he was singing just to them in arenas, and tonight he would be doing just that.

"How are you feeling? Are you ready?" Molly Stein, who handled his PR and earned every cent he paid her, usually the hard way, tentatively asked.

"I can't wait to get out there. Best high in the world." He chuckled, "And this time I'll actually enjoy and remember it."

"I can feel the buzz from the crowd. Even back here." She peeked through the curtain to the front of the house.

Jesse smiled at her. "Isn't it amazing? You can actually feel energy. It's like everything is vibrating faster. Please, tell the house manager to make sure when Kylie gets here that security escorts her right up front. I want her near the front of the stage on my left side."

"So, stage right, coming from the back of the floor?" She confirmed.

"Yeah, exactly. I want her a little off-center. Make sure that is where security puts her." In his mind's eye, he knew exactly where he wanted to look to see her face and the crew needed to make sure that happened precisely as he instructed.

"I'll make sure he knows," Molly promised.

When the frenzy on the floor hit a feverish pitch, the house lights dimmed and the crowd went wild. A single spotlight followed a tall man to the microphone center stage.

"How are you all doing tonight? I'm Johnny V from WNYC's NightRock." The crowd went wild. "This has got to be one of the most special shows I've ever introduced. He's one of the biggest names in music, we've all seen him play stadiums and arenas, and tonight, for one night only, we get to enjoy an intimate evening of new and old favorites with the one, the only, possibly the sexiest man in rock 'n' roll, Jesse Winslow." He ended with a flourish and a second spotlight followed the infamous rocker to center stage where the two men quickly hugged before Johnny faded into the black.

Bursting into raucous applause and cheering, the tone for the evening was set. The crowd had their boy back after months and months on hiatus and their love freely flowed to the front of the house, giving Jesse Winslow the most amazing charge.

"You missed me?" He yelled out to his fans.

A resounding 'Yes' and 'We love you, Jesse' shook the room and they were rewarded with his glorious smile, as he paced the stage, feral energy, pent up for months, shrouding the room, straight to the bar at the back of the floor, captivating all. Looking out at the crowd, he noticed on his right side, Dr. S. and the crew from L9. Scanning the left side, as he paced back in that direction, there was still no Kylie, but he knew it would take a while to get there from Kennedy airport.

"So, as you probably already all know, I've taken some time off after a well-publicized, and very public, meltdown. Yeah, I kinda do things in a big way. But since that time, I've gotten sober." The crowd cheered. "Thank you. I'm closing in on two hundred and seventy days here." More cheers. "I'm not gonna lie, it's been rough. But it's been great and I've had some wonderful people at my side, helping me succeed." He looked over to Claire and smiled, then nodded an acknowledgement to the L9 gang. Chuckling, he lifted his worn black tee-shirt showing the crowd his well-defined abs and a peek at the V disappearing into the top of his worn-out jeans, "So, you can see, I've gotten really healthy." The women in the crowd were in a frenzy and he laughed at their reaction.

Walking toward the back of the stage, he grabbed one of the acoustic guitars, wrapping the strap over his shoulder he plucked a few strings to check the tune on it, before making some minor adjustments.

Approaching the mic, he took a moment and smiled at the audience. The women were digging their fingernails into the arms of their best friends standing next to them and sighing, "Look at him."

"So, since I'm here with a group of old friends tonight," more cheers, "let's start off with an old friend." By the second chord the audience was going berserk.

Stepping to the mic, Jesse and the crowd sang along together to the classic Winslow tune--everyone lost in the moment before they even hit the first chorus.

*I'd still take you back.*

*With your sweet sighs*

*Punctuated like poison arrows to my heart.*

*I know you're killing me.*

*Slowly killing me*

*I can tell by your smile*

*But I just can't stop myself.*

*Baby, if I could have just one more night....*

Keeping up the high-energy pace, the second and third songs were also Winslow classics and by the end of the third song, the crowd was one-hundred-percent behind him, ready and willing to go anyplace he wanted to take them. They were on the journey.

At four songs in, the house was positively silent, when the first chords he plucked on his acoustic were ones they didn't recognize. Listening intently to the words they were hearing for the first time, Jesse premiered the title track of his upcoming release, *Fade to White.*

With his eyes closed, a single spot capturing him center stage, he was up in his falsetto, delivering the final chorus. The majority of the audience was holding their collective breaths and wiping tears from their eyes, this new, hauntingly beautiful tune rocking them to their cores.

*A movie scene fades to darkness*

*But our score never ends*

*After a brilliant crescendo*

*It's always 'til we meet again*

*Fade to White*

Slowly, the stage lights rose, bathing Jesse in pure white light until all that was visible of the rocker was a shadow in the blinding glow.

*'til we meet again*

*Fade to White*

Every light in the house came on, momentarily blinding the teary-eyed fans. There was a moment of absolute silence as the audience processed what they had just witnessed. And then pandemonium. Every person in the crowd knew Jesse Winslow's powerful solo performance would be the benchmark for every live show they ever saw again.

Approaching the mic with a smile, he strummed a few chords. Looking out into the crowd, his eyes widened in surprise, "Okay, let's have an unconventional moment here. What would a Jesse Winslow concert be without an unconventional moment or two? I have not seen my girlfriend in over a month, we've both been traveling. And she just got here. So, excuse me while I say hello."

Jumping off the stage, he waded three-deep into the crowd until he got to Kylie as the crowd cheered. Wrapping her in his arms, he pulled her into a deep embrace, "Toots, I've missed you so much," he whispered in her ear.

Letting her go, he took her face in both hands, looked into her eyes for a long moment and then planted a soft kiss on her lips.

The crowd went wild at the impromptu, swoon-worthy moment and Jesse gave everyone another huge smile before turning and climbing back up on the stage with the ease of a mountain goat.

"Ahhh," he said into the microphone. "All is now right in the world."

If his fans hadn't adored him before, tonight sealed the deal. He was just a guy, in love with his girl.

"Hmm, I think I'll play something a little different here. This is probably from before any of us were born, but I'm guessing, every one of you," he pointed out to the audience, scanning right to left, "can sing along with me and not miss a single word. This was one of the great New York City bands of the fifties. Hey, Kylie," he looked at his girlfriend with a shit-eating grin, "Save the Last Dance for Me."

Erupting with glee, the audience, as Jesse had predicted, sang every word of the classic tune at the top of their lungs and the club turned into an oversized frat party. From there, Jesse played a few Winslow classics to keep the energy up, before taking the energy down to introduce a new ballad.

Walking to the piano, he sat down, and adjusted the microphone. "So, I wrote this the other night on the plane flying back to New York. I was in London, recording at Abbey Road Studios," the crowd cheered, "which, by the way, was very cool. Why am I telling you guys? You probably already all know this. The pictures were all over the Internet. So, anyway, I was flying home and I wrote this. It's still a work in progress. If I were a writer, I'd probably be calling this my first draft. Hope you like it." He stopped after a few keys, looked at the audience and smiled, "Did you guys know I play piano?" the guitar player inquired, almost as an afterthought and then went back to the tune.

Opening with an extended and ethereal piano solo, Jesse had the audience's rapt attention and he was soon lost with them to someplace the music took only him. When he began to sing, the crowd stayed absolutely silent, taking in every nuance of the emotional ballad the rocker was sharing for the first time.

*I walk the studio floor at night*

*Searching for a shadow that holds a memory of you.*

*But in the darkness, all I find*

*Is an empty reflection of the scenes in my mind.*


*I may never know how our story ended,*

*The final chapters were ripped from the back of that book.*

*Still I yearn for a glimpse of two hearts that were mended,*

*But I'll always be at a loss as to where to look.*

*So, I reach for a moment that doesn't exist*

*Hoping to pluck out some truth.*

*And, Rachel, I fear I'll never know of your fate*

*'Cause our paths won't be crossing again.*

*Not tomorrow, not someday.*

*Oh, Rachel.*

*You told me I taught you about love and healing*

*Well, baby, you taught me more than that.*

*But right now, all I've got are memories trapped in time*

*Of that sweet, brief moment when I called you mine.*

*Oh, Rachel.*

*High in the hills above Jerusalem,*

*The wind howls like a lone wolf's cry.*

*Maybe if I listen hard enough,*

*I'll find our love on the edge of time.*

*Oh, Rachel, I know you're out there somewhere*

*Or maybe it's just in my mind.*

*I keep reaching and reaching and reaching*

*To grab hold of a love on the edge of time.*

*Rachel*

*You told me I taught you about love and healing,*

*Well, baby, you taught me more than that.*

*But right now, all I've got are memories trapped in time*

*Of that moment when you were still mine*

*Oh, Rachel.*

*How I wish you were mine.*

*I'll keep reaching and reaching and reaching*

*To grab hold of our love on the edge of time.*

*How I wish you were mine.*

*I want you to be mine.*

*Oh, baby, please tell me that you're mine.*

When the houselights came up, the audience went wild. "That's called Rachel," he said softly into the mic before standing and taking a little bow. As he headed back to the mic at center stage and picked up a guitar, he glanced over toward Kylie, hoping she understood about him writing a song about another woman, as with their separation and the crazy time zones, they hadn't yet discussed that regression, but surely, she would understand from the lyrics that Rachel was part of his work with Dr. S.

It took him a moment to spot her, she was facing toward the other side of the audience and was making her way through the crowd. Scanning across, he could see Claire facing Kylie and mouthing something. And then all hell broke loose. Kylie pounced on Claire like a jaguar attacking its prey. Grabbing a handful of the other woman's hair, Kylie yanked it hard with one hand and backhanded her cheek with the other, slapping her to the ground.

Coming up behind Kylie, her coach, Zac, grabbed and restrained her as his dad kept Claire at bay.

Jesse quickly mouthed to his closest security, "Get them in the back right now."

Grabbing the microphone, "Hey folks, we're going to take a

quick break." And the lights went out.

Heading backstage, Jesse was confused and in shock. *What the hell had just happened?*

As he approached his dressing room, he could hear Kylie's raised voice behind the closed door, "You knew. You freaking knew. You let me walk out of your office destroyed, you saw what that last session did to me and you freaking knew the whole time, you sadistic bitch."

Zac had Kylie on one side of the large room and his dad stood with Claire on the opposite end. Two of the club's security were also there. Jesse looked from Kylie to Claire and then back to Kylie.

"Thanks for your help, gentlemen. I think the three of us can take it from here." This was a conversation to which no outsiders needed to be privy.

As soon as the four men vacated the room, Jesse turned to the two women, "What the hell happened out there?"

"Would you like to tell him, Claire, or should I?" Kylie stared the woman down.

"You know I am legally bound..." she began.

Kylie cut her off, "Oh, stop with that legal bullshit. You are so full of it. What about being morally bound, Claire? Clearly, that means nothing to you. You fucking knew," Kylie's voice choked.

"What is going on?"

"That song."

Jesse looked at Kylie. "Did it upset you?"

"Not for the reasons you're probably thinking. But, yeah, it upset me deeply."

"I thought you'd understand if I wrote about another woman, but it was clear that the context was from a regression. I'm sorry if..."

"Don't be sorry. The last thing you said to me, David, was that you'd find me. And you did. You found me." Kylie was almost at the point of hyperventilating.

"What?" He looked from one woman to the other.

"And she knew," Kylie pointed at Claire. "She knew Daniel and I watched as you were marched to your death, the last time I saw you, you and three other rabbis were crucified, and she didn't have the decency to tell me that you found me. Just like you promised that day." Anger had turned to pain as she sobbed out the last words. "Your final words to me were, 'I'll find you.' That was your promise to me and you did, you found me."

"Daniel," he mouthed the name before turning to Claire. "Is this true?"

"It's not as simple as she is making it out to be. I am bound by HIPAA laws."

"Oh, my God, you are so full of shit, you despicable bitch. I bet you just wanted to keep us apart." Kylie screamed.

"Is this true, Claire? Is Kylie Rachel?" Jesse's jaw was hanging open, his own breath ragged.

"She appears to be," admitted the doctor, who remained the calmest of the three.

"Dr. S., I'm sure you have a good reason for not sharing this with us." Jesse's eyes were pleading for a valid reason.

"Well, I haven't really seen you," she justified.

"No. Not true. You haven't seen me. But you've held sessions with Jesse every week. Did you tell him? No. And you knew before I left for Australia and you made the conscious decision to keep this from us. You didn't want us to know. You never wanted us to find each other."

Claire's lips began to move, but no sound came out. The silence was then broken by a knock on the door.

"Yes," Jesse called out.

The house manager opened the door a crack. "Jesse, you're due back on stage."

"Okay," he sighed, "give me another two to three minutes."

When the door closed, Kylie continued, "What else have you been keeping from us, Claire?"

"Kylie, you know I can't discuss another patient with you," her tone was condescending.

"It's not what you can't do. It's what you don't want to do. Which tells me you are hiding something. I already know you were Cassius Petronius, Lord knows what other wicked roles you've played in this crazy little psychodrama. I'm done with you, Claire. You should be brought up to the medical review board and have your license revoked."

"Are you threatening me?" The psychiatrist's tone was indignant.

Kylie shook her head. "I don't need to threaten you. The universe will take good care of you. Of that, I have no doubt."

"There's a lot of talking that needs to be done," Trying to play peace maker, Jesse looked from Kylie to Claire. "But I've got to get back on stage. I've gotta go and finish this show."

"Yeah. Well, I've gotta go, too. Permanently. You can forgive this bitch all you want and buy all her bullshit excuses. That's your choice. And this is mine." And Kylie pushed past Jesse out of the dressing room toward the front of the club without so much as a backwards glance.

· · · · · ·

"Toots, it's me. Pick up your phone. I'm back at my apartment and all your luggage is here, but no you. Did you go home? We need to talk. My head is spinning right now. I'm in total shock. Where are you?"

· · · · · ·

"C'mon, Kylie. Where are you? I'm worried about you. I'm worried about us. Oh, I forgot to tell you, I spoke to Dr. S. last night and she agreed not to press any assault charges. But I think you're probably going to need to find another shrink. Call me, I'm worried about you."

· · · · · ·

"Okay, I'm giving you fair warning, I'm coming over to your apartment to make sure you're still alive. Why aren't you speaking to me? We need to talk now more than ever. I don't know if you realize this, but you called me David the other night. I swear my heart just stopped beating at that second. I felt like I'd been Tasered. Well, you are not answering and I'm coming over."

Kylie: Don't come over, Jesse. I don't want to see you and I don't want to talk to you. The door is chained from the inside, so your key won't do any good.

Jesse: Okay, excellent. We have text action. You are alive. Chained in your apartment. All your shit is over at my apartment, come here where your stuff is. We need to talk, Kylie.

Kylie: I need space. Lots and lots of space. Please, have my stuff sent to me. Enjoy your sessions with your psychiatrist. I'm bowing out of this evil little triangle and you two can live in karmic bliss.

Jesse: What the hell are you talking about? Evil triangles? What is it you know? Or think you know?

Kylie: I know nothing. Clearly. Please have my stuff sent.

Jesse: So, that's it?

Kylie: Yup. That's it.

Jesse: Just remember this was your call, Toots.

. . . . . .

Jesse: Two weeks and still radio silence. Can you at least tell me what I did wrong in all of this? I don't understand why you are pissed at me.

Kylie: Not pissed. Just want you out of my life.

Jesse: Ouch.

# Chapter 17

Enough was enough.

Every day had been torturous, checking his phone a thousand times for messages that never came and not understanding why this would make her run, when all he wanted to do was talk about it and see what they could discover by sharing details.

"You might have to come to terms with the fact that she is choosing not to have a relationship with you in this lifetime and move on." Claire had told him in their last session.

But he was not anywhere near remotely ready to do that. This was his Kylie. And now his Rachel. And she was running. Running scared. Hiding was out of fear. He knew that in his gut. Getting her across the threshold and alleviating what was causing this extreme anxiety was the answer. She had dealt so well with regression analysis, so now why this behavior? It was not like her to not want to confront everything head on and get to the bottom of it. Underneath the tough, New Jersey girl exterior, something had her so freaked out that she literally locked and chained the door.

Moving on was not the answer. And he was starting to resent Claire for saying that to him.

And as far as giving her time and space, that was a freaking chick thing and he was done with it. Kylie wasn't the only one with the license to call bullshit. He was now calling it. And he was fed up with it.

Enough was enough.

And that is how he found himself banging on her apartment door.

"C'mon, Kylie. Open the door. You do know I have a key." Pounding the door again, he shook his head, thinking exasperated didn't even begin to describe it. "Kylie, open up."

Hearing a click from behind him, he quickly turned. Two twenty-something neighbors of Kylie's peered out to see her famous boyfriend pleading for her to let him in. "Hi, Jesse," they giggled, almost in unison. Without really looking, he lifted his hand to wave and turned back to the door.

"I'm not going away, so you need to let me in." He paused, "And when I need to use the bathroom, I'm sure the girls across the hall will help me out."

The door across the hall opened an inch. "We will." One of them yelled, before the click of the door closing and giggles from inside.

Without another word being spoken or anymore pounding, the door to Kylie's apartment opened, with Kylie tucked behind it where Jesse couldn't see her. He stepped inside the apartment, peeking behind the door to find a tear-stained redhead almost cowering. Kylie, cowering? Jesse's heart hurt looking at her. This truly was destroying her and that was what he could not understand.

"Toots," he reached out for her, only for her to back away. "No. No. No. Come here." Taking her face in both hands, he asked, "Do you think I'm going to hurt you?"

"I know you are. That's the way it's always been. Don't you see that? I will be left devastated. You will destroy me again."

*What the hell was going on in her head?* He had initially misread the situation, thinking it was just pissed-off, ballsy Kylie, but as time went on, he wondered. Anger would have worn off and that made him fear something more serious. And he was right. He knew it. He could feel it, feel her, even with the absence and distance.

Her haunted eyes were but a mirror of her haunted, and now jaundiced, heart and Jesse knew if he didn't find a way to get to her, this time he would lose her forever. "I'm not going to hurt you, Kylie. We now know, so together we can figure this out. Knowing is a gift. We can figure out the broken pieces and fix them. We're going to change our fate this time. Karma is on our side."

Her face was still in his hands, as she shook it no. "I didn't want to fall in love with you to start with. I knew what a risk you were and I was just setting myself up to be decimated. I knew that. But I couldn't stop. I was the addict here, Jesse, not you. You were the drug, the sweet high that elevated me to a new plane, spun me around and released me to fly. One dose of you and you're impossible not to crave."

She was retreating. He could feel it. He went to speak, but she cut him off.

"I have lost you so many times and I'm always the one left behind to deal with the pain. The pain of losing you, the slow death where I'm begging it all to end. Every time, Jesse," she was almost screaming at him, anger mingling with the desperation of heartache. "Every time you leave me in Hell. Well, not this time. I'm not accepting that fate this time. I'm not going to love you the way I loved Bruno and David and Gaius, who I'm assuming were all you."

Reeling, Jesse dropped his hands from her face, and stumbled backwards. "You–You remember loving Gaius?"

Kylie's hand flew to her mouth, realizing the words she had spoken, chills running up both arms, meeting at the stiffened hairs on the back of her neck. "I don't know. Maybe it's because of what you've told me." But in that moment, she knew it wasn't. Standing before her was the man who came back for her again and again. "You came for me," she sobbed out the words.

"Forever and always," he repeated the promise it felt like he had made to her only yesterday. A promise born in the shadows of Rome's ancient aqueducts. Saying a silent prayer, he hoped, on some level, his response clicked another moment, another memory into full-technicolor for her.

Silently, she nodded as if remembering. *Forever and always.* It meant something to her.

Searching her glorious green eyes, he hoped for a passage, that sliver of a path that would lead her back to him quickly, before the fear robbed her from him again. Jesse knew he had to strike. "Let's figure this out, Toots. You've got half a puzzle and I've got half a puzzle and it was no coincidence that we both ended up as patients of Dr. S. But this time we're going to put it together and we're going to have our happily ever after. Because we'll know all the shit we've gotten wrong over the lifetimes and we'll fix it. We're going to fix this, here and now." Taking a step toward her, he opened his arms. "I promise," he was shaking his head yes.

"You promise?" She needed reassurance.

"I do," and he nodded again before she went to him. Holding her tightly, "Toots, I'm not going to let anything happen to you and I'm not going to let anyone hurt you. That, I promise. If anyone tries to hurt you, they'll have to break through me. We know. Kylie, we know. It all makes sense now. Us meeting. And now that we know, we're invincible. It's not about how our love began, or what we've been through, it's about how we choose to rewrite it now. There is no death. Ponder that one, babe. We never end. You are mine forever."

Holding her this time felt different. He was holding Kylie. He was holding Julia. He was holding Rachel. And the realization became too much. He'd always thought of Kylie as a gift and now he knew why. That one last chance to hold Julia. To be with Julia. Again. The ultimate gift. And Rachel. Oh, to feel her in his arms one more time. Finding her, again.

Burying his face in her neck, he was overwhelmed by the myriad of emotions slamming him from different points throughout the eons and exploding as hot tears. It was too much to comprehend. Too much to bear, and right now he was only focused on the good.

"I'm getting you soaked," he pulled away to look at her, shocked at her lack of emotion. He was feeling every moment his soul had ever lived and Kylie had seemingly shut down on him again. Grabbing her hand, he pulled her to the couch, stopping short of sitting down. "Do you have paper and pens?" She nodded and headed toward the bedroom while he pulled out his chariot journal.

Coming back, she handed him the pens and paper and just stood there. "Sit, Toots. I'm not going to bite you."

Kylie didn't crack a smile.

"Before we start this, I just want you to think about this, okay? Never will there be a moment that is our last. Never. Just think about that, Toots. We didn't know that before, and being separated killed us, but we know it now. I can't even describe the comfort I feel in that. If we had known this all those other times, it would have made the hell we've gone through less painful. All you have to know is I will love you forever. I've already loved you for thousands of years. And I think probably for many lifetimes. And you and I, we're still on this journey together. We will always have so much more to share. Always and forever." He smiled his lopsided smile as a thought came to him. "If this doesn't help create some brilliant tunes, then I need to hang up my rock 'n' roll shoes," he finished with a rough laugh.

Spreading out the sheets of paper on the table in two columns, he titled one, Kylie, the other Jesse.

"We've told each other bits and pieces, but we've never really gone in-depth with one another about the details of our regressions." Handing her a pen, "Start with the first ones and the images you saw and then on to the more complex ones. Let's do where, when, people we knew, landmarks we can identify, details like clothes."

"Smells and scents," she added, her nose twitching.

"Yeah," he encouraged, glad to see she was going to partake. "It might be the littlest thing that spurs a memory." He went back to his list, writing details from clothes to food to monetary denominations. Looking out the corner of his eye, he watched for a moment as Kylie neatly created her list, knowing if he could keep her talking, working with him on the puzzle, that the exile she'd imposed on him, trying to avoid the danger of love, would finally be conquered.

After about thirty minutes, Kylie stood and stretched before disappearing into the kitchen, only to return with two bottles of cold water.

"Thanks, Toots." Jesse grabbed the bottle and went back to his list.

They worked for another hour before Kylie broke the silence. "How do you want to do this?"

Picking up his water bottle, he headed for the couch and kicked off his shoes. "I'm going to lie back and close my eyes, just read your list. I'm going to try and keep my mind clear and see what happens."

"Okay, that sounds good." She waited for Jesse to get comfortable and for his breathing to settle before beginning on the list. The first few items were just from visuals and feelings she had in the early sessions: being left out on the frozen tundra from one session, a steep hill leading down to the beach in another session, and spiky mountains in a third.

Her regression with Gunther brought more detail as she described the canals of Strasbourg and the bright-colored flowers hanging in baskets that swung in the breeze, flower petals catching the glowing sunlight, beckoning the honey bees. The contrast of those visions to the inside of the hospital where she worked, were stark. The hallways smelled of antiseptic and death, the air never taking on a fresh breeze.

She glanced over at Jesse, wondering if he was still awake. Then she began to tell him about her life as Geneviève. And there was so much to tell. The slight pulsing of his jaw muscles let her know that he was taking in every word, but didn't utter a sound of his own.

*We lost our parents in a fire.*

*It was just us, my brother, Bruno and me. He had to raise and protect me,* she read, peering over the paper, swearing she saw the tic in his jaw again.

*I attended the church school at Saint-Eustache and then worked for Mme. Michaud, a rich woman who gave me mending and house-work to do.* The line of his lips went straight, she was sure of it. To test him, the next 'fact' she revealed was, *my brother used to give me a coin every day to buy an éclair from Patisserie Stohrer.* The edges of his lips pulled up and she knew what she was witnessing were actual reactions and this last one was probably based on nothing more than the treat he had brought her back from Paris.

*Bruno, my brother, did handyman work for Mme. Michaud for extra money.* She laughed, *And to make sure I stayed employed and fed, he also, umm, serviced her.* The line of his lips resumed their straight line and his nostrils flared as he breathed in deeply, exhaling raggedly.

*Does he remember any of this,* she wondered? And went on, *He was also involved with the man who ran the charcuiterie.* She paused and laughed, *He was quite the player. Simply irresistible.* She could almost see Bruno's handsome face in her mind's eye.

*And then one night he didn't come home. I was worried sick, I couldn't find him anywhere and I soon found out he'd been arrested for being caught with Mr. Diot, the charcuitier, for having sex in a public place. And I never saw him again. Not until his execution, but he was already dead by then. They'd broken their necks before burn-ing them at the stake.*

So focused on her memory, Kylie had not glanced at the couch to note Jesse pulling off his shirt in a ripping motion.

His eyes were closed, his face screwed in agony. "That smell," he wailed. "That smell." As he rose from the couch, his hands moved from his tattered shirt to his spiky hair, pulling at it.

"Jesse," Kylie screamed. "Jesse. Stop."

His eyes shifted rapidly as he opened them, searching for a place to focus, orient, and anchor himself. With a series of short rapid sniffs, he asked, "What is that smell?"

"Sulphur," she replied, although there were no odors present in her apartment.

Nodding, he repeated, "Sulphur, yes." With his hands in his hair, now wet with sweat at the roots, he walked in a circle twice before sitting back on the couch.

Silently, Kylie watched his face, a portrait shifting as if the painter were applying broad, altering brush strokes, before he tilted his head to the side, a thought clearly capturing him as his eyes widened and he frantically dug in his pants' pocket for his phone.

"There's a plaque, Kylie. Have you ever seen the plaque?"

Shaking her head, "I don't know what you're talking about."

"There's a plaque on the street where the bakery is. It's set into the sidewalk. I saw it last time I was there. The day I got you the éclair. What was your brother's name again?" he asked.

"Bruno Lenoir," her voice was soft, arms crossed over her chest, hugging herself.

He stared at his phone for a moment, "When was the last time you were on that street?"

"Rue Montorgueil?"

He nodded.

"Let me think. I was in Paris about two years ago, but I wasn't in that area. Probably the last time I was at Patisserie Stohrer was on a trip with my parents. My father and I went there. He loves their Baba au Rhum."

"When was that?"

"Um," she thought. "A while back...2011, maybe. We were there in April that year."

"Can you be sure?"

Kylie nodded, heading down the hall to her bedroom. She came back, flipping through the pages of her passport.

"Here it is. We got to Paris on April 8$^{th}$, 2011 and left on the 15$^{th}$. What does the plaque say, Jesse?"

"According to internet articles, the plaque was placed in the sidewalk in 2014, so if you were last there in 2011, you wouldn't have seen it."

Without uttering a word, she held out her hand for his phone, sensing his reticence at surrendering it to her.

And there it was, set into the sidewalk. Chills ran up her arms again as she read of her brother's fate.

"You saw this?"

Jesse nodded. Sitting back down on the couch, he put his forehead in his hand. "I stopped to read it and my French is good enough to get the gist of it. And I had a crazy reaction to it, Toots. I couldn't breathe. I ripped my scarf off because it felt like it was strangling me. I *lost* it, Toots. I felt like I was being asphyxiated."

"They stuffed their shirts with sulphur." Tears streamed down

Kylie's face, an exquisite portrait in pain.

"The complete destruction of their bodies to mere dust, implied at the end of time that they would not resurrect, stopping them from taking part in eternal life." Jesse was not sure how he knew that, but it was a fact planted somewhere in his mind.

Kylie smiled for the first time. "Well, the fuckers got that wrong."

"Yes. Yes, they did."

Jesse paced the room, his lips moving, but no sound emerged, as Kylie watched him, looking for something, anything, that gave her solid proof that he was the brother who loved and protected her.

"Mon moitié," she mumbled, barely audible.

Stopping in his tracks, the rocker spun around to face her, a myriad of emotions battling one another for control of his expression. "I failed you in that lifetime, too, didn't I? I was there to protect you and my own selfish behavior got in the way, leaving you to a horrible fate as a small child. I failed Geneviève just like I failed Julia and Rachel. I've always been so wrapped up in my own agenda, that those I love most are collateral damage for my risk taking. No wonder you've been so afraid of me since we found out. I couldn't understand why. But now I do."

"But, Jess, don't you see that I am not that victim anymore. I fought my own battle with Blaise Collins and you were there ready to protect me, you didn't let me down. You laid it on the line for him and I stood up to him on my own. He's not going to metaphorically starve me and blackball me. I'm going to beat all of them at their own game. And you're not abandoning me. Yes, you have to go off and record and tour, but you are not leaving me in a compromising position. I'm not allowing myself to be a victim."

As they continued pouring through the lifetimes, the themes kept continuing. The suffering and degradation she experienced upon losing him. His feelings of invincibility. Third-party involvement in his demise. The tragedy just played on and on.

But now they knew. And destiny was theirs for the taking.

. . . . . .

His mumbling in his sleep woke her. It felt good to have him back in her bed again. She couldn't deny that. His warmth and presence made her realize how much she had missed and needed him. Something she wouldn't let herself acknowledge before that point. But her world was complete when Jesse Winslow held her in his arms. And now she understood why.

Softly, she ran her fingers through his spiky hair, enjoying the rush she still got every time she looked down at him and saw this famous man off in his dreams next to her, his face magnificent in repose. It had always been deeper than his notoriety and beauty. He was truly the missing piece to the completion of her soul. *Mon moitié.*

Stirring, he opened his eyes and smiled up at her. "You okay? Can't sleep, Toots?"

"I'd rather look at you." She continued to pick at his spiky hair.

"At me?" he chuckled. "What do you see? Or maybe I should ask, who do you see?"

Smiling down at him, "I see you, Jesse. I'm glad for all the others. They're like missing shards in a panel of stained glass. But the picture they create is distinctly you."

"I like that." He stretched, tangling his feet with hers.

Moving her hand from his hair, she cupped his cheek, "Thank you for nearly knocking down my door today. And thank you for not giving up on me."

Putting his hand over hers, he moved it to his lips, softly kissing her palm. "Kylie, you have been my love forever. Literally. And I loved you before I even knew that. Knowing what I know now, I feel blessed. Yeah, blessed, not a word I use a lot, but blessed that fate has not only brought us together again, but revealed the truth to us. Walking away was never an option for me. Even if I didn't know the truth about us, did you ever think I'd let you go?"

"I love you." She moved down on the pillows so that she was face to face with him. "I love you." The words were finally out.

He was silent.

"I know what you are thinking," she continued when he didn't respond. "You're thinking, does she love me or love them?"

Smiling, "You know me too well, Toots."

"I loved you long before I knew you had anything to do with them. I think I fell in love with you when you brought me the éclair. Yeah, that far back. You brought me a gift because you were thinking about me and I was just so moved by that. In your busy life, you went out of your way to do something to make me smile. So, yeah, it's you I love. But now that I know our truth, it just takes that love and amplifies it. Jesse, I feel like my heart is going to explode. I am so overwhelmed."

"C'mere." He pulled her into a tight embrace, tangling their legs even deeper.

Shifting, so that she could look in his eyes, the words tumbled out without any forethought. "Marry me." It was neither a question nor a statement.

"You want me to marry you?" His lopsided grin already told her his answer.

"We never got to do it. Not Gaius and Julia, nor Rachel and David. That was a dream we never fulfilled. And I want the dream. I want you to marry me." Kylie's eyes were alight in the semi-dark room. And what she didn't say was as powerful as what she did say.

"Toots, I will marry you tomorrow if we can. But are you sure?

You just spent weeks refusing to see me, telling me we were over. I'm reeling in a good way now, but I won't lie to you, I have been in hell since the concert."

"I'm sorry. I'm so sorry that I hurt you. I know it doesn't make it any better, but I was miserable, too. And all I could think was that I'm going to lose you again, so do it now and get it over with. Don't fall any deeper in love with him. Get out now."

"And how did that work out for you?" There was the sound of pleasure in his throaty laugh.

"Not so good. I thought about you day and night. I missed you so much it physically hurt. I knew the pain of losing you and I thought if I have to go through this again, it will kill me. So instead, I was slowly killing myself. I cursed the day I met you in Claire's waiting room. And begged the cosmos to give me a break and not love you so much. But they didn't listen. It sucked. It sucked so bad. And I was in Hell knowing you were out there and not with me. I'm sorry I tried to run and hide. And I'm sorry for hurting you. I ache knowing I caused you pain, Jesse."

Rolling away from her, he reached for his phone on the nightstand. After a moment of looking something up, he said, "It says we have to get a license and then there is a twenty-four-hour waiting period. Let's get it tomorrow morning." He smiled his lopsided grin. "And then go back the next day and get married. We can do however big a wedding you want afterwards, but let's just do this quietly first so nothing fucks it up. This way, by the time people find out we're getting married, we're already married."

"Can Hayley be our witness?"

"Sure. Do you want your parents to come down?"

Kylie shook her head, "No. They can come to the party when we throw it. I just want this to be you and me. And Sip."

"I'm getting married," he laughed. "I'm marrying some pushy

New Jersey broad who asked me to marry her and I said yes, after she ignored me for weeks. I'm such a fucking pushover."

"You are a lucky son of a bitch." She laid her head down on his shoulder.

. . . . . .

They needed a second witness.

Jesse looked out at the rows in the courtroom, "Hey, anyone want to be our second witness?"

What ensued was practically a stampede at a rock concert with fans rushing the judge's bench instead of a stage, with a none-too-happy judge calling for 'order in the court'.

His name was Jason and he was a bass player in a local band, there in court to get married that morning, too. It seemed perfect since he was a fellow musician and now would have the ultimate rock 'n' roll story to tell forever. *"Did I ever tell you about the time I stood up for Jesse Fucking Winslow at his wedding?"*

In a black suit and skinny tie, with his new clean-cut look, Jesse looked more model than rocker. She was in a white silk drape dress, resembling a stola. It wasn't a coincidence. With her hair pulled up, titian curls framing her face, Kylie was a vision, ethereal and timeless.

By the time they emerged, hand in hand, onto the courthouse steps, the paparazzi had been alerted to what had taken place in the court-room and were waiting for the newlyweds.

"I'll meet you two later to celebrate," Hayley kissed them both goodbye and effortlessly disappeared into the crowd.

"Jesse, over here. Did you two just get married?" The popping flashes blinded them.

"I'd say I'm a bit overdressed for a traffic ticket," he kidded.

"Are you and Kylie really married?" It was a reporter from *Rolling Stone.*

"Well, we were hoping to tell her parents first before you found us, but yes," he turned to Kylie, his trademark smile and eyes singing a love song of their own. "Please, meet my fantastically gorgeous, smart, beautiful-hearted, and lovable bride, Mrs. Jesse Winslow."

The crowd cheered as the once world-famous playboy bachelor took his bride's face in both hands and smiled at her before going in for a kiss that would satisfy all the media outlets and be broadcast throughout the world in mere minutes. But even more importantly, as they stood at the top of the famous marble staircase in lower Manhattan, it did not elude either of them that the fairytale they'd wished for-- to be husband and wife, once upon a time, on gleaming white marble steps, before the destruction of Herod's second Temple in Jerusalem, and once upon a time, among the intricate marble staircases ascending the Seven Hills of Rome--had finally come true.

Had the soul work they had done in this lifetime been enough to alter the fate that had continually kept them separated lifetime after lifetime? Was this possibly their karmic retribution, their day in the sun?

As they separated from their kiss, the cheer of the crowd was deafening as the first citizens of the world celebrated their union. Pulling her close, Jesse held Kylie tight, softly rubbing his cheek against hers until his lips caressed her ear.

Feeling his warm breath against her skin was comforting amongst the growing pandemonium surrounding them. Above the noise of the crowd, she clearly heard his whisper in her ear as he proclaimed a promise, one that she had waited for over the course of millennia.

*"Forever Mine, ma moitié."*

# Chapter 18

"You know we just started a shit storm," laughed Jesse. "Let's call security, so they're waiting for us at my building, and can get us in the door," he told the driver.

"And I'd better call my parents. Damn, I thought we were going to be able to stay under the radar with that."

"Slight miscalculation," the driver said and they all laughed.

"What do you want to do tonight? It's our wedding night." Jesse was beaming.

Kylie laughed. "We really didn't think about this, did we? Why don't we invite some friends and family over and order in a bunch of Chinese takeout?" She wondered if he'd go for it.

"Perfect, Toots," he quickly replied, looking down at his buzzing phone. Answering it, "Yes, I know you want to kill me. You're supposed to know about things first, so that you can manage the press." He looked at Kylie and mouthed, Molly. "Yes, it's true. We're married. A statement? Okay. Today I married the love of my life, Kylie Marie Martin, the former Miss New Jersey and the current, and forever, Mrs. Jesse Winslow. I have been blessed in finding my soulmate, the one person who, in this lifetime, I am meant to be with, forever. I'd like to thank everyone for their warm congratulations. How does that sound, sound good?"

Next to him, Kylie was on a call of her own. "Hi, Mom. How are you?... Have you seen the news yet this morning?... Okay, well you might want to turn it on…No, everything's okay… actually everything is fantastic." She turned to Jesse and whispered, "She's turning on the TV." Smiling, she was waiting for the scream on the other end of the phone. "Yeah, try CNN…" Kylie held the phone out and not ten seconds had gone by when she heard the screech through the phone. Kylie put the phone back to her ear, "She's calling me a little stinker," she told Jesse. "Mom, Jesse and I want you and Dad to come over tonight. We're having a few people over. Very casual. We think we're going to bring in Chinese food…. Sake? Sure, bring it. Come on over about 7:30 or so…. Yes, we'll talk about a reception. Mom, Jesse wants to talk to you."

She handed him the phone, "Hi, Mrs. Martin… Oh, okay, Fiona… Yes, I'm very excited. … No, this was a surprise for me too…. Well, I didn't expect your daughter to ask me to marry her… Yeah, she did." He laughed. "How could I say no?... We will see you tonight… Bye."

He handed Kylie back her phone. "Are you going to tell everyone I asked you to marry me?"

"Toots, you bring new meaning to the feminist movement. You'll be an inspiration to girls and women all over the world." And then out of the side of his mouth, "Rock stars everywhere will be stalked by their future brides." He could barely contain his laughter.

Giving him a side-eyed glance, "Don't make me regret you finding me."

"Don't make me regret saying yes, Mrs. Winslow. Now, shut up and kiss me." He pulled his bride into his lap, the space on the seat between them too much for him to bear.

······

"I found out the two of you knew one another when I saw it on TMZ," Fiona started. "I recognized the mystery woman from Starbucks as my very own daughter. Then I found out you were dating on Facebook news."

"I'm glad you have such reliable sources to keep track of your daughter," Jesse laughed.

"And now you're married and I'm meeting my son-in-law for the very first time." Fiona was on her third sake. A tall, natural redhead like her daughter, Fiona Martin was still a head turner.

Kylie rolled her eyes at her mother, she knew, more than anyone else on the planet, that her momma was the ultimate, control-freak, stage mother. Having a daughter who was Miss New Jersey was one of her greatest accomplishments in life. That daughter marrying one of the world's most famous and handsome men was clearly a result of her mothering. Or so she thought. And would continue to let everyone know.

"I loved him, Mother. I did not want you to run him off."

"You loved me?" Jesse asked with a huge lopsided grin.

Kylie backhanded him in the arm. Catching her hand, he pulled her to him, kissing the side of her head.

As the evening went on, and more calls and texts of congratulations came in from close friends and business associates, they continued to invite people over. The question of can we bring anything was answered with, "Chinese food, champagne, sparkling cider."

By nine p.m., there were nearly thirty people in the apartment celebrating the surprise nuptials.

"Are you going to have a big reception or is this it?" was the question on everyone's lips and while both Kylie and Jesse would have been more than happy to make their impromptu Chinese potluck the beginning and end of their wedding festivities, Fiona was having none of it. She would make sure her daughter and son-in-law had a wedding that paparazzi would be clamoring for their spot to get a glimpse of the most beautiful bride they'd ever seen.

"I'm going to put together a list of venues here in the city," she began early in the evening.

"You could do a destination wedding," suggested Hayley.

"Isn't tonight good enough?"

The heat in Fiona's face slowly rose from her chest to her neck and up her face and Kylie knew her mother was seeing red. There was a deep satisfaction in it, payback for years of being paraded out on a stage. Kylie had no doubt in her mind that this was the ultimate stage mother moment for her. Fiona had never expected anything like this.

"I'm not going to even speak to you. Hayley, I know with your good southern breeding, that I can count on you to help me with these decisions."

Putting her hand on Fiona's forearm, she smiled warmly and drawled, "It would be my pleasure." Turning, she smiled at Kylie.

"Turncoat, bitch," she muttered. "Okay, just get it down to the final choices of venues before you start dragging me all over God's creation."

"Fine," her mother acquiesced with an attitude.

"Zac," Kylie perked up. "I'm so glad you came." Standing to greet him, she gave her trainer a big hug.

"Congrats, Red. I am so happy for you two. You were the hot topic at L9 today. People were gathered around the juice bar watching the TV and talking about how they'd seen you both at the club."

"I'll bet." Kylie laughed. "Zac, this is my mom, Fiona, and my best friend, Hayley, aka the reigning Miss Mississippi. Mom, Zac is responsible for getting me healthy and into shape."

The tall, handsome blond shook his head, no. "Kylie, you are the only one responsible for getting healthy and into shape. I just made you sweat. So nice to meet you both," he said to the ladies and then introduced the woman with him, "This is my good friend, Liz van der Heyden."

"So nice to meet you, Liz. I'm glad you could join us." Kylie welcomed the petite woman at Zac's side.

"Congratulations. What an exciting day for you." The dirty blonde had a warm vibe that Kylie immediately liked.

"Are you of the Darien, Connecticut, van der Heyden's?" Fiona could sniff out Social Register families like a bloodhound.

"Yes, I am."

"I chaired a fundraiser for Autism with Neelie van der Heyden a few years back."

"Neelie is my mother."

"What a lovely woman. She is quite a prolific fundraiser." Fiona extolled a rare compliment.

Hayley looked on silently, not taking her eyes off Liz, until Liz could no longer ignore the stare.

"Nice to meet you, Hayley."

"The pleasure is all mine," Sip was dripping southern honey. "Would you two like something to eat? Let me show you where everything is?" And with a crook of her finger Zac and Liz followed.

"What a nice-looking couple." Fiona smiled after them.

"I think they are just friends, Mom. My bet is that she will end up as Hayley's next conquest. Did you see that look Sip was giving her? It was like, excuse me, how are you ignoring me? I'm standing right next to you. Nothing else should matter."

"You think so?" Fiona was shocked.

"I have not seen Sip act like that." Kylie was amused.

Excusing himself from their guests, Jesse walked into the bedroom for a moment. Sitting on the edge of the bed, he took a deep breath and smiled. *Married. Whoever would have thought it.* He had never even considered it before. Not with Claudine or any of her predecessors. Marriage just didn't fit his lifestyle. Not until he changed his lifestyle and met the woman he promised he'd find again. What a trip. And it was their secret. People would think they were nuts, if they knew.

Jesse laughed out loud. Yes, nuts. Crazy, in-love nuts about her. Just as he had been about Julia and Rachel. And now Kylie. Finally, their time. It may have taken two thousand years and a bunch of lifetimes, but this time they got it right. Tonight, after all their guests left, he would make love to his wife. Finally.

Pulling out his phone, he began to check messages. Congratulatory message after congratulatory message. Even one from Bongo that sounded sincere. All the good energy coming his way was uplifting. Until he got to hers.

**I wish you would have spoken to me before going ahead with your spontaneous plans. I'm deeply concerned with your well-being and the ramifications this might have for you. Obviously, I'm prohibited from disclosing certain things, suffice it to say, my concern with what you did today runs very deep. We need to talk. ~ Dr. Claire Stoddard**

Seriously? That's the message she sent him on his wedding day. He was annoyed that she would encroach upon his happiness, on today of all days, and do something to bring him down emotionally. There was certainly an ex-patient of hers with whom he would not be sharing this little missive. Seeing Kylie grab the woman by the hair once might have held a little bit of excitement, if he was being honest about it, but a second altercation would probably result in assault charges.

Heading out of the bedroom, he tried to shake off his mood. It was his wedding night for God's sake. The apartment was filled with friends and colleagues he loved and he knew he needed to get back into conversations that lifted his spirits. *But that text…* it really stuck in his craw. So, instead of Jesse Winslow, newlywed, entering the living room, it was Jesse Winslow, rock star, who rejoined his guests, because that guy knew how to put on a show and hide himself in the process.

It was nearly dawn by the time the last guests were straggling out.

"It's not our wedding day anymore." Kylie stuck out her lower lip in a pout. "We never made love on our wedding day."

"And you think I won't make this up to you?" The look in his eyes made her thighs clench. "But right now, I'm starving. We ate that Chinese food hours ago. Diner?" he suggested to Kylie and their three remaining guests, Hayley, Zac and Liz.

"At this hour, you can actually probably get out of the apartment without the paparazzi camped out.

"Let's do it. There's that great twenty-four-hour place on 8$^{th}$ Ave."

Emerging from the building onto the empty sidewalk into the chilly, pre-dawn, Jesse looked at Zac, "You were right. The paparazzi are asleep."

"They think we are, too." Kylie laughed, taking her husband's hand on what was feeling like the perfect ending to the perfect day.

Two eggs over easy, bacon, rye toast and wonderfully greasy home-fried potatoes later, Mr. and Mrs. Winslow finally crawled into bed together for the first time as husband and wife.

Spooning together, Kylie suggested, "Can we sleep for a few hours before consummating this relationship, because as hot as you are in bed, I know I'm going to fall asleep in the middle of it, even if I'm on top riding you."

Kissing her neck, he laughed, pulling her tighter into him, "We are so not rock 'n roll."

Slipping her hand into his and bringing it to her lips for a kiss. "Another one of our many secrets it's best that the world does not know."

"You got that right, Mrs. Winslow."

# Chapter 19

He had received three additional texts from her, all similar in tone to the one she sent on their wedding night. Like the initial one, he chose not to share them with his bride. After cancelling two consecutive appointments, he decided on week three to keep his Wednesday appointment as scheduled and finally make the break. It needed to happen. Claire was not going to be happy, but she really wasn't of concern to him. Kylie was his only concern and her animosity toward Claire had taken on a life of its own, as she had a strong gut feeling that Claire played a role greater than just as a psychiatrist in their current lives.

"I don't think she wants us together, Jess, and I don't think this is the first time that's happened. Do you think she's in love with you?"

"Well, that would be highly unethical, Toots. I'm a patient of hers." But there was something in Jesse's gut that told him Kylie was very astute and probably on the mark. Women could read other women in a way that men were clueless to understand. It was the way Dr. S. looked at him, always found opportunities to physically touch him, as innocuous as those motions seemed, they happened with regularity at every session. And although what appeared to be her growing feelings for him had crossed his mind, he swept them away

This was his first time seeing her since he and Kylie had gotten married, and frankly, he just wanted to get it over with. Opening the door to her office, she greeted him professionally, welcoming him in.

Something was different. Her blouse was cut a little lower, her skirt a little shorter and tighter and her long hair was curled into loose waves that fell about her shoulders. She gestured for him to take a seat and just looked at him, waiting for him to speak first and surrender the position of control. Sitting back on the couch, he silently continued to look at her.

Finally, she spoke, giving into him, "Is there something you want to say to me?"

"Obviously, there's a lot I want to say to you. Let me start with the text you sent me on my wedding night. What *were* you thinking? It was incredibly inappropriate as were the subsequent ones you've sent."

"You are my patient and I'm looking out for your well-being and when I see red flags, it is my responsibility to alert you to them."

"Just like you did with David and Rachel's regressions?"

"I have to be very discreet with my patients' private information."

Waving her off with a hand, "Dr. S., I think it's time you refer me on to someone else to continue treatment. This is not healthy. And the relationship between you and my wife has taken a very hostile turn and I really don't want to get any more of your texts maligning her. She is my wife."

As if there was a string pulling her from the top of her head, Claire's spine straightened to its full-sitting length, "Jesse, I can absolutely recommend someone else for you to talk to, although I think you are acting hastily and there is still important work you and I could be doing. We've had a lot of success in our association, have we not?"

"Yes, I'm clean and sober and I could not have done that without you. I will forever be grateful."

"I don't want your gratitude. I want you to maintain your health, I want you to continue healing through self-discovery and sobriety. I think the most stable way to achieve that is for us to continue our work together."

"I think that would be something that would upset my wife greatly."

"If she truly loves you, she'll want what is best for you and that is not to have a disturbance in the treatment that has been so successful for you." Although Claire was selling hard, she was attempting to give off the opposite appearance.

Shaking his head, Jesse realized that today, he was hearing the words the doctor was saying to him very differently than he might have heard the exact same statements in the past. He was now hearing them as a married man, with a responsibility to love and protect his woman. The single, narcissistic, lone beast was gone. In his place was the alpha of a newly formed pack. His mind quickly flashed to Rachel's wolf, whose innate instinct was to protect those he loved. He had become the wolf.

"Are you questioning Kylie's love for me and her commitment to my health?"

Crossing her legs the other way, Claire was quiet for a moment before she spoke, "I do not think she would consciously want to sabotage you. I'm just afraid her feelings toward me might cloud her ability to separate what is best for you."

"We always look to alleviate our stressors, right?" He paused, his eye contact direct with the doctor. "Right now, the stressor is you, Dr. S. Moving on would remove the stressor on several levels."

She sat there silently for a beat. "I hope you know the only thing I want here is what is best for you. It is my only motivation, Jesse. I am your doctor. It is my job to help you help yourself get and stay healthy. And to see you have any kind of relapse," she shook her head and waved her hand in front of her face, "would be a horrible situation to watch and know that I couldn't help you." Then, without missing a beat, she posed, "Here's something to think about. I know Kylie and I have had a major falling out, but she and I have also done some important work together that has helped her get her life back on a solid path. Would the two of you consider, at least as part of your treatment, being treated jointly? I really don't know what that would look like, we can discuss that and build a protocol that would work for you both and it might give us more answers to your past history together."

As she threw out the last piece, she was certain it would be the irresistible lynch pin to reel Kylie back in and to hold onto Jesse as a client. Her sole motivation.

"I'll talk to her. That's the only thing I will commit to. I'll talk to her."

. . . . . .

"So, this is the list. Hayley and I have culled it down to seven." From a folder already two inches thick, Fiona pulled a single sheet of paper and placed it on the table in front of her daughter.

With the briefest of glances, Kylie responded, "I can make it five for you immediately. You can pull off there right now both The Plaza and The Pierre."

"I think you should go see them," Fiona's protest was cut short.

"Don't waste your breath, Mom. Neither of those places say Jesse and Kylie. We need a place where if in the middle of the wedding, Jesse and his buddies decide they need to do a set, it's totally cool. The Plaza and The Pierre are too white bread formal."

Reading a text on her phone, Sip was smiling, "Liz said if you're interested, her parents can sponsor you to use the Wee Burn Country Club in Darien. They are members."

Kylie laughed out loud, "Tell her it was very nice of her to offer, but we're going to have to pass. Or they may end up getting their membership revoked.

"Wee Burn is very elite," Fiona informed them, picking at her farro and grilled chicken salad.

"It ain't rock 'n' roll, Ma." Kylie laughed. "You and Liz's mom have the same taste."

"Taste alike," Hayley muttered under her breath, snickering at the thought.

Changing the subject, Kylie asked, "So, what is going on between you and Zac's cute little friend?"

"She is cute, isn't she?" Hayley wanted corroboration.

"Very," Kylie agreed, "And I like her a lot. She just fit right in that night, like we'd known her and been hanging out with her forever."

"So, you are seeing the young lady Zac brought to Jesse's apartment?" Fiona was still trying to wrap her head around the fact that she wasn't Zac's girlfriend.

"Well, I don't know if I'd call it seeing yet, but we're definitely getting to know one another." Putting her hand up to her mouth, she whispered to her friend's mother, "You might get to go to that Wee Burn wedding someday." They both laughed at the joke, as Wee Burn was a bastion of conservativism.

"Okay, so the two sticking out to me here are either Gotham Hall or Capitale. It's funny that they were both originally built as banks by great architects, with big rotunda rooms and Corinthian columns. Look at the details in both venues. They're magnificent." Kylie spread the press kits out on the table. "I think Jesse would love either space and both lend themselves well to setting up a stage, just in case."

"Will his bandmates be there?" Hayley asked.

"He's heard from the entire band, including Bongo, congratulating us and saying they were looking forward to coming in for the wedding and to getting back into the studio." Kylie continued to pour over the information from the two sites.

"That has to make Jesse feel good."

"It really does. It's a weight off him and I know not worrying about that is really significant for him." *Now if we can only get rid of Claire,* she thought. Jesse had come home from his last appointment *still* a patient of *'The Evil Doctor,'* Kylie's new nickname for her. Claire now wanted to treat them together, which, while it could provide them with so many answers about their souls' journeys, meant they'd still be tied to her and that set off all Kylie's red flags. But the chance of knowing more was still intriguing.

Kylie knew, beyond a shadow of a doubt, that this was not their first rodeo with Dr. Claire Stoddard. Oh, no, none of this was a coincidence. Jesse had always been in the middle of them somehow and that woman did not like losing. She would go to any means not to be perceived as the loser. Of that, Kylie was sure. As the vision of Mme. Michaud looking down on her standing in the street, a twelve-year-old begging for her help, crossed Kylie's mind's eye, a hatred erupted from deep within, causing her to shiver. If that was really her, she left a twelve-year-old orphaned with no family to care for her, knowing the child's future would hold rape and abuse and most likely death. *That was it,* she had to tell Jesse she couldn't go back to Claire for joint sessions. Although she had no hard proof that the two women were, in fact, the same soul, she knew in her gut they both needed to stay as far away from her former shrink as possible.

"You're shivering and have goosebumps," Fiona rubbed her daughter's forearm where the pale golden hairs were standing straight up.

Someday she and Jesse were going to need to share this other part of their lives with those they loved. She yearned to share that side of herself, but the time wasn't right yet. And she didn't know if it ever would be.

"So, you've already visited all these places?" Kylie reentered the conversation, leaving eighteenth-century Paris, on just the other side of the veil.

The two women nodded.

"Of course, we have," Fiona's tone was indignant.

"Well, you two have been busy little beavers." Again, Kylie looked back between the brochures. "But seriously, thank you for doing this for me. What you have done in under a month would have taken me eight months to complete."

"Everyone wants to do your wedding, so we totally got the royal treatment everywhere," shared Hayley. "It's actually been a lot of fun."

"So, between these two, did either stand out head and shoulders above the other?"

"They are both gorgeous venues, depends if you want to do midtown or downtown on the Bowery," her mother offered.

"A Jesse Winslow wedding screams Bowery to me. You know, home of CBGBs. The whole punk movement was born down there, it's kinda just the right vibe. And it was designed by Stanford White, which adds another level of intrigue. But, I guess I should see them both," Kylie acquiesced.

"Who's Stanford White?" Sip asked. "And how do you know about this building from the 1890s?"

"There's been books and movies about him. If he were around now, the paparazzi would be all over him. He was a notorious playboy obsessed with this woman, Evelyn Nesbit, who was basically America's first supermodel, right around the turn of the century. She was a teenager and he was in his forties. And then she married this totally crazy rich guy who was flipped out that she lost her virginity to White. The husband became totally fixated on it and ended up shooting and killing Stanford White at Madison Square Garden," she ended dramatically.

"That is totally creepy and that White guy sounds like a pedophile," the look on Sip's face portrayed disgust. "Now I think you should take the other place and forget this one."

Kylie laughed. "He wasn't killed in that building, so I think we're safe. No ghosts to sabotage the wedding."

Fiona stood. "Let me call both places and we'll see if we can do walk-throughs. We need to get this booked."

. . . . . .

"Dr. Stoddard's office," the receptionist answered.

"Hi, this is Jesse Winslow, is Dr. Stoddard available?" It was his appointment time and he wasn't there, so he knew she was in the office.

"Hello, Jesse. Is everything okay?" Claire was on the line.

"Yes, everything is fine, Dr. S. I just wanted to let you know that Kylie and I have given serious thought to having you work with both of us together and we really feel, at this time, that it is in both our best interests to move on and work with another psychiatrist."

The pause was long and tense. Jesse was just glad he'd gotten it all out there, uninterrupted.

"Are you saying that you will no longer be seeing me individually as a patient, in addition to me not working with you as a couple?" Claire's usually melodious voice was tight.

"Yes. That is what I'm saying. I appreciate all you have done for me, especially with this last detox and how successful it was, but circumstances have changed and it's really in everyone's best interest if we part ways. I hope you will still provide me with names of other doctors. I do, however, wish you the best."

Her sigh was loud. "Jesse, you are making a huge mistake. I know you think you know Kylie and that you are soulmates, but I don't think this is a wise decision. Down the line I think you will be very happy and comforted should you continue your individual sessions as my patient."

"I appreciate your concern. I do. But I won't be coming back and I look forward to you sending me an email with information for other psychiatrists that use hypnosis therapy."

"Jesse, you are making a grave mistake."

"Claire," he called her by her given name, a first, "I'm sorry. But honestly, I think staying would be much more damaging. Take care of yourself."

When she didn't respond, he hung up the phone.

· · · · · ·

"Let's work out in the private gym," Zac suggested, based on the number of eyes on them. "We've always had high-profile clientele, so paparazzi is permanently camped out front, but I swear it's tripled since you and Jesse got married. Everyone wants the scoop on the wedding."

Kylie laughed as she got down on the mats to begin stretching, "I know, it's crazy. I see a few guys when I come in, and then when I leave it's double, and it's both the paparazzi and Jesse's fans. How do they find out so quickly?"

"They have apps on their phones. So much of the stalking is in near real time with these entertainment shows. Once their guys have got the pictures and statement, they upload it and it's splashed in their breaking news section...and their app subscribers are getting text alerts. Stuff like *Update: Jesse Winslow pumping iron and drinking smoothies at L9/NYC.* So, by the time you're leaving here, millions of people know it."

"That's really so bizarre. We were just talking last night about bumping up security because it has gotten so much more intense, just from the time I first met Jesse."

"It is so crazy. I don't know how you guys deal with it. Okay, let's do twenty on the treadmill." He programmed the machine. "We're going to do a little foothills action here." He finished pressing the buttons. "Jesse always had a crowd that followed him here, which was why this room was perfect for him, but it was never like it is now. And not to stroke your overinflated ego any more than it needs to be," he smiled at her, "but the public never gave a shit about Jesse and Claudine the way they do about you and Jesse. It's a totally different fascination."

"Really? You think?" *How could that be?* Kylie wondered. The woman was at the top of the top supermodels.

"Oh, definitely," he scoffed. "Red, you are so much more accessible than Claudine. She's like not even real. And you're this girl who's had struggles with her weight the way they have, you're real, and in a way, one of them. So, that makes Jesse more real for them, too. When he was with Claudine, it was like they were some pre-packaged thing nobody could relate to. Did people love Brad and Jennifer more than they liked Brad and Angelina? You bet they did. Although Angelina does great charity work, women don't relate to her, where they want to be drinking coffee with Jennifer. She's real and warm. And that's you."

"I'm warm?" Kylie was surprised to hear that.

"Mmm, maybe warm is not the right word, but you're snarky and funny and definitely real. Face it, you ate your way out of a pageant title. What woman isn't going to love that? That is like the best story ever. Okay, think about this, how much did the world adore Oprah through her diets. They loved her. They dieted with her. They gained weight with her. She was real, with real-life weight problems, just like them. Jesse has always been a mega-star, but the two of you together bring this crazy fascination, the likes of which I've never seen before."

"I feel bad that you've had to put ropes up at the front entrance to keep them back." Kylie was out of breath. "What the hell did you do to this incline?"

With a self-satisfied smile, Zac laughed. "You've just started a new program, babe."

"Oh, yeah, what's that?" She was huffing and puffing.

"Program *I need to look hot in my wedding dress*." He stood there with his arms crossed over his muscular chest.

"This is why we went to City Hall. But no, you, my mother and Hayley, you're all going to torture me and make me do this big lavish wedding."

The treadmill slowed to a halt and Kylie stepped off and headed straight for the refrigerator, grabbing a cold bottle of water, she pressed it against her forehead. "That was murder."

"You ain't seen nuthin' yet," he smirked. "So, where's the wedding going to be? Have you decided?" He pointed to the biceps/triceps chair.

Kylie was happy to take a seat. "The two that I'm considering are Gotham Hall and Capitale. It's funny because they were both initially built as banks and are ornate and built around a center rotunda space, so there's a similarity between the two. Obviously, I've got a style of architecture that I like. We've got sit-downs with them over the next two weeks to look at the nitty-gritty and availability and then make a choice."

"Those spaces sound like L9," he commented.

Kylie thought for a second. "You're right. No wonder why I'm attracted to those two places."

"You should get married here."

"Here? What and come down the aisle between the treadmills and ellipticals?" She laughed.

"Yeah, we'll just seat guests in rowing machines," Zac laughed. "We've done a load of big events here and they've been great. Obviously, the equipment disappears and tables move in. My dad and his partner, Yoli Perez, work with Elan Gerstler of Claret Productions, and he handles everything. If you're interested, you should talk to my dad."

"Wow. I hadn't even thought about this. I'll run it by Jesse."

. . . . . .

It was the fifth text he'd gotten in the three weeks since he'd told Dr. Stoddard he was no longer going to be her patient. He'd never received a list of other doctors, but that wasn't really very surprising.

The texts, however, were a total surprise. The woman had, for the most part, been very professional and he thought she would let it end that way.

But apparently, he was wrong.

**I really need to speak with you. I've gone through some regressions with my supervisor and I have more answers for you.**

She was playing hardball now, throwing out hooks she was certain he and Kylie would not just want to nibble on, they'd want to bite hard and feast upon. To know more of their story, the shared history and love and how it had played out over the ages was something they yearned to discover. And Claire Stoddard, of all people knew that.

For the first time, Jesse responded to her text with one of his own.

**Enough, Dr. Stoddard. This needs to stop. Your behavior has**

**become highly unprofessional. I am asking you to cease and desist contacting me directly. If there is any reason you need to get a message to me, please do so by contacting my manager, Jon Fritz at Fritz Music Management.**

His decision not to tell Kylie about the ongoing texts was to protect her from this unpleasantness and let her enjoy her special time planning their wedding. He wondered if they'd ever done that before. Jesse and Kylie had concluded that she was, in fact, the other redhead in his life, Julia, and as they had learned through Jesse's Gaius regression, their plans to marry never came to fruition. That was a dream that had been robbed from them over and over and over again.

Although Kylie had given Hayley and her mother responsibility for much of the wedding planning, she became more and more involved in the process, as if with each day, she finally had the confidence to allow herself to dream a dream that wouldn't be stolen from her, with the man who would forever be hers.

"Having writer's block?" She snuggled into him on the couch. His ancient deck of cards was spread on the coffee table before him in a vanishing cross solitaire formation.

Looking up, he quickly kissed her lips. "Yeah, I'm stuck on some lyrics. I need to clear my mind so that they'll come."

"Well, I've got something I want to run by you."

Putting the remaining cards in his hand down on the coffee table, he turned to her. "Shoot."

"I was working out with Zac today, who by the way is going to kill me. He's on a mission to get me into a smaller sized wedding dress. But that's another story. So, we were talking about venues and I told him that I was down to two: Gotham Hall and Capitale, and that there was a similarity between the two properties. Like the grand architecture, they were both built as bank headquarters, the ornate Corinthian columns, the main rotundas, and that I clearly had a type of building that I liked. Well, he pointed out to me the similarities those two spaces have with L9. Which is probably what attracted me to those two spaces and he was telling me that they've done events there where they clear out equipment and an event company comes in and takes over." Kylie stopped to take a breath.

"Okay." Jesse just looked at her smiling. She finally was truly acting like a bride. The fear, which he knew she never actually acknowledged, was no longer clouding her ability to move forward and live in the now.

"Well, is that something you'd be interested in?"

"It's a great space. You and I really got to know each other there, so there's tremendous sentimental value. It's part of our shared history. The Jesse and Kylie history," he clarified. "I think it's worth a conversation and I'd like to see pictures of other events done there so that we can get a feel for it and decide if it's right for us."

Smiling at him, she leaned in for a kiss, "I love you."

"I love you, too, Toots. So, let's contact whoever we need to at L9 and check it out."

· · · · · ·

The paparazzi was waiting for them when they arrived at L9.

"Jesse, Kylie...have you set a date?"

Kylie was always amazed at how responsive and open he was with the press. While others snubbed them, Jesse made them his friends and fans by giving them what they wanted and they loved him for it.

"We're working on it. Well, actually Kylie's working on it."

The crowd laughed.

"Do you have a place picked out?"

"You know you guys are going to have the answer to that before I do. I'm going to find out from you."

Again, laughter from the crowd which had already grown in the few minutes since they'd gotten there.

"Any plans to go on tour?"

"Will it be solo or with Winslow?"

"Next tour will be solo and then after that you can expect to see Winslow back in the studio again." The crowd reacted positively to that news.

"We've got to head in," Jesse waved goodbye to the reporters.

"One more question. Any little Winslows planned?"

This time it was Kylie who turned around to answer the question, with a huge smile and a dip of her head, in true pageant-girl style, she wowed the crowd. "C'mon, you guys. You know how I've struggled with my weight. Let's get me looking gorgeous in a wedding dress first before we start talking babies." And she did that little shoulder thing, pageant girls do.

"We love you, Kylie," more than one reporter screamed.

"We love you, too," she yelled over her shoulder at the crowd as she and Jesse entered L9's massive wooden doors for their meeting with Elan Gerstler, founder of the award-winning Claret Creative Event Agency.

"Wow, that was quite a crowd," Jesse commented.

"Wait until you see the size of it by the time we leave. They have apps that alert them. And this time, it's the two of us together."

"I want your arms," Kylie announced to Yoli Perez, L9's President, as she led them up to the second-floor executive offices.

"We'll get Zac to start working you on free weights," Yoli

laughed, looking down at her very toned arms.

"You can wear anything sleeveless and look great."

Yoli leveled a glance at Kylie, "If I looked like you, my arms would be the last thing people would be noticing."

Entering a large office suite, a dark-haired man rose from a distressed driftwood conference table and came around to great them.

"Hello, I'm Elan Gerstler," his voice was warm and slightly accented. "It's a pleasure meeting you both."

After a few minutes of pleasantries, Elan asked, "Do you pretty much know what you want or are you open to creating a new concept?"

"We're open," Kylie and Jesse said simultaneously, and then looked at one another and laughed.

"Okay, let's start by taking a look at other events we've done in both this space, as well as others, and see if there are elements that resonate with you, things you are drawn to and we can build upon that so the night really expresses who the two of you are and what your journey is all about."

Pressing her thigh against Jesse's, Kylie smiled. "If we told people about our journey they would Baker Act us."

Elan's look told them he was not familiar with the American term and Kylie laughed as she explained, "It means to commit someone involuntarily to a mental health facility."

He laughed, "By the time weddings take place, brides and grooms are usually voluntarily committing themselves to escape their relatives."

Elan began with a digital slide show projected onto the wall. "I'm going to first show you a few different themes we've created for this space."

The first group of pictures were bathed in blue light, bare branched white trees and twinkling white lights captured the beauty of winter.

"I love that," Kylie squeezed Jesse's hand.

"I like that a lot, too," he agreed.

The next set, transformed L9 into an Alaskan wilderness with an everchanging sky of Northern Lights.

"This looks like where I was up shooting. We have to go up there together."

The cool colors disappeared with the next set of images, replaced by bright oranges, yellows, pinks, and greens as Elan transported everyone to the streets of a Caribbean island. Although they were just taking in the visuals, it wasn't hard to imagine steel drums calling out a beat that would have shoulders and hips swaying all night long.

The next few events he shared were more formal and not theme driven, but all very elegant.

"I had no idea this space was converted for events." Jesse sat back in his chair.

"We don't do it often," Yoli advised. "Typically, it's for a charity that Schooner and his wife, Mia, are very passionate about, or an event for a club member they have a relationship with."

"Here it is," Elan had been searching files on his laptop. "It was misfiled."

As they looked back up at the wall, Kylie heard Jesse's intake of breath. The scene was ancient Rome. Not Rome as ruins, but a depiction of Rome in its glory. With a three hundred and sixty-degree view of the Seven Hills.

"How do you…" Jesse began.

"Holograms," explained Elan.

He scrolled through a few photos so that they could see it from different vantage points, the details exquisite in each, from the rough-hewn cobblestones lining the street to the aqueducts.

Leaning in to Jess, "Are you okay?" She whispered.

Squeezing her hand under the table, he nodded. "Yeah."

"How did you recreate this time period in all its splendor versus the way we see it now in ruins?"

"To originally build this was about three years' worth of research before we even began the graphics."

"It's amazing and very realistic," Jesse remarked. *More than you know.*

Turning to Jesse, Kylie smiled. "We're not waiting that long. Imagine dealing with my mother for three years over this."

Everyone laughed.

"My mother is a pageant mom, Elan. And everything you have heard about pageant mom's is true. You have been officially warned."

"Have any of these themes resonated with you? Felt right?" Elan asked.

"All of them, to some extent." Kylie looked to Jesse for his input.

"Toots, I am good with whatever you love."

"Does the Rome set belong to someone?"

"Yes. To us. All of this is the proprietary property of Claret. If you're interested in Rome, we can take what we have as a base and add elements, if there is something you are really looking for," he explained.

"Would that add a lot of wait time for production?" As much as Kylie wanted her wedding to Jesse, she also wanted it behind her.

"No, not necessarily. With as much in place as we have, we can create additional elements in about a month."

"We have a lot to think about." Kylie gave a big sigh and smiled at Jesse, who was being a great sport through this. "Can we go out into the club and take a look at how the logistics would work. From the bridal and groom suites to how things would work if we did the ceremony and reception here."

"Sure," Yoli stood. "First let me show you the rest of the executive office space up here, because that would be for the bride and bridesmaids, and you'll see why when we get outside. Jesse, the private gym that you and Kylie use would be reserved for the groom and groomsmen."

Following Yoli, the executive office space was much more expensive and posh than she'd expected. There were multiple areas with bathrooms and couches and mirrors. A must for a bridal party.

"You both know the owner of L9, Zac's dad, Schooner Moore. His entire business operation, including a foundation he runs, is housed out of this facility and he did an amazing job renovating the office space that existed here. Out-of-town business associates can actually stay on premises."

Moving out onto the mezzanine overlooking the rotunda, Kylie marveled at the view. "I usually don't get to see the club from this vantage point."

"I'll never get tired of it," Yoli admitted, as they spent a moment looking over the club's main floor. "Okay, so you would come out of the bride's suite through this door here, which puts you at the top of the marble stairs. And that will make quite an entrance as you descend the staircase and have Jesse come up a landing from the main floor to meet you."

Turning to smile at Jesse and say, "Fiona is going to have an orgasm. She is going to love this." Kylie never got to express those words, because something caught her eye. Was it the glint of silver in the club's intricate lighting or the cold blue of Claire Stoddard's eyes? She would never know for sure, no matter how many times she replayed that moment in her head. She would remember thinking, "When did she become a member here?"

The instantaneous fading of the smile on Kylie's face and the shock and fear in her eyes caused Jesse to immediately turn around to see what had caused her reaction, but all he saw was Claire Stoddard lifting her arm and instinct told him to protect Kylie. Shield Kylie. Save Kylie.

Stepping in front of his wife, Jesse Winslow was thrown back, like a ragdoll, as the bullet entered his chest. Together the two rolled down the marble staircase, a grotesque tangle of blood and limbs. Neither aware of the commotion at the top, as club patrons restrained the gunwoman.

In the distance, Kylie could hear calls for a doctor and 911. Pressing her hand over Jesse's wound, she tried to stop it. But there was so much blood pumping from his chest. He was losing it fast as it rushed around her fingers like a river tripping over fallen branches.

"Stay with me, Jess. Help is on the way." The words were barely recognizable amongst her sobs. "This can't be happening to us. We did the right things this time. We changed so many of our mistakes from the past. I thought we'd changed our destiny, Jesse."

Putting her ear close to him, she could make out his words in the gurgling. "Me, too, I thought we'd figured it out."

"Please, don't leave me, Jesse. I can't do this again without you."

"Yeah. You can. This time you're strong. So strong."

"You promised," she choked on her sobs. He was going fast. She could feel it, a transition painfully familiar. That agony in her heart was closing in. Again. The familiarity choking her. "You promised you wouldn't go."

"And I never will." He was struggling for breath.

"Stay with me, Jesse. Please, stay with me," she begged, her tears falling onto his cheeks.

"I'll find you, Toots. You know I will."

"No. No. No. No. No. No. No. I can't do this again. I can't." Her wail would haunt everyone who was witness to the brutal slaying, and although they didn't know the details of a love that had flourished over thousands of years, they would feel it to their core, understanding they had witnessed a tragedy so great, a loss so profound, that they would forever feel as one with this young woman.

Looking up from her beautiful husband's face to the top of the stairs, Dr. Claire Stoddard was being handcuffed. She smiled at Kylie, a smile that made Kylie's blood run cold, for she had seen that very same self-satisfied grin before, looking down at her from a window with a newly repaired sash.

# Epilogue

*Two Years Later*

In a corner office with two glass walls, high above the streets of Manhattan, three women all had huge smiles on their faces as they listened intently to the lawyer on the speakerphone in the middle of the desk, as he shared the good news.

Cutting it close was an understatement.

Tonight was the big party celebrating their deal. Over three hundred industry people would be in attendance and they were down to the wire, sweating it, that the deal, which should have been completed more than six weeks ago, would still be stalled. But in the eleventh hour, with their threat of pulling out, it had finally worked out, just within the last hour. And now the company was theirs.

Hanging up the phone, the three flew out of their chairs, hugging and kissing and jumping around the room, looking more like middle-school teens who had just been asked to their first dance, than professional business women who owned a corporation.

"Oh, my God, we did it. We finally did it." Kylie was beaming.

Hayley picked up a picture of Jesse from her friend's desk and smiled warmly at it. "He would have totally loved this moment."

"Yes, he would have," Kylie agreed, trying not to let her eyes mist over. "For many reasons, including the fact that he despised Blaise Collins and the way he treated me, so seeing the three of us as the new owners of Siren would have made him proud."

"We are going to turn this industry on its ear." Liz was stoked. "All sizes. All colors. All persuasions. Straight. Gay. Dyke. Trans. All beautiful. And all celebrated. This industry had better be ready for us, because *we* are the new Siren." She grabbed Hayley's hand and kissed her palm.

Sip's shoulders did a little dance in response to the spontaneity of her lover's genuine affection.

Between the three of them, they now owned sixty-seven of Siren's stock. Buh-bye, Blaise.

"Are you going home to change?" Hayley asked.

"No. This is it. This is what I'm wearing. That's why I had the invite say business attire," Kylie laughed.

"I love that jacket. I've never seen anything like it before," Liz complimented Kylie's colorful garment with its watercolor paint splashes.

"I had it made in Italy when I was there. I just love this fabric, plus there are all these cool, useful hidden pockets, so I don't need to carry a purse. Check this out," she opened the jacket to show them the inside, "there's a breast pocket inside on both sides. It will fit my cell, keys, wallet, and sunglasses and with the way the fabric drapes, you can't even see that I've got anything bulky in there, so I'm not carrying a purse tonight." She laughed, "And that's better than going commando."

"I need that jacket. Or maybe I can borrow yours...permanently," Sip laughed.

"Umm, or not." Kylie gave her the evil eye.

Liz looked at her watch. "Do you want to ride over with us?"

"No, go on without me. I've got a few things to finish up here first before I leave. I'll meet you over there."

"Okay. Come on, plus one," Sip kidded, as she reached for Liz's hand. "See you over there, Gracie."

In the quiet of her office, Kylie sat back in her chair. Today was a big day. It was a good day. Good days were happening every so often now. Tonight was going to be even a bigger night. She'd be fine. Until she got home.

Picking up the picture of Jesse that Hayley had moved, she couldn't help but smile looking at his beautiful face.

"Oh, Jess, I really wish you were here to see this. And you probably are, huh? I'm guessing that you know everything that's going on and maybe even have been providing some divine intervention. I wouldn't put it past you. I know you'd be proud of me. Unlike the past, I didn't get beat down and abused by men once you were gone. I've stayed strong and turned it around and beat an asshole at his own game. Pretty badass of me, right." She nodded at the picture. "And now, Hayley, Liz, and I are business owners and we're going to empower people who have been disenfranchised. Quite the opposite of my previous destinies. I know this is what I was supposed to do, Jesse. This is how I'm going to help people. With you, it was your music. It gave people life and hope and joy. I hope what I do helps people love themselves and have the confidence to stand up for who they are." She paused, thinking for a moment.

"But, you know, I still wonder, what didn't we get right? You grew and were no longer putting your own agenda first, I was no longer a victim. So, the only thing I can think of is we were only taking ourselves into account and we didn't factor in the third variable, who would not stop short of killing if she didn't have you. Do you think that's it? It's the only thing I can come up with. The lawyers promise me she won't see the light of day again in this lifetime, but she's a crafty bitch, so I don't trust that she won't be granted parole at some point. Next time, babe, we are taking her down. I promise you that. This is the last time that witch gets the best of us.

"Look at me talking to your picture." A short laugh turned into a sob as the bravado from the moment before vanished and tears welled up from her heart. "Tonight's a rough one without you, Jesse. I'm not going to lie. Sometimes it feels like you're right here with me, that you're a part of everything, just like twenty minutes into the future, on the other side of the veil, and I really do good at those times. And then there are nights like tonight, where I just feel so alone and I miss you so damn much. I just wish I knew that you were by my side. I want you with me walking into that celebration tonight. Me and you. The way it's supposed to be. We belong together, Jesse. We do. And I feel so freaking alone tonight. I'm happy, the company is a great accomplishment and the start of something big, but the emptiness just feels amplified by a million, because you're not here to share it with. I want you with me, Jesse." Her voice trailed off to a whisper, "I just want you here with me."

Putting his picture down on the desk, she wiped her now red and swollen eyes. *A great look for a new company owner*, she laughed, and swiped under her lashes one more time with the side of her fingers to ensure any raccoon-like rings were erased.

Grabbing her keys, wallet, and phone, she turned off the office lights and took a deep breath. Time to pull it together and be a kick-ass Jersey girl.

Stepping out into the hall, as she turned to lock the door, the toe of her shoe crunched something on the metal threshold. Looking down, she could see blue plaid sticking out from under her right pump.

"What the…" She bent down to pick it up.

The card was a faded blue plaid, the white no longer bright, but yellowed with time, the edges worn. Turning the card over, a sound that was a combination of a gasp and a sob erupted from deep in her chest, as the image slammed her heart, lodging the flutter of a missed beat at the base of her throat.

Silent for a moment, she blew out the air she'd been holding in her lungs before taking a deep breath that she hoped would restore her voice.

"Yes. Yes, you are," she whispered. The tears flowed freely now, falling onto the antique picture she held in unsteady hands.

Nodding her head, knowingly, she smiled through her tears at the handsome face on the vintage playing card, as she spoke. "You are my King of Hearts. You always have been and you always will be." Closing her eyes, she acknowledged, "Okay, okay. I get it. Sometimes I just need a reminder."

Opening her jacket, she slipped the card into the inner breast pocket on the left side, patting the soft fabric down over her heart. "Tonight, you're going to be my plus one." And with a smile on her beautiful face, they were on their way.

*Fade to White*

*A movie scene fades to darkness*

*But our score never ends*

*After a brilliant crescendo*

*It's always 'til we meet again*

*Fade to White*

Hello Readers,

Have you read **THE NEEDING MOORE SERIES** yet?

IF YOU HAVEN'T, I've got the first book, **Searching for Moore, free** for you. The series is an epic second chance romance about the one you just never get over.

**Click this link** and sign up for your **FREE** copy of the book - https://dl.-bookfunnel.com/oielzjh2mo

IF YOU HAVE read the Moores, make sure you check out the first chapter of my next book, **Moore than a Feeling**, a stand-alone romance about Holly Moore.

**Click this link** for the **FREE** first chapter of the book - https://dl.bookfun-nel.com/m2uw0f6tjo

Enjoy!

Julie

# Author's Note

In my lifetime, there have been three things I've wanted to be: an astronaut/astronomer (very first career choice), a psychiatrist (talked out of by my tenth-grade English teacher, who wanted me to be a writer), and a writer. So, based on that, it's probably not surprising that reincarnation and regression analysis have been lifelong fascinations of mine. I don't remember a time in my life where I wasn't drawn to these topics and exploring them.

There are some members of the spiritual community, who have been tremendous influences on me and to whom I'd like to give special acknowledgment...

Reading the works of Dr. Brian L. Weiss was life-altering for me. His books chronicle regressions he conducts with his patients, and the information is fascinating, as under hypnosis they provide detailed accounts of past lives. While reading his book *Same Soul, Different Bodies,* there was a segment that involved Dr. Weiss and I knew what a description of something very specific was going to be, before I'd even read it, as I saw it in my mind's eye first. Every hair on my arms stood on end. *Could I have possibly been there with them? How did I know this piece of information? And why could I see it?*

Before I began writing *Love on the Edge of Time,* I was very fortunate to be able to cross something off my bucket list – a Past-Life Regression Workshop led by Dr. Weiss at the Omega Institute in Rhinebeck, NY. It took place over a weekend, my birthday weekend, which I interpreted as a sign to give myself an amazing gift. And I did.

I'd like to thank astrologer Chani Nicholas for allowing me to use her quote at the beginning of the book. Weekly, Chani pens the most amazing, prolific, in-depth and on-target horoscopes I have ever come across. They are like no one else's, as her writing is magnificent and a joy to read. I highly encourage following her at http://chaninicholas.com and signing up for her weekly newsletter. She will blow you

358 | Julie A. Richman

away.

James Van Praagh, thank you for giving me the sign to focus on my signs when I got stuck. The irony didn't escape me that the sign I was looking for was a sign. Go figyah!

John Edward, for keeping my peeps in touch with me. Sometimes we all need that little reminder to keep the faith, just like Kylie got from Jesse at the very end of the book.

Diane Hogan – our paths were supposed to cross that weekend for a reason. Follow the guideposts and stay on your path.

And Bryce Draper... the first time we exchanged messages, I knew you had to be the face of Jesse Winslow. Your journey is taking you down a very select road, one that you are ready to travel. Thank you for being part of this project. And I look forward to seeing where your journey takes you.

'til we meet again,

Julie

# Acknowledgements

Without the readers and the bloggers in the Indie community, this world would be a whole lot less colorful, and I'd probably be working for some asshole. So, thank you, thank you, thank you! Seriously, thank you.

So, you know how you look back on a period of time and think, "I would have loved to have lived then." Whether it was with Hemingway and the flappers in the 20s, beat poets in the 50s, hippies in the 60s or 300 years ago, there's something about certain historical periods that make you feel you were born too late (or too soon).

I think for those that come after us, the skyrocketing of the Indie Publishing community, post-2010, will be a time people cite as one they wished they had been a part of, as a reader, a service provider, an author – or any combination of the aforementioned.

The Indie Romance Community is the female version of the Wild West. It's morphing and growing and taking shape before our very eyes. Can you actually think of a more fun place to be than that? I can't. So, thank you all for being part of it with me. This is one hell of a ride we're on and I can only hope the words I pen bring you hours of enjoyment.

So, thank you readers, bloggers, service providers, and my amazing Rogue BBCs for allowing me to do what I love. If you keep reading 'em, I'll keep writing 'em.

To Vi and Penelope – If this truly is the Wild West, you two are the posse I want by my side navigating uncharted territory and making memories. I love strong women who support other women and the two of you are shining examples of dignity and grace.

To Cleida and Kristen – Your friendship and support is appreciated more than you can ever imagine. Being able to bounce things off the two of you is an incredible reality check that I am blessed to have.

To Jenn Watson, Sarah Ferguson and the SBPR Team – Thank you so much for making my life easier and alleviating my stress. It is truly a delight to work with all of you.

To Elaine, Elena and Shannon – Big thanks for finding all those pesky, hide and seek-playing errors and making it all look wonderful.

To Jena – Wow, we started this one a million years ago and most of the elements were timeless. But like a fine wine, this one got better with time. Thank you for your brilliant creativity and wonderful friendship.

To Shaun – Your vision is irresistible and tells a story most photographers just dream of capturing. Be prepared for a beach shoot – in winter, for the cover I want YOU on.

To Brigette and Naiman – Goldilocks here thanks you for creating a space that was "just right" when you conceived of the Corona Coffee Co.

To Mom, Mark and Max – With all my love for all the weekends I say, "Sorry, I have to write…edit…proof…

To Mindy – When do I get a book? LOL. Umm, how about now. This one is for you. The ultimate journey. Pick your fellow roadtrippers wisely – because the journey needs to be freaking epic. Nothing short of that will do.

We done good.


'Til we meet again…

   With deep love, respect and gratitude to all…

     Julie

# About the Author

Author Julie A. Richman is a native New Yorker living deep in the heart of Texas. A creative writing major in college, reading and writing fiction has always been a passion. Julie began her corporate career in publishing in NYC and writing played a major role throughout her career as she created and wrote marketing, advertising, direct mail and fundraising materials for Fortune 500 corporations, advertising agencies and non-profit organizations. She is an award-winning nature photographer plagued with insatiable wanderlust. Julie and her husband have one son and a white German Shepherd named Juneau.

### *Contact Julie*

Twitter
@JulieARichman

Website
www.juliearichman.com

Facebook
www.facebook.com/AuthorJulieARichman

Instagram
www.instagram.com/authorjuliearichman

# For the Reader

Thank you for purchasing and reading this eBook. If you enjoyed it please leave a short review on book-related sites such as <u>Goodreads</u>. Readers rely on reviews, as do authors.

Made in the USA
San Bernardino, CA
24 November 2017